ALSO BY M.J. TROW

SCHOOLMASTER MYSTERIES

Book 1: Maxwell's House
Book 2: Maxwell's Flame
Book 3: Maxwell's Movie
Book 4: Maxwell's War
Book 5: Maxwell's Ride
Book 6: Maxwell's Curse
Book 7: Maxwell's Reunion
Book 8: Maxwell's Match
Book 9: Maxwell's Inspection
Book 10: Maxwell's Grave
Book 11: Maxwell's Mask
Book 12: Maxwell's Point
Book 13: Maxwell's Chain
Book 14: Maxwell's Revenge
Book 15: Maxwell's Retirement
Book 16: Maxwell's Island
Book 17: Maxwell's Christmas

# MAXWELL'S CHRISTMAS

M.J. TROW

*A Schoolmaster Murder Mystery Book 17*

**Previously published as *Maxwell's Crossing***

JOFFE BOOKS

Revised edition 2024
Joffe Books, London
www.joffebooks.com

First published by Allison & Busby
as *Maxwell's Crossing* in Great Britain in 2012

This paperback edition was first published
in Great Britain in 2024



Cover art by Imogen Buchanan

ISBN: 978-1-83526-655-7

## A NOTE TO THE READER

Please note these books were published in the 2000s, when social attitudes were different.

# CHAPTER ONE

The email was, as ever, terse. Maxwell, as ever, found it with seconds to spare. 'Meeting in my office, second period, Monday. JD.' Because Peter Maxwell always thought of his esteemed Headmaster as Legs, he had to think for a moment who this JD person was. Then, with an inward tut, he remembered that the man's given name was James. His surname was Diamond, but anyone less like a geezer it would be difficult to find. Maxwell glanced up at the clock in his office that ticked away between the film posters of Audie Murphy and Randolph Scott, a reminder of the days when Men were Men. The second period of the day was only ten minutes old — most of his colleagues would be on phase two of the eight-phase lesson by now — so he decided that he would be magnanimous and turn up. He pushed his chair back from the desk and spun round to face into the room.

The last week of the Autumn Term was always a little depressing. The tinsel, put up with such enthusiasm and about a pound of Blu-Tack, was beginning to sag. The Christmas cards were leaning at rakish angles on any flat surface, the preponderance of an image of a slightly psychopathic-looking robin giving testament to a special offer on at Poundland. An exquisitely wrapped gift inexpertly hidden at the back of a shelf proved that Helen Maitland, Maxwell's trusty Number Two, was as organised as ever. It had been in position since just before half-term, Helen not being a person given to last-minute decisions. The Head of Sixth Form sighed and reached for his scarf and hat. County Council cutbacks had resulted in a school as cold as the Arctic. Classrooms met national guidelines, so the little dears didn't keel over with hypothermia, but to get from A to B meant using dogs, sleds and a backpack of glucose supplies. And all this in the face of Global Warming. Legs Diamond, of course, having banned conkers three years ago, had now given a new directive: should it snow, anyone found snowballing or creating an ice slide, or a snowman with recognisable features of any member of staff, was to report to his deputy, Bernard Ryan, for a good letting off.

Mindful of the wind chill along the Mezzanine corridor which housed his domain, Maxwell closed the door of his office behind him. In the silence of the room a little more tinsel wafted gently to the floor and the Christmas card lovingly inscribed by Jonelle Squabb of Seven Ell Queue slid quietly down behind the radiator, another link in the urban archaeological site which was Peter Maxwell's office. The long-dead faces from the posters on the walls watched him go — a man on a mission. Impossible? You'd better believe it.

* * *

Maxwell bounced enthusiastically into James Diamond's office. After the tundra of the foyer, it was like a sauna. Diamond sat in his shirtsleeves — the racy devil — behind his desk. Paul Moss had obviously been in there since the bell went; he had had time to shed his jacket and undo the cardigan he had taken to wearing underneath. Diamond looked pointedly at the clock above the door. Maxwell screwed his head round to follow his gaze then pushed the door to and sat down next to Moss, taking off his scarf and hat and throwing them under his chair.

'Mr Maxwell,' Diamond said, flatly. 'Thank you for coming.'

'Thank you for inviting me, Headmaster,' Maxwell beamed. 'Should I know why we are here?' He looked enquiringly at his Head of Department.

Paul Moss still looked like a twelve-year-old, although now the hair that skirted his ears was greying and the smile creases at the outer edges of his eyes threatened to turn silently into crow's feet when no one was looking.

'As you know,' Diamond began, 'Paul is to leave us temporarily at the end of term to take part in a cultural exchange with an American teacher.'

'Yes indeed. What an excellent opportunity for him.' Maxwell sounded as though he was reading from a cue card. It was, to his mind, neither excellent nor an opportunity, but he was a civil man and saw no need to say what he felt, in this case something along the lines of 'What, are you nuts?'

'Indeed, indeed,' echoed Diamond, following the great man's lead. 'An opportunity. However,' he dropped his voice, 'there has been a slight problem at the other end.' He fiddled with his pencil and looked up at Paul.

'A problem?' Maxwell brightened. Could it be that his prayers were to be answered and in fact they were not to be saddled with what could only laughingly be called an American History teacher?

'The other half, as it were, of this arrangement, has had to pull out.' Diamond looked at Maxwell dubiously. 'You doubtless remember my email on the subject.'

Maxwell cocked his head on one side and looked brightly at the man. He looked not unlike the psychopathic robin reproduced so many times along his shelves. 'Hmm?'

Diamond and Moss sighed as one. Paul Moss had a sneaking suspicion that Maxwell was perfectly aware of what went on in the Leighford High School Super Highway, but played along anyway.

'My replacement was to have been a very senior teacher from Los Angeles, who would, with a little guidance no doubt from you, Max, have been quite capable of taking on most of the Head of Department work. She has, however, been elected to the State Legislature. This has apparently been an ambition of hers for some years and, obviously, it can't be postponed, so she is no longer coming over.'

A very old joke rose in Maxwell's throat, but he beat it back. He tried to keep the joy from bubbling out as he spoke. 'So, we'll have a supply, will we? No probl—'

'Indeed not!' Diamond was aghast. The budgetary implications alone made him want to reach for his tablets from the doctor. 'No. We will still be having a teacher from across the Pond,' he smiled tightly, to invite the others to join him in his hip command of language. 'But he . . . umm . . .' he consulted the paper in front of him, 'Hector Gold is younger, less experienced and so, Max, to cut a long story short, Paul and I were hoping you would be able to take on the mantle of Head of History for a year.'

There was a silence so complete that the creaking of the foot-long icicles hanging outside Diamond's window could clearly be heard. Then, having controlled his amusement, Maxwell spoke.

'I'm sure I could manage that, Headmaster,' he said. It seemed that Diamond was the only person in the school not aware that, to all intents and purposes, de facto and every which way, Maxwell already *was* the Head of History. Paul Moss shot him a grateful glance. His family were already packed and ready to go, to the land of sun and foot-long hot dogs, so if Maxwell had let him down at this late stage, he was wondering if it would be safe to go home.

'No extra remuneration, I assume?' Maxwell asked pleasantly. He hated to bring up the sordid subject of money and was not remotely surprised when Diamond smiled apologetically and shook his head.

'If I had my way, of course . . .'

Maxwell understood that Diamond already had his way, but he smiled back beatifically.

Diamond shot out of his chair, relief all over his usually unreadable face. 'Max, thank you so much,' he said. 'I was . . . that is, Bernard and I wondered if . . .'

'What with me being four hundred years old, whether I could manage it?' Maxwell completed the sentence for him. 'Oh, yes, Headmaster. I'm sure I will manage. I have vague memories of the Year Seven syllabus.' He screwed his head round to look at the clock and felt his neck click. He didn't wince; it seemed inappropriate in a spry young thing like him. 'Well, time's a-wasting. I'm sure Mr Moss and I have a lot to discuss. Are we still doing Tudors and Stuarts for A Level, Paul, or does that depend on the latest initiative from Sir Keith Joseph?' He grabbed his scarf and hat and flung open the door, to the discomfiture of Pansy Donaldson, who had been leaning her ear against it. 'Sorry, Mrs Donaldson, do come in.'

The woman was thinking fast to concoct a reason for her sudden entry and so didn't react as Maxwell and Moss swept past her and scurried through the ice house to the staffroom fug. As the Headmaster's door swung to, they heard her launch into a spurious tale of wrongdoing to cover her confusion.

'She's good,' Maxwell murmured to Paul Moss. 'Especially bearing in mind that at this time of the morning she is probably still half-cut.'

'Apparently not,' Moss said. 'It's not like you to be behind the times, Max. She's on the wagon, by all accounts. Alcoholics Anonymous.'

'And the Anonymous part is?' Maxwell asked.

Moss laughed. 'This *is* Leighford High, Max. Jack Jackson in my tutor group has an auntie whose next-door neighbour is half-sister to the wife of the man who opens up the church hall for them on a Wednesday.'

Maxwell nudged the man in the ribs. 'Don't make it up,' he admonished. 'I have a bit of a soft spot for Pansy, one way and another.'

Moss laughed and pushed open the staffroom door, releasing a wave of heat and yesterday's tuna sandwiches. 'It's true. Well, I may have simplified it, but that's basically the link. Seven degrees of separation. It's the oil that keeps the wheels of gossip turning.'

'I'll miss you,' Maxwell said, and meant it. 'I think this Hector Gold may turn out to be rather boring after you.'

Paul Moss blushed slightly and stored the moment away for later. He had always secretly felt rather dull compared with some of the larger-than-life characters with which Leighford High was peopled. Although, on the other hand . . . Paul could always see the ointment and the fly and this made him the man he was.

He toyed with saying something valedictory, something which would ring in Maxwell's head when he, Paul, was on the other side of the world, up to his waist in the mighty Mississippi or fightin' off pesky varmints like skunks or realtors. He settled for something rather more mundane. 'Coffee?'

'Why not?' Maxwell said, flinging himself down in the comfiest chair in the room, which nonetheless challenged even the most robust spine after a while; Deputy Reichsfuhrer Bernard Ryan's secret method to prevent lingering. 'Since it's nearly Christmas, I may also indulge in a biscuit.'

Moss looked dubiously in the tin. 'There's only Rich Tea,' he said. 'And half a Garibaldi.'

'Ah, you historian, you! Aren't there any mince pies?' Maxwell asked, plaintively.

'You don't like currants,' Moss said.

'I know that,' Maxwell said, slightly testily. 'But I'd defend another man's right to a mince pie to the death. And besides, where there are mince pies, there are often other festive foods. I'm thinking chocolate log, Tunis cake, things of that nature. I haven't had my cholesterol fix today yet.'

Moss tried another tin. 'Good guess,' he said, diving in with an only slightly smeary knife. 'Chocolate log it is.'

Maxwell leant back, fingers interlaced across his stomach, padded for the internal weather with more layers than normal. 'Thank you, Paul,' he said, politely. He mulled over whether he would have time to train Hector Gold in the space of three terms to reach this level of service provision. Americans were a polite people, he had heard, although he had never knowingly had any truck with such a creature. It might turn out all right . . .

There was a splashy clink as Paul Moss put down his burden of mugs and chocolate log on the table in front of Maxwell. He sat in the chair opposite, hoping it was the one with the springs intact. There had been a nasty incident the previous week, involving a member of the Art Department, sticking plaster, Dettol and Nurse Sylvia Matthews, which none of the men would forget in a hurry. He was in luck.

'So, Paul,' Maxwell said, stirring himself enough to be able to reach his mug. 'Do we know anything about this Hector Gold person?'

Moss took a sip of his coffee to give himself time to think. 'Not really, Max, to be honest. I only heard about the change the day before yesterday and the bio his school has sent is very brief. It has meant a change in accommodation for us, though. Hector and his wife have no children and so they live in quite a small condominium . . .'

'Flat,' muttered Maxwell.

'. . . in downtown LA . . .'

'The town centre.'

'. . . which wouldn't be suitable for us at all.' Moss ploughed on regardless. Maxwell refused to speak Amerenglish for anyone and Hector Gold was just going to have to learn to live with it. You give a nation the finest language in the world and look what they do to it! Ingrates! 'So, Hector's in-laws are coming along as well, so that we can have their house, which is larger and nearer to Long Beach, which will be nicer for the kids.'

'Longer drive for you, though, is it?' This remark was thrown in for politeness sake. Long drives were for other people; to all intents and purposes, Maxwell's world was bounded by the strength of his leg muscles and the stability of White Surrey's infrastructure. The bike was getting on a bit, not to mention the muscles, but most of Leighford and the surrounding area were still on the menu. The ancient machine lay padlocked to the north of Classroom Two. Actually, the padlock didn't work but everybody knew whose bike it was and wouldn't dream of touching it. Retro-crap meant nothing to the average fourteen-year-old and no bicycle thief would be seen dead riding anything like that.

'I'm not sure what constitutes a long drive over there,' Moss said. 'If you go by American sitcoms . . .' here he paused and glanced covertly at Maxwell, but the Head of Sixth Form was still looking at him with a pleasant smile on his face, as befitted a long-time devotee of Comedy Central. 'American sitcoms, yes, if you go by them, apparently, no one ever walks. Not even to the end of the road.'

'So, there will be quite a little party arriving, then?'

'Yes. As I understand it, there is Hector, his wife, Camille, her mother, Alana and her father . . . um . . .'

Maxwell, overwhelmed by the sheer West Coastness of the names, added, 'Rock?'

'Pardon?' Paul Moss had been lost in a fugue of trying to remember details he had only skimmed himself some hours before. 'Oh, Hector's father-in-law? Ha. No. Jeff, I believe. They sound very nice people.' It was hard to tell whether the last sentence was a statement, a question or a deeply felt hope, but Maxwell let it go.

'They sound wonderful, Paul. When are they arriving?'

'Well, that's just it, really. They didn't want to travel over Christmas, because it is much more expensive.'

'So, when are they arriving?' Maxwell brushed cake crumbs from his lapel and sat up straighter. Years of reading the subtext in his Head of Department's remarks had suddenly made him feel a little edgy.

'Well, with the weather we've been having,' Paul Moss shivered extravagantly and rubbed his hands together as if at an invisible brazier, 'travelling isn't so easy, is it? Can't take even Heathrow for granted, dear me, no.' He smiled, hopefully.

Maxwell leant forward. He beckoned to the man who sat opposite him to come nearer and when they were almost nose to nose he asked his question one last time. 'When. Are. They. Arriving?' Then, to sound less testy, he added, 'Paul.'

The Head of History smiled, but only with one corner of his mouth. He licked his lips. 'Today?'

Maxwell sat back, satisfied. He hadn't lost his touch, that was good, but he was saddened to hear Moss already using the moronic interrogative. 'Today. So. Where are they staying?' He was not by nature suspicious, but he had been married to a Woman Policeman for some time now, so he had had suspicion grafted on. And, of course, he had been a teacher for at least a thousand years, so his nose for prevarication was finely tuned. He felt a sleepover coming on.

'No, no, Max. I wouldn't ask that of you. Heavens no.' Moss tried a smile and this time the whole of his mouth was in working order. 'No, we're going to my parents' place for Christmas anyway, so we're just going a bit earlier, that's all. We were packed and everything as well — well, you know Manda, always organised.'

Maxwell did know her. Pleasant enough in her way, but she put the O in OCD. He had no doubt that they had been packed since the first day of term, just to be sure. 'That's all right, then.' He tried, almost successfully, to keep the relief out of his voice. 'Jacquie would have been more than happy . . .'

'Of course, yes. I know that.' The two men muttered platitudes over each other for a few more moments, then, honours even, turned to the knotty problem of the History Department, running thereof.

# CHAPTER TWO

'So, they're here already?' Jacquie lolled back on the sofa, nursing a coffee. 'That was a bit sudden, wasn't it? How did they get organised so quickly?'

'Good question, Inspector Carpenter-Maxwell,' her husband replied, with a grin. The 'Inspector' bit was still new enough to give him a little thrill up his spine. He had rarely been so proud of anyone in his life, although the sight of Nolan's determined little back as he went in to face the rigours of Mrs Whatmough of a morning ran it close. Metternich's vole capture count had gone off the scale years before.

She acknowledged his smile by burying her nose in her mug, but he could see by her bunched cheeks that it still gave her a kick as well.

'I think that the intended victim—'

'Did you just say victim?' she asked, sharply.

He looked alarmed. 'Did I?' He looked at the ceiling and reran the sentence. 'Yes, I did. Freud, eh? Tchah! Where was I? Yes, the intended *exchange colleague* knew she wasn't coming ages back, but they kept it to themselves so we wouldn't make a fuss. Bit like Pearl Harbor in reverse. They say Churchill knew all about the Japanese attack beforehand but kept it under wraps so that Roosevelt would have to come into the war. These exchanges are sorted out very carefully, you know — people are vetted and each side has to agree, that sort of thing. UN Security Council, the Politburo has to be consulted — oh, and the Pope has to give his blessing, of course.'

'I hope that doesn't mean they are trying to get this Hector person in under the wire, then.'

'I checked with Paul. We can refuse to keep him, if he's that bad. But . . . would he be that bad?' He smiled at her hopefully but she just raised an eyebrow in reply. 'Yes, I know.' He sighed. 'We've had some corkers, haven't we, even after a two-day interview.' He blew out his cheeks and looked doleful. There was that Mrs Whatserface of the Methodist persuasion; that little bloke with the high-pitched voice and the Cornishman Who Never Spoke. Amongst others even more distressing.

Jacquie smiled across at him and thanked every lucky star. Maxwell looked so like Nolan in this mood it was uncanny. In certain moods, he also looked like the cat; in others, like a curmudgeonly old git. But they suited each other, by and large. She dug her toes into Metternich's side, as the great black and white animal snoozed at her feet. He acknowledged her with a chirrup and a flex of a claw. 'Do you want to have them round?'

He looked up. 'Nah,' he said, in flawless Nolan. 'Too near Christmas. Mrs Whatmough lets her prisoners go tomorrow and, let's face it, Nole is manic enough without introducing a clutch of American strangers.'

'Just strangers will do, Max,' she said, slightly sharply. 'Remember what we agreed about flagrant xenophobia?'

'Oooh, Inspector Carpenter-Maxwell,' he purred. 'Are you sure you're a policeman? Using words like "flagrant", and such?'

She cocked her head at him, a sign that planning mode was now in place. 'He'll just have to learn that Christmas is not just for him,' she said.

'Isn't that an animal charity's slogan?' Maxwell wondered. 'Near enough, at least.'

'No. It isn't. It means that we can't let our son think that just because the house looks like an explosion in a tinsel factory and that Mrs Troubridge has enough parcels with his name on under her tree to stock Hamley's, that he can avoid spreading a little goodwill to all men. I *know* we don't usually do much entertaining once you guys have broken up, and I *know* that we fobbed my mother off with tales of me being on call, and I *know*—'

Maxwell knew he was beaten and reached for the phone. 'I'll ring Paul, shall I?' he said.

'Do. And then we have to get going — if anyone's late for the Carol Concert, apparently Mrs Whatmough tells Santa they have been bad and he just leaves coal in their stocking.'

Maxwell looked up from the receiver as the phone peeped the number into his ear. 'Coal? When I was a lad, we'd have given our eye teeth for some coal. Why, one year, I remember — Oh, hello, Paul. That was quick.' He grimaced at Jacquie who went out laughing to get their coats. 'Are your visitors with you yet?' There was a squawk from the receiver. 'Yes, now you come to mention it, I can hear them.' Maxwell's heart began a tiny downwards slide. 'I'm ringing with an invitation . . .'

* * *

The candlelight flickered on the diamante on the wings of Rosemary Whatmough's glasses as she stood outside the little church to welcome the parents to the Carol Concert. She looked more like a character from *The Nightmare Before Christmas* than one of Santa's jolly helpers, but the snow newly fallen on the ground and the general goodwill of the end of term reduced the effect to one of mild peril, familiar to any watcher of a PG DVD.

'Mr Maxwell, Mrs Maxwell,' she said, scarcely moving her lips. She was in a bit of a quandary over the Maxwell family in general. Nolan was obviously incredibly bright, but he burnt with a light in a spectrum she scarcely recognised and she didn't know how to bend the beam to her will. Nolan's father was just too peculiar for words and she had a horrible feeling that Nolan was simply a chip off that old block. The mother, now, she was a nice woman; Nolan looked just like her, lucky child, and she seemed to be relatively normal, but she *was* a policewoman and Mrs Whatmough had heard that the police were ever vigilant for the smallest infraction, not that anyone every infracted on Rosemary Whatmough's watch. But still, it paid to be careful.

'I've reserved you some seats at the front,' she said, gesturing. 'So you get the benefit of Nolan's performance.'

The Maxwells didn't miss a beat as they smiled, nodded and made their way down to the front. A small child dressed as a sheep waved them into their seats and it was only when they were safely seated that Maxwell turned to his wife.

'Performance?'

She shrugged. 'I have literally no idea,' she said. They sat in silence, each one going over conversations with their son in the last month or so, filtering for any mention of a performance. There was none.

Jacquie smiled at Maxwell, a little uncertainly. 'He's probably a lamb or something; an ox, maybe.'

'Most likely,' Maxwell said. He knew his son and how easily a performance could become a Performance. On his day, he could give any diva a run for her money. The next thing he had to say was sensitive and could go either way. 'If he isn't an ox, though, or a camel or similar, you won't cry, will you?'

She fixed him with an eye already filling up. 'Not if you don't,' she agreed. They linked little fingers and waited as the lights went down slightly and the firm footsteps of Mrs Whatmough echoed from behind them as she made her way to the front. She paused, in much the same way as a galleon in full sail loses way and steadies itself against the swell, and surveyed the ranks of parents, mentally noting absentees.

'Thank you all so much for coming,' she boomed. 'The children and staff have been working for many weeks as you know.' She leant forward waggishly. 'Some of you mums,' and she smiled condescendingly at them, 'may have been wondering why you hadn't had the usual request for costumes this year.' There was a pause to give these women time to nod and reinforce their status as star mum. 'Well, some of you may remember the Camel Debacle of last year,' pause for sycophantic laughter, 'so we have made all the costumes ourselves this year, to avoid a repetition.'

There was a muffled sobbing from the back as the Third Camel's mother from the year before could hold her tears back no longer. The Maxwells breathed a sigh of relief as one. So that was one thing they could tick off their 'Haven't Done' list.

'But, enough of that,' Mrs Whatmough suddenly boomed, making a rather nervous grandmother in the third row wee herself ever so slightly. 'I give you . . .' she flung her arm out in an expansive gesture, 'The Carol Concert.'

To a tumult of applause, the lights went down the rest of the way. Then came on again. Then went down again and stayed down. In the flickering health and safety mock candlelight that was left, there was a shuffling silence, followed by a reedy single note from a recorder, then the hesitant beating of a drum. Then, a voice that made the hairs on the backs of the Maxwells' necks stand up and take notice. It wasn't trained, or powerful. It wasn't even always dead on the tune. But it was a voice which meant what it said, and it was the voice of their son.

'Twas in the moon of wintertime, when all the birds had fled,' it sang. Then, on the rush of a gathered breath, 'That mighty Gitchi Manitou sent angel choirs instead. Before their light, the stars grew dim, and wondering hunters heard the hymn,' then, joined by all the other little voices of Year 1, 'Jesus your king is born, Jesus is born, *in excelsis gloria*.' Then, Nolan, in full regalia, war bonnet on his curly head, had drawn level with them, beating his drum. He didn't look at them, but as he passed, Jacquie saw his left eyelid drop in a secret wink.

'Within a lodge of broken bark, the tender babe was found.' Somehow, Maxwell and Jacquie managed to keep the sobs in their throat. 'A ragged robe of rabbit skin enwrapped his beauty round. But as the hunter braves drew nigh, the angel song rose loud and high, Jesus your King is born, Jesus is born, *in excelsis gloria*.' Nolan took the opportunity of the chorus to wipe his nose on his sleeve. Maxwell was impressed — good, authentic pre-Colombian stuff.

The Huron Indians had reached the chancel steps now and turned to face the audience. From behind them, from the vestry, a little band of travellers emerged, from Year 4, looking huge by comparison with the little ones in the front. The hunters parted in the middle, leaving Nolan and his drum still facing the audience.

'O, children of the forest free, O, seed of Manitou, The Holy Child of earth and heaven is born today for you. Come, kneel before the radiant boy who brings you beauty, peace and joy. Jesus, your King is born, Jesus is born, *in excelsis gloria*!' A triumphant drum roll finished their song, and in the ringing silence a single sniff was heard. Only her secretary, sitting with her at the back, knew it came from Mrs Whatmough.

And so the Carol Concert wound its way through the story of the Nativity, from the angle of distant lands. As a theme it was sometimes a little stretched, but from the Huron Indians to the inevitable Dylan Thomas, it was a roaring success. Mrs Whatmough was flushed with pride as she stood in the doorway to usher the parents into the church hall for a mince pie and coffee. She bestowed a smile on the Maxwells.

'Did you enjoy Nolan's performance?' she said, archly. 'It was so good of you to rehearse with him; you must be very tired of that carol by now?'

Maxwell wasn't lying when he said, 'It was as if I was hearing it for the first time tonight, Mrs Whatmough.'

The woman looked as if she wanted to pat him on the head and say 'well done'. As an answer it had ticked all of the boxes, from polite to pithy and it also had the bonus of being totally true. Fighting with glutinous pastry, Jacquie could only smile her recognition of a gaffe well avoided.

The doors from the church crashed back and the children poured in. One child had refused to remove her costume and so would have to go home dressed as a pine tree, but otherwise they were all back in mufti. Nolan's head swivelled as he looked for his parents and then he bounced over to them, a rather circuitous journey as he had to be hugged by various grannies and mothers trying to show they weren't jealous. Eventually, he was at their side. He turned a beaming face to them.

'D'you like it, Mums, Dads?' he said, bouncing lightly on his toes.

Jacquie was torn, in the mothers' dilemma. Did she pick him up and bury her nose in his hair, sniffing up the little boyness of him, while yelling, 'This is my boy — isn't he wonderful'? Or did she say, 'You were pretty good, but did I hear a bum note in the third verse'? She settled for silence and a curl ruffle.

Maxwell was the one who bent down and picked him up for a hug. 'Mate,' he breathed in his ear, 'you were amazing!' His teacher's sensibilities meant it was done so fast that most of Nolan's friends missed it, but it was that or cry. 'I have to ask you one thing, though, if that's all right?'

Nolan looked quizzically at his father. At this time of the year you couldn't be too careful. You heard things about Father Christmas, knowing if you're good or not, that kind of thing. So he settled for, 'Mmm?' and a bright smile.

'Practising.'

Still the bright smile, one eyebrow perhaps a little raised.

'The carol.'

Nolan breathed again. 'Oh, yes. I did it with Mrs Troubridge. On Tuesdays.'

Troubridge Tuesday had become an institution and although it wasn't always necessary for the mad old trout to watch Nolan after school it had somehow become carved in stone. Plocker's mother — Maxwell felt sure that he had once known both her name and that of her son, but now could remember neither — would drop Nolan off at Mrs Troubridge's door and watch while she came down and let him, and usually a lurking Metternich, in. Then he would have his tea with her and, after doing his homework and having a bit of a chinwag, would run downstairs, out through her front door, and with a quick wiggle through where the hedge met the wall, would be home again, ringing at the bell by jumping up and fetching it a thwack with his satchel, Nolan Maxwell being the last child in the Western world to own a satchel. He would then ring up Mrs Troubridge to say he was home safely and that would be another Tuesday done and dusted.

'I didn't know Mrs Troubridge could sing,' Jacquie ventured. 'And you should have told us, Nole,' she said. 'It would have been nice to invite her.'

'I did 'vite her,' he said, drawing himself up a little. 'She said she would cry, so could she have a copy of the DVD.'

Maxwell rumpled his son's hair. He could see that this could turn nasty, given half a chance. He bent down to him and gave him an extra kiss on top of his head. 'Sometimes, mate,' he said, 'I wonder who has been bringing you up. Whoever it is, they're doing a bang-up job. Well done. Very thoughtful all round.' He gave Jacquie a warning glance. When she was feeling a bit fragile, she often became what she thought was businesslike but could seem to a five-year-old a bit policeman-like.

'Well, I thought so,' muttered the forty-year-old that seemed to live in Nolan's little body sometimes. 'The DVDs are fifteen pounds,' he said, addressing himself to his mother. 'Nana wants one as well.'

'Does she?' was all Jacquie could say, weakly. 'How does she know about them?'

'I told her last week, on the phone.'

'Ah.' Jacquie reached for her purse. 'I wonder if it's buy one get one free.' A glance in the direction of Mrs Whatmough, beaming in the corner with her hand full of tenners, answered that question. 'You guys get in the car, while I buy some lovely DVDs.'

* * *

The first day of the Christmas holidays had always followed a certain pattern in the Maxwell household and this year was no exception. Get up. Add some more tinsel to any lingering bald spots in the decor. Go out and buy more tinsel. Remember that no one had ordered a turkey. Go out and order a turkey. This year another dimension was added: go out and buy nibbly bits and some cheap but stylish presents for the visit that afternoon by the Gold family party. Nolan was excited; he always tended to be a bit of a method actor and his Huron Indian persona still lingered, so Americans were very much the order of the day. Maxwell was getting by on deep breathing and concentrating on Jacquie's instructions to stop saying 'Howdy' all the time. They had invited Mrs Troubridge. The DVD was a great success and somehow, in all the cooing, and the aahing, someone — and Maxwell feared it may have been him — had asked her round. Still, as he told Jacquie, in for a penny, in for a Troubridge.

'She can hand things round,' he added as an extra encouragement. 'Olives. Buffalo wings. Things of that nature.'

Huron Indians have razor-sharp hearing. 'Have buffaloes got wings?' Nolan said, materialising at his father's elbow. 'They seem a bit big to be able to fly.'

'And think of the poo,' Maxwell added, leaping on to his son's train of thought as effortlessly as a hobo onto a boxcar.

Jacquie looked up from her list-compiling. 'I was thinking of keeping the food a bit more traditional,' she said. 'Mince pies. Sausage rolls. Umm . . .'

'Mini pizzas,' Maxwell offered. 'Filo-wrapped king prawns. Satay chicken onna-stick.'

Jacquie screwed up her face. 'You're right. What is traditional these days? I think I'll just have a bit of a mooch round M&S — that's traditional, isn't it?'

‘Absolutely,’ Maxwell said. ‘And don’t overdo it. The Golds’ll only just have got over Thanksgiving. While you’re out, Nole and I will tweak the decorations.’

That seemed like a good deal to Jacquie — the thought of shopping with two overexcited Maxwell men did not appeal at all. She grabbed her handbag and was down the stairs like a rat down a pipe, hauling on her coat as she ran. ‘It’s a deal,’ her voice floated up to them. ‘See you later.’ And with a crash of the door, she was gone.

# CHAPTER THREE

The sound of the Mosses' people carrier drawing up outside 38 Columbine was the innocent precursor to possibly the oddest Christmas drinks party the Maxwells had ever thrown. That it was the only Christmas drinks party the Maxwells had ever thrown was only part of it. Mrs Troubridge was waiting at the door to greet what she had decided to call 'Our Transatlantic Cousins'. This had confused Nolan at first, whose life was pretty devoid of cousins, having only a couple of the species — girls who were too old to play with and too far away to know. Jacquie had explained the reference and it hadn't helped much, but at least now he wasn't expecting the cast of *Hannah Montana* to tumble out of the people carrier.

Maxwell and Jacquie took their places at Mrs Troubridge's side, with Nolan between them. Maxwell feared they may strike the Gold family as a bit of a cliché, but it was too late now. First out of the car was a woman so manicured and coiffed it was a wonder she could move her head, let alone speak or blink. She was tiny but not, as Jacquie told her mother later, in a good way. Everything spoke of gym and surgeon, and as she got closer, it was clear that she was carrying a few more years than it at first appeared.

Mrs Troubridge rose to the occasion, stepping forward and speaking very clearly, as befitted someone who was divided from the guest by a common language and six thousand miles. 'Hello,' she trilled. 'I am Mrs Troubridge, Mr and Mrs Maxwell's neighbour. Welcome to Leighford.'

The woman looked down at her, but only slightly. It was unusual for anyone to be almost Mrs Troubridge's height and it gave them the appearance of an optical illusion. 'Hi,' she drawled. 'Camille.' With that, she walked forward, making the Maxwells break ranks, and she made her way to the stairs. 'Up here?' she asked and Jacquie hurried to follow her in.

The next to appear was a man built so differently that he appeared to be another species. He was huge, with wide shoulders, powerful thighs and a bull neck on which his head, buzz-cut to the scalp, appeared to balance like an egg in its cup. The general effect of scarcely controlled power and aggression was slightly offset by a huge gut which preceded him by some way as he came up the path to the by now fragmented welcoming committee. Maxwell felt Mrs Troubridge shrink into his side and he shared her trepidation. If this was Hector Gold, he would be going off sick for a year. At least.

The man thrust out a hand which seemed at least as big as the turkey now taking up half the fridge upstairs. 'Jeff,' he boomed. 'Jeff O'Malley. Glad to have you know me.'

Maxwell's knee pressed lightly into Nolan's back. Many viewings of *The Aristocats* had made J Thomas O'Malley almost seem like a member of the family, and although this huge man was not much like him to look at, Maxwell knew his son and a bit of a reminder at this early stage could prevent some serious embarrassment down the line. A faint humming of a familiar tune from just above knee height confirmed that this early intervention had not been wasted.

Trying to keep the relief from his voice, Maxwell took the proffered hand and shook it back. 'Peter Maxwell. Delighted to meet you.' He stood aside and ushered the man through. 'Do go up. I'll be with you in a minute.' The Head of Sixth Form glanced down, checking that Nolan and

Mrs Troubridge had not been swept up in the giant's passage. They were both there and he could give his attention to the next arrival, a woman so colourless and insubstantial that she was hardly there at all. She was clearly the wife and mother of Jeff and Camille in that she was cowed enough and skinny enough, but there was little else to say about her. Maxwell sincerely hoped that, should the woman go missing during their stay, he wouldn't be called upon to describe her, because he would not have been able to do it.

Mrs Troubridge leapt into action, having finally recovered from the volcanic eruption that was Jeff O'Malley. She extended a tiny hand and said gently, 'Hello, I am Jessica Troubridge, Mr and Mrs Maxwell's neighbour. And this,' she put a hand on Nolan's shoulder, 'is Nolan, their son. Come with us, there are mince pies upstairs. And sherry.'

Maxwell was a little disconcerted to see a flare of interest light the woman's eyes. He hoped that it was because she loved mince pies.

'Alana,' the woman breathed. 'Alana O'Malley.'

'How lovely,' chirruped Mrs Troubridge and she shepherded her little flock towards the stairs. Maxwell looked at her fondly; despite all her strange little ways and the years of bridling and unbridled nosiness, she was almost as much a part of his family now as Metternich, although she didn't tend to bring in quite so much dismembered livestock of an evening. He was brought out of his reverie by a soft touch on his arm.

'Mr Maxwell?' The voice was apologetic and gentle. It was like being tumbled headlong into an episode of the *Prairie Home Companion*. Looking up, he expected to see a Garrison Keillor lookalike, tall and gangly, hunched over from the Minnesota winters of his Lake Wobegon childhood. Instead, a small neat man stood there, his thinning blond hair stretched smoothly across the top of an almost impossibly high forehead. His eyes, behind his gold-rimmed glasses, were pale and apologetic, but his smile was real and he was the only one of the four who seemed genuinely glad to be here. It was probably the snow making him feel at home.

'Hector?' Maxwell smiled back. He had to fight to keep the relief out of his voice. 'My dear chap, how lovely to meet you. Come on in.'

'You have a lovely home,' Hector told him, gently. 'Please call me Hec, all my friends do.' And so they made their way up the stairs, with Hector finding time to exclaim about some small thing on almost every step. Metternich, scooting down at a rate of knots, was scooped up and admired from nose tip to tail tip. To Maxwell's amazement, he didn't take the man's face off with one swipe, but tolerated it as the lesser of two evils. Metternich didn't usually do strangers. He ate them occasionally, but only if they were of the rodentular persuasion.

Upstairs was becoming a little hard to take. Now Maxwell had time to listen, the noise levels had reached something approaching a large jet on its final descent, made up in equal amounts of Jeff O'Malley's strident roar and his daughter's descant whine. He looked round at Hector Gold, who was following him with a smile of pleasant vacuity on his face. He had clearly learnt over the years to filter the noise out and to rise above it. Maxwell was heartened; this should mean that Leighford High and the perils of Pansy Donaldson would hold no fears for a man who could live with the rest of this particular family. Squaring his shoulders, he led the way into the sitting room, temporarily become the Seventh Circle of Hell.

At Christmas, the Maxwell sitting room always seemed smaller than usual, because with every year of Nolan's life, the tree had got bigger and bigger. When the extra tinsel and various manifestations of Santa were taken into account, it was only just adequate for a party of normal people, but when the party involved Jeff O'Malley, it seemed genuinely cramped. He was standing, legs apart in a positively Henrician posture, with a mince pie dwarfed in one massive hand, a glass of sherry looking like a toy in the other. He turned as Maxwell went in.

'Hey, Peter,' he yelled, 'I was just telling the little woman here how I like your little home. Cute as a bug, ain't it?'

'We like it,' Maxwell smiled through gritted teeth. He was not used to being called Peter at the best of times, and when it appeared to be spelt with a 'd' in the middle, it was even worse.

'Ah, you English,' O'Malley shouted. 'You're always so polite. Say, can I call you Pete?'

'Er . . . no,' Maxwell said, still smiling, still with teeth gritted. 'But you can call me Max, everyone does.'

'Max it is, then,' the big man said and spread his arms still wider, to engulf everyone in the room it seemed. 'Ain't this swell? Christmas in England. I never thought I'd do it. And snow as well. It's just perfect.' He smiled around the room. 'And new friends too.' He threw the mince pie in whole and Nolan had to be shushed covertly; he knew these people were guests but he also knew bad table manners when he saw them. O'Malley chewed twice and swallowed. 'What the hell — oh . . .' he threw a glance at Nolan, 'sorry, little feller, what in blazes is in these things? I've had I don't know how many since we got here and I don't think two have been the same.'

Maxwell, who avoided mince pies as if his life depended on it, started compiling a list of ingredients in his mind, but the look in Jacquie's eye stopped him from sharing. 'Mincemeat,' he said. 'Fruit. Suet.'

O'Malley swirled a sausage-sized finger round between his teeth and gums to remove the glutinous remains. 'Is that so? Well, I think I've had enough of them now to know I don't really like them.' He glanced at Jacquie. 'No offence, little lady,' he said dismissively. 'Just don't like them.'

Maxwell was appalled to think that he and O'Malley had anything in common, and to cheer himself up, turned to Hector, but no sooner had he opened his mouth than O'Malley was off again.

'I was saying, as you came up the stairs, Max, what was it your little gal here did for a living? Camille here was saying that surely she didn't stay at home all day, with you just being a teacher and all. Camille has her own business at home, because of Hector being a teacher and only bringing home enough to keep her in shoes, more or less.' Maxwell had never actually seen a man castrated in his own sitting room before, but he supposed there had to be a first time for everything. The man paused, and finally Jacquie spoke.

'I am a Detective Inspector,' she said.

'What's that?' drawled Camille. 'You have people to inspect detectives over here? Isn't that a bit specialised?'

'No, honey,' O'Malley said, fetching her a slap on the shoulder which should have felled someone her size, but she had obviously been brought up to it, because she barely flinched. 'A Detective Inspector in England is the same as a Lieutenant in LA. Sort of.'

The woman looked vaguely at Jacquie as though she were some exotic creature in a zoo. 'Don't say,' she said. In the silence that followed, she added, 'I run a nail bar.' She threw a glance at her father. 'Daddy bought it for me, when he retired.'

'Retired from what?' said Jacquie politely.

'Why, from a Lieutenant in the police,' he laughed. 'Didn't old Hec tell you that on all those forms he filled in?'

'I don't believe that there was a space for father-in-law's profession,' Maxwell said quietly and turned to where Hector had been last, just behind him. The man had wandered away and was nodding gentle approval at a *Spy* cartoon of Gladstone which was just peeping out from behind the Christmas tree. 'How long have you been retired, Jeff?' he asked.

There was a tiny noise, as though a very quiet mouse had snorted, and only Mrs Troubridge heard it. It came from Alana, who was sitting on the arm of the chair Mrs Troubridge was occupying, with Nolan tucked down the side, like a cushion. The old woman looked up sharply and saw a smile just fading on Jeff O'Malley's wife's face. 'Retired?' she heard her say. 'Retired?' and the tiny snorting mouse snorted again. Mrs Troubridge looked down at Nolan, who did a whole body shrug which could mean so much between them. On this occasion it meant that he, Nolan, knew that she, Mrs Troubridge, thought that something was odd and that he acknowledged her right to do so. But, that said, he had no idea what she was thinking and if she wanted to tell his mum, now was the time, because she was forgetful and he was only five.

'Oooh, five or six years now, hon, isn't it?' O'Malley appealed not to his wife, but his daughter.

'More like seven,' she said. 'Because, if you remember—'

Nolan could see this going on for ages. 'Mums,' he suddenly announced. 'Mrs Troubridge would like to see you in the kitchen.'

'Really, darling,' Jacquie said, brightly. 'Well, all right, then. Help her up, poppet.' Nolan wriggled down behind his friend and hoisted her up by pushing with his knees.

Mrs Troubridge popped out of the chair like a cork out of a bottle, nearly dislodging Alana, whose balance didn't seem to be all it might. 'Yes,' she said, 'it's about the stuffing.'

Jacquie flicked a glance at Nolan, who looked innocent, and at Maxwell, who for once actually was innocent. O'Malley and his daughter were stalled in a conversation about realtors, Alana was looking glazed and Hector had wandered still further, in search of a little culture now he was nearer to it than he had been in years. The party was pooped, well and truly.

In the kitchen, Mrs Troubridge sat down at the table. 'I'm sorry, dear,' she said. 'I don't think it's anything to make much of, but I don't *like* that man.'

'Heavens above, Mrs Troubridge,' Jacquie said, pouring some gin into her sherry glass and knocking it back. 'I didn't need to come out here to glean that piece of info. None of us like him.' She looked over her shoulder in sudden horror, to see Hector standing there. 'Oh . . . I do apologise . . . well . . .' she stuttered to a stop. 'Mr Gold, what can I say? I'm so sorry.'

'Please,' he said and his smile slowly spread to light up his face. 'We all hate Jeff. Go right ahead.' And he wandered up the corridor in search of more history. 'And do call me Hec,' they heard him mutter, 'everyone does.'

Jacquie and Mrs Troubridge were transfixed and it took the younger woman a moment to get the conversation back on track. 'Where were we?'

'I can't remember, dear.' Mrs Troubridge looked confused. 'I'll retrace my steps. Hold on.' She closed her eyes and her lips moved and her arms waved as she bobbed and ducked her metaphorical way back into the sitting room. Her eyes opened. 'I remember, dear. It was Alana, poor soul. She was *very* sarcastic when her husband and daughter said he had retired. I wondered if there might be a story there, something we should know if these people are going to be living nearby.'

Jacquie looked at her neighbour quietly for a few seconds. Her gossip-gleaning skills had been honed for years on the grindstone that was the life of Peter Maxwell. She didn't miss much. 'Thank you, Mrs Troubridge,' she said. 'I'll bear it in mind.'

The general hubbub across the landing reached a kind of crescendo and Nolan came into the kitchen and leant nonchalantly on Mrs Troubridge. 'The Count has brought a vole in,' he remarked. 'He gave it to Meal.'

'Meal?' Mrs Troubridge asked.

'Camille,' Jacquie told her, in an aside. 'And that's Mrs Gold to you, young man.'

'S'right, Meal,' said Nolan, intent on the story. 'She is screaming quite a bit, so they are all going home. Dads said to come and say.'

'And of course we must go and say goodbye,' Jacquie said, scooting round the table and heading for the door.

'Yes, indeed,' said Mrs Troubridge, adding to Nolan as he helped her up, 'before they change their minds.'

* * *

The silence was so profound that the Maxwell family could almost feel it still ringing in their ears. Mrs Troubridge had left with the Gold O'Malley brigade, helping Alana down the stairs and quietly removing the almost empty sherry bottle which she had secreted in her bag. Mrs Troubridge had identified a troubled soul and she and the American woman had bonded in the silent fellowship of lonely people everywhere. Although Mr Troubridge had been noted for his quiet elegance and self-effaced courtliness, his widow could still feel some fellowship with Alana O'Malley: years of lonely nights, knitting furiously and pretending that you didn't care that he hadn't come home. Mrs Troubridge had had no children; Alana had had Camille, but she was so much a daddy's girl that it was doubtful that she had helped the loneliness much. At least when Mr Troubridge did get home from his absences, he could give his attention to his wife — Mrs Troubridge blushed to even think the word 'attention' with its attendant implications — but she imagined that in the O'Malley household it would be difficult to get a sheet of paper between Camille and her father, let alone a whole wife, no matter how thin. So she had seen them off at the door with an understanding pat on Alana's shoulder, and had then gone back to her own house. Apart from anything else, she suspected the sherry had run out apart from the dribble in the recovered bottle and there was also the risk of washing up.

Maxwell looked around and could hardly believe that a room could empty so quickly. He gathered up a few glasses and made a cursory search for the sherry bottle, which appeared to have gone missing. Nolan was taking plates out to the kitchen one by careful one. Jacquie was out in the garden, disposing of the vole. Maxwell turned as he heard footsteps on the stairs. Something about the combined voices of Jeff and Camille had made him jumpy.

'Oh, it's you,' he said to his wife as she came in, voleless.

She couldn't be bothered to do the murder mime they usually did in honour of the television crime cliché that normally preceded 'What are you doing here?' and a knife/axe/bullet to the head. Instead, she settled for, 'Who else were you expecting?' She went over to the fire and rubbed her hands together in front of the flames.

He shrugged. 'Who knows, after this afternoon? That was a strange experience and no mistake. Have you seen the sherry?'

'Mrs O'Malley put it in her bag,' Nolan informed him from behind the sofa.

'Quisling,' Maxwell muttered, but he was proud of the boy's observational powers nonetheless.

'Ah,' Jacquie said, with the air of someone putting two and two together.

Maxwell cocked an eyebrow at her and then looked at Nolan, in a significant sort of way.

Jacquie sighed. There was little her son didn't spot; she sometimes suspected he might have the house comprehensively bugged. She sat down and hauled her son onto her knee. 'I sometimes think we put too much on this child.'

Maxwell looked round the room, spinning round and looking under clocks, table mats and behind the curtains before asking, 'What child is that?'

Nolan laughed like a loon and flung himself back onto the sofa. Jacquie made his hysteria worse with some well-aimed tickling. Eventually, they all calmed down and Nolan, slipping two fingers into his mouth and squeezing his ear lobe, said solemnly, 'I think I'll go and have a bit of a quiet moment,' and left the room heading for his bed, followed by the cat.

They watched him go and Maxwell reraised his eyebrow.

'Mrs T seems to have taken to Alana,' Jacquie told him, 'and heard her make a sarky comment when Jeff and Camille were talking about when he retired.'

'I can't see how a comment, be it never so sarky—'

'Yes, I'm with you there,' Jacquie agreed, 'but I must admit I have my doubts about Jeff O'Malley, Police Lootenant. He seems a bit like a character from a sitcom.'

'Heavy on the sit, fairly light on the com, I think, don't you?'

'They're horrific. Hector seems all right, though. And can't stand his father-in-law.'

'He told you that?' Maxwell had heard that Americans could be rather blunt about things, but on a very short acquaintance it seemed a bit much, even for an American, and a Minnesotan at that.

Jacquie blushed and told him about her little faux pas. 'But he really didn't seem to mind, Max,' she said. 'I mean, I hope you would at least pretend to stick up for my mother . . .'

'Dearest heart, I *would* stick up for your mother. I *do* stick up for your mother.' There was a brief silence as they both remembered the incident at Jacquie's cousin's wedding the previous summer. And he *had* put in a good word for her at the Nuremberg trials. 'Did he not, then? Hector? Not stick up for your mother, obviously, but I'm sure you catch my drift.'

'No,' she said. 'He said, "We all hate Jeff," and then just asked me to call him Hec.'

'Hmm, apparently everybody does.'

'He seems a genuinely nice chap,' she said.

'He is. And Alana seems nice as well. We mustn't judge her just because she nicked the sherry. She deserves it, in my opinion. And Mrs Troubridge has taken to her, you say?'

'So it seems. So, as I said, she was sitting next to her through all the retirement conversation when she heard her mutter to herself and I think she got the impression that the retirement was not quite all that it seemed.'

'Kicked out, you mean?'

'Nail on head as always, precious,' she said, kicking off her shoes and curling her feet under her as she leant back. 'Perhaps I'm just embroidering for the sake of it, but he really was a piece of work, wasn't he? Thank goodness we won't have to meet him ever again.'

'I must say, I'm hoping not,' Maxwell agreed. 'But I have a horrible feeling that they might turn out to be the kind of family that go around together in a flock, or pack, or whatever Attenboroughian phrase you like to use.'

'Shoal.'

'As in piranhas?' he asked.

She inclined her head with a smile.

'Then we little sticklebacks must learn to hide in the weeds until they have passed by, mustn't we?'

# CHAPTER FOUR

Maxwell, Jacquie, Nolan and Mrs Troubridge sat back from the remains of the Christmas dinner and let out a collective sigh. The portions had varied, Mrs Troubridge eating a plate of food which would not have taxed the robin on the chocolate Yule log, but they had all had ample and just a tiny bit more and were, to quote Nolan, as full as eggs.

'Darling, that was spectacular, as always,' Maxwell told his wife, then turned to Mrs Troubridge and risked what she would count as a slightly risqué sally. 'Darling, so was your contribution,' he told her. Mrs Troubridge had provided the stuffing and the trifle, both home-made, both absolutely stiff with alcohol, much to Nolan's relief. He hated both stuffing and trifle and being forbidden to eat them was an extra Christmas treat.

Mrs Troubridge blushed coquettishly and gave Maxwell what she considered a hefty whack on the arm. As a killer blow it left a lot to be desired, but he flinched theatrically and smiled at the old trout through the endorphin-fuelled haze of a huge meal. 'Mr Maxwell,' she said, 'you really are funny.' She looked round the table at them all and her eyes misted over. 'I love you all, you know,' she whispered, then, taking herself in hand, scraped her chair back from the table. 'I must be away, though, because Araminta is phoning from some far-flung outpost and I mustn't miss her call.' She dropped a kiss on Nolan's head, air-kissed Jacquie and fluttered her fingers at Maxwell before scurrying to the stairs. They all sat with bated breath until they heard the door slam at the bottom. She wasn't quite as steady on her feet as she had been, but their care had to be at a suitable distance. The tap on the wall on the landing told them that she had also negotiated her own stairs and normal service resumed.

'May I get down, Mums?' Nolan asked, feet already on the floor and only the slightest sliver of bum still in contact with the chair.

She nodded and he was off like a greyhound. The mound of presents from under both the Maxwells' and Mrs Troubridge's trees had resolved into his favourites and the rest. One of the topmost favourites had been a rather scary battery-powered hamster, which would by definition be somewhere under the sofa mauled by Metternich by Boxing Day, so he was making the most of it while the going was good. Soon, distant chuckling could be heard from his bedroom and his parents could relax.

'Mrs Maxwell,' the Head of Sixth Form said, 'you do a mighty fine Christmas.' It was Alan Ladd out of *Shane* and not at all like Jeff O'Malley.

'Even without blueberry pie?' she asked. She didn't get all of his film references, but this one had been with her, Constable and Inspector, for long enough now for it never to be missed. It wasn't a very good Jean Arthur, but you couldn't have everything.

'I couldn't eat a blueberry pie right now for ready money,' Maxwell told her. 'For a start, I am drunk as a skunk on the trifle.' He lowered his head and looked sideways along the table. 'Look, if you line it up against a light background, you can see the fumes.' He looked up at his wife and cocked his head on one side. 'Have you had anything to drink with the meal?'

'No. I didn't fancy it.'

He straightened up. 'You're on call, aren't you?'

She lifted one shoulder and avoided his gaze. 'I might be,' she said.

'Might be?' he asked. 'How long has this hypothetical situation been the case?'

'A few days,' she said. 'Henry rang while the O'Malley lot were here.'

'The Gold lot,' Maxwell corrected.

'That's not how it felt,' she said, 'but then, yes. Did I not mention it?'

'Not really,' he said.

'It probably slipped my mind. Anyway,' she went on hurriedly, 'it's nearly half past three and I'm only on until nine. Then one of the others takes over. Bob Thorogood, I think.'

Maxwell knew the rules about tempting fate, but he did it anyway. 'Let's hope there's no murder and mayhem today, but if there is, let it be at one minute past nine,' he said.

'If I had a drink, I would drink to that,' Jacquie said, raising an imaginary glass.

'Clink,' said Maxwell, waving his real glass at her. 'Scrabble?'

'Don't mind if I do,' she said and they pushed back their chairs and went across the landing to the sitting room. 'No proper names, nothing foreign and absolutely *nothing* historical. You cheated last time with "defenestration".'

'Only because I inadvertently put two effs in it.'

Metternich listened carefully from under Mrs Troubridge's abandoned chair for the faint pop as the gas fire was lit, then crept out stealthily. He was allowed a lot of leeway, he realised, especially now he had experienced Happy Paws cattery and all that that had entailed, but he knew that even he would be pushing his luck if he licked the gravy off the plates in full view of everyone. So he waited a while longer and then, when the tiles had been shaken out and Jacquie had let out her usual wail when Maxwell could get rid of all seven letters on the first go, he sprang onto the table and started with the dregs in the gravy boat. Ah, the hint of turkey!

* * *

It was eight fifty-nine and the Maxwell house was quiet. Nolan had gone to bed without a problem, clutching his hamster to his chest, and Maxwell had done the washing-up while Jacquie dozed in front of *The Sound of Music*. She couldn't stand the film, but Maxwell hated it with a mad passion, so it amused her to watch at least the beginning whenever it was shown. The Scrabble had been a rout as usual, the cold turkey and bubble and squeak a mere formality as they were all so full still, and so Christmas Day had wound its usual uneventful way down to night, sleep and Boxing Day.

Maxwell was sprawled on the sofa, with Jacquie sprawling the other way, so that he could massage her feet and she could refrain from tickling his. Metternich was tucked neatly in where their bodies crossed in the middle and something totally mindless was happening on the television. God was in his heaven and all was right with the world. They both tried not to look at the clock.

Nine o'clock, and all was well. Jacquie heaved a sigh of relief and Maxwell wordlessly passed her the gin and tonic, poured while he was last on his feet, against the day. She raised it to her lips and muttered, 'Cheers.' He raised the amber glass of Southern Comfort.

Then three things happened, so close together that to a casual observer they all seemed to happen at once.

The phone rang.

Metternich leapt out from his cosy nest, severely clawing both Maxwell and Jacquie in his passage.

And Jacquie Carpenter-Maxwell, Detective Inspector with the Leighford Police, said, 'Bugger and poo — what's the matter with them? Can't they tell the time?'

She scrambled off the sofa and reached the phone by lying on the floor and pulling it off the coffee table. 'Yes?

What? But I'm . . . Now, just hang on . . . Well . . .' She frowned at Maxwell and ran a finger across her throat. 'I think I should ring DCI Hall . . . Oh, is he?' This time she sighed. 'I'm on my way.'

She rang off and rolled over, lying on the rug with arms splayed out to her sides.

Maxwell wasn't sure what the correct length of pause was in situations like these, but after what he judged to be the right length and time, he said, 'Problem?'

'Yes. A shooting, out on the Barlichway.'

'Of course there is,' he said. 'It's Christmas, the time of peace, goodwill to all men and getting tanked up and taking a potshot at the neighbours. Why do they need you? More to the point, why have they called you? It's gone nine.'

'Two reasons. Bob Thorogood "forgot",' and Maxwell could clearly hear the quotation marks as she spoke, 'that he was on call after nine and is lying insensible in the remains of the Christmas pudding, according to his wife. The other reason is that the shot man is an old friend of mine, well, ours actually, as he went to Leighford High. Henry and I had him in court finally last October; you may remember the case, it was in the *Advertiser*. We finally had enough on him for child abuse, mental, physical and sexual, a horrible case, but he got off on a technicality.'

'A technicality?' Maxwell was appalled all over again.

'His wife was the main witness, and she changed her testimony. We had no other witnesses, the medical evidence was a bit equivocal and so the case was thrown out. I have rarely seen Henry so mad.' She was gathering herself together, running her hands through her hair and generally checking her clothes for gravy dribbles and chocolate smears. She held out her arms and faced Maxwell. 'Do I have to get changed?'

'You're fine,' he told her, 'although you might want to take off the Santa earrings. So, the wife did it?'

'Who knows. I would if I was his wife. I've been tempted married to you, so I can only imagine what she must be feeling. Her children have been taken into care and she had to choose between him and them. Not a choice I would care to make, especially at Christmas.'

'If the case failed, though . . .'

'Social Services work independently of the police and the case is still ongoing. They have a child protection procedure underway, and until it has gone through all the stages, it can't be stopped. Like us they are sure of their ground, although there is no longer any corroborating evidence, so they are dragging their feet on this. The children are quite little, so they can't be witnesses, but if they are away from their father for long enough without showing any signs of bruising or anything, that will mean that the chance of accidental bruising becomes less and non-accidental more.' While she was talking, Jacquie was scrabbling under the sofa for her other shoe. 'I hope it isn't her, I have to say. She seemed a nice enough woman, just very weak.'

'So, she probably hasn't done it, then, this Mrs . . . ?'

'You don't catch me like that,' Jacquie said. 'Even the *Advertiser* understood the need for anonymity. So do I.'

'An old Leighford Highena, though . . .'

'Yup.'

'I can't think who . . .'

'A lot can go on between GCSE and . . . however old this man became before tonight.' She grabbed her bag and left the room, blowing a kiss as she went. 'I don't expect I'll be long. Henry's meeting me there.'

'Henry is? He was having Christmas off, I thought?'

'Yes. That's why I took the days on, really. It's the first Christmas with the boys back from university and I think Margaret wanted to do the family thing. She's a bit empty nest, love her.' Jacquie spoke with the confidence of one whose empty-nest days were long in the future.

'So . . .'

'He felt it badly, like I did. Those kids were covered in bruises and cowered whenever he came into the room. He is built a bit like their dad, same colouring as well. They are totally traumatised.' She coughed to cover a sob. 'We couldn't help comparing . . .'

'I know, sweetie. Sooner you're gone, sooner you're back. Love to Henry.' He waved her off and listened as her footsteps went the wrong way along the landing, to Nolan's room at the foot of the second flight of stairs. She just had to do it, he knew. Having their son was the best thing they had ever done, but it didn't make her job any easier.

She blew another kiss into the sitting room as she passed the doorway, ran lightly down the stairs and in no time he heard the car start and she was gone.

* * *

Detective Inspector Jacquie Carpenter-Maxwell, with her glug of gin in mind, drove sedately across the Dam, heading for the Barlichway Estate. It glowed faintly in the distance, pulsing slightly as the million Christmas light bulbs flashed on and off, the Barlichway version of kneeling before the radiant boy. She glanced down at the GPS screen and saw that the address she needed was at the far side of the estate, through the rabbit warren of affordable housing and burnt-out garages that a large proportion of Leighford's population called home. She turned down the volume on her Christmas CD which Nolan and Maxwell insisted on having permanently installed in the car for the whole of the season and squared her shoulders. 'Merry Christmas, everyone,' she mouthed along with Shakin' Stevens as she took the slip road, away from Christmas and into hell.

Henry Hall looked up as she drew up outside the house. No Christmas lights here, making it look like a black hole in comparison with the condensed Blackpools on either side. The door stood open and faint light spilt down the path, giving the DCI a halo as it caught in his hair. There was a sprawled shape on the path, with a dark pool at the end where the head had so recently been. On the snow to either side was a spray pattern, looking dark in the faint light but,

Jacquie knew, in the arc lights the forensics boys were setting up it would look an eerie grey and red with sparkling spicules of white bone. Hall was wearing white coveralls and latex gloves and looked like a snowman from a horror movie, flanked as he was with piles of grey scraped-up snow from the greasy road. His usual immaculate three-piece was hidden away under that lot but he didn't look out of place. For both Henry and Jacquie this was gear they both wore all too often. He raised his hand in greeting.

She got out of the car and stood on the pavement until one of the forensics team standing at the back of their van handed her a coverall. Hall wandered over to her as she struggled into it. She looked up at him and saw her expression mirrored in his face. That he had an expression at all was a surprise and showed how this case had affected him. It was unfair — and inappropriate — to liken the DCI to something out of *I, Robot* but there were those who did. 'Merry Christmas, Henry,' she said, softly. There was a faint question in the statement.

'I think so, yes,' he said. 'I don't want to speak ill of the dead,' he said, 'but I'm certainly not sorry to see this today.'

In her head, Jacquie heard Maxwell's voice say 'Each man's death diminishes me' but she ignored it; even John Donne would not be sorry to see this man dead. She focused on the task in hand. 'Did his wife do it?' she asked.

'Hmmm, now there's a question,' Hall mused. 'No, I don't think she did. He was shot from quite close range with a large handgun, something along the lines of a .44 Magnum, or the forensics team think so at least. His head is gone, more or less, and there isn't much else that can do that amount of damage. There's no sign of the weapon, but with the snow, it may be lying close by and we wouldn't see it, so that's nothing really. But the wife was still in her slippers when we got here, and they were dry. They would be soaking if she had faced him from the path. The footprints were pretty scuffed; neighbours came running, if only to applaud, so we'll get nothing there.'

Devil's Advocate J Carpenter-Maxwell put in her ten penn'orth. 'She could have changed her shoes. She could have hidden the gun.'

'She's distraught.'

'She could be acting.'

Hall looked at her, light clouding his glasses, one eyebrow raised. 'Jacquie, you've met this woman. She can hardly walk and chew gum, let alone put on a performance like this. Come inside, tell me what you think when you've seen her.' He held out a hand to her. 'Watch where you step. The path is a bit . . .'

'I'm fine,' she said, but she took his hand all the same. 'I hope she didn't do it, Henry,' she said quietly, 'but if she didn't, who did?'

Hall waved an arm to encompass the Barlichway, if not the world. This was the sink estate they had tacked on to a sleepy south-coast resort thirty years ago, believing presumably that nowhere had a right to be safe and secure. Affordable housing was a euphemism for drug dealing, pit bulls and — as of today at least — a gun culture which the architects of yesteryear had not dreamt possible.

Jacquie nodded and followed him inside, skirting the mess on the path.

Going inside the house was like going through a wrinkle in time. There was nothing to suggest that it was Christmas — no tree, no decorations, no presents, no lingering smell of turkey and sprouts. The only thing the room had in common with festive settings all over the country was a table with loads of bottles of sundry booze; the difference was that for this house, they were a normal fixture, like a fruit bowl might be elsewhere. Curled on the broken-backed settee was a small woman, folded tightly in a foetal position, a crumpled tissue held to her red nose. Her eyes were swollen with weeping and every now and then she gave a shudder, accompanied by a whimper. A policewoman in uniform sat on the arm of the settee at the woman's feet and tried to look sympathetic while not touching anything. It was a hard trick and she was not quite pulling it off.

Jacquie went and crouched at the woman's head. 'Mrs Hendricks? I'm Detective Inspector Carpenter. Do you remember me?' Henry noted the dropping of the 'Maxwell'. The Barlichway was no place for two surnames, unless one was an alias. 'I'd like to ask you some questions, if that's OK.' She paused, but the woman didn't react at all. Jacquie put out a hand and touched her arm, and the woman flinched and gave a little cry. 'I don't want to hurt you,' Jacquie said. 'No one will hurt you.' It was with an effort that she bit back the 'now'. 'Can we get you a cup of tea? Coffee?' She glanced at the table of drink. It was mostly extra-strong lager and whisky, in a bottle with a plain label which said simply 'whisky'. There were a few sticky-looking alcopops and some liqueur, but nothing that was appropriate for shock brought on by your husband having his head shot off.

The woman struggled upright and gave her nose a decisive blow. 'Got no tea. Jim didn't like tea, so we never got it in.' She looked at Jacquie and the DI saw that her eyes were not just swollen with tears, but were blackened with bruises old and new. A tiny ghost of a smile touched the woman's mouth. 'I would love a cuppa, though.'

Jacquie looked up at the policewoman who was standing now the big guns were here. 'Constable, can you nip next door and borrow a tea bag?'

'I can do better than that, ma'am,' she said and put her hand in her pocket. She pulled out a tea bag in a little envelope. 'It's Twining's Breakfast Tea,' she said, 'if that's OK, Mrs Hendricks?'

Jacquie was amazed on more than one level: firstly that the woman had a tea bag in her pocket and secondly that she wondered whether it was the right kind. 'I'm sure that will be fine,' she said, smiling. She looked down at the new widow. 'Sugar?'

'Ain't got none. Jim . . .'

'. . . didn't take sugar. But do you?'

'Two.'

Jacquie looked up at the policewoman and was rewarded by the appearance of two sugar sachets from the same pocket as the tea bag. She was tempted to ask for a rabbit and a tiger to see if she could produce those as well, but this was no time for frivolity. Without taking her eyes from the magic pocket, she said, 'Milk?'

'Got that,' the woman said. 'Jim drank a lot of milk. For the calcium. He was . . . he was very healthy, Jim. He said his body was a temple.'

Jacquie nodded to the policewoman who went out towards the kitchen, squeezing past Hall as she did so. He looked on; despite not being old enough, he felt like a proud parent when Jacquie was going through her paces. She could charm the birds out of the trees and get information out of the least promising witness. Having wound her up, he would just let her go.

'Mrs Hendricks . . . can I call you Linda?'

The woman looked puzzled, as though she had almost forgotten that that was her name. Jacquie remembered that her husband had routinely referred to her as Bitch, both to her face and when referring to her, even in court.

'S'pose. Yeah,' the ghost of a smile flitted again, 'that would be nice. Linda. Yeah.'

'Well, Linda, can you tell us what happened here tonight?'

'We was watching the telly. It was some programme, hundred best something. Christmas telly, you know the sort of thing.'

Hall and Jacquie exchanged glances. If this call had had just one good thing about it, it was because it was saving them from Christmas telly.

'The bell went. We couldn't work out who it was, because . . .' she dropped her eyes and then flicked a glance at Hall. 'You know how it's been, Mr Hall. Eggs and dog shit, all that.'

Hall had seen the reports, taken down verbatim, the obscene rants from Hendricks on the phone, in person at the station, demanding protection which was, apparently, his right. He knew his own rights, just not those of anyone else. He inclined his head to her and motioned her to go on.

'Well,' she sniffed and Jacquie offered her a clean tissue, 'Jim went upstairs and looked down. You can see the front step from the bedroom window. He came back down again and said he couldn't work out who it was, but he thought he knew them. He just couldn't remember where from.'

'Did he describe them to you? To see if you knew who it was?'

Linda Hendricks laughed, a sound more like a bark, as though she had forgotten how to do it and was practising. 'He wouldn't expect me to know who it was,' she said. 'Anyway, he went to open the door.' She closed her eyes and leant back. Tears leaked across the yellow and blue of the bruises and she pressed the already sodden tissue to her mouth. Jacquie and Hall waited for her to compose herself and after a minute she lifted her head and went on. 'I heard him say hello, like a question, you know? Hello? Like that. Then . . . there was a bang.' She paused, eyes unfocused, remembering. 'No, not a bang. Not really loud. More a kind of pop. Like a really big balloon going off, if you know what I mean?'

Hall and Jacquie made mental notes: something to silence the gun, or a lie.

'Then . . . Jim didn't come back in. It was cold with the door open, so after a bit I went to see what had happened.'

'After a bit?' Hall asked. 'How long did you wait, Linda?' He knew Hendricks well enough to know that she would not have done like most wives and simply kicked the door shut with a foot. That would probably have got her a re-blackened eye at the very least. When Matthew, known as Jimi, known as Jim Hendricks left a door open, that door stayed open or he would want to know the reason why.

The woman shrugged. 'Five minutes?'

'Are you sure?' Jacquie asked. 'Five minutes is a long time to wait.'

The woman hung her head, then shook it. Tears were dripping off the end of her nose and flew from side to side. She wiped her eyes with the back of her hand. Her voice was a whisper. 'He didn't like me to interfere. He said I was too stupid . . .' She cleared her throat, and when she went on, her voice was stronger. 'I went out and at first I couldn't see anyone. Then, I looked down . . . I didn't know what had happened to his head! I knew it was him, from his clothes, but he didn't have a head! I screamed. People came running . . .' She started to scream again, a thin wail that went on and on, not rising or falling except when she drew a ragged breath.

Jacquie patted her arm and Hall went outside for a paramedic who had arrived with the ambulance. He came in, a green saviour, and rummaged in his bag. Jacquie got to her feet and went outside with Hall.

He looked down at her. 'So, did she do it?' he asked.

She set her mouth for a moment, to recover from being in the path of that eldritch wail. 'No, guv,' she said. 'No, she didn't do it.'

Skirting the tarpaulin stretched over the bloodstained snow, Hall turned and spoke over his shoulder. 'We'll look for the person who did, then, shall we? But not today.'

'Not?' Jacquie was staggered. Henry Hall's watchword — or one of them at least — was to not let the grass grow under his feet.

'No. It's Christmas still, you've got a home to go to. So have I. So has everyone here. Let's salvage what we can of the evening and meet tomorrow eight sharp and see what we can do. Have you had a good one, so far?'

'Fabulous, actually; Christmas was never much of a thing when I was a kid, but Max and Nole certainly know how to party. They have single-handedly caused a tinsel shortage in Leighford. We had some awful people round a few days ago; I told you about the exchange teacher, I think, didn't I?'

'You mentioned it, yes. Some woman.'

'She backed out. It's a bloke now, seems nice. But the extended family . . . well, sooner him than me, I say. Nolan was disappointed. The father-in-law is called O'Malley . . .'

Hall had sat through The *Aristocats* far more often than even Jacquie and Maxwell and unexpectedly hummed a bar of the song.

'Yes,' Jacquie chuckled. 'Unfortunately, only the name is the same.'

'How's Mrs Troubridge?' Hall had a soft spot for the old lady.

'Having a whale of a time now Nole is bigger. She adored him from the first, of course, but now they are inseparable, pretty much.' She stamped her feet in the cold and blew on her hands.

'You're cold,' he said. 'Let's get off home until tomorrow.'

'I won't argue with you, Henry,' she said. 'I would like to wind Christmas Day up properly. Cold turkey and pickles at midnight, or it isn't Christmas.'

Hall almost smiled. 'Fried Christmas pudding for Boxing Day breakfast in our house. In fact,' he paused with the door of his car half open, 'Let's make that nine sharp, shall we?' He raised his voice so his team could hear. 'Nine o'clock tomorrow, everyone. Can you make sure everyone knows? Thanks.' Then, to Jacquie, he said, 'In answer to your much earlier question, Jacquie, yes, it *is* a merry Christmas, I believe.' And he climbed into his car and was gone.

# CHAPTER FIVE

As Jacquie drove down the sweep of Columbine her heart rose a little at the glow of light from behind the curtains of Number 38. Maxwell didn't always wait up, on her instruction, but on Christmas Day there were certain traditions to be followed and if there was a man in the world who followed tradition, that man was Peter Maxwell.

She walked up the stairs quietly, not creeping exactly, more a case of moving not loudly, and poked her head around the door of the sitting room. Maxwell was stretched out on the sofa, Metternich lying along him, mirroring his position and both spark out. Taking care not to clink, she poured a gin and tonic even stronger than the earlier aborted one of what must have been the same evening, but felt like years ago. Easing a slice of lime down the edge of the glass so that the splash didn't wake anyone, she sat down in the chair next to the fire and gazed into the flames. Metternich flicked an ear, which may have been a greeting or something happening in a dream. Otherwise, the room was still, the only sound the faint hiss of the fake flames. She cradled her drink and sank deeper into the chair.

'Matthew Hendricks,' Maxwell suddenly said, not moving. Metternich extended a warning paw, but otherwise didn't move either.

Jacquie sat up as if he had screamed in her ear. 'What?' she said, sharply. The words had echoed so precisely what she was thinking that it made her feel a little dizzy.

'Matthew Hendricks,' Maxwell repeated. 'Known, inevitably, as Jimi, later shortened to Jim.' He got up carefully, dislodging Metternich claw by painful claw, and turned, propped on one elbow, to look at her over his shoulder. 'The dead man, am I right?'

She gathered herself together. 'I couldn't possibly comment,' she said, but her attempt at an Ian Richardson in *House of Cards* was woefully short of the mark.

Maxwell flopped back down and brushed off his front, where Metternich had left his scattered black and white calling cards. 'Thought so,' he muttered, smugly, and closed his eyes again. Then, he sat back up and turned to her properly, smiling. 'Where are my manners? You must be hungry. Turkey and pickles?'

She nodded, still not speaking.

'Just a mo', then. Branston or onions?'

'Both, please.'

'Pig. Cold roasters?'

'What, are you nuts? Of course.'

'Hang on, then.' He went out and she could hear him across the landing, humming as he assembled their Christmas supper, as if one of his Old Leighford Highenas was not lying dead on Dr Astley's slab, waiting for his assistant Donald to have a good old rummage in his abdomen and have a go at piecing together his head. *Bones* had a lot to answer for, one way and another, although a 22nd-century lab full of beautiful people all flirting with each other and undergoing counselling was as far from Dr Jim Astley's establishment as you could possibly get. Soon he was back, closing the door behind him with a deft flick of his left bum cheek. He passed her the plate.

She took a few mouthfuls and then looked across at him. He was sitting on the sofa, spreading piccalilli on a slice of turkey as though butter wouldn't melt in his mouth. 'So, how did you know it was Matthew Hendricks, then?' she asked him.

'It wasn't that hard, as a matter of fact,' he said, putting down his fork, so he could count off on his fingers, 'aside from the fact that I am a genius of rare talent. Firstly, I tried thinking of all the boys I have taught in the past million years who would behave the way this one has, and it came to too many. So, secondly, I thought of all of the above, but who would be aged between, say, twenty and thirty.'

'Why that age range?'

'Well, you said the children were too young to give evidence, so they are under, shall we say, ten. I assumed that the couple in question would probably have had their first child quite young, so I just chose those ages to cut the numbers down.'

'OK, go on.' Jacquie tried not to let it show that she was impressed. Matthew Hendricks had been twenty-seven.

'That cut the numbers down quite a lot, so that was a helpful device. So then I thought, of all of the ones I was left with, which ones had an abusive parent.' He held his hand up to stop her speaking. 'Yes, yes, I know that isn't always the case, but as I say, I had to cut it down somehow.' He looked a little crestfallen. 'As a matter of fact, that cut them all out, so I had to backtrack. This time, I asked myself if any of them had ever been involved in any cases of child abuse outside of the family and, as they say in the Modern Languages Department, *voilà*! Matthew Hendricks.'

Jacquie bit down on a pickled onion in a rather threatening manner. 'Ah ha, Mr Clever. Matthew Hendricks has no record of being involved in child abuse.'

'No indeed, Woman Detective Inspector. But he does . . . *did* . . . have a record of accusing someone of child abuse.'

'Really? We didn't know that.'

'It wouldn't have helped, I don't expect. We dealt with it internally — it was clearly a pack of lies. He accused the whole SLT, male and female, of doing unspeakable things to him when he was in detention. His mother threw a wobbly and came in ranting at Legs and so we had to have an enquiry but it was clear from the start that it wasn't true. On the other hand, he showed a remarkably accurate knowledge of some rather strange sexual practices which alarmed us. We did send a report to Children's Services, but I'm afraid at this remove I can't remember what happened.'

'Well, it must be ten years ago now, surely?'

Maxwell pursed his lips and did some maths in his head. 'How old was he?'

'Twenty-seven.'

'Sixteen years ago, then.'

'He was *eleven*?'

'Possibly twelve, but he was certainly in Year Seven, yes.'

Jacquie slumped back in the chair. 'Oh, great. If this comes out . . .'

'Well, no one will hear it from me,' her husband assured her. 'So, did the wife do it? Mmmm . . . Linda, was it? Mousey hair, blobby nose?'

'Yes, Linda. But, how did you know that?'

'Control freaks mate for life, you should know that. We had trouble with them from the start. Linda McGarry she was, then. Inappropriate behaviour in class, that kind of thing. She would do anything he told her to, without question.'

'No change there, then,' Jacquie muttered, taking a big swig of her drink. 'Why did we not *know* this stuff? Isn't there some kind of procedure?'

'Of course,' he reassured her. 'Reams of paper get filled with reams of information every week. Pages and pages of concerns, questions, requests for feedback. But at the end of the line, there has to be a human to deal with them and that's what we're short of. It takes a whole load of people to make a perfect world and sadly only one to spoil it again. And after five years we have to bin the lot anyway. So,' he thought he would try again, 'did the wife do it?'

Jacquie thought of confidentiality. She thought of children crying in the night with no one to hear. She thought of

Linda Hendricks' black eyes, one superimposed on another and on another. 'No,' she told him. 'The wife didn't do it.'

'Got anyone in the frame?' Maxwell asked her, gathering up the plates and making for the door.

'No, not really.'

'It sounds like a mousetrap situation to me,' Maxwell said from the doorway.

'Mousetrap?' Jacquie was tired and the evening had taken a very unfestive turn.

'Yes, you know, the mousetrap. *The* mousetrap. Agatha Christie. *The Mousetrap* — the policeman did it.'

Jacquie went pale. Yet again, Maxwell had read her mind.

* * *

Boxing Day was, as Boxing Days tend to be, a bit of an anti-climax. Nolan's hamster still worked, which was an unexpected relief, and so he and Metternich played happily with it for most of the morning, CBeebies burbling happily along in the background. Jacquie had gone off to work before either of her men were dressed and, in fact, was destined to return while they were in their pyjamas, but again, rather than still.

While the cat and his boy kept each other amused, Maxwell got his head down in one of the books which Santa had delivered; he had a lot to choose from, he must have been really good that year. Jacquie had long ago given up the unequal struggle of trying to make his presents look interesting by packing rolled-up socks in the same package as a DVD. These days, his presents looked like a mini ziggurat at the bottom of the tree as large and scrummy illustrated books on the Crimea gave way to biographies which gave way to books of silly pictures which in their turn gave way to DVDs and CDs. To some it might be boring; to Maxwell it was heaven.

But this Boxing Day he couldn't seem to get last night's events out of his head. The book — a biography of Cleopatra, enjoyable and readable enough — held his attention for pages at a time, but the mental picture of an eleven-year-old with old, old eyes kept rising in front of him and obscured the text. He tried to remember which staff had been involved in the drama at the time. The Head of Sixth Form had been at the periphery only, as the boy had been in Year Seven, but it had been a trivial incident in one of his lessons which had kicked the whole drama off, so he had been copied in on all that had happened later. He closed his eyes and conjured up a mental picture.

Legs Diamond had obviously taken the brunt, as a Head Teacher always will. Bernard Ryan had not come out of the whole thing with too much dignity intact, but that was Bernard for you. He had been younger then, of course — as had they all — and was still clawing his way up the greasy pole, before it got just too slippery and he settled for Deputy Head at Leighford High School in perpetuity. He tried to remember whether Deirdre Lessing had been there and decided that she had. He tried not to think of her as poor Deirdre; before death had claimed her she had been as vicious and ambitious as anyone he had ever worked with and so sympathy was pretty much wasted. She wore a halo now, but there was a time when live snakes coiled in her hair and she was a creature of a different culture. In fact, thinking harder, he realised that Deirdre had featured in almost all of Matthew Hendricks' more lurid accusations. They were unfounded but the boy had had no idea at the time, any more than had her colleagues, as to how near to the truth he had inadvertently come. Now . . . who else? Maxwell whistled softly as he looked at the ceiling, thinking.

'Dads? Dads!' Suddenly the present was very present in the shape of his son.

'Hmm? Sorry, mate,' he focused on the child in question. 'What can I do you for?'

'My hamster has gone under the sofa and the Count has gone after it. He won't eat it, will he?' The big eyes were wide with worry. It seemed only yesterday that all Nolan could manage of the cat's name was Nik, and now he gave him his title. Ah, the miracles of modern education.

'Are you worried about the Count or the hamster?' Maxwell asked, playing for time.

The fear flickered and Nolan's father realised he had made an error. Before, the boy had only been worried about the hamster. Now he was worried about the cat as well. The child's mouth opened in preparation for a short burst of incoherent crying; this was a rare sound inside 38 Columbine and Maxwell was keen to nip it in the bud.

'They'll both be all right, Nole,' he said, jumping up. 'I'll get them out.' He knew this would probably involve some probing with the walking stick they kept in the kitchen for closing the window without falling out; always a good plan when you are on the first floor. The hamster wouldn't fight back but Count Metternich was an altogether different proposition, and Maxwell had the scars to prove it. 'Look, why don't you pop downstairs and see if Mrs Troubridge would like to see you today? It's a bit lonely for old people at Christmas.' He didn't really want Nolan to see him sweeping under the sofa with a stick. The boy was too young to have seen *Willard* and that was about rats rather than hamsters, but you couldn't be too careful. Maxwell and Metternich knew there was no harmful intent, but it would damage his credibility at a later date, he knew. His son was like an elephant, not because he was large, grey and wrinkled but because he had forgotten nothing since birth, or so it sometimes felt.

Nolan's face was a picture of indecision. He had known his father pretty much all his life and knew the old chap inside out. He could spot a bit of misdirection a mile away and sometimes he decided to let it go and sometimes he didn't. But it was Christmas after all and he was minded to be generous. Not to mention the fact that Mrs Troubridge was truly rubbish at any board game you cared to mention, so he knew that his victories were one hundred per cent genuine. He decided. 'Yes, I will. She'd like that. Do I need to put my coat on?'

'I think so, mate. It's been snowing again. Pop your wellies on as well, but take your slippers. You know how women can be.'

Both the Maxwell men made a clicking noise with their tongue and rolled their eyes. They both loved the women in their lives and respected all the others that came their way, up to and including Mrs Whatmough, but they liked to play the chauvinist when they were together, for the solidarity. Maxwell helped Nolan wrestle his way into the duffle coat Mrs Whatmough's establishment insisted upon, and after a slight sidetrack involving mittens on a string, he was ready. Maxwell watched from the landing as his boy negotiated the stairs and let himself out.

'Don't close the door until Mrs Troubridge answers,' he called down.

'No probs, Dads,' Nolan called and Maxwell could hear him talking to himself as he waited. Then, he heard him say, 'Merry Boxing Day, Mrs Troubridge. Can I come and visit you so you aren't lonely?' Distant twitterings betokened Mrs Troubridge's pleasure and Nolan called out, 'It's OK, Dads. She says I can visit. See you later,' and with the slam of two doors, he was gone.

Maxwell turned back to the task in hand and advanced, twirling the cane in his best Charlie Chaplin, on the sofa and the cat.

'Come out, come out, wherever you are,' he cooed and knelt down to peer under the furniture. Two baleful yellow eyes looked back at him from the dark and Metternich gave him his warning siren, a growl so far back in the throat it was the sound of the sabretooth tiger which lurks in every household moggie. 'Metternich! Let go of the hamster and come out with your paws in the air. Well, not that, because you wouldn't be able to walk then, I'm not an unreasonable man. Don't make me use the stick.' He brandished it in a firm but unthreatening way. The yellow eyes widened a little but otherwise the cat gave no sign that he was at all put out.

Maxwell decided to try a little reverse psychology. He'd long ago realised the pointlessness of 'Step away from the settee' and reading the cat his rights.

'I think I'll pop up into the loft for a bit,' he remarked, to no one in particular. 'See how the glue is drying on TSM Linkon.' He genuinely was dying to get cracking on Captain Bob Portal of the 4th Lights, his 54-millimetre present from Jacquie's mother after a rather hefty hint from her daughter, but he had to be strict with himself. No starting on a new one before he had finished the one before had been his watchword throughout his long years of modelling. The Charge of the Light Brigade or, more correctly, his diorama of the moments before the balloon went up in the battle, was coming along nicely and he was beginning to wonder what he could do when it was finished. There had been dark rumblings about the spare room needing a lick of paint, but it wouldn't be the same. And if his encyclopaedic knowledge of cavalry charges was anything to go by, wasn't there a little thing called the Heavy Brigade too? He hadn't the heart to tell Jacquie they'd have to move to accommodate it. Scarlett and Scarlett's three hundred may have to wait.

He backed away across the carpet, painfully finding one of the missing monopoly pieces as he did so; aren't top hats hard? Muffling an oath and scrambling to his feet, he hummed a little as he walked along the landing and was only on the first step of the next flight of stairs when a black and white streak whizzed past him, mercifully without a piece of mangled orange nylon fur in its jaws. Chuckling, he doubled back and retrieved the hamster and hid it in a drawer in the kitchen, where it could lie in wait to give him a nasty turn the next time he was looking for a teaspoon. Then, because the idea was in his head and Nolan was safely stowed with Mrs Troubridge, he turned and made his way up to the War Office to do a bit of gluing, muttering as he went, '"Forward, the Light Brigade. Was there a man dismayed?" You'd better believe it.'

* * *

Henry Hall tapped gently on the whiteboard behind him with the marker he had been using to write out the salient points. He glanced over the people gathered in front of him and made a few mental notes. There were a few missing who would have some explaining to do. Some of the messages on his voicemail that morning had actually been quite amusing, and this morning Henry Hall was in the mood to be amused. Pete Spottiswood's mother-in-law had been taken ill over the Christmas pudding and so he would not be back until New Year. There were several things about this message which would be clear to any policeman, even one without Henry Hall's many years' experience. Firstly, what had she been taken ill with that would take exactly a week to recover from and secondly, and perhaps most importantly, Pete Spottiswood's mother-in-law had been buried with two weeks' pomp and circumstance only last September. No wonder she wasn't feeling well. And Bob Thorogood, who had 'forgotten' that he was on call . . . well, Bob might well be heading for either Traffic or early retirement. Hall decided he would wait and see on that one; he didn't want his good mood caused by the removal of a boil on the arse of mankind to sway his judgement. He tapped a little harder on the whiteboard.

'If I could have your attention? Thank you.'

'. . . buggered if I care.' Bob Thorogood's voice rang out alone as everyone else stopped talking.

Hall's mind was made up. Traffic it was, then. Retirement was too good for him. He glanced at Thorogood and gave him a disconcerting half smile. Henry Hall never smiled. His eyes were unreadable behind his glasses and Bob Thorogood's blood ran cold.

'Hopefully you have all read the briefing notes which were left in your pigeonholes for you this morning. If you haven't had a chance to, then the outline is that Matthew, known as Jim, Hendricks was killed last night by a single gunshot to the head. His wife found the body a few minutes later. There are no witnesses and no suspects.'

'The wife, surely,' someone said from the back of the room. The body had been found on the Barlichway. It had to be a domestic.

'Yes,' Hall said. 'We thought that too. but no. No gunshot residue on her hands, and in fact we believe, having spoken to the psychologist who has been treating Mrs Hendricks, that she would be totally incapable of committing this crime. We are looking for a third party.'

'Family.' This time the interjection was less certain. It was still the Barlichway.

'Again, a good idea,' Hall said. 'Linda Hendricks had lost all contact with her family on her husband's instruction.' His voice, always colourless, was as smooth as glass. 'We are under the impression that possibly she has been in contact with a sister, but we haven't been able to confirm that yet. She is in a women's hostel at the moment, pending possible inpatient psychiatric intervention.' He forestalled any comments by adding, 'I don't think it really matters how truly repellent your husband is, it will still be a shock to find him spreadeagled on the path with no head.' He looked around the room. 'Questions, anyone.'

Bob Thorogood, with a head full of cotton wool and unnamed fears, had been trying to think of something intelligent to say ever since Henry Hall had caught his eye. He moistened his lips and diffidently raised his hand.

'Bob.' Never had a syllable had less emphasis, less to go on. Thorogood was totally unnerved.

'Well, guv, as you know, it was actually my shout last night, but for some reason despatch called DI Carpenter . . .'

There were catcalls and general rhubarb in which the most audible word was 'pissed'.

'. . . and I had worked on the case before,' Thorogood persisted. 'We all knew he was good for it, if it hadn't have been for his missus changing her evidence.' Thorogood stopped as he heard the next sentence in his head and knew it was probably rubbish. But he had to say something now he had started and so, speaking more quickly to get it over with, he said, 'I reckon it might be one of us, you know.' He twisted round in his chair to grimace at his colleagues, to make it sound less like his actual opinion. 'It sounds daft, and I don't mean one of *us*,' and he took in the room with a sweep of his arm. 'I mean one of the good guys.'

And to his relief and surprise, no one laughed. Especially not Henry Hall.

* * *

In the loft at 38 Columbine all was peace and seasonal good-will. Troop Sergeant Major John Linkon of the 13th Light Dragoons was coming along nicely and would soon be glued to the saddle of the bay that would be killed in the mad charge the real man had ridden back in the October of 1854, when Peter Maxwell had been limbering up for his O Levels. The TSM had gone on after the Charge to be a drill instructor with the Hampshire Yeomanry and then a man from the Pru. Downhill all the way. Had he lived longer, he would probably have become a Deputy Head.

The snow covering the skylight gave an eerie glow to the room, warmed as the cold light reached the desk by the pool of yellow that lit Maxwell's endeavours. Metternich was stretched out on the ex-laundry basket, moulded over the years to his increasing girth and as comfortable as a hammock to the great black and white beast. Maxwell and his cat echoed each other in a little sigh of pleasure.

Then, Metternich's least favourite noise, the ringing of the phone, broke the companionable silence. Maxwell had TSM Linkon in one hand and a paintbrush in the other. He dithered for a moment, then clenched the brush between his teeth and picked up the instrument.

'Or O-i,' he said, indistinctly.

'What?' roared the voice on the other end of the line. 'Who the hell is that? I want to speak to Mr Peter Maxwell. Put him on.' It was so loud that Maxwell swore he could feel the hair stir on the non-phone side of his head. Metternich sat bolt upright, ears flat and eyes staring. Maxwell swore that Linkon's plastic horse whinnied and trotted away. It could only be one person. He removed the brush from his mouth and tried again.

'Jeff,' he cried with as much enthusiasm as he could. 'Sorry about that. I had something in my mouth. How can I help you?' He raised his eyebrows at the Count, who turned round three times and settled back to sleep, but with his back ostentatiously turned.

'Well, we're all here, wondering what the hell there is to do here in Leighford. Nothing's open, just some hardware stores and a bookshop.'

Maxwell had never heard such contempt in two syllables as Jeff O'Malley managed to get into the word 'bookshop'. 'It's Boxing Day,' he ventured.

'Yeah, we heard of that. What does it mean, anyway, Boxing Day? Is there boxing somewhere?' His voice brightened. 'I was a useful pair of fists, back in the day.'

'No one's quite sure where the name comes from,' Maxwell said. 'It's tradition.' He wasn't anxious to cast any more detailed pearls of wisdom in the direction of this particular swine.

'Oh, tradition.' Maxwell could tell from the tone that O'Malley had turned to his daughter and that they were laughing at the quaint old English ways. Hector Gold had better be a really good teacher to make up for this. And yet, with this family as his choice, what were the odds? 'Well, I said to Hec, I said, I know old Max will know what's what. He strikes me as a man who knows how to have a good time.'

Maxwell was briefly speechless wondering how he had managed, standing in his tinsel-laden sitting room, in a cardigan and slippers, in the company of his elderly neighbour, his young wife and small son, to nevertheless give the impression of a man who knew how to have a good time. 'What kind of good time did you have in mind?' he eventually asked.

'A game?' Jeff asked wistfully.

'Leighford United might be playing today,' Maxwell said, doubtfully. He knew football happened, but happily only to other people. He had been a rugger bugger through and through. Rucks, mauls, incomprehensible rules and the last man in the shower's a cissy.

O'Malley was suspicious. 'That sounds a hell of a lot like soccer to me,' he said.

'Yes, soccer, that's right. I believe there is sometimes ice hockey at the rink down on the Esplanade.'

'Ice hockey! Canadian rubbish!' said O'Malley, the Californian through and through. 'No baseball? No proper football?'

'This is Sussex, Jeff,' Maxwell felt it necessary to tell him. 'Yea, Sussex by the sea. And it's Boxing Day.' He thought for a moment. 'Have you considered a trip up to London, perhaps? I'm sure there is a lot going on there, even today. Sales, for example. A few bargains to be had, I'm sure. Didn't one of your fellow countrymen pick up London Bridge for a snip not so long ago?'

'With your economy, everything is more expensive than back home.' O'Malley's mouth shut with a snap.

'Walk on the beach?'

'Call that a beach?'

'Perhaps you can find some American football on the television.' Maxwell was now clutching at straws, as he knew a smack in the mouth could often offend.

'Ha!' O'Malley's scorn nearly burst Maxwell's eardrums. 'I can't find any sport at all. There only seems to be about thirty or so channels. Hasn't anyone got cable around here?'

'Cable isn't so common in England,' Maxwell said. He thought furiously; surely Paul and Amanda had Sky? A sixth sense told him to think very carefully before his next remark. 'We have Freeview. That's where all the channels come from. There are some sports channels on that.'

'Nothing I'm interested in,' O'Malley said, dismissing the entire television output of the country in four words. 'Say, didn't I see a dish on your house? You got satellite?'

'Gosh, no,' Maxwell said. 'Used to have. Had it taken out. Didn't get the use out of it. No, no, ha, no, we've just got the old Freeview.'

'Hmm.' The ex-policeman sounded unconvinced. 'Little lady in?'

'Pardon?' Maxwell was suddenly at a loss. What was the man talking about?

'Jacquie? Is she in?'

'No, she's at work today. A murder last night.'

'Just the one?' O'Malley sounded dismissive.

'As I may have mentioned,' Maxwell said, somewhere between exhausted and curt, 'this is Sussex, Jeff. We usually manage with just the one a day. If that.'

'Call that a murder rate,' O'Malley said. 'Well, if you've got no ideas, I'll let you get on with whatever you're doing.' There was a pause. 'What are you doing?'

Maxwell decided to take the bull by the horns. 'I'm sitting in my attic with my cat painting a small plastic soldier.'

O'Malley guffawed. 'Sure you are,' he said, and at last the phone went down.

* * *

'So he said,' Maxwell told his wife, curling a lock of her hair round his finger, '"Sure you are" and rang off.' It was a perfect Jeff O'Malley.

Jacquie snorted and turned her head, almost pulling the hair out as she did so. 'Ow.' She slapped at his hand and he changed the lock. 'I don't believe you.'

'Yes. It's all true. Apparently,' and Maxwell gave a small mock preen, 'I look like a man who knows how to have a good time.' He smiled at her. 'Do you know,' he said, 'if you were a cartoon you would have an exclamation mark and a question mark over your head right now.'

'Make that two question marks,' she said. 'You've just gasted my flabber.' She gave one last flap at his hand and moved away slightly. 'But, seriously, Max, don't you worry about how Hector is going to settle in?'

'I did, for a while, but I think he will fit in really well. He is obviously totally different from the O'Malleys, and I count Camille as an O'Malley, because that is how she counts herself. How on earth they ended up together I can't imagine. The Count and I had a long chat today and he can't see it either. I think Hector will consider his hours at Leighford High each day as a pleasant interlude in the rest of his awful life.'

The idea was so poignant that they both sat and stared into the flames for a moment. Then, Jacquie broke the silence.

'Poor man,' she said.

'Too right,' said Maxwell. 'Poor man indeed.' After another silent vigil for Hector Gold, the Head of Sixth Form leapt up and rubbed his hands together. 'Drinkie?'

'You're very bouncy, standing there in your 'jamas, all washed and brushed. If you think dressing as Nolan is going to get you all the details of today, think again. And yes, I will have a drink, thank you. Something sticky and Christmassy. Benedictine. That would be nice.'

Maxwell turned to the drinks on the side table, where drinks had been placed in his house at Christmas since time immemorial. His eyes had a predatory gleam. While her husband poured her drink, Jacquie marshalled her thoughts. The day had been long and fairly fruitless. Sharing her added knowledge with Henry Hall had taken a while, and while he was grateful, it had advanced the case not even an inch. Even so, it had given them a slightly longer list of suspects, all of whom were immediately struck off again, by virtue of being dead, out of the area visiting far-flung families or, the last man standing, Peter Maxwell. There had been the usual sighs and glances when his name had come up, but a murder enquiry without him would not have seemed like Leighford at all.

She looked up to find him standing there, proffering her a glass. 'Oh, sorry. Miles away.'

He flung himself down in his chair and picked up the dregs of his Southern Comfort from earlier. 'Thinking about the case, I expect.' He smiled, innocently, or so it would have seemed to anyone but his wife.

'Case?'

'Yes. The case.'

'I'm starting my New Year Resolutions early. No more talking about cases. I'm an Inspector now, all grown up. You have heard your last case notes, Mr Maxwell. It's a brave new world.'

Maxwell narrowed his eyes. A challenge for the new year. Oh, goodie!

# CHAPTER SIX

There were not usually too many new kids at Leighford High at the start of what was amusingly called the Spring Term. This year, there were fewer than usual, due to the fact that another Coldest Winter Since Records Began had the whole of the South Coast in its vicious grip and the near peninsula that was Leighford even more harshly than its softer, more cradled cousin Brighton and Hove. Quite a few school buses had not even left the garage, let alone arrived with their cargo, and Pansy Donaldson and her depleted staff had telephones permanently glued to their ears, phoning out to outlying parents and taking calls from most of the rest. The stalwarts who had arrived were being marshalled into something approaching year groups and the staff were being allocated as best they could be.

Maxwell was there (albeit without the less-than-trusty-these-days White Surrey) because Nolan had gone in to school; and anyway it gave him yet another opportunity to point out how absurd the concept of Global Warming was. Mrs Whatmough had personally phoned every single parent the previous day and her message was clear: be there or there would be serious trouble. No matter that polar bears were rifling through the rubbish bags outside. She didn't give a hoot that the glaciers were marching, creaking and calving, across the downs. Ymir may be leading his frost giants down the High Street, but Mrs Whatmough would not be making allowances for anyone who was absent on the first day of term.

Jacquie was also at work. The case had not progressed much and the usual Christmas family feuds had almost knocked it off most people's desks, but enquiries were continuing, if a trifle sluggishly. No one felt much like catching someone who, in their opinion, had done the whole town a favour. 'They should give him a bloody medal' and 'Remind me again why they abandoned the death penalty' were just two muttered phrases that captured the ethos of the day.

Hector Gold was also at work. He was a little taken aback that so few people had come in to school, seeing as how there were just a few measly feet of snow on most roads. He was only a Californian by residence; he was a Minnesotan by birth and a workaholic by constitution. He had walked in, as the O'Malleys were stuck in the house, looking out wide-eyed at the snow. Coming from Los Angeles, they had heard of snow, of course. They went looking for it at reasonable expense twice a year, with skis tied to the top of the car. The idea of it coming to them was rather novel, though, and they had decided to wave Hector off and think about going out later.

Hector was currently enjoying James Diamond's hospitality. He was used to a Principal who sat behind an enormous desk with not a single piece of paper on it, with a picture window overlooking the softball pitches yelling orders into the tannoy system that permeated every corner of the school. Although James Diamond liked to consider himself rather a hard taskmaster, in fact his approach left Hector wondering when the real Principal was going to arrive. Surely this bland quiet man could not be in charge?

'And so, Mr Gold,' Legs Diamond concluded, 'I'm sure Mr Maxwell, or Max as I'm sure you will end up calling him, will look after you well. Our Mr Maxwell is a backbone of the school and you will learn a lot from him, I'm sure.' During this speech, he had come round from behind his desk and was ushering the man to the door. 'Any problems, my door is always open.'

Hector Gold found himself standing in the corridor. Remembering his manners, he turned to say thank you to the man he would never learn to call Head Teacher, only to find that the door had been closed oh-so-gently behind him. Ahead of him was another door, half glazed with frosted glass, although the school building was so cold that he wondered if the frost was not in fact the real thing. He knocked tentatively.

'Yes.' It wasn't a question. He only knew it was a word because he doubted that English schools kept Rottweilers on the premises. He knocked again. 'Yes!' Now the voice, or dog, sounded annoyed, so he summoned his courage and went in.

Sitting behind a desk was a huge woman, with a face like a big and angry scarlet moon. 'Yes? What is it?' She looked more closely. 'Who are you?'

'I'm . . .' Hector was on familiar ground with bullies and in a strange way he felt calmer than he had since setting out that morning, slipping and sliding in his thin Californian shoes across town to the school. 'I'm Hector Gold, the US exchange teacher you may have heard of me I'm here to teach history I've been to see Mr Diamond . . .' He ran out of breath at the same time he ran out of punctuation and the room swam a little.

Pansy Donaldson leapt out from behind her desk, her maternal and first-aiding buttons having been well and truly pressed by the fragile-looking man standing there. 'You poor man,' she said, as she grabbed his hand. 'You're frozen. And your shoes and trouser bottoms are soaked.' Turning her head she called over her shoulder to Emma, the morning receptionist, the girl who Maxwell always called Thingee One. 'Leave the phones, fetch Mr Maxwell, fetch a cup of coffee, fetch a towel, fetch Nurse Matthews, fetch Mr Diamond.'

Emma sighed and turned from the switchboard. 'In any particular order?' she asked.

Pansy was incensed. 'All at once, of course,' she said. 'Mr Gold may be suffering from hypothermia. He comes from sunnier climes and I'm afraid our winter doesn't suit him.' She put a beefy arm around him and gave him an encouraging squeeze. 'I shall have more than a few words to say to Mr Maxwell, making the poor man make his way in in such weather.'

Hector Gold opened his mouth to explain that in fact Peter Maxwell had rung the night before to tell him that attendance was scarcely mandatory in the prevailing weather and that whenever the roads were clearer would be more than adequate. He would also have liked to say that he would rather crawl over broken glass than stay another day in what still struck him as a poky house with inadequate sanitation with his in-laws. He sometimes thought of his wife as one of his in-laws as well, so little did she seem bonded to him, but thought that this kind of conversation was perhaps one which could come later in their acquaintance, if at all. He decided that it would be better not to say anything, and he shut his mouth with a small snap.

While they waited for Emma to fulfil all of her tasks, Pansy Donaldson filled him in on the ways of Leighford High School. Had his hair not been ultrashort, ultrafine and thinning, it would have curled. He had been told that schools in England were soft and easy options and here was this gigantic woman — who seemed to wear the same perfume as his mother-in-law as the general ambience was very similar — telling him of drug dealing, sex, violence and worse. As far as he could tell, she was implying that these all took place in the staffroom, but her embrace was beginning to stop the flow of blood to the brain, so he may have got that bit wrong. He heard voices and hurrying feet coming down the corridor outside and then — heaven be praised — there was Peter Maxwell, smiles and wiry hair in equal measure, bearing down on them and finally Pansy Donaldson's death grip was released and he almost fell into the Head of Sixth Form's arms.

'Hector, my dear chap!' Maxwell led him away, leaving Pansy protesting in their wake. 'I wasn't expecting you today.' He glanced down at the man's feet. 'Did you walk here in those shoes?'

'In these shoes?' Gold asked. 'I don't think so . . . sorry, I couldn't help that.' He smiled his unexpected Californian smile.

'Kirsty MacColl fan?' Maxwell asked.

'I am. I sometimes can't help finishing quotations, even when it makes the conversation nonsense. I mean, of course, yes, I did walk here in these shoes.'

'Don't you have anything . . .' Unusually, Maxwell was stuck for a word. Thicker? Stronger? More suited to a country where it rains more than it doesn't and that's when it isn't snowing?

Gold raised one foot then the other, ruefully examining shoes ruined beyond repair. 'Jeff said we didn't need anything else. That we would be driving everywhere. That Britain had a moderate climate . . .'

'And you believed that?' Maxwell was aghast. The man was clearly a moron and yet here was his son-in-law hanging on his every word.

'Well,' and the smile flashed on again. 'No, of course not. Jeff is an ass.' He left Maxwell to decide whether he was meaning ass as in donkey or ass as in arse; either would fit the bill. 'But Camille . . . well, you may have noticed how it is with her and her dad. She did the packing. There is a perfectly good pair of walking boots in the closet at home, I guess. Unless she gave them to the Goodwill. Or exchanged them for something more appropriate. Perfume. Lingerie. Something useful.'

Maxwell looked at him sideways. 'I thought Americans didn't do irony,' he said.

'Oh, no, Max,' Hector said, straight-faced. 'We *do* irony. We just can't pronounce it.'

Maxwell laughed and clapped the man on the back. 'Do you know, Hec,' he said, pushing open the door to his office to the welcome blast of hot air, 'I think we're going to get along really well.'

'I'm glad about that, Max,' Hector said. 'Really glad.'

A head with bronze curls popped round the door. 'Hello, Max,' it said. 'Emma told me we had an American dying of hypothermia.'

'Sylv!' Maxwell crossed to the woman and kissed her. 'You know Thingee. Always keen to make a drama out of a crisis. I'd like you to meet Hector Gold — Paul Moss's exchange for the year. Hec — this is our very own Florence Nightingale, Sylvia Matthews.'

'Charmed,' Hector smiled and shook her hand.

'You and me both,' she smiled back. 'You're looking pretty well for somebody at death's door.'

'Pioneer stock, ma'am,' he drawled for her benefit. 'Pioneer stock.'

Sylvia Matthews and Peter Maxwell went back a long way. She'd loved him for years but he hadn't really noticed and now that she had Guy and he had Jacquie — not to mention Nolan — her love had mellowed to that between two very good friends. Hector Gold didn't look much like Daniel Day-Lewis in *The Last of the Mohicans*, she couldn't help thinking, but you couldn't have everything.

'How was Christmas, Max?' she asked.

'Great,' he said, adding mentally to himself, except for this man's family. 'Yours?'

'You don't really want to know.'

But she told them both anyway.

* * *

Mrs Whatmough was not amused. She rarely was, but at that moment she was so far from amused she very nearly came out the other side. The woman standing in front of her in her office was close to tears, but tears were just a waste of salt as far as the Headmistress was concerned and she was having none of it.

'Sarah,' she said, her voice a little colder than the icicles outside her window, which tinkled in sympathy. 'This is not some kind of . . . *pawnshop*.' She said the word as though it were poison. 'I do not give advances on salary. I have no say over salaries, you know that. Was there an error in your last payslip, perhaps, that you find yourself so financially embarrassed now?'

The woman shook her head and muttered, 'No, Mrs Whatmough.'

'Then why, in only the second week of January, are you saying you have no money?'

The woman shrugged her shoulders. 'I just don't have any, Mrs Whatmough, and . . . well, I have a pressing need for some.'

The Demon Headmistress pushed herself back from her desk, arms straight, and looked down at the single sheet of paper in front of her. She stayed like that for a moment and then seemed to come to some kind of decision, but clearly not a happy one. 'Sarah,' she said, 'I am not an unreasonable woman. I am not, I hope, an unkind woman.'

To Sarah Gregson's surprise, she realised that this was so. All of Mrs Whatmough's apparent coldness came from her wish to make everyone perform to the best of their ability, to help them make a silk purse out of what may otherwise be a sow's ear. 'No, Mrs Whatmough, you are not,' she said.

'Thank you, Sarah. So, because you are clearly upset and because I do not want you to be working at anything other than your utmost in my school, I am prepared to make a loan to you, to help you out. This is not from the school, you understand. I have governors and shareholders to consider. This is a personal loan, from me.' She reached down and picked up her handbag, the size of a small suitcase and never far from her side. Staff and pupils alike believed that she slept with it. The Reception Class thought she slept *in* it. She snapped open a clasp and brought out her purse, which looked like a calf of the handbag. Another snap, and it was open. She looked up, enquiringly. 'How much?' she asked.

Sarah Gregson swallowed hard. Her mouth had gone horribly dry. 'I didn't want you to . . .'

Mrs Whatmough brandished her purse. 'It is this or nothing, Sarah,' she said. 'I will not involve the school in this. When you are feeling better, perhaps you can explain to me why this money is needed so urgently.' A wintry smile crossed her face. 'When you pay me back, perhaps. Now, how much do you need?'

'Two hundred and fifty would be very helpful, Mrs Whatmough,' the teacher said.

The Headmistress's eyebrows rose. 'But you would like . . . ?'

'Five hundred?'

There was a pause. 'Very well.' The woman opened the purse and to Sarah Gregson's amazement pulled out ten fifty-pound notes, one after the other. Mrs Whatmough looked up. 'Please close your mouth, Sarah. It is not attractive to stand there with it open. I don't usually have this much cash on me, as a matter of fact, but I have bills to pay this evening on my way home, so got some out this morning on my way in. With the weather so inclement, it seemed unfair to pay by cheque when people might not be able to get to the bank. Never mind, that will have to do now.' She held the notes out. 'There you are.' She shook them at the woman, impatiently. 'Take it. Pay me back when you can. I trust you to do so at the first opportunity.'

The teacher stepped forward and took the money gingerly, as though it might suddenly spontaneously combust. A tear crept down her cheek. The Headmistress was looking down, making terse marks on the piece of paper. After a moment, she looked up.

'Why are you not in class, Sarah?' she asked, as though nothing of the last few minutes had happened.

'Sorry, Mrs Whatmough,' she said and turned for the door. 'Thank you.'

The Headmistress flapped her away with one hand, not looking up. When the woman had gone, Mrs Whatmough leant over and opened a drawer. She pulled out a small notebook and opened it. Checking her watch, she made a note and replaced the book in the drawer, then resumed the checking of the piece of paper. Her face showed nothing, but her hand was trembling, very, very slightly.

* * *

Maxwell's xenophobia was taking quite a hit the more time he spent with Hector Gold. Physically the two could hardly be more different. Hector's accent sounded like someone doing a bad take-off of someone doing a bad take-off of an American, so clichéd was it. Maxwell, of course, spoke nothing but received pronunciation, even though the words he chose were sometimes not always what might be expected on the Nine O'clock News, so the pair were very nearly two buttocks of one bum. They sat that lunchtime in Maxwell's office, their postures perfect mirrors, their coffees both white, no sugar, their unwrapped Kit-Kats balanced on one knee, and chatted about this and that. In the Sixth Form Common Room across the landing, the dulcet tones of The Coast were belting out the retro numbers that Maxwell rather liked. The Sixth Form had voted unanimously for Radio Appalling but Maxwell had vetoed it — after all, they were not called Maxwell's Own for nothing. And he deliberately misquoted Winston Churchill — 'Democracy is the worst system in the world.' What he 'forgot' to add was 'except all the others'.

They had forgiven him, of course. They knew that Mad Max would go through the shredder for each and every one of them.

'Max,' Hector said, 'I can't tell you how much I envy you Jacquie and Nolan. Even your cat . . . Talleyrand, is it?'

'Metternich,' Maxwell said with a smile. 'Close, but not quite a cigar.' The man was a good historian, then, and knew his nineteenth-century European survivors, even if he didn't have much of a memory for names.

'Metternich, of course. Even your cat is an amazing animal. He looks as though he understands every word you say.'

'He'll be disappointed to hear that,' Maxwell said. 'He likes to think he is rather inscrutable. But I will pass on your kind words; he'll like that. Do you have pets?' Maxwell knew the answer, but thought it would be polite to at least ask.

'No, no pets. The condo board don't really allow pets, although people do have them, of course. Fish. Turtles. One guy had a parrot, but it got to be a bit of a nuisance and since we have parrots flying wild in LA, or just outside it, perhaps I should say, he had to let it go.' He smiled. 'I don't mean he stopped employing it, I mean . . .'

Maxwell was smiling already. He had a picture in his head of a parrot being given the sack before Hector Gold had finished the sentence. 'We have parakeets in Sussex, too. In lots of British counties, as a matter of fact.'

'Doesn't the cold kill them?' the American asked. 'I wouldn't have thought this snow would suit them too well, poor little fellas.'

'It probably thins them out a bit,' Maxwell said, 'but there have been feral parrots in Britain since Victorian times, so they must manage somehow.'

'That sounds swell. I'll maybe take . . .' Hector Gold paused. He knew it would not sound at all realistic to suggest that he and Camille would be going out birdwatching, so he changed tack. 'Do you come from a big family, Max?'

'Not really. I have a sister, Sandie, and she has two children, but we don't see each other much. Her husband works abroad a lot — something hush-hush in the Diplomatic Corps — and they only come home once in a while. My parents are both dead; they rode into the sunset years ago. Jacquie has a mother, Betty.' He crossed his fingers in the air against the Evil One, then laughed. 'Actually, we get on well enough, but because we are the same age, it would be a surprise if we didn't.'

'Yeah,' Hector said, a blush shading his pale sharp face just slightly. 'We wondered about that. Second marriage, huh?'

'Well, yes, but not how you think, probably. My first wife and our little girl, Jenny, died in a car crash a long time ago.' Maxwell was not often so open with a relative stranger. Dark wet evenings still made his heart ache for his lost family, even now he had Jacquie and Nolan. When the rain lashed at the windows and the Count crossed his legs and thought of England before he would go outdoors, Maxwell found himself checking that Nolan was still asleep in his bed. Some nights he almost wore a groove in the carpet, checking back and forth, but Jacquie said nothing, simply holding him a little tighter when he slid back into bed. He realised he had sat for a few moments without speaking. He cleared his throat and went on. 'So, yes, a second marriage. A different marriage, but happy. And Nolan is our pride and joy, as you may have spotted.'

'Gee, yeah. I'd be proud to have a child at all, but one like Nolan would be a special pleasure. A great little man, and like his mother.' He reran the sentence. 'And you, of course. I didn't . . .'

Maxwell laughed. 'We're all glad he looks like his mother,' he agreed. 'But surely, you haven't decided not to have children already? Not at your age?'

Hector Gold glanced behind him to check the door was closed, put down his mug and leant forward. 'Max,' he said. 'You're an intelligent man and I doubt much gets by you. You must see what my life is like.'

Maxwell was disconcerted. That Hector Gold's family made his life a misery was clear. That he had noticed, he had hoped was a little more subfusc.

'My wife is what they call a "cougar" in the States. She likes younger men and . . . well, that's how that happened. She was out to get me and I guess I wasn't really concentrating.' He smiled his flash of a smile. 'That'll teach me not to pay attention. I met Jeff and Alana after the wedding — we went to Vegas, by the way. Not quite all it's cracked up to be.'

Maxwell marshalled his received information on Vegas weddings, mostly gleaned from American sitcoms, his secret vice. 'I'd always assumed that Vegas weddings were really rather tawdry and tasteless,' he remarked, 'officiated over by people who got ordained over the net for ten of your Earth dollars.'

'Yes. As I say, not quite all they're cracked up to be. So, anyway, we got back home and we moved into her condo. It's in a nice enough area, but we are pretty much surrounded by singles and so the pool parties and so on tend to go on pretty much 24/7. That's why Jeff and Alana came with us, so Paul and his family can have their house.' He managed to say the whole thing with no inflection in his voice at all, but Maxwell detected hidden depths; Hector had these in shoals, unlike his wife, who only had hidden shallows.

'So, you get on well with Jeff and Alana?' Maxwell thought he probably knew the answer, but asked out of innate politeness.

Gold snorted and shook his head. 'Max,' he said, 'you are so British, really! No, of course I don't get on with Jeff and Alana. Well, Alana I might, I suppose, if I had a chance, but when she isn't drunk she's so cowed by Jeff and Camille she hardly speaks and when she's drunk she's . . . well, she's drunk. I guess I'm lucky, really.'

All Maxwell could do was raise an interrogatory eyebrow.

'She's a falling-down drunk, not a mean drunk. *Jeff's* the mean drunk.'

Maxwell reached forward and touched the man lightly on the knee. It was all part of the Special Relationship. 'Hec,' he said. 'May I phone a friend?'

Gold bridled slightly and said, with frost in his voice, 'I didn't know I was keeping you from something else, Max.'

'No, no, for heaven's sake, that's not what I mean at all. It's just that Sylv is a whizz at all things like this and she could probably help with the address of a meeting, or something, if Alana and Jeff are missing their group.'

'Elegantly put, Max,' Hector said. 'I apologise for snapping. I would like to speak to Sylvia, yes, but Alana doesn't have any backup. Jeff and Camille refuse to accept she has a problem and what they say goes. Jeff doesn't have a drink problem as such; he just takes a drink once in a while and it's no improvement, sadly. No, Jeff's little problem is gambling.'

Maxwell's earlier conversation with Jeff O'Malley sprang into sharp focus. 'Horses, dogs, that sort of thing?'

'Oh, no,' Hector smiled. 'Jeff thinks that betting on sports is a mug's game. Jeff plays cards.'

'Serious cards?' Maxwell asked.

'Oh, yes,' Hector said, grimly. 'To the death, Max. To the death.'

'Not literally?' Maxwell's antennae were waggling madly.

Hector shrugged his shoulders. 'Not so far as I know. But with Jeff, that means nothing.' Then he smiled again. 'Hey, let's not talk about Jeff. He's not a good subject for my karma. Say, the sun is shining, the snow is snowing. It's like old times for me, except that back in Minnesota I used to walk to school in proper footwear! Is there something I can borrow in the lost property cupboard, do you think? I've a mind to go for a walk.'

Maxwell was aghast. 'There's nothing you'd want in the lost property cupboard, Hector. Trust me.'

* * *

The room was very dark, except for a single dim bulb over the table. It was so low that the people hunched around the baize could feel the heat. A pile of money was in the centre and it had been growing steadily over the past fifteen minutes. One by one, the players dropped out until just two were facing each other, cards gripped in hands slippery with tension. Even the non-players, the ones who had folded through lack of funds or from a sudden rush of common sense to the head, were tense, with fingernails pressed into palms slick with the sweat of excitement turned to disappointment. Some looked longingly at the housekeeping money which made up part of the pile and would never now go through the tills of Messrs

Tesco. One was looking at a sunshine break in the Balearics; he could almost smell the suntan oil wafting from the heap.

Balearic man bulged through his clothes. Hours of pumping iron left him edgy and with too much time to think. Here in the pool of light on the baize he could realise some, at least, of those dreams he dreamt as he strained on the weights and sweated in the sauna. Here was sweat of a different kind, the adrenalin surging through him as though he was in front of an Olympic crowd roaring him on to win. But he had the sense to know when he was beaten. He glanced at the girl to his left.

She was leaning forward now, focused, heart thumping like a hammer in her scrawny chest. Balearic man was twice her width but he didn't have the sharp intensity of concentration that she had. Perhaps she was rooting for the woman still playing, in some bond of sisterhood; perhaps she wanted, as he did, to see the arrogant bitch taken down a peg or two. She licked her lips and looked across to the third folded player.

He sat motionless, his chin resting on his hand. All night long he had been watching the latest addition to their game, the big American whose advent had already seen off three other players; his style was too rich for their blood. Newcomers unnerved him. You couldn't read them; maybe you could beat them, but not tonight. But he was good at waiting and surely, one day, his turn would come.

Despite the excitement of the game, the pile of money in the middle, they all regretted the old days, somehow. They called them 'the old days', but they were only weeks ago. Bowls of crisps on the table. Folded players chatting quietly in a corner while the high rollers played for a pound a point. But the big American had changed all that in what was only slightly more than a syncopated heartbeat, rough with the fear of losing the mortgage money again.

The two players played on, raising each time until the last twenty was in the pile. The man, hulking in the dim light, spread his cards triumphantly out, to low hisses from the others.

'Straight flush,' he grated out, already reaching for the pot. 'King high.' The diamonds almost seemed to glow and pulse as he fanned the cards back and forth.

'Coincidence,' said the woman. She spread her cards, but deliberately, one at a time, putting each one in place with a small click as the pasteboard hit the baize. The other players craned round to see what she had in her hand. They held their breath as her opponent leant up on his hands to see. There was a ten of hearts, followed by a Jack, Queen, King and Ace. 'Not a perfect coincidence,' she said quietly. 'Mine's a *royal* flush, of course. But well done, Jeff. Very well done.'

The words were scarcely out of her mouth when the American stood up and grabbed the edge of the table, flinging it over, money flying everywhere. He stormed out of the room, setting the light swinging, and slammed the door. They could hear him thundering down the stairs and then another door slammed. Then silence.

The remaining players stood or sat as he had left them for some minutes. Then, suddenly, they all came to life, crowding round the woman, who had caught most of the money in her lap as the table went over. She looked like a leftover from a Greek wedding. They all picked up the notes and squared them in their hands. Balearic man picked up the table and stood it in front of her.

'Here, Sarah,' he said. 'Use this. To count your winnings.'

'I know what my winnings are, Tim,' she said. 'This is my last game. I've had a bad fright, the last few days. I've been spending . . . well, more than I could afford. More than I *have*, really. I've got someone who I owe a big favour to, and I don't want to let them down. If you lot have any sense, you'll pack it in as well. Jeff O'Malley has changed us, even in the last week. We used to have fun. We used to talk to each other, put the world to rights. Remember the muffins we used to bring for birthdays? Popcorn? Twenty-pound table limit?'

There were nods and grunts of agreement around the table.

'Well, I've had enough. If any of you want to come back here and play with him again, that's your affair, but I won't be here. There're always people wanting to join. There won't be a gap for long.'

The only other woman in the room stood back from the table and looked as though she might burst into tears. She had only joined this card school because Sarah had joined and she was in an agony of indecision. She had come up through the ranks of playing the National Lottery, playing bingo online to playing poker online to here. She wasn't sure whether she could go back to being fixated on the computer day and night but she knew she couldn't keep on coming here without Sarah Gregson.

'Sarah,' she said, trying to keep her voice level, 'Don't be hasty. I'm sure when you've slept on it—'

The teacher raised her head. 'Sandra,' she said sharply, as though to a naughty child. 'I haven't slept since Jeff O'Malley joined this group and I would love to have one, just one night of sleeping without worry.' While she was speaking, she was counting the money into piles. Finally she was finished and she looked up. 'Right, I was spent out, so five hundred of this is mine.' She pushed the pile to one side. 'I know O'Malley was spent out as well, so five hundred is his and I think that's mine as well.' That pile joined the other. 'The rest,' and she waved her hand over the remaining piles, 'must by definition be yours. I know that Sandra was spent out, so one of those piles is hers.' There was silence and no one moved. 'Take it, Sandra. I'm not joking.' Tentatively, the woman reached out and picked up the money, shoving it into her bag without looking.

One of the men, a short, weaselly-looking creature with glasses mended at the side with Elastoplasts, cleared his throat. 'I have fifty left, but, honestly, Sarah, I don't need you to give me the money back. I wouldn't gamble with what I couldn't afford to lose.'

She refused to believe that he had money to burn. For a start, who wore glasses mended with plasters if they had enough money? She knew his job didn't pay very well, though he was cagey about what it was exactly. Rumour had it that he was a traffic warden for the council, but he always denied it. Perhaps if she were a traffic warden, she would deny it too. So she took two twenties and a ten from the top of one pile and pushed the remainder towards him. 'Even so, Mark. That's yours, then. And this one,' she put the notes on top of the last pile, 'must be yours, Tim. Go on, take it.'

'You won it fair and square, Sarah,' he said. 'I don't gamble to get my money back as a present.'

'Tim, don't come the he-man with me. I know that money is your holiday fund.' She pushed it to him again.

'How the hell do you know that?' he snapped.

'Because . . .' She paused. They all tried to keep their private lives as private as they could, but sometimes poker and reality had to collide. 'Because I happened to bump into your wife, who happened to tell me that you were probably going to have to cancel your holiday because so many of your colleagues were off sick that you had had your annual leave refused.'

Tim Moreton stepped forward and for a moment Sarah felt quite intimidated. The man was built like a brick privy and until Jeff O'Malley had joined the group had been the hulk at the table. He was a training instructor at the local council-run gym and, or so rumour had had it, had once been a bit of a lad with the women. As he had hit forty his charms had begun to fade as his hairline had retreated, and his extra training sessions with a guaranteed happy ending had brought him in fewer and fewer tips from grateful clients. He could ill afford to lose this money and so, after a suitably macho pause, he took it.

Sarah Gregson pushed her chair back from the table and stood up. 'Well, I won't say I'm sorry to be leaving you all, because that would be a lie. But I have enjoyed our Saturdays and Wednesdays over however long it's been. I'm just sorry that I ever clapped eyes on Jeff O'Malley and am just glad that I will never have to see him again. If you are wise, you won't be here on Wednesday, but I doubt you'll listen to me. Just remember before you drag some other poor soul into this room to take my place that you should check that they can afford it.' She turned away and started to collect the glasses on the small counter at the back of the room. Turning her head, she said, 'Off you all bugger, then. It's my turn to sort the room out. No need to change that.'

Muttering collective thanks and generic farewells, the three made their way to the door and she was alone. She methodically collected the glasses and empty bottles onto the tray, wiped the counter, tucked the chairs round the table and went over to the door. She turned out the light and took one last look at the room in the faint glow from the street lights coming up the stairs. There had been some good times here, some good friends made and lost — playing cards for money isn't a good way to keep friends, she had found — but she wasn't sorry to be going; Jeff O'Malley seemed to hang in the room like a sour fog. Maybe, in the real world out of the pool of light, Tim could drop a weight on his foot, Sandra could feel his collar or at the very least Mark could give him a taste of the Texas Boot. She shuddered and turned to go, pulling the door shut behind her. Her footsteps died away down the stairs and the room settled down to wait for the next time.

As she reached the car park she had no trouble remembering where her car was; it was the only one on the top floor, except for one which had clearly been there for days, with a crisp rectangle of snow still on its roof. The frost sparkled on her windscreen and she watched the twinkling lights out to sea where strange and silent tankers slid through the night waters like ghosts. After she opened the door to get the scraper she turned the key to get the blowers going to warm the inside up. Finally the windows were clear and she walked around the car to get back inside.

Silently, a dark figure detached itself from the shadow of the nearest pillar, and walked round widdershins to meet her.

'Hello' was the last word she heard. The last sound was the grunt as the air left her lungs as she was pushed over the edge of the roof. The last sound she made was a sickening thud as her head hit the pavement below. Her blood ran for another minute or so, freezing into the slush on the ground. One last breath smoked on the air and she was still.

# CHAPTER SEVEN

Jacquie Maxwell snuggled under the covers until just one curl was showing on the pillow and tried to make the morning go away. The Christmas Day shooting was still rumbling along, making no headway, or so it seemed. The forensics had been held up by the repeated falls of snow and so it had been two steps forward, three steps back. The SOCO team had identified at least nine sets of footprints in the fall that lay on the night in question. One was the dead man's. Another the shallow depressions of his wife's slippers. Then the snow had started again and the detail had gone to the devil.

The *Leighford Advertiser* had a field day. After the usual endless round of panto reviews and speculation on what the New Year would bring vis-à-vis the projected wind farm, a mindless shooting was a breath of fresh, if bitter air. The Nationals had got wind of it too. 'Drive-by shooting in seaside town.' Nottingham had come to Leighford. Yet none of it made sense. The bullet case came from a large-calibre weapon, a .44, the sort of thing you'd expect in Chicago or LA, but never in Leighford. Had the world, after all, gone mad?

Apart from all of that, the usual festive domestics had hit a new high this year, with families who could usually stomp off separately to the pub being snowbound together with too much booze and far too much turkey. Heads were bound to roll and it had only been sheer good luck that that had not literally happened. The shelters were full of bruised and battered wives and husbands, where I'm Going Home To Mother And I'm Taking The Goldfish was not an option, but slowly, surely, Leighford was returning to what its denizens called 'normal'.

From the kitchen, she could hear the muffled shrieks and laughter that meant that Maxwell and Nolan were making breakfast. From the weight on her left foot, she knew that there was not any meat on offer, as Metternich had decamped to his second favourite place on a Sunday morning. This must mean pancakes, so her intervention was not required and she could enjoy another ten minutes, probably more. Easing her foot from under the cat, she curled up in a ball and closed her eyes. She could still hear the phone, sadly, but when it began to ring, she decided to ignore it. It was Sunday. She had worked ten days straight and even more if you discounted the single afternoon she had had off the week before last. She heard Maxwell pick up in the kitchen and the questioning burble as he found out who it was on the other end. She waited, fists clenched, for the happy burble which would mean it was a friend or family member. Although she tried to make it sound different, there was no mistaking the sudden clear words.

'Oh, hello, Henry. She's still in bed. Is it urgent?'

Jacquie lay quietly and counted the seconds of silence. Ten for a call to check that paperwork was up to speed for Monday. Fifteen would be a request for a meeting to sort out some lingering staffing issues, particularly Bob Thorogood. Twenty was—

Twenty-three seconds after the silence began, the bedroom door opened apologetically and Maxwell was suddenly in the room.

'Soz, Mrs Maxwell,' he said, quietly. 'Henry's on the phone. It sounds a bit urgent.'

She didn't speak, just held her hand out from under the duvet at the side of the bed. She felt the phone being gently placed in it, then heard the door softly close. It was only the combination in the kitchen of Nolan, a frying pan, pancake batter and syrup that had forced Maxwell to be on the other side of it.

Still in her warm nest, she pressed the phone to her ear. 'Guv?'

'Where are you?' he asked. 'You sound as if you have your head in a bag.'

'I'm under the covers, to tell you the truth. I was planning on making a bit of a morning of it. But that obviously isn't going to happen.' She struggled upright and spoke again. 'That better?'

'Yes,' he said. 'You sound better upright. I didn't want to do this to you on a Sunday, especially after the couple of weeks we've had, but we've got a bit of a nasty one.'

Now she was all attention. 'Where?'

'Town centre. Woman found this morning, on the pavement. Seems to have jumped from the roof of the multi-storey car park.'

'Suicide?' Jacquie frowned. It wasn't like Henry Hall to call her on a Sunday anyway, not if he could help it. And for a suicide?

'Well ... possibly. It certainly looked like that at first. Can you come straight here? There are elements of this I need a bit of brain for, and what I've got here isn't really cutting the mustard.'

'Bob?'

'Hmm.' Henry Hall was inscrutable as well as professional.

'He *is* trying hard, isn't he? I'll be over asap. Can I have some breakfast first?'

'As long as it's not too many courses. She isn't going anywhere, but there are things I want you to see before we move anything. Just to make sure I'm not seeing things. We're on the High Street side. Halfway along. Pray for no more snow.'

Jacquie didn't have her guv'nor down for the praying kind, but she knew the place well. In her mind she saw the chemist's on the corner and the pet shop with the electric fish that Nolan had to have a look at every time they passed. Just an ordinary street in an ordinary town. Now it was a crime scene. And soon it would be a shrine with plastic flowers and bedraggled teddy bears. She thanked him and pressed the red key to ring off. Only Henry Hall would think it necessary to tell her precisely where the police investigation would be taking place, as if there might be three other white tents along the pavement that day. She slid out of bed and dressed in the clothes she only seemed to have taken off a couple of hours before. Maxwell reappeared in the bedroom door as though by magic.

'Breakfast is served, modom,' he said, in his best Jeeves. 'Or do you want that to go?'

'No, I can eat it here,' she said, dragging a brush through her hair. 'I'll be down in a mo', I just need to quickly wash my face and brush my teeth and I'm done.'

'So much for the leisurely day,' Maxwell said, sadly, not feeling it right that morning to upbraid her for her split infinitive.

'I know,' she said, going through into the en suite and talking over the hum of the toothbrush and through a mouthful of foam. 'Iz a ugger.'

'Indeed it is,' Maxwell agreed. 'A ugger.'

Down in the kitchen, he doled out a stack of pancakes and drooled on the maple syrup. He sliced a banana over the whole thing and set it down in Jacquie's usual place. Nolan was halfway through his and the maple syrup was already slicking his ear lobes. This was what came of letting the child eat a pancake like a slice of watermelon, but it was Sunday after all.

Jacquie came in and slid into her seat, cutting through the stack as she did so. 'I'm so sorry, guys,' she said. 'It's a pig on my day off, but . . .'

'We understand, Mums,' Nolan said indistinctly. 'We'll have a nice day together, but we will miss you too.'

'What a nice child you are,' she remarked.

'Thank you,' he said. 'And you are a nice . . .' he was stuck for a description, 'Detective Inspector.'

Maxwell stifled a laugh. 'What about me?' he said. 'Am I a nice anything?'

Nolan looked at him for a long minute. 'You're nice too, Dads,' was what he settled for and another diplomat was born.

* * *

Henry Hall was not usually a man who dressed for the weather. Summer and winter, he turned up for work immaculate in a suit and crisp white shirt. They were still there on this freezing January day but his wife, a mother hen temporarily chickless, had wrapped him in a thick coat bought in the hopes that one day they would go on the long-awaited cruise to the Arctic and had topped it off with a scarf that reached up from collar to lens. The gloves he had managed to lose in the car on the way over but the scarf seemed to have become an integral part of his face and resistance was useless. He left it where it was, pulling it down each time he needed to speak. Not for Henry Hall the Maxwellian type of neckwear, the Jesus College scarf worn with bravado and just a hint of snobbery. Hall also had hiking boots on, which were proving far more treacherous on the glassy surface of the pavement than any shoe would have been, and he stayed near to the railings which skirted the margins of the car park, to have something to hold on to. He had resisted the white suit and was staying well back.

Jacquie joined him there, at the back of the crowd, dressed in a sensible ensemble, it seemed to him, of padded jacket, rubber boots and a rather natty hat with a tassel. Nolan had insisted on the hat, but otherwise her clothing had been her own idea.

'Guv?' She peered between the bent backs of the forensics team to see what was going on. 'Jumper?'

Hall was wearing one of those too, as part of his many layers, but knew this was not what she meant. 'Yes. At least, that's what it looks like.'

His voice was rather muffled and Jacquie gave him a quizzical glance. 'Can I help you with that scarf?' she asked.

'Would you? Margaret is afraid I'll catch cold.' Jacquie reached behind him and undid the intricate knot, memorising which Girl Guide extravaganza it was, so that she could put it back again at the end of the day. Hall flexed his neck, colder but far more comfortable. 'That's better. Right. It looks like she was a jumper from down here, but it is up there that I am interested in. Shall we?' He ushered her through the pedestrian door, into the mixed smells of urine, cold metal and weed that made up that popular air-freshener fragrance, L'eau de Garage Parking.

Jacquie pushed the call button of the lift.

'Not working,' Hall remarked, as he pushed open the door to the stairs with his shoulder. 'Let the door swing to; they haven't dusted here yet.'

Without speaking again, their lungs straining on the biting cold air, they made their way to the top. Just inside the door, a uniformed Constable, snug in his cape, kept watch.

'I hope it's all right, DCI Hall,' he said, 'if I stand inside. It's bitter out there.'

'Can you see everything from in here?' Hall asked the man.

'Yes, sir. The car is over there.'

'Stay in here, then. We don't want you to die of hypothermia and this might be a bit of a long job. Have they dusted up here?'

'Yes, sir.'

'Good. This way, then, DI Carpenter-Maxwell.' Hall was always punctilious about formality in the company of uniform. 'It's that car, over there.'

Jacquie listened. It was easier than looking; the snow had started up again and evil little frozen grains hit her in the face and lodged in her tassel. 'Is the engine running?'

'That's right.'

She walked over to the car, treading in the footprints of the SOCO team who had preceded her. She walked around the vehicle, looking carefully. 'That's peculiar,' she said, at last. 'She'd cleared the windscreen. In fact, she'd cleared all the windows.'

'Yes. And she'd turned the engine on to warm the car while she did it. It's been here all night. There's no new frost on it and the exhaust has even melted some of the snow on this abandoned job next door.'

'It wasn't suicide, then, guv, surely?'

'No, it wasn't. But not just for these reasons.'

'There's more?' Jacquie had opened the door and was looking around the interior of the car.

'Pick up the bag and look inside. It's OK, it's all been checked by SOCO.'

Jacquie reached inside and grabbed the handle of the bag which was in the passenger footwell. She opened the clasp and looked in. 'Good God, guv,' she said, on an intake of frosty breath. 'How much is in here?'

'One thousand pounds,' Hall told her, his voice flat and expressionless.

'Is there a note?' She already knew there wouldn't be a note, but it had to be asked.

'No, not that we can find. Someone from uniform is round at the house going door to door while SOCO do the inside, but there's nothing yet. There's an ex somewhere — I gather that he is on his way to the station to talk to us. We'll get back there now you've seen this. I just wanted you to see what was what.'

'That's good of you, guv.' She paused. 'Do I gather you are in the minority here?'

'Yes,' he said. 'I'm afraid so. I'll be logging it as suspicious, no matter what the forensics boys say. They are having to put warm bags round the body to unfreeze it from the pavement. They'll be a while. Jim Astley's still on his way. Let's go and talk to the husband. I'm parked round the corner. You?'

'I'm behind you,' Jacquie said. 'I'll just quickly ring Max and tell him not to hang on for lunch and then I'll be along.'

'To tell him not to hang on for lunch.' Hall managed to get a world of meaning into that simple remark.

'Yes,' Jacquie said. 'Precisely that. We have a brave new world at 38 Columbine this year, where I don't tell him about any of my cases.'

'Not even Matthew Hendricks?' Hall raised an eyebrow.

'*He* told *me* about that,' she protested but didn't add that technically that didn't count because it was last year. 'We haven't discussed it since.'

Hall was sceptical, but he knew Maxwell as a man who could bide his time. If an iguana on a rock knew something that Maxwell wanted to know, Hall knew who he would have his money on as to who blinked first. But that could wait. 'Make your call, then,' he said. 'I'll see you at the station.'

Jacquie went to the far corner of the car park to maximise the signal and pressed '1', the speed dial for home.

'Carpenter-Maxwell residence.'

'How very formal,' Jacquie said.

'Hello, sweetness. How're things?'

'Cold.'

'Are you wearing a vest?' Maxwell asked, with a tut in his voice.

'Many vests. It's still cold. I'll be home later this afternoon, I think, but don't wait for lunch. The forensics is going to be important on this one, and we're going to have to be patient on that because the body is totally frozen.'

'Frozen? What, as in stored in a freezer?'

'No, as in . . . Wait a minute. Remember my resolution?'

'Yes, I do.'

'Well, so do I. I'll be home as soon as I can. Make sure Nolan does his homework.'

There was a puzzled silence from the other end of the phone. Jacquie could almost hear the cartoon question marks growing and popping over her husband's head.

'Sorry. You know. Just . . .' Sometimes she just hated her job and missed her boy more than she could say. At all other times she knew she would be a basket case if all she did was stay at home and dust. It just happened that today, she was in the missing mood.

'Don't worry, petal. When you get home he will be done and dusted and ready to play. See you later. And . . . Jacquie?'

He didn't often use her name and her heart skipped a beat. 'Yes?'

'Be careful, driving. It's a bit slippy today.'

'I'll be careful,' she said. 'I'm always careful. And then I'm a bit more careful, for you.'

She heard him chuckle. 'Thanks. See you later. Bye.' And the phone went down. She put her mobile back in her pocket and took a last look over the parapet, at the hunched white-clad bodies beavering away below, then walked very carefully across the half-frozen ruts of the car park, through the icy snow-carrying wind, back to the relative comfort of the staircase.

* * *

As Detective Inspector Jacquie Carpenter-Maxwell drove away, she was watched out of sight by one of the SOCO team, one so large that he had his own personal stash of specially ordered coveralls in the back of his car. Donald, Jim Astley's gargantuan amanuensis, had carried a torch for Jacquie since way back when he only weighed a mere seventeen stone. He had pined quite badly for a while when she first married Maxwell and colleagues worried that he might never get back to his five-McDonalds-a-day norm, but after that one afternoon of being off his fodder, everything was back to normal. He sighed and turned back to the job in hand, cross with himself for missing an opportunity to exchange some witty banter. Angus, whom everyone secretly thought of as the *real* forensics guy, was trapped in Chichester by the weather so they had fallen back, metaphorically, on Donald. Falling back on Donald would have been relatively comfortable, but some of the sticklers in the team wished that he didn't shed crumbs all the time. It was going to screw up a case one of these days.

Pete Spottiswood, back from nursing his mother-in-law, followed the line of Donald's gaze and smirked, loudly. Spottiswood was one of the few people who could smirk audibly and Donald hated him with a passion. The big man knelt in the melting bloody slush and wished him to hell. As for Sandra Bolton, she might just as well have not come. She had been heaving her guts out at the end of the road almost since she had got there. Donald had never been sick in his life. He had the constitution of an ox, and other things in common with the animal, like size and, some would say, thought processes. But he had occasional flashes of near brilliance and for those the team liked having him on board. Angus might be better trained, but the THC was beginning to take a bit of a hold, and since that time he absent-mindedly ate a cake that was about to be entered as evidence in a domestic because he had the munchies, they had been glad to have Donald around.

His brain was buzzing a bit now. He turned to Spottiswood and crooked a finger.

Without moving, Spottiswood said, 'Yeah, Donald? What? You peckish?'

Well, of course he was, but Donald knew a sarky bastard from a hole in the ground, so ignored him. 'What's the matter with Sandra?'

'Sick, I should think,' the constable replied, without looking at the woman, who was leaning on the wall at the end of the block, head back, eyes closed, breathing hard. 'It's Sunday morning. I'd bet most of us are feeling a bit fragile.'

Fingers rose here and there from the team in silent agreement. Donald had never had a hangover either, but was prepared to believe them. 'I think she's a bit over the top, even so,' he said. In his role as the pathologist Jim Astley's assistant, he inhabited a hinterland between medicine and crime and sometimes medicine won. 'I think you should go and check on her, see if she's all right.'

Spottiswood looked down at him for a full minute, but the big man's gaze didn't waver. Then the policeman straightened up from his habitual slouch and picked his way over the glassy pavement to where Sandra Bolton stood. Donald watched the conversation, but couldn't hear what was said. But he did see Spottiswood reach into his jacket pocket and drag out his mobile. He jabbed one number and spoke urgently into the phone. The next thing Donald saw was the two hurrying round the corner to their cars. He smiled a small triumphant smile. Donald strikes again, he thought. I ought to get a consultancy fee, like Monk, or Patrick Jane on the telly. And they got all the smart totty. The rest of the morning passed in a happy mist, cold and wet notwithstanding, as Donald dreamt of a life in sunny California, as he impressed beautiful women and important men with his amazing feats of logic. His beatific smile was creeping out his colleagues, but that was nothing new, down among the dead men.

* * *

At Leighford Nick, Henry Hall and Jacquie had shed what seemed like dozens of layers of clothes and were feeling more comfortable. The dead woman's ex-husband was waiting in an interview room, but he was warm and in the dry so he wouldn't suffer if they stopped for a cup of coffee, just to warm themselves up. Jacquie warmed her hands around the mug and she sipped it gratefully.

'What do we know about this woman, then, guv?' she asked Hall.

'We're working on the details, but her name is Sarah Gregson, she is separated but not divorced from her husband, Charles. Someone from uniform is looking into him as we speak. It seemed quite amicable, no domestics lodged, that kind of thing. She works as an unqualified teacher,' there was a small question in Hall's voice as he said the last sentence.

'That is someone who has the initial qualifications, a degree in other words, but not a teaching one. There are quite a few at Leighford High because they're cheap and Legs

Diamond is on a cost-cutting mission.' A sudden thought struck her. 'She isn't from Leighford High, is she?'

'No,' Hall's response was fast and grateful. 'She seems to teach younger kids . . . I can't remember the school right now. It wasn't where the boys went, I know that. Anyway, we'll drag the Head out today if necessary, but if it has no bearing, we'll leave it until tomorrow. She used to be a social worker, but got out before the stress got to her. That's according to the door to door at her address. She hadn't been there long, so there wasn't much gossip. No men, by all accounts. Doesn't go out all that much. I've only got notes on that so far, no details. I'm hoping the ex, if that's what he is, can fill in the gaps.'

Jacquie put down her mug, most of the coffee undrunk. The coffee at Leighford Nick was only good for warming your hands on; it wasn't really meant for human consumption. 'Let's go down and see him, then, shall we?' she said. 'Or does it need both of us?'

Henry Hall looked at his immaculate desk. He always left it on a Friday afternoon as if he would never be returning. There was just one very slim file on it, containing the notes from the door to door and a precis of the contents of Sarah Gregson's handbag. 'I'll do it. Why don't you go home, try and salvage something of your Sunday?'

'Are you sure?' Jacquie didn't want to argue in case he changed his mind, but it seemed rude to leap up without at least a token resistance.

'Yes, off you go. I'm sorry I called you, really, but I wanted to copy you in on the circumstances, give you a heads-up before tomorrow. I'll let you know at home if anything dramatic turns up.'

Jacquie was already in her coat and making for the door.

'Drive carefully,' Hall said.

She didn't turn, just waggled her fingers as she went through the door before he changed his mind.

* * *

Henry Hall followed more or less in her footsteps, down to the interview room where Sarah Gregson's husband was waiting. He pushed open the door and went inside, to receive rather a surprise. Sitting at the table, engrossed in a book which Hall quickly identified as the Gideon Bible from the window sill, left there some time before by a crusading special constable, sat the vicar of All Souls, the nearest church to the Halls' house. Henry realised to his embarrassment that he didn't know the man's name and he certainly didn't know he was married. Well, he knew his name now, of course, it was Gregson, but despite having been dragged along to Harvest Suppers and various other events, he had never logged his name in his head.

'Reverend Gregson, hello. First of all, I would like to say how sorry I am for your loss.'

The vicar stood up. 'Thank you, Mr Hall. I had no idea you were a policeman.' He held out his hand to Hall, who shook it. 'Dear me, that sounds rather insulting, I'm afraid. I certainly didn't mean it to.'

'That is perfectly all right, Vicar,' Hall said.

'And also, perhaps before we start, I should say that my name isn't Gregson. My name is Mattley. Giles Mattley. Sarah went back to her maiden name when she changed jobs last year. We weren't intending to divorce, or at least, that was my intention, but she wanted to . . . remove herself a little for a while.'

'I see,' said the DCI, pulling out a chair and gesturing for the man to sit. 'Or rather, I don't think I do see, not quite.'

'Sarah and I separated quite amicably, Mr Hall. I still love her very much, but she had some personal demons which she needed to sort out before we could really progress at all and she preferred to do it alone. She had worked as a social worker in Brighton for some years, then moved to Leighford about eighteen months ago, to have less travelling to do. She had a very distressing case to work on and she became rather depressed, so I encouraged her to make a career move and last September she got a job as unqualified teacher in the Reception class of a very nice little school not far from home.' All this had come out in a torrent, but it was measured, controlled, as though the man had been rehearsing it for some time.

'And then you separated?' Hall wanted to get the details clear. This case wasn't at all clear so far.

'Um . . . no. We separated while she was still working in Children's Services. That would be around Easter time last year. But, as I say, it was amicable and, as far as I was concerned, strictly temporary.'

'I suppose your job would make it difficult to—'

'My job, as you put it, DCI Hall, had absolutely nothing to do with it. I loved Sarah. I still do love her. I wanted our lives together to continue, and if she needed time, then that was fine by me. A year or two out of the marriage if it meant we would be together for ever was a small price to pay, to my mind.' He looked down at his hands, still clasped around the Bible, as if he had never seen them before. 'Of course, that's . . .'

To Hall's embarrassment, a fat tear splashed onto the man's hand and trickled down to stain the matte red leather of the book. Why had he sent Jacquie home? She was good when people cried.

Then Giles Mattley pulled himself together and looked up at Hall, wiping away a lingering tear with the back of his hand. 'I think I am supposed to think she is in a better place, DCI Hall. I know that is what I tell my parishioners at times like this. As if there are times like this . . . I gather Sarah committed suicide. I had no idea she—'

Hall was quick to cut in. 'I don't know where that idea came from, Reverend Mattley,' he said. 'Your wife didn't commit suicide. My colleagues and I have very good reason to assume that she was murdered.'

The man went white and swayed in his chair.

'Are you all right, Reverend Mattley? Would you like a glass of water?' Hall's hand strayed to the buzzer on the table.

'No, no, thank you. I'll be all right in a second, but . . . murdered? Who would want to murder Sarah? She was the loveliest, the kindest of women.'

'She had one thousand pounds in her handbag, Reverend. Can you explain that?'

'A thousand pounds? In cash, you mean?'

'In very used notes. It was neatly counted out, like they do in banks with all the notes facing the same way and the twenties, tens, the odd fiver all in stacks. We were wondering if you could shed any light?'

'Why would . . . ? Blackmail, are you saying?' The Reverend Giles Mattley watched a lot of TV. 'Sarah was being blackmailed?'

'Or was blackmailing someone.' Hall spoke without emphasis, but watched his man intently.

'My Sarah? A blackmailer? Don't be ridiculous. She didn't even like to gossip. That's what finished her in social work, in the end. She always believed the best in people. And almost always was let down, of course.'

'Of course.' Henry Hall had been a policeman for a lot of years. He knew what it was like to be let down. A bell rang in his head, way at the back, where all the most important bells hung out. 'I don't suppose you know what the case was, the one which made your wife leave social work?'

'Confidentiality, DCI Hall. Confidentiality. You must know about that. Police. Church. Social workers. Teachers. The list goes on. All bound by confidentiality.'

'I don't expect names as such, Reverend Mattley. Just the gist.' Henry Hall held his man's gaze. 'Didn't she let you know even a hint, when she was so depressed?'

Giles Mattley hung his head and it was a few seconds before Henry Hall realised the man was praying. Whatever guidance he received, it was in Hall's favour.

'She told me it was a man, not very old, who had been abusing his children, mentally, physically and sexually, since they were tiny. He had been abusing his wife for years, since they were at school, as far as she could tell.'

Henry Hall sighed. 'I know the case.' He looked down too, but if he was praying it was to the God of Coincidence, who he knew to be a figment of his own imagination. He stood up. 'Thank you, Reverend Mattley. We'll be in touch, and again, I am sorry for your loss.'

'What about the thousand pounds?'

'We will have to discover if it is . . .' there was no good way to say it, 'the proceeds of a crime. If it isn't, then I would imagine it is yours, if you are your wife's heir.'

The man shook his head and turned for the door. 'Have you ever lost anyone you love, Mr Hall?' he asked.

Hall swallowed the lump in his throat. 'My mother,' he said. 'My wife, almost, once.'

'Ah, and there you have the advantage of me,' Mattley said and this time didn't brush away his tears. 'Almost, once. I have lost mine not once, but again and again and again. When you finally give her back to me, Mr Hall, please make sure it is for good.' And he was gone, the door swinging behind him.

# CHAPTER EIGHT

Jacquie Maxwell called from the foot of the stairs as she got in, stamping the snow from her shoes. There hadn't been a winter like it for years, the Met Office kept assuring everyone, causing Maxwell to mutter darkly about the fiction that was Global Warming and wondering again how any of 'those people' slept at night. Nolan had done a project on Global Warming in his first few weeks at Mrs Whatmough's estimable establishment, although to be fair, bearing in mind the age group, it had mostly been a collage of pictures of polar bears. Nolan had included a fairy in his, which his teacher had found quite endearing until he explained that his daddy thought the whole nine yards was just a fairy story to worry the readers of the *Daily Mail*. His teacher had given him a long look and written something cryptic in his permanent record which may or may not come back to bite him when he applied for his father's old college in the years ahead.

'Hello, chaps,' she called. 'Anyone in?'

She was rewarded by scampering feet and her son's head appeared around the corner at the top of the stairs. 'Mums!' he called. 'That was quick! Did you catch the man?'

What a lovely simple view her son had of her job, she thought, climbing the stairs towards him. He was, as always, gathering himself together for a leap into her arms. 'Not till I'm on the landing,' she said, raising a warning finger. 'Remember what happened to Mrs Troubridge.'

'*I* didn't make her fall downstairs,' Nolan said, outraged.

'I know you didn't, poppet,' Jacquie said, scooping him up. 'But she did fall down them, didn't she? Stairs are dangerous if you don't take care.' And we have so many, she thought. We must be crazy, living in this tall house with a small child and a psychopathic cat whose newest hobby was waiting until you were halfway up or down a flight and then leaping out at you. He'd be sorry if his meal ticket broke its leg. 'Where's Dads?'

'He's making lunch,' Nolan told her, squeezing round her neck with one arm and giving her a wet kiss on the cheek.

'You're very cuddly,' Jacquie laughed. 'I'm suspicious.'

'You're a Woman Policeman,' Maxwell told her, appearing from the kitchen. 'You're meant to be suspicious. Come and join us. We are just about to sit down to lunch.'

Jacquie sniffed the air. There was no smell of Sunday roast or anything approaching it. She went into the kitchen. 'Pasta shapes on toast?' she said, appalled. 'Where's the Sunday dinner?'

'Still in the fridge,' Maxwell said. 'You caught us out. We were going to cook it later, so you could eat it with us properly, rather than heated up.'

'And with the time we save,' Nolan said importantly, sliding down his mother and climbing onto his chair, 'we were going bogging.'

'Bogging?' Jacquie was confused.

Maxwell was dividing the pasta-covered toast in front of him onto two plates. Pushing one of them towards Jacquie, he said, in explanation, 'Tobogganing.'

'Tobogganing,' Nolan echoed. 'What I said.'

'Oh, sledging!' Sometimes their geographical differences made all the difference.

Maxwell smiled. 'I suppose it depends on whether you use a sledge or a toboggan. As it turns out, we will be using a toboggan.'

'We don't have a *sledge*,' Jacquie said, with a forkful of pasta halfway to her mouth. She had just realised she was hungry.

'We do,' Nolan said. 'Hec . . . Mr Gold has got me one. He rang up this morning and said he hadn't seen snow like this since he left . . .' he glanced at his father for confirmation, who mouthed 'Minnesota' at him, 'since he left where he used to live. So he got a boggan and we're going to the Dam and going bogging. He's checked and there is lots of snow and that's where we're going.' He shovelled in another mouthful of pasta and started on the tomatoey toast. 'Aren't we, Dads?'

'Indeed we are. Are you coming?' he asked Jacquie. 'It should be fun.'

'Just Hector?' Jacquie asked.

'Let's hope so,' he smiled. 'I don't think the Californians born and bred are very enthusiastic about this weather. According to Hector, it has seriously impeded Camille's attendance at the nail bar. She likes to keep her nails maintained, apparently.'

Jacquie looked down at her hands, her nails short, neat and clean but not what anyone would call maintained. She thought for a moment. 'Let's do it,' she said. 'I can't remember the last time I went sledging. It was always a bit difficult when I was a kid. We didn't really have many hills. My dad used to have to drag me along the road. It's not the same.'

'Tell me a story about my granddad,' Nolan said. 'Tell me the story about when he fell over on the beach and it looked like a monster had crawled out of the sea, you said. Tell me about when he used to try to fly a kite.'

Sometimes, Maxwell found it sad that his little boy had started life with just one grandparent, although the redoubtable Betty was quite enough for any child all on her own. He had fond memories of his own grandparents and even a few hazy recollections of a sweet-smelling little old person sitting quietly in a corner who he realised later was his great-grandmother. Nolan would miss all that when he was older, a whole page missing in his family history. But for now, they were going bogging.

‘Talk while you eat, Mums,’ Maxwell said, suiting the action to the words. ‘Hector will be here in . . .’ he glanced up at the clock, ‘about three minutes and we’ve got to get our woolly combs on yet. Chop chop.’

‘Dads! That should be chomp chomp!’ Nolan could hardly eat for laughing.

‘Whatever,’ drawled Maxwell. He usually hated smart-arses but the fact that this one was his son just underlined the basic truth of genetics so he let it go. ‘Let’s just do it. We don’t want to miss an afternoon’s bogging, now do we?’

* * *

Henry Hall was not much given to introspection, but his interview with the Reverend Mattley had made him thoughtful. He had come down without a notepad and fished in his pocket for a piece of paper. The man’s obvious distress and love for his wife had removed him from the list of suspects in Hall’s view, but he realised after the man had gone that he had not asked him the reason for their separation. To remind himself to ask these questions later, he wrote ‘demons’. Then, after a bit of thought, he underlined it and added a question mark.

There was a tap at the door and Pete Spottiswood stuck his head round. ‘Guv?’

Hall looked up. ‘Shouldn’t you be back at the scene? What are you doing here? Auntie’s dog been taken ill?’

Spottiswood smiled grimly. He knew it would be a long time before he lived down his faux pas over Christmas. He was a frequent liar, just not a very good one. He could never remember what he had said. He decided to play it straight. ‘No, guv. It’s fine, thank you. A sure-fire bet in the 6.30 at Brighton next Thursday. I’ve brought Sandra back with me. I think you’ll want to hear what she has to say.’ He reached behind him and produced the WPC like a rabbit out of a hat.

‘Guv.’ She stood there, still pinched from the cold, eyes red with crying.

‘Sandra.’ Hall had an idea that some of the rookies were scared of him, but they didn’t usually cry.

Spottiswood was reluctant to give up the limelight. ‘Sandra knew the dead woman, sir. She has something to tell you.’

Hall looked down at the piece of paper on the table in front of him and folded it twice and put it in his pocket. Standing up, he said, ‘Let’s get out of here, Sandra. We’ll go up to my office. Pete?’

‘Yes, guv.’

‘Can you get us a couple of cups of coffee, please? Then you can get back to the scene. See if SOCO have any preliminary thoughts. Did I see Donald there?’

Spottiswood personally thought he would be hard to miss. ‘Yes, guv.’

‘See if he can give us a time for the post-mortem report being ready. We’ll need toxicology, alcohol, that sort of thing.’

‘There’ll be alcohol,’ Sandra Bolton said. ‘I was with her last night and we had a few drinks. Only a couple, so after all this while there won’t be much. She was certainly not over the limit to drive.’ She started to cry again, quietly.

Hall looked at her and his face was even more set than usual. ‘WPC Bolton, are you telling me that you were out drinking with Sarah Gregson last night and you have taken . . .’ he glanced at the clock on the wall, ‘you have taken over five hours to tell anyone?’

The woman nodded, miserably.

Hall sighed. ‘Come on, then,’ and he ushered her out. ‘Up to my office. Pete, get someone to come and minute this.’ He turned to Sandra Bolton. ‘You do understand that we have to take this seriously, Sandra? It may go further and we have to have a record.’

‘I’ll minute, guv,’ Spottiswood said, eagerly.

‘Thanks, but I’ve seen your shorthand. Send someone from the front office. And don’t forget the coffee.’ He led the way up the back stairs. He wished he hadn’t sent Jacquie home. He had a feeling that this was going to need a woman’s touch.

* * *

The phone was ringing when the Maxwells tumbled in through the front door. They were all wringing wet, but had had a marvellous time with Hector, who was indeed an expert tobogganer. He had even coined a new word for their experience, which covered both Jacquie's and Maxwell's vocabulary: slebogganing. The American and Nolan had bonded immediately and just as well because Maxwell and Jacquie had turned out to be a major disappointment on the makeshift piste on the slope behind the Dam. It hadn't helped that half of Year Nine from Leighford High were there, the lads jeering (though quietly) at Maxwell's Winter Sports efforts, the girls cooing over Nolan who was still little and cute enough to bring out the incipient mother in them all. He was now slung over his father's shoulder like a deadweight and Jacquie answered the phone in the kitchen.

On his way into the sitting room where he planned to crash into his chair, having decanted his sleeping son on the sofa, Maxwell could only here a muffled hum of a very one-sided conversation from across the landing. After a moment or two, Jacquie appeared in the doorway, holding the phone away from her and mouthing at Maxwell.

He mouthed back, 'What?'

She tried again, but still with no success. She was clearly enunciating at least four syllables, but they didn't seem to make any sense.

'What?' he mimed, in the silent version of a slightly testy shout. Marcel Marceau would have turned silently in his grave.

She gave up, dropping the arm holding the phone to her side. 'It's Mrs Whatmough on the phone, *dear*,' she said. 'Apparently, although she knows that I am a very senior police person, she would prefer to speak to you.'

At the sound of his Headmistress's name, Nolan twitched in his sleep and made a lemon-sucking face. Maxwell stopped his task of stripping off the soggy siren suit and stood to attention. 'Mrs Whatmough?'

'You can say it out loud now, Max. I find it helps. Here you are.' She held out the phone. 'I'll take Nolan's wet clothes off.'

Maxwell made frantic hushing sounds. 'We're probably not allowed to get him wet.'

'He's not a Gremlin, Max. Are you going to take this call?' She shook the phone at him in a this-is-your-last-chance sort of way.

Maxwell took off his hat, ran his fingers through his hair and gave himself a relaxing shake from shoulders to toes, as taught in music and movement at his infant school so many millennia ago. Then, with tummy and tail tucked in, he took the phone and reluctantly put it to his ear.

'Mrs Whatmough! Hello. We were just drying him off, so he doesn't get a chill . . . Nolan. Yes, tobogganing.'

The phone gave an impatient quack.

'Yes, he had a helmet on.' He raised his shoulders at Jacquie, trying to make her complicit in the lie. 'Yes, indeed. Exhausted. Anyway, how may I help you?'

Rosemary Whatmough was not quite herself on this Sunday afternoon. Her Pekinese, around whom her non-school life, such as it was, revolved, did not like having wet belly fur, so had had to be accommodated on newspaper in the utility room, and she was not sure who hated it the most, but she suspected it might well be the dog, who was making its extreme bad temper manifest by disembowelling a sofa cushion. In the middle of this outrage, Mrs Whatmough had received a phone call which had made the snow pale into insignificance and almost her first thought had been to call Peter Maxwell, for whom she secretly carried a bit of a torch. Not so much a torch, possibly, more of a glimmer, but she was not one to wear her heart on her sleeve in any case, so that was not the issue. No, she wanted to get to the bottom of the inconvenient behaviour of one of her staff and she knew he had a bit of a knack in that direction.

'I beg your pardon?' Maxwell said, aghast, at the end of her monologue. 'Murdered? I had no idea . . .' He looked down at Jacquie, kneeling on the rug removing Nolan's soggy shoes and rubbing his feet dry. Catching the look in her eye, he backed out and continued the conversation on the landing.

'I did know there had been a murder, of course, but I didn't realise . . . No, my wife doesn't tell me things about her work. Confidentiality, Mrs Whatmough, confidentiality.'

The angry quacking from the telephone made it clear that Mrs Whatmough understood all there was to understand about confidentiality and indeed had more or less written the book on it. Her point was that a teacher from *her* school had been murdered and . . . a strange sound made Maxwell listen harder.

'Mrs Whatmough, are you all right? Are you crying?' The Head of Sixth Form almost felt that he should look outside, to see if a flock of pigs were flying overhead. It was certainly cold enough for Hell to have frozen over. 'Mrs Whatmough, please. This isn't getting us anywhere, is it? Are you able to get the car out?'

A muffled sob implied that the Whatmough drive was always snow-free.

'In that case, why don't you come over here and tell us about it? Jacquie — Mrs Maxwell — will probably be able to advise you better than I. Do you know . . . yes, I'm sorry, of course you do. We'll see you shortly, then, shall we?' He rang off and stood there for a second or two, tapping the phone against his chin. Then he went through into the sitting room. 'Tidy away that child,' he ordered. 'Mrs Whatmough is coming over.'

'Mrs Whatmough?' Jacquie hissed. 'What, are you nuts?'

'She was crying,' he told her, simply.

She looked at him for a long minute, then scooped the sleeping Nolan up in her arms. 'I'll just tidy away this child,' she said, making for the door, then turned. 'But you owe me, big time.'

* * *

Sandra Bolton eventually stopped crying, blew her nose, took a huge gulp of something which may have been coffee and looked at Henry Hall. 'Are you going to ask me questions, or shall I just tell you stuff?' she said.

‘Let’s try a mixture, shall we?’ Hall suggested. ‘Start by how you met Sarah Gregson.’

‘That’s easy,’ the WPC said. ‘We met at Zumba classes, at the council health club. She was working for the council at the time and my other half works for them as well, so I have a family membership . . .’

‘Let’s try and keep the details to what we need, shall we, Sandra?’ Hall said, in a slightly frosty tone.

‘Sorry, guv. Well, we met and afterwards we would have a drink or something. Zumba is very exhausting, you lose a lot of fluid and . . .’ she caught the look in Hall’s eye and stopped.

‘When was this?’ he asked, to get it all back on track.

‘About a year ago, maybe a little less. She was a social worker and she was finding it all a bit stressful, so when she asked me if I did any other clubs or anything apart from the Zumba, I told her about poker.’

Zumba, Hall had heard of. His wife had briefly toyed with it as a way of losing weight, but the constant Latin music coming from the spare room had finally led to a frank exchange of views and she had switched her allegiance to the rather quieter option of fat-reduced meals from Marks and Spencer to help her battle of the bulge. For a moment he wondered what Poka was then realised what she was talking about. ‘Poker? You mean, as in . . . poker? Cards?’

‘Yes, guv. Well, not always poker, actually. Not then. Depending on who turned up, we sometimes played canasta or cribbage. We had a room we used above the Red Lion off the High Street. Someone who used to play cards knew the landlord, ages ago, and it had just carried on.’

‘For money?’ Hall could not believe his ears. This woman, this *girl* who was hoping to make a career in the police, was playing cards for money in a room over a pub.

‘Well, not much, guv. Just enough to make it interesting, you know. Penny a point, that kind of thing.’

Hall leant over his desk and she instinctively drew back. ‘Sandra. You do know that Sarah Gregson had one thousand pounds in her bag at the time of her death?’

Sandra Bolton nodded miserably.

'And she won that playing cards, did she?'

Again, the nod.

'At a penny a point?'

This time there was no nod, or shake, just another storm of tears. Henry Hall pushed the box of tissues across the table and waited; and eventually, she resumed her story.

'A few weeks ago, we had a new chap join us. I'm not sure who introduced him, he just seemed to appear from nowhere. An American chap he was, said he was over here for a while and was looking for some action. I . . . I'm not sure how it happened, but by the second Wednesday, he had us agreeing to no table limit. We put our foot down,' she paused a moment, wondering why that didn't sound right, then carried on anyway, 'and said we would have to have a limit of some kind. We agreed at five hundred pounds.'

Henry Hall had never been one of those policemen who complained about how much he earned, or rather how little. Even so, he would have been hard-pressed to take five hundred pounds to a poker game once a month, let alone more often, as this seemed to be. He asked, 'How often did you play?'

Sandra Bolton sniffed loudly and wiped her nose. 'Twice a week, but I think that sometimes Jeff got another game going in between.'

'Twice a *week*?' Hall's famous imperturbability was being stretched to the limit. 'So, how many times have you played with this kind of stake money?'

She rolled her eyes up and appeared to be calculating. 'Last night was the fifth, I think. Or sixth. I can't remember.'

'So, let me get this right,' Hall said. 'Sarah Gregson had played at least five times since Christmas, with a five-hundred-pound stake. Was she lucky at cards?'

'Not usually,' the WPC said. 'Jeff usually won, and sometimes Mark ended up about even. The rest of us lost, as a rule.'

Hall was aghast. 'You've lost two and a half thousand pounds in less than a month? How could you afford that?' His reply was a storm of crying. 'Oh, I see. You couldn't afford that.' He pushed himself back from the table and walked across the room to look out onto the snowy car park. Winter Wonderland was not the first phrase that entered your head as you gazed over the rooftops of Leighford. 'What happened last night?' he asked quietly.

'Well,' she said, pulling herself together, 'there were only five of us last night. There had been as many as eight, but the others had dropped out when the money got too much. Sarah won the pot and Jeff stormed out.' She blew her nose with a finality that made Hall hope that it really *was* the last time in this exchange. 'He isn't a very nice man, guv. He is a real bully and doesn't like to lose. He drinks a bit as well . . . not to be roaring drunk, you know, but just a bit more than the rest of us. Anyway, he lost. We all did, except Sarah. Jeff overturned the table and the money went everywhere. Then he left.'

The scratch of the shorthand minute-taker's pen was all that could be heard for a while, then Hall spoke, carefully, gently so as to not upset the woman. 'I'm not a card player myself, Sandra,' he began, sitting back down behind his desk. 'Just the odd hand of Hearts or Newmarket at Christmas, perhaps, so I don't really understand this but, if everyone but Sarah lost and the limit was five hundred pounds . . . why did she not have two and a half thousand pounds in her bag?'

'She gave us ours back,' Sandra Bolton told him. 'Mark, Tim and me, she gave it back.'

'But not . . .' he paused, 'do we have a surname for this Jeff?'

'No. The rest of us all knew each other in various ways. For example, Tim works at the health club, Mark is with Highways in some capacity. He's always chasing some kind of promotion, always talking about it but I don't know what he actually does these days.'

'Yes, I see. So how did this American chap come into the picture?'

'I don't know. He must have known someone, perhaps one of the ones who has dropped out.'

Hall was thoughtful for a moment. 'You were telling me about her giving the money back.'

'Yes. She insisted. She knew we couldn't really afford to lose that much and she gave it back. She said she wouldn't come anymore either, and that we shouldn't. I wasn't going to go back. I wouldn't have been comfortable without Sarah.'

'What about the others?'

'I'm not sure. When she gave us the money back, we all went home. We . . . we left her to clear up and we all went home.'

'Had Jeff left the premises?'

'He may have been in the pub, but there isn't anywhere else he could have been. The room doesn't connect with the pub, there's just the room and the stairs and he wasn't on the stairs. We heard the door slam when he went out and he wasn't outside when we left. The door doesn't open from the outside once we're there. The landlord lets us in and then that's it.'

'It all sounds a bit hole-and-corner, Sandra, for a card school at a penny a point.'

She smiled wanly. 'I know. I think the boys liked it. It was a bit James Bond.'

Hall conjured up a picture of the Red Lion in his mind. If the room upstairs had anything in common with the actual pub, James Bond was not the first thing that came to mind. More toothless old men playing dominoes still whingeing about that Margaret Thatcher and how she was ruining the country. 'So he had gone, then, had he? You're sure?'

Sandra Bolton went white. 'Do you mean that it was Jeff? Who killed Sarah?'

'No ideas yet, Sandra.' He looked at her for the longest minute of her life. 'Go home. I am suspending you from duty as of now, but I will have to ratify that with HR tomorrow. Please don't leave Leighford, we'll be needing to chat. Meanwhile, have you no contact details for any of the other three?'

'I know where Mark and Tim work. I don't know Mark's surname and I'm not sure of Tim's. My partner will know that. I don't know Jeff's surname or where he lives.'

‘Not to worry,’ Hall said. He had a look of a man whose internal filing system had just come up trumps. ‘I think I may know a woman who does. Off you go now, Sandra. We’ll probably need you tomorrow, but I’ll send a car.’ He looked down at his tidy desk and the minute taker got up and left. Sandra Bolton knew when she had had a lucky escape and was through the door before it had closed behind the woman.

Hall sat there in silence for a moment and then reached into his pocket and took out the piece of paper. ‘Demons?’ he read, then screwed it up and threw it into the bin. ‘Well, that answers that question.’ He pulled the phone towards him and punched in the Maxwells’ landline number. After ten rings it went to the answerphone and he replaced the receiver. He could try her mobile, but this was one that would wait. If the man he was looking for was who he thought he was, he was going to need a long time with the Maxwells to find out all he could first and he needed all the calm he could muster before involving Mad Max in this one. Another New Year Resolution had already bitten the dust and the year was scarcely two weeks old. He decided to break another and headed for the chocolate machine in the rest room. May as well be hanged for a sheep as a lamb.

# CHAPTER NINE

Betty Carpenter had always kept a tidy house and one of the things that she had instilled into her daughter was that as long as the sofa cushions were straight and there was no fluff on the carpet, you could make any room fit for visitors in less than five minutes. With the kitchen door closed on the toast-crumb/tomato-covered plates and a quick squirt of something down the loo, the house was Whatmough-ready in no time.

And in what seemed no time at all, there was a brisk ring at the bell, followed by two sharp raps.

Maxwell, who had hardly been relaxing in his chair anyway, leapt to his feet and dashed down to open the door. Unlike most of the audience of the old Monty Python sketch, he *always* expected the Spanish Inquisition. On the step, Mrs Whatmough had recovered her composure and nodded her head graciously to Maxwell, as if she were the householder and he the importunate visitor.

'Mr Maxwell,' she remarked, with no inflection.

Maxwell decided to be a good host. 'Mrs Whatmough! Come on in out of the cold.' He stepped aside to let her pass and she went up the stairs without a backward glance. He heard Jacquie greet the woman on the landing and he took three deep breaths before going up to join them.

As he went into the sitting room, Jacquie was helping Mrs Whatmough out of her coat, which she handed to Maxwell without a word. He disposed of it tidily across the back of a chair and ushered the woman to a seat by the fire. They all sat round for a moment or so, with the Headmistress surveying the room, now detinselled but still bearing the signs of a recent Christmas, with board games still out and a by now slightly mangled ginger battery-driven hamster on the mantelpiece. She smiled as far as she ever did.

'What a pleasant room this is,' she told them.

'Thank you,' Jacquie said and sat waiting patiently for the point of the visit to be broached. Then, when nothing else seemed forthcoming, she added, 'We like it.'

'Is Nolan not here?' Mrs Whatmough asked.

'Having a nap,' Maxwell said. 'We've had rather a busy afternoon.'

'Oh, yes. Tobogganing,' she said. 'Although we always called it sledging when I was a child. I hope he will be fully rested for school tomorrow.'

Jacquie gave Maxwell a small triumphant smile. The sledging-versus-tobogganing question had been settled by the best possible authority. 'He'll be up shortly,' she said. 'Then it will be supper, bath and bed. He likes his routine.'

'Routine is the key,' Mrs Whatmough said, but without much enthusiasm. Unspoken sentences hung in the air of the room like smoke.

Maxwell was never one to hang about when a murder investigation was pending. He had not been able to get any details out of Jacquie all afternoon, not even by attaching questions to casual remarks or placing lighted matches under her fingernails. His best attempt had been 'Just look at those two fly down that hill, was she pushed do you think or did she fall?' He was agog to know what Mrs Whatmough had to do with the whole thing but had been too polite to ask her on the doorstep. But enough was enough. Even so, he wrapped it up a little.

'I'm sure that, like us, you don't want Nolan to hear this conversation, Mrs Whatmough. Would you like to ask anything? Tell us something, perhaps?'

This was the opening they had all been waiting for. Taking a deep breath, the Headmistress began.

'I received a telephone call from the estranged husband of one of my staff this afternoon, a Reverend Mattley.'

'May I interrupt, Mrs Whatmough?' Jacquie said.

'Do, please, call me Rosemary.'

'Er . . . Rosemary. . .'

'Only in this context, of course. Not in school.'

Jacquie knew the rules. 'Of course not. Where was I?' she appealed to Maxwell.

'Interrupting.'

'Yes. The dead woman's name was not Mattley. I wonder if we are at cross purposes.'

'No, her name was Gregson. She and her husband had separated just before she came to work at my school,' Maxwell would have sworn he could hear capital letters on those two words, 'and I must say I was uncomfortable about having a woman in such a situation as a teacher, but as we all know these days, marriages don't always last.' She blushed faintly under the uncompromising layer of powder and carried on. 'I received a call from him, and it was to tell me that his wife was dead. I think he was just trying to do the right thing, to let me know she wouldn't be in on Monday.' She stopped speaking and swallowed hard, as if the situation had just hit her. Telling the staff. Telling the children. It was not a task she relished, if only because of its unfortunate effect on discipline and routine. She coughed and continued. 'Of course, I was shocked; she was only a young woman. When he told me the circumstances I was . . . well, Mr Maxwell, Mrs Maxwell, I was rather upset.' Again, the small cough. 'I had had some . . . personal contact with Sarah Gregson on Thursday and the more I thought about it, the more I was convinced that I should speak to someone. But—'

Maxwell cut in. 'But you didn't want to go to the police and you thought that we might be the next best thing.'

'Not really,' she retorted. 'I know I will have to speak to the police. But I doubt they will be doing much about this death, which I assume they will assign in the final analysis to suicide. I don't think it was, Mr Maxwell, and I had heard that you . . .'

'Interest myself,' Maxwell offered.

'Pokes his nose in,' muttered Jacquie, then, louder, 'You don't have to worry, Rosemary. We have decided that this is murder. Officially.'

Maxwell looked at his wife out of the corner of his eye. She had obviously made the decision to share in the interests of finding something out. With luck, she would end up the better for it.

Rosemary Whatmough let her guard slip, even if only for a moment. 'You agree? But why?'

'There were various things at the scene which have made us lean towards conducting a murder enquiry,' Jacquie said. 'But, Rosemary, I would be interested to know why—' Her head snapped up. 'I'm sorry, can you wait while I go and see Nolan? I can hear him on the move. Unless . . .' She looked meaningfully at Maxwell, who smiled and shook his head.

'A boy needs his mother,' he said, smugly.

'Indeed,' Mrs Whatmough agreed.

Jacquie shot Maxwell a venomous glance and left the room.

Maxwell waited until he heard her talking to Nolan along the landing and then turned to Rosemary Whatmough. 'So,' he said, 'as Jacquie was about to ask, why do you think it was murder?'

The Headmistress flicked a glance to the door. 'Well, Mr Maxwell, I . . . To be quite frank with you, I thought that I would be at loggerheads with the police, but now that I find that they also suspect murder . . .'

Maxwell decided to go out on a limb. He affected a hurt expression and said, 'As they suspect murder, you don't need my amateur bumbling.'

'No, no, good heavens, no. I just mean that I should share my knowledge with Mrs Maxwell, as a senior police officer, rather than . . .' She glanced up, met his eyes and made a decision. She folded her hands in her lap and leant forward. 'On Thursday, Sarah Gregson came to me in great distress and asked for an advance on her salary.'

Maxwell smiled. 'Christmas is always an expensive time, Rosemary.' He knew exactly how far teachers' salaries went.

'Of course,' the woman agreed. Her small capon had been ridiculously overpriced, but had kept her and Yan Woo in leftovers for some days, to be fair to Messrs Waitrose. 'But this seemed more than that. She was desperate and clearly didn't have anywhere else to turn.' She raised an unexpectedly self-aware eyebrow. 'I can hardly imagine any of my staff would come to me with such a request unless they were quite, quite desperate, Mr Maxwell.'

This was clearly a rhetorical remark, and he let it go without reply. 'How much did she say she needed?' he asked, instead.

'She *asked* for two hundred and fifty, but I lent her five hundred pounds.'

Maxwell's jaw dropped. He indulged in a moment's imagining that he would be lent five hundred pounds by Legs Diamond and somehow the picture refused to take shape. Only the usual squadron of pigs roared and squealed their way across the sky, vapour trails entwined. 'That was . . . incredibly generous of you, Rosemary.'

'I happened to have it on me. I wouldn't have, as a rule. I assumed she was being blackmailed.'

'That's a very unusual conclusion to which to jump,' he said, wondering again what sort of people had been unleashed to teach his son. 'And also, if I may say so, would that not, were it true, be a very good reason for suicide?'

Rosemary Whatmough looked at the man before her, at his trousers, slightly baggy at the knees and still bearing a faint trace of bicycle clip creases at the cuffs; at his jumper, pulled at random places by Metternich's rare expressions of affection; at his barbed wire hair, his side whiskers, newly trimmed for a new term; at the questioning half smile. But most of all, she looked into his kind knowing eyes and found herself to be in floods of tears.

Maxwell was immediately on his feet. He passed her a box of tissues from the coffee table and stood by her side, a hand hovering over her shoulder, which he finally decided to risk patting. The contact seemed to pull her together and she recoiled slightly, leaving him to return to his chair, hostly duties performed to perfection.

She blew her nose. 'I apologise,' she said. 'I have been through a rather worrying time lately.'

'It hasn't shown,' Maxwell said. He knew that he could bestow no greater compliment.

She heaved a huge sigh. 'Thank you,' she said. 'I'm glad. My school means everything to me and I have been worried that . . . well, it means everything to me.'

The light went on in Maxwell's head. 'Rosemary,' he said gently. 'Are *you* being blackmailed?'

'Ha.' The attempt at a laugh was mirthless. 'Whatever would anyone be able to blackmail me about?'

'Well, I have no idea,' Maxwell told her. 'I assume it is a secret, or how would you be being blackmailed?' It seemed pretty obvious to him.

'You are a very intelligent man, aren't you, Mr Maxwell?' she said. 'Not just intelligent, but you know how to put two and two together.'

'Maths is probably my weakest area,' Maxwell said, 'but following the analogy, I do indeed know how many beans make five. Would you like to tell me about it?'

She blew her nose again, in a ladylike fashion. 'Not really, Mr Maxwell.' She leant down and picked up her handbag and started to get up. 'This was a mistake. I should go, really. Please give my apologies to your wife.'

The door opened and Jacquie walked in. 'Apologies?' she asked, taking in the woman's tear-stained face. 'What for?'

The Headmistress stood up and went towards her coat. 'I made a mistake. I must go home. Please don't speak of this, Mr Maxwell. I assure you that as far as I am concerned it is forgotten already.'

'But, Mrs Whatmough. Rosemary,' Maxwell said, touching her arm. 'Jacquie can help you, I'm sure.'

'No. Please. I must go.' She struggled into her coat and was through the door and off before either of them could stop her. The door at the bottom of the stairs slammed behind her, and in the ringing silence, Jacquie turned to her husband.

'Was it something I said?'

'No, and it wasn't something I said, either. My gob is, however, metaphorically smacked. Is Nole getting up?'

'No. He's decided to stay in bed and watch a DVD with a bowl of Coco Pops. I keep meaning to ask you, as a bit of an expert on children: are they all this easy?'

Maxwell thought briefly of his last experience of fatherhood, but knew that wasn't why she asked the question. 'By the time they get to me, they have passed through so many hands it's hard to tell. Half of them are degenerates, a quarter sociopaths and I don't even want to think about the other forty per cent. But Nole certainly seems to be little trouble, I'll give him that. What's he watching?'

'He was trying to decide between *Despicable Me* and *Howl's Moving Castle*. Nightmares either way, but the way he is about choosing, he'll be asleep before he watches either. Anyway, that's enough prevarication. What was Rosemary's problem? What did you say to her?'

'Well, I began with asking her why she thought it was murder.'

'And why did she?'

'It all took a bit of a funny turn from then on. She, Rosemary, suspected that she, Sarah, was being blackmailed.'

'That's grounds for suicide, surely.'

'As a rule. But Rosemary Whatmough has her own set of rules. And if she hasn't committed suicide because of blackmail, she doesn't really see why anyone else would. I think that was the gist.'

Jacquie leant forward, her mouth open. 'Mrs Whatmough's being *blackmailed*?'

'She didn't say so, but . . . yes.'

'You do know that I'll have to follow this up? I can't ignore it.'

'Yes, I know you can't ignore it, but can I follow it up? Pretty please.'

'Max—' The phone shrilled and they both looked round wildly trying to locate the handset. Jacquie remembered first and dashed into the kitchen. Maxwell heard her say, 'Oh, hello, guv.' There was a pause and then, 'We were out on the Dam, sledging. We've not been back long.' Maxwell noted with pleasure that she didn't mention Rosemary Whatmough. 'Well, of course,' he heard her say. 'We'll be here. 'Bye.'

She came back into the room, the phone still in her hand. 'Henry's coming over,' she told him. 'Apparently, he thinks we might know the murderer personally and he wants to have a chat.'

Their eyes locked and their minds echoed each other with the same phrase. 'Surely not Mrs Whatmough?'

* * *

Henry Hall was a methodical man above all else and he sorted out his desk before he headed off to 38 Columbine. As is always the way of it, this meant that he got caught by umpteen people who had been trying to catch him all week, and so it was gone seven by the time he rang the bell. Jacquie opened it, on a waft of roast chicken. Hall was not a policeman for nothing, and noting the smell and the small drool of gravy on her chin, he apologised at once.

'You're eating. I'm sorry; I'll come back later.'

'Don't talk rubbish, Henry. We've saved you some. I rang Margaret and said we'd feed you, if that was all right with her.'

'And was it?'

'Yes. Apparently she had already had a low-fat cauliflower surprise.' Jacquie paused halfway up the stairs and looked back at him. 'It sounds delicious.'

'Does it? Well, now, that's something I suppose.' Hall realised that he had had nothing except chocolate since a snatched breakfast. 'Do I smell stuffing?'

'Of course. Here at the Restaurant at the End of the Universe, all the trimmings means exactly that. Having only thrown the turkey out last week I think it may be a little soon to have poultry again, personally.'

Henry Hall had learnt in what he called the Diet Years, in other words every single day that had passed since his youngest son was weaned, that it was never too soon for stuffing and followed her gratefully up the stairs. At the kitchen table there was a fourth place set, with wine glass already half filled with a thoughtfully parsimonious half a unit of wine. Wouldn't do for a Detective Chief Inspector to be breathalysed by One of his Own. Nolan was leaning on his elbow at one of the other places and seemed to be asleep halfway through a Brussel sprout.

Jacquie picked him up and removed the speared Brussel from his unresisting hand. 'Get Henry's dinner on the table, would you, sweetheart?' she asked Maxwell. 'I'll just put Sonny Jim to bed.'

Maxwell sketched a kiss at his son who waved a tired hand in everyone's general direction.

'Night night, Nolan,' Hall said. He had forgotten, through all the spotty teenaged years of his own boys, how endearing they had looked at Nolan's age. He sat down to his dinner, freshly out of a warm oven. 'Max, you're a lifesaver. I didn't know I was so hungry.'

'You're in luck,' the Head of Sixth Form-turned-Masterchef said. 'We usually eat at lunchtime on a Sunday, but we went out instead.'

'Yes,' Hall said, slicing into a chicken leg. 'Jacquie said you had been out at the Dam.'

'Yes, we went with Hector Gold, our exchange teacher. American, but very nice chap. He and Nole get on like a house on fire.'

If Maxwell noticed Hall pause in his chewing, he gave no sign.

'Jacquie did say you had an exchange teacher. Who is he in exchange for?'

For the briefest of moments, Maxwell saw a grim black and white 50s noir moment, of spies passing each other on bridges somewhere in central Europe. The reality was a little less colourful. 'Paul Moss. I think you've probably met him from time to time.' Both men knew that this meant from the occasional murder case, but they were still too deep in social mode to say so.

'History,' Hall said.

'That's right. Hector is a very good European historian as it turns out, bearing in mind his colonial pedigree. It's a shame. His family are the in-laws from Hell, so we won't be seeing much of him. His wife is a panther, or some such feline.'

Jacquie came in at this point. 'I think you must mean cougar,' she said, sliding back into her seat.

'That's the critter. Anyway, she is a bit older than Hector.' He paused in a gentlemanly way to give Jacquie time to snort.

Jacquie snorted. 'A bit!'

'She is older than Hector by a fair old margin and that's all you're getting out of me. Alana, his mother-in-law, is more or less permanently drunk as far as I can tell. She pinched the sherry when they came over before Christmas. Mrs Troubridge did some detecting and found out for us. The father-in-law . . . Well, I'll let Jacquie take over on this one.'

'Yes. Hector's father-in-law. Where to begin? We'll leave out any personal prejudices I may have and just say that he is a sexist bully. He was a police officer in the States, but was removed from his post for various as yet unspecified misdemeanours.'

'Malfeasance,' muttered Maxwell.

'Mr Maxwell,' Jacquie explained to her boss, 'has taken the opportunity to do lots of take-offs of Francis McDormand in *Fargo*. I must apologise. Where was I?'

'Jeff O'Malley,' Hall prompted.

'That was clever.' Maxwell was on him like a ninja. 'I don't remember telling you his name.'

'I'm sure Jacquie mentioned it,' Hall said, smoothly imperturbable as always.

Maxwell narrowed his eyes, but gestured to Jacquie to continue.

'His son-in-law obviously hates him and quite rightly. When Mrs Troubridge took me into the kitchen to tell me about something she had noticed about Alana . . .' she raised an eyebrow at Hall to see if he was with her so far and he nodded, 'Hector just let it drop in conversation that everyone hates Jeff. His wife — Jeff's wife, that is — was similarly indiscreet when Jeff claimed to have retired. That's really the only reason I think he was removed, that and the fact that I don't like him. But why are we having this conversation? We thought you were here to ask about Mrs Whatmough.'

'Who on earth is Mrs Whatmough?' Hall asked, genuinely confused.

'Nolan's Headmistress,' Maxwell said. 'We thought you might have her in the frame for Sarah Gregson's murder.'

'How do you know who has been murdered?' Hall said, glaring at Jacquie.

'Not from me,' Jacquie said. 'It was Mrs Whatmough. Who told him, I mean. I don't think she did it.'

'You've said she's strict,' Hall said, 'but surely not as strict as that.'

'She's being blackmailed,' Jacquie said. 'And Sarah Gregson had a thousand pounds on her. But then it turns out that Mrs Whatmough had lent her five hundred only last week. She thought that Sarah Gregson was being blackmailed as well. We can't decide for sure, because she came over all unnecessary and left, but we thought perhaps that she was afraid that the blackmailer might be the same one.'

Hall looked at the two, so different and yet, at this moment as they looked at him eagerly over the wreck of a Sunday dinner with all the trimmings, they could have been Tweedledum and Tweedledee. 'I will ignore the use of the word "we" in this conversation and if I have to repeat it, I will change it to "I",' he said, dryly. 'So, she's afraid that the blackmailer would be coming for her next. That's an unusual view of blackmailers. They usually like to keep the golden goose alive and laying.' He could hardly believe his own ears. Every time he came into this house he sounded more and more like a Grimm Brother.

'No, no,' Jacquie said. 'You really need to know Mrs Whatmough before you understand this, but we think it is because she doesn't want him found. Or at least, not before she has found him. Or her.' Discretion stopped her from telling her boss that the Headmistress had come to 38 Columbine to secure the services of Maxwell, PI. 'She knows that if you find him, you'll find out what she's being blackmailed about, and that is more than she is going to put up with. She is quite a forceful lady.'

'I see. Does she gamble, do you know?'

'*Gamble?*' Jacquie said.

'*Mrs Whatmough?*' Maxwell added.

'Well, Sarah Gregson did,' Hall told them. 'That's where the thousand pounds came from. And so does—'

'Jeff O'Malley.' Maxwell finished his sentence for him. 'Sarah Gregson was playing cards with Jeff O'Malley. Bingo.' He stopped to listen to what he had just said and regretted it. The others didn't even hear it as the potentially tasteless joke it could have been in other hands and so he let it pass.

'That's right. Sandra Bolton also played . . .'

'Sandra from the nick?' Jacquie asked. 'But she was at the scene. Why didn't she say anything?'

'That's for another day,' Hall said. 'There were a couple of others there, but this O'Malley is where my interests lie at the moment. We're tracking the others, but I just wanted to sound you out about O'Malley. This Mrs Whatmough has rather muddied things, though. You see, before I spoke to Sandra, and now you two, I had had an interview with Sarah's husband. He's the vicar of our nearest church, in fact, so I know him slightly. You know, bazaars and similar. He's absolutely not in the frame, of that I'm sure, but he did say she used to be a social worker.'

Jacquie was all attention. 'You mean, this could be linked with the Hendricks killing?'

Maxwell looked at Hall. Surely coincidence had not entered his life at this late stage.

'I thought possibly, because of the way Hendricks died. It was an execution, as far as we could tell. But this isn't that kind of killing, and anyway, she wasn't even working for social services by the time it came to court, so I think that is just a red herring. I think that O'Malley was so wild that he had lost for once, he just tossed her over the parapet. Big guy, I gather.'

'Enormous,' Jacquie said. 'Run to fat a bit, but still very strong. And angry. Aggressive. I can see him hitting first and thinking later.'

'Right.' Hall drained the dregs from his glass and pushed himself back from the table. 'Thanks, people. It has been very useful.' He turned to Maxwell and forced out two words. 'As always.' Maxwell acknowledged them with a nod. 'But I think I have some work to do tonight before I go to bed. Thanks for dinner.'

Jacquie stood up as well. 'I'm coming, guv. Let me get my coat.'

Hall looked at Maxwell, then turned to Jacquie. 'Not on this one,' he said. 'It might be . . . awkward. With his son-in-law, and everything.'

'Don't worry about Hector,' Maxwell said. 'If he has time, he will arrange a ticker tape parade to see him off the premises. And anyway, I think Alana might need a friendly face. She has had enough trouble being married to Jeff O'Malley as it is. This might be the straw that breaks her back. I suppose there is one saving grace, though.'

'Which is?' Jacquie said, muffled by the scarf she was winding round her face.

'That at least it won't drive her to drink. She's already parked the car in the car park and gone inside.'

# CHAPTER TEN

The plate flew across the dining room and shattered on the wall, drooling melted cheese and tomato down Manda Moss's immaculate decor. A shard of fried tortilla took out a small figurine of a teddy bear holding a chocolate in a winsome way and the guacamole made interesting patterns on a lampshade. Apart from a slow drip as pieces of cheese lost their grip one by one and fell to the floor, the room was silent.

Alana O'Malley started to get up, eyes downcast, in order to clear up the mess.

'Sit down.' The order from her husband was not a command. He seemed to be able to make any words sound like a threat and he did so now. 'Don't anybody move.' He was carrying his head low and his eyes flicked from side to side. Then, almost as if nothing had happened, he said, 'With all those cooking programmes on the TV, why can't you cook anything else but chimichangas?'

His wife looked wildly at her daughter, who avoided her eye. 'You don't like anything else I cook,' she said. This was bold for her and Hector narrowed his lips slightly, ready for the storm to come.

'That's because everything you cook tastes like shit,' her husband said. If an eavesdropper whose native tongue was not English had heard it, they would have assumed it was an endearment, so at odds was the tone with the content. This was O'Malley's way of making the perp feel confused. It broke men in custody within hours. Alana O'Malley had heard it daily for forty years and the fact that she had not totally broken yet was a credit to her. But if not broken, she was tired out by it and most days hung on by a thread and a bottle or two of vodka. All she could do after her initial bravado was shrug.

Camille had been a witness to her father's behaviour all her life so for her it was the norm. The buffeting of life with Jeff O'Malley had left her perhaps the most damaged of them all, but she didn't seem to know it. She looked up from pushing a salad around her plate. These days she just didn't seem to find food very tasty. A tomato was plenty for an evening meal for anyone, she felt. Why her family seemed to insist on more was a mystery to her. But this was a conversation about food, which seemed to matter to other people, so she thought she might just as well join in. They seemed to expect it.

'The food's OK here, Dad,' she said. 'I found a great smoothie place down by the nail bar in town.'

'That's great, kitten,' O'Malley purred. 'That's swell.' It was as if a tiger had come in and sat down at the table and decided to behave itself for a minute or two before it ate everyone. 'But,' and his fist crashed down, making the crockery jump and breaking a glass, 'but I'm talking about the food I get *here. That* food tastes like shit!'

He looked around the table, and being a man ruled by his emotions, his face showed what he thought of his family as his eyes settled on them one by one. For Hector and Alana, there was naked contempt, although for Hector he added a sprinkling of pure hatred. When he thought of all the great guys his little princess could have had it tore at his guts that she had ended up with this little weasel. He didn't like to think about what went on between them. Man and wife. It was an atrocity he could hardly bear. The veins stood out on his neck and his anger was fuelled by Hector's look of calm acceptance. His wife just got the contempt; she wasn't worth anything else, the dried-up, drink-soaked old woman. How come he was married to an old woman? He was in the prime of his life and he could name a dozen women who would tell him so. But for Camille, his little princess, he managed a smile. Only he and Camille would recognise the love in it. To everyone else, it looked like the smile on the edge of a razor. He drew a breath to tell his wife just what he thought of her damned cooking, but was stalled by the doorbell ringing.

Camille got up. She was always expecting the call from Hollywood, no matter where she was at the time. She knew she could be a star and she had heard so often that when opportunity knocked, you had to be ready to let it in. In her nail bar, back home, she had done the nails of many stars; well, not necessarily the stars themselves, but people who knew the stars, and they all said the same. As if echoing her thoughts, there were three sharp raps on the door and another ring of the bell.

'Sit down, sugar,' O'Malley said, flapping a hand at his daughter. 'Sounds a bit rough to me. I'll get it. It's probably some—'

A muffled voice from outside drew everyone's attention from what he had been about to say. It was English, it was polite, but it brooked no argument. It was Henry Hall at his most impressive. 'Mr O'Malley. If you are in the house, could you please come to the door? This is important and we would like to speak to you.'

Everyone inside looked at everyone else. Alana, three parts drunk and four parts dispirited, turned her haunted eyes on her husband. It was all happening again, or was it? Was she dreaming this, or was it real? It wasn't quite like the last time. The voice outside was polite, there didn't seem to be guns. She wasn't spreadeagled against the wall, with the hot breath of a policeman on the back of her neck and the cold muzzle of a Glock tickling her ear. But in most other ways, it was the same as had happened before. And don't forget the time before that. A tear stole slowly down her cheek.

Camille used the look she had once used when she had been caught out in a childish misdemeanour. It had worked on her father since time immemorial. It had worked on teachers, employers and then, eventually, Hector and his many predecessors. But time had not been kind to Camille's signature look and now it was as though a small and bewildered child, none too bright but horribly cunning, looked out through the eyeholes of a beautifully painted but rather grotesque Halloween mask. She couldn't understand why men kept coming to find her father. These cases of mistaken identity really should be clamped down on. Even the girls at her nail bar back home sometimes said bad things about him, but she had the answer to that. They had their marching orders P.D.Q. and no mistake. No one worked for Camille O'Malley Gold for long if they said bad things about her father.

Hector just looked smug. He'd been here before and he expected to be here again. But each time it happened, he got a tiny excited glow inside a happy bubble just behind his ribs that told him that perhaps *this* time, they could make something stick.

The knock came again and Hector pushed back his chair. 'I'll go, shall I?' he said and walked off down the hall and opened the door.

The waiting O'Malleys held their collected breath.

'Oh, Jacquie,' they heard him say and they let their breaths out, prematurely, as it turned out. 'Or should I say Detective Inspector Maxwell? Since you are here on business, am I right?'

'Yes, I'm afraid so. May I introduce Detective Chief Inspector Hall? DCI Hall, Hector Gold. I think I may have told you, he is a colleague of my husband.'

God, thought O'Malley, these Brits are really stiff. If it was a bust of mine, I would have been in here with nightsticks by now, making them assume the position and talking Mirandas. There they are, chatting like at a tea party.

'May we come in?' The man spoke, and he was still polite, but somehow it didn't sound quite like a question.

'Of course.' Hector stood aside and let them in. He turned and led the way to the dining room. 'Folks,' he said, and Jacquie would have sworn he became more Minnesotan with every syllable, 'it's Detective Inspector Maxwell and Detective Chief Inspector Hall. I assume they are here to see you, Jeff. Would you like to see them in here or through in the family room?'

Jacquie looked around and was aghast. She had been to many a dinner here, exquisitely cooked and prepared by the immaculate Manda Moss. The Gold-O'Malley ménage had been in charge here for less than a month, and yet the place was a wreck. Every surface had at least one glass-ring on it, there were clear signs that someone was smoking heavily in there; it didn't take a Detective Inspector to work that out, with laden ashtrays everywhere, which on closer inspection turned out to be saucers from Manda's prized wedding present tea service, the remains of which were leaning drunkenly in the leaded glass-fronted cabinet in the corner. But the *pièce de résistance* of the O'Malley redecoration scheme was the striking mural of tomato and cheese decorating one wall. She hoped that O'Malley didn't choose to go through into another room. The least she knew about the devastation of Manda's pride and joy, the better.

O'Malley leant insolently back in his chair, which creaked protestingly. 'What I have to say to these people, I can say here,' he said.

'That's thoughtful of you, Mr O'Malley,' Hall said, smoothly. It was the first time he had spoken since he had been on the other side of the door and Camille pricked up her ears. He was old, of course, old for a woman with her tastes and obvious charms, but he was a man and she automatically preened herself. But he was a gentleman, and that was what had attracted her to Hector Gold, in the days when she was attracted to Hector Gold. Henry Hall was saying more stuff and she forced herself to listen.

'That's thoughtful of you, Mr O'Malley, but I'm afraid we won't be interviewing you here. We would like you to come down to the station with us, if you would? We have a few questions we would like you to help us with.'

O'Malley leapt to his feet. 'You arresting me, fella?' he growled.

'No, not at the moment,' Hall said. 'We would just like you to come down and be interviewed. You will be under caution, but not arrested.'

'What kind of guff is this?' O'Malley said, looking round his family for support. 'I done nothing. I've been here all day. Stuck in this stinking hole because Hector here needed the car.'

'There are two cars here,' Jacquie pointed out. She was trying hard not to judge this man before she had the facts. But if ever she had wanted someone to be guilty, that moment was now.

'Call that a car?' O'Malley cried, incredulous. 'That thing, I could put it in my pocket. It's only got two doors, for one thing.'

Jacquie had sold her beloved Ka to Manda as a runaround and felt very protective towards it, but it was quite true that O'Malley would have been hard-pressed to even get inside. She damped down the mental picture that she had of him looking like Fred Flintstone in the vehicle and turned to Hall.

'It isn't necessarily today we want to speak to you about, Mr O'Malley,' Hall said, smoothly. He looked at Hector, who he had rightly identified as the only normal one of the family. 'Could you fetch Mr O'Malley's coat, please, Mr Gold?' he asked him. 'There is another sharp frost tonight and it is very cold outside.'

Hector Gold almost skipped down the hall to fetch his father-in-law's coat. He had been waiting for this moment practically since the day he first met Jeff O'Malley, and even if they didn't lock him up and throw away the key, he was enjoying all this immensely.

Not so Camille, who hurled herself into her father's arms, weeping extravagantly. He unwound her gently and said, 'It's all right, kitten. These hick coppers will soon realise they have the wrong guy. I'll be back before you know it. And with the money I get when I sue their asses for wrongful arrest, we'll go on a holiday, huh? Just you and me. Somewhere nice and warm, with none of this cold and wet. Huh? OK, kitten?'

The sight of a woman who wouldn't see forty again nodding like an appeased child was somewhat stomach churning, but Hector Gold was back with the coat, and the tableau broke up, much to everyone's relief. O'Malley shrugged into the windcheater and growled at his wife.

'I'll be back sooner than you think, so get some decent food for me then. These people,' with a glare at Jacquie and Hall, who both returned his stare impassively, 'will arrange my transport, so don't worry about that, everybody.' He turned to Hall. He had decided to ignore Jacquie as being beneath notice. 'Shall we go? Sooner we get there, sooner I can start suing your ass.'

'Indeed,' Hall said and gestured to the door. 'After you.'

O'Malley stamped down the hall and flung open the door. If he was surprised to see the police van backed into the drive, complete with flashing blue light and two policemen in Kevlar jackets standing shotgun on either side of the open doors, he didn't show it. With admirable aplomb, he walked up to it and climbed inside. He turned to the policeman on the right. 'Call this a police wagon?' he said. The policeman turned and closed the door in his face.

'Straight to the station, guv?' he asked.

'Straight there, yes,' Hall said. 'We'll be along shortly. Put him in . . . well, put him in whatever cell someone was sick in last.'

The policeman smiled. 'Will do, guv. I'll phone ahead and call off the cleaners,' and he sprinted round the side of the van and jumped aboard. The van screeched off, siren wailing. It wasn't strictly necessary, but it made Jeff O'Malley feel at home.

Hall turned back to the house, to find Hector Gold standing right behind him. Jacquie knew how he felt; the man could creep up on you quieter than Metternich. 'I'm terribly sorry, sir,' Hall said. 'That was unprofessional of me.'

Hector Gold punched him lightly on the arm, an expression of extreme delight, because Hector didn't go in much for physical contact these days. Camille had pretty much knocked that trait out of him. 'Don't mention it, Mr Hall. Don't even give it a second thought. Umm . . . I don't know how to phrase this, but . . . how long are you planning on keeping him? What's the rule here? I know you can ask for longer, for example, but longer than what?'

He was clearly trying to keep the glee out of his voice and Jacquie smiled at him, a smile he returned in his usual dazzling camera flash style.

Hall looked at him for a long minute. 'I'm not sure what our timescale is, Mr Gold,' he said at last. 'Enjoy your evening. Please say goodbye to your wife and to Mrs O'Malley for me. Thank you.' And Henry Hall walked down the drive to his car, parked on the road outside.

Jacquie turned to Hector. 'Hector,' she said. 'Whatever can I say? Not sorry, obviously, because this must be quite a day for you.'

'Too right, Jacquie. It'll hit Camille hard.' He added no other words to describe how he felt about that. 'Alana is pretty much pickled. I don't think she's been properly sober since that day at your house. And she wasn't what I'd call real sober then. Jeff won't let her get help, because, of course, he is the reason for her drinking and he doesn't want to face that.'

Jacquie was suddenly reminded of Mrs Whatmough and her fear of exposure, although two people less alike than O'Malley and the Headmistress it would be hard to find. 'Don't worry, Hector. I'll ring you when I can with news. Meanwhile, if you need anything, ring home. Max is there, he will be able to help you.'

'I will,' Gold said, reaching out and giving her shoulder a tentative squeeze. 'You're good friends, Jacquie. Thank you.' Again there was the flash of a smile and he gently closed the door.

* * *

At Leighford Nick, O'Malley was treating the staff to some rough music. Hall had rightly guessed that his behaviour on the journey would earn him some cooling-off time in the cells and so he and Jacquie had not hurried to get ready for the interview. O'Malley had discovered that there were not many opportunities for his usual destructive behaviour in the cell, as there was nothing in there that was not bolted down, so he was making his presence felt by yelling every obscenity he could think of at the top of his not inconsiderable voice. A slight echo of it seemed to reach into even the most distant parts of the building, reverberating through pipes and conduits and making the wax shift in the ears of those close by. In Henry Hall's office, it was just a distant hum.

Hall shrugged out of his coat and hung it behind the door.

'Seems like a nice chap,' he remarked to Jacquie.

'O'Malley?' She was confused.

'No, no. Mr Gold.' Another man would have laughed at her mistake, but the man in question was Henry Hall so he just inclined his head slightly, to show his amusement.

'Oh, yes, Hector is a very nice man. He doesn't deserve his family, I know that.'

'Mrs O'Malley, what do you make of her?'

'Drunk. Defeated.'

'Domestic abuse there, do you think?' Hall was getting all his ducks in a row. He was determined to get O'Malley for something, anything; he hardly minded at this juncture.

'I would imagine so,' Jacquie agreed. 'But not lately. He hardly notices her these days, I think. She's only here because she would have been more trouble to leave behind. It's the daughter he dotes on.'

'Just dotes?'

'Hmm . . . well, just dotes these days. Perhaps not always.'

'It's a bugger of a family, but it's grand,' Hall quoted, unexpectedly.

'Guv!' Jacquie laughed. 'I never had you down for a rugby man!' She had spent many an hour as a teenager glued to the side of a rugger hearty from the posh boys' school down the road and some of those songs were engraved in her brain. Maxwell often hummed one or two of them as accompaniment to the washing-up.

'Not the game, just some of the songs,' Hall explained. 'My DCI when I was a sergeant was a fan.'

Jacquie realised that she had never thought of Henry Hall as a sergeant. In her mind, he had sprung fully formed as a DCI after a planning meeting somewhere at Hendon. A sudden thought drove the image from her mind.

'Guv, I know this is against the rules, but can I just ring Max about this? He knows most of it anyway, but I need to keep him up to speed, in case Hector rings.'

Hall flapped a hand at her. He paid lip service to reminding her that she mustn't tell Maxwell so much as the time of day, but in practice he was more than well aware that that was not how things happened at 38 Columbine. 'Yes, but keep it to a minimum. I'm sure Mr Gold is quite capable of telling Max all he needs to know.'

Jacquie went into the corridor and rang the home number, which was engaged. And engaged. And engaged. She went back into Hall's office. 'It's engaged. I think Hector is probably quicker off the mark than we thought. Not to worry — I'm sure you're right about that. Hector will fill him in.' She looked at her watch. 'Have we left him to stew long enough, do you think?' she asked him.

Hall cocked an ear towards the door, checking for sounds filtering up the stairwell. 'He seems to have gone quiet . . . Oh, no, there he goes.' He sighed and got up. 'We'd better go, though. He'll be asking for the Embassy in a minute if we don't. Do you want to come in with me? I only ask because you do know him, if only slightly. I don't want you to feel pressure.'

'That's a nice thought,' she said, grimly. 'My only pressure will be preventing myself from hitting him. He is totally objectionable. Perhaps I had better not come in. I might be prejudicial.'

'After the last hour or so, there's no one in this nick that isn't prejudiced. We'll do it together.' He picked up the phone.

'Steve? Oh, sorry, Jim. Yes, could you take Mr O'Malley to Interview Room 3 for me, please? We're on our way down.' He listened for a moment. 'Yes, he is, isn't he? Thanks.'

Jacquie smiled. 'Quick character study from the front desk?' she asked.

'You could say that,' he said. 'Quite short words, but very descriptive. Come on, we can't put it off any longer. After you,' and he ushered her through the door, carefully switching off the light as they left the room, to preserve polar bears for his grandchildren, as his wife was always telling him.

* * *

Camille Gold was clinging to her husband in a way that she hadn't done since Vegas. And that was only for the photographs, taken by a rather elderly Elvis, whose hair had left the building.

'It can't still be engaged,' she whined as her husband put the receiver back for the umpteenth time.

'Well, it is,' he said. 'People do have lives that don't revolve around you, you know.'

Camille Gold was outraged. That was not a thought that crossed her mind very often. 'Daddy is in the precinct station,' she said, as if they didn't all know. 'Mother is passed out in the dining room. The place is a mess, all covered with food.' Her lip quivered and it wasn't a pretty sight. Hector was certain he could see her lipstick moving slightly out of synch with the flesh. 'Somebody has to *do* something!'

Hector Gold was hard to move to anger as a rule and in fact he wasn't really angry now. But he was as near to it as he liked to come. Sharing a continent with Jeff O'Malley had made him more aware than even his domineering mother had made him that uncontrolled anger was not a pretty sight and he tried not to inflict it on people. So he was gentle with Camille as he pushed her away. She, however, reacted as though he had punched her in the face and fell to the ground, weeping uncontrollably. He looked down at her and heard the small snick of the last piece of mortar falling out of the wall that had been his marriage. He felt a lightness of heart that made him feel sorry for her and he leant down to help her up, but she flinched from him as if his hand was on fire.

'Suit yourself,' he said quietly, and went into the dining room to check on his mother-in-law. She was still passed out in the ruins of the meal of which no one had eaten so much as a mouthful. He shook her gently by the shoulder and spoke softly to her. 'Alana. Alana, honey. Wake up. It's Hector.'

The woman whimpered and frowned in her sleep, but didn't wake. Hector went back into the hall and stirred his still-weeping wife with his foot.

'Your mother is unconscious. I've never seen her this bad before. I think we ought to get her to the hospital.'

Camille O'Malley Gold, soon to be just O'Malley again, although she didn't yet know it, looked up from her position on the floor. 'We can't leave,' she whined. 'The police might bring Daddy back while we're out. How will he get back in?'

Hector personally thought this unlikely, but his wife had stopped weeping and this was a plus, so he decided to humour her. 'Look.' He squatted by her side. 'Why don't you get up, wash up, put your face back on and try and do something about the state of this place while I drive her there myself? That way, if they do bring him back tonight, not only will you be here but Jacquie Maxwell won't be quite so horrified at the mess. This house belongs to friends of hers, don't forget. It was immaculate when we got here and your father has wrecked it, like he wrecks everything he touches.' Camille gathered herself up for a wail. 'Don't go there, Camille. I've had enough. I like the people here. I want them to be my friends and you and your family are doing your damnedest to prevent it. Now,' he pressed on his knees and got up, 'I am going to take your mother to the hospital before she dies. You can do as you like, but I would be grateful if you could move so I don't have to drag your unconscious mother over you to get to the door.'

Without another word or backward glance he walked away and she could hear him in the dining room, muttering words of encouragement to her mother as he manoeuvred her into her coat. Then she heard 'Coming through' and she scrunched her legs round to the side as her husband and his deadweight burden made for the door. They went out and the door slammed behind them, leaving her alone. She tried crying, but no one was there to hear. She lay there for a moment, inhaling the smell of carpet shampoo which was still just in the ascendant over the smell of her father's cigarettes and her mother's despair. Then she gave herself a shake, got up and dusted herself down and went into the lounge to read the paper. There was an article on the newest crackle glaze nail varnish which she wanted to read. Camille and a goldfish had a lot in common, and it wasn't just a slightly artificial-looking golden tan; in moments she had forgotten all about the drama of the evening and was happy in a world of nails.

# CHAPTER ELEVEN

Henry Hall and Jacquie had just reached the bottom of the stairs when the Duty Sergeant popped his head round the door from his office and crooked a finger at them. With his voice lower than strictly necessary, he told them that Sarah Gregson's old man was waiting in the lobby. Henry Hall craned his neck to see, and sure enough, the Reverend Mattley was sitting patiently on one of the hard upright seats, under a poster warning about the perils of sneezing.

'What does he want?' he asked the Sergeant. 'I'm surprised to see him back here so soon, especially on his busiest day.'

'He says he may not have made himself clear earlier,' said the Sergeant, in the tone of someone who wants to make sure he has the words right. 'Something he said about his wife. He wants to clarify, he says.'

Henry Hall thought quickly about the things the vicar had told him and remembered the piece of paper he had thrown in the bin upstairs. Were the demons the demons of gambling, or something else? It wouldn't take a moment to find out. He turned to Jacquie. 'Can you hang on a minute, Jacquie?' he said. 'I think I know what this may be about.'

'OK, guv,' Jacquie said. 'I'll try Max again while I wait. Can I borrow your phone, Jim?'

The Sergeant nodded and pushed the door open further. He gestured to a phone on a desk at the back. 'Use that one,' he said. 'It's not the emergency number, so you don't have to worry about snarling the system up if you use that.'

'Thanks, Jim. I won't be a minute, anyway.' She picked up the phone and stabbed out the numbers. The phone rang — thank goodness he was off the phone. Who had it been for such a long call?

'War Office.' His voice had the slight echo it had when he answered the phone in the attic.

'Max, whoever have you been on the phone to all this time?' she asked, trying not to sound like a nagging wife.

'Sorry, that was the Count.'

'Max, I love him dearly, but I don't believe that even Metternich can use the phone.'

There was a silence. 'I'm shocked to hear you say it, but in fact on this occasion he wasn't using the phone. He had knocked the receiver off the one up here and it wasn't till I came up just now to do a bit of quiet painting that I realised he'd done it. It's his lack of opposable thumbs that causes the problem. Was it something urgent you wanted?'

'No, not really.' She looked over her shoulder at the Duty Sergeant, but he was dealing with a motorist outraged at getting a parking ticket in the car park of the cinema. In vain did the Sergeant try to explain that the ticket didn't come from a council traffic warden but from a private company, but the man would not be placated. The last words Jacquie heard as she turned back to face the wall was that all traffic wardens ought to be castrated and then shot. In that order. Slowly. She dropped her voice nonetheless. 'We took Jeff O'Malley in for questioning, as we planned,' she said. 'It didn't go very well, as you can imagine. They have virtually trashed Manda's lovely house, by the way.'

'She'll go apeshit,' her husband said, as always getting to the nub of the sentence.

'At least,' Jacquie said, remembering the saucers used as ashtrays and the cheese on the wall. 'Alana was absolutely smashed.'

'Of course.'

'Yes. And Camille was . . . well, actually she was quite creepy. Like thingy in that film. Thing. Baby something.'

'Bette Davis in *Whatever Happened to Baby Jane?*' It was a perfect Joan Crawford, but Jacquie missed it.

'That's the one. She is an odd one and no mistake.'

'But did you ring me to tell me about the O'Malley Golds and how odd they are? Because if so, it was a wasted call; I already knew that.'

'No, I rang to say that I told Hector that if he needed any . . . support, I think I was thinking, really, he was to give you a ring. When you were engaged, I assumed it was him.'

'No, he hasn't rung. He might have done, because I've only just discovered the phone was off the hook.'

'He'll be fine, I'm sure. It's just that Alana was really in a state and Camille was off the wall.'

'As I may have said, if not just now then at least in the recent past, *plus ça change, plus c'est la même chose*.' Maxwell hated speaking French (he hadn't forgiven them for winning the Hundred Years War) but there were times when the bastards simply had the *mot juste*.

'Too right. I've got to go. Henry was just seeing someone, then we've got to tackle O'Malley. Don't wait up.'

Maxwell was thoughtful as he put the phone down. So, he was 'O'Malley' now, was he? A small but significant difference in nomenclature. He knew his Woman Policeman and he recognised the signs of someone banged to rights. And yet . . . and yet . . . how could someone who had only been in the country for a few weeks have established himself as a blackmailer? Was the blackmailer a red herring? Did Mrs Whatmough kill Sarah Gregson and make up the blackmailer? Or did Sarah Gregson in fact throw herself off the top floor of the municipal car park? He turned to Metternich, who was lying in an abandoned posture across the top of the laundry basket, legs out straight and his tail curled modestly across his boy's bits.

'You know, Count. I don't think he did it.'

The cat raised an eyebrow at him.

'You're right.' Maxwell turned back to the painting task in hand. The buttons on RSM Linkon's jacket were a bit of a bugger. 'He's done something, that's for sure, so I'm sure that the cosmic karma will all balance out in the end.' He picked up a small piece of horse and put the paintbrush in his mouth for safe keeping. It felt curiously wet and soft. 'Bugger.' So it had happened at last. He had put the wrong end of the paintbrush in his mouth. Was this how senility began, he asked himself? And is cadmium yellow as poisonous as it sounds?

* * *

'Reverend Mattley,' Henry Hall said, crossing the lobby towards the man. 'Shall we go into an interview room?'

The vicar stood up and shook his head. 'It's just a small point, Mr Hall,' he said. 'It came to me tonight, at Evensong. I got rather sidetracked earlier today. I was . . . upset.'

'You've just lost your wife,' Hall reminded him. 'Upset is allowed.'

The man compressed his lips in what may have been meant to be a smile, but the wobble changed it. 'Yes. Thank you. I said that she had some . . . I think I said, personal demons.'

'Yes,' Hall said. 'I assumed it was the gambling, when I found out about that. But thank you for coming in to clarify.'

'Gambling?' Guy Mattley was surprised. 'Sarah didn't gamble. I meant about her mother.'

Now it was Hall's turn to be surprised. 'Yes, Reverend. I'm afraid Sarah did gamble. Recently, at least. And for quite high stakes. But what was the issue with her mother?'

The other man was adamant. 'I'm sure Sarah wouldn't gamble,' he said again. 'We didn't even have board games in the house.'

'Her mother?' Hall asked. This conversation could go on like this for hours if he didn't get it back on track.

'Yes. Her mother, lovely woman, was very ill. She had cancer and she had ignored it. By the time she went to the doctor there was hardly an organ in her body which was not affected. It was in her bones as well; she was in terrible pain.'

'That must have been distressing to watch.'

'Yes. Sarah and her mother were very close. One night, when Sarah was at her mother's house — she stayed sometimes, overnight, so that her mother could have a few days of privacy without a nurse there — her mother asked her if she would help her to die.'

For several heartbeats, there was a thick silence. Henry Hall knew what it was like to see someone you love in pain. He had often wondered what he would do if his mother asked him just that favour, but she had died naturally in the end, of a heart attack, quick and clean but devastating for those left behind. He swallowed and said, 'And what did she do?'

'She lifted a pillow from the bed and held it in her hands for a moment, praying. She was a devout and loving daughter, Mr Hall. And so in the end, she put the pillow down and made her mother as comfortable as she could.'

Hall waited for the rest of the story.

'In the morning, her mother was dead. She had been saving up her sleeping pills and had taken them all. Sarah always blamed herself for driving her mother to do it. She had wanted to die by a loving hand, and Sarah had failed her. Or at least, that's how she felt. She felt like a murderer.'

'As she would have been, had she used the pillow.'

Guy Mattley smiled ruefully and nodded his head. 'Exactly, Mr Hall. I said they were demons.'

* * *

Jacquie was waiting back at the foot of the stairs when Henry Hall had shown the vicar out.

'Ready?' she asked, motioning towards Interview Room 3, where the noise had started up again. This time it was a rhythmic thump as Jeff O'Malley pounded on the table. 'Did the husband have anything useful to add?'

'No. Not useful. Just that Sarah Gregson didn't gamble.'

Jacquie was confused. 'But . . .'

Henry Hall heaved a sigh. 'Yes, I know. But. I don't think it is important, but still, it makes it less clear than it was. It doesn't have any bearing on this, though. Come on. We can't put this off any longer. Did you get through to Max? All well?'

'Yes. The cat had knocked the phone off the hook.'

'That's OK, then. As long as there was no problem. With the Golds, I mean.'

'No. Everything is fine. Hector hadn't spoken to him when I rang. I'm sure once everyone calmed down, and by "everyone" I mean Camille, it would all be fine.' But she didn't believe it as she said it, any more than Henry Hall believed it when he heard it. This was a very damaged family and it would take handling with kid gloves. He pushed open the door of the interview room and they walked into a wall of sound.

Jeff O'Malley was sitting at the table in the middle of the room and it was obvious that had it not been made of metal and bolted down it would have been in pieces by now. He leapt up as they came in and at once the two Constables standing against the back wall moved forward.

'So you got here finally,' he spat at Hall. 'Where you been? Giving little Mrs Goody Two Shoes here a good time? Husband old as hers, only to be expected.' He looked Jacquie up and down with a leer.

Hall sat down opposite the man and gestured for him to take a seat. Jacquie sat next to Hall and pressed a button on the recorder on the table and leant in slightly to the microphone. 'This is Detective Inspector Carpenter-Maxwell and also present is Detective Chief Inspector Henry Hall, Police Constable Andrew Davis and Police Constable Neil Moran. The interviewee is Mr Jeff O'Malley, a United States citizen, in Britain on a one-year visa, which has eleven months and two days to run. The interview is timed at twenty-one forty hours and is being videotaped for the record.'

O'Malley looked contemptuous. 'Tapes can be fixed,' he said. 'Don't think I don't know that.'

'We don't fix tapes, Mr O'Malley,' Hall said, 'and you are not arrested, as I am sure someone will have explained to you. You will have been read the customary caution as you are being questioned in relation to a crime. We have not accused you of anything at the moment, and what happens next will be dependent on your answers to our questions. Now, firstly, for the record. What is your full name?'

'Jeffery Patton O'Malley.'

That figures, thought Jacquie. Just wait till Max hears that.

'And your date of birth, please.'

'May ten, nineteen forty-six.'

'Thank you. And your current address.'

'Hell, you know that. You came hammering at my door to drag me here.'

'For the record.' Hall was persistent.

'Hell, I don't know. I don't write to myself. Some pansy name to the house and some drive or another. I don't know. She knows.' He pointed at Jacquie. 'She knows the folks who live there.'

Jacquie nodded at Hall and wrote the address down on the form in front of her as he continued with the questions.

'A local woman, Sarah Gregson, was found dead in the town centre this morning.' Hall and Jacquie watched carefully for signs of surprise on O'Malley's face and saw none. 'She had fallen from the top of a multi-storey car park and had died instantly. We have reason to believe you knew her. Did you?'

'I've only lived here five minutes,' O'Malley sneered. 'Why would I know her?'

'Are you saying you don't know her?' Jacquie asked.

O'Malley looked at her as if the chair had spoken and addressed his answer to Hall. 'I know someone called Sarah, yeah. Don't know if her surname was . . . what did you say it was?'

'Gregson.'

O'Malley screwed up his face in ostentatious thought. 'No help. Sorry. Got a picture? I'd prefer before rather than after, but I can handle after. I've seen hundreds of jumpers.'

Hall had always privately considered that the jumpers were not a problem. It was the landers that weren't so pretty. He turned to Jacquie, who held out a picture, clearly cropped from a wedding photo. He held it up to O'Malley, who leant forward to focus on it.

'Yeah. Sarah. I know her. Don't know why she jumped, though. She scooped the pool last night. Two thousand pounds, she won from us.' He made a clicking noise with his teeth. 'Damn shame. I was looking forward to winning that back.'

His answers had rather knocked Hall from his planned route. He had been expecting at least a little prevarication, but the man seemed to have nothing to hide. 'We have reason to believe also that you were extremely angry last night, when you lost.'

'Five hundred, I lost. Could you lose that much and not get mad?'

'It's not something I have ever had to consider,' Hall said. 'I suppose if I couldn't afford it, I might be angry, yes. But I suppose no one should gamble if they can't afford it.'

'Ooh, wise words,' O'Malley mocked. 'What are you, some goddamn Bible-puncher? If you can afford it, where's the buzz? But, as it happens, I could afford it. Not so sure about the other three, though, and I know damn well Sarah couldn't afford it.'

'How could you possibly know that?' Hall was repelled and intrigued by the man.

'Just the look in her eye. You get to know the signs.'

Hall decided to ignore that. 'But you could afford it?'

'Yeah. I've been on a bit of a winning streak, y'know. And I don't have many expenses. Old Hec, he picks up the bills and Camille, her business is doing fine back home, so she has plenty. I've got my . . . pension, so we do OK.'

Hall flicked a glance at Jacquie to see if she had noticed the tiny pause in front of the word 'pension' and from her notes he could see she had. 'And the others. You say you don't think they could afford it, either. Why did they play, then, for such high stakes?'

O'Malley leant forward and rubbed his thumbs and forefingers together. 'The buzz.'

Hall looked back at him, face blank. He waited for a half-minute, leaving O'Malley to lean back and stop the gesture, looking awkward to be left with no response.

Like many people when faced with a silence, he felt compelled to fill it. 'So, if you're looking for somebody to pin this on, it sure ain't me. One of those others. I reckon the woman. What's her name? Sandra? Yeah, Sandra. Probably her.'

'We have spoken to Detective Constable Bolton, thank you, Mr O'Malley. But we will note your comments, of course. Do you have any views on the others?'

'Policewoman, huh? I never had her pegged for that. Well, it could still be her. Wouldn't be the first time, won't be the last. How about the guys, then? That Tim, built like a shithouse. He could toss her over a little low parapet like that, no problem.'

'You are familiar with the top of the municipal car park, Mr O'Malley?' Jacquie asked him.

He decided it was time to bring the little lady into the conversation, seeing as how they would be discussing girly matters. 'I drove Camille in to town the other day. She needed her nails done and she didn't want to drive in all the snow. We don't get this weather at home; she's no experience. I parked at the top. That people thing that the Mosses drive, it's a bit big to park in those itty-bitty spaces further down.'

Hall was surprised. It wasn't what he would have expected from Jeff O'Malley, to admit that he couldn't park a car.

'I mean to say, call that a car park? You could only park those silly little town cars in there. My SUV wouldn't fit in two of them spaces. And as for the Winnebago, don't go there.'

'You have a Winnebago?' Hall asked. 'My word, Mr O'Malley, American police pensions are more generous than here. I'm in the wrong country.'

O'Malley shrugged. 'We do OK,' he said.

Jacquie made a note and underlined it with several heavy lines. O'Malley craned over to see, but she turned the paper over, with a smile.

'You were talking about the other people at the card game,' Hall reminded him.

'Yeah. Tim. Don't know his other name. Real big guy. Works somewhere, some gym or other? I don't know. He seemed to know Sandra anyways. I gave him a lift home one time. He'd walked in, jogged maybe? It came on to snow, so I dropped him home. He only lives down the road from where we're staying. Same kinda house; ticky-tacky. He didn't seem to worry too much the first few games, then he got . . . don't know what you'd call it . . . edgy. Come to the end of his savings, I guess. Wife leaning on him probably. If she knew. Most don't.'

'Does yours?' Jacquie asked him.

His eyebrows shot up towards the remains of his sandy hair. 'Alana?' He snorted. 'You've both met Alana. She doesn't know where she is or when, let alone how much I win or lose. It's no business of hers, neither. She has all she needs. Vodka's dearer here than at home, but still she's cheap to keep.'

Hall decided to keep the momentum going. 'And the last member of your card school. Who is he?'

'I know a bit more about him, seeing as he's single, so he has more time after the game. We've had a few drinks together. Mark — don't know his other name, though. He's something to do with the police, well, not the police as such. Security. Something like that. He lives in town, in a flat over a shop. No. That's wrong. A flat over a taxi firm, something like that. I went there, must have been after the second game, and I could hear the radio, you know, that "over and out" thing you get. With cells nowadays I don't know why they do it, but I guess they're all geared up and don't see the need for change.'

'Cells?' Hall was confused.

'Cells. Phones. Oh, Jeez, I forgot. Mobiles.'

'Ah. So, you don't know Mark's surname, but you know where he lives.'

'Hell, no. I just went there. I don't know where it is. I couldn't find the house where I'm living unless someone takes me there. This town is not built right. The roads are all over the place. Where's the grid? The common sense? Take where you live, now,' he threw out a hand in Jacquie's direction. 'What the hell is going on there? It's a new estate, right? So why aren't the roads in straight lines? I can see why roads are all over in somewhere old like Stratford,' he pronounced it with the emphasis on the second syllable, 'but why here? We've got older places at home, and it's not often a Californian gets to say that.' He slammed his hand down on the table and roared with laughter. Jeff O'Malley had decided they could all be cops together.

Henry Hall had not decided that and made a few cryptic notes on his piece of paper before looking up at O'Malley. 'Well, Mr O'Malley,' he said at length. 'You have been very frank and I thank you very much for that. But until we speak to the remaining members of the group from last night, I'm afraid we'll have to ask you to wait here. I'll arrange some coffee and sandwiches if you like. I seem to remember we interrupted your supper when we called on you at home.'

O'Malley's brow darkened and he rose to his feet, like a mountain out of the sea. 'I don't have to take this—' he began.

'Yes,' Hall said, calmly but with a snap to the word. 'I rather think you do. Constable Davis here will get you anything you want. Good evening.' And he gathered up his papers and left the room.

Jacquie closed the meeting on the recording and followed her boss out into the hall.

'Damn,' he said. 'I was sure it was him.'

'Isn't it?' Jacquie said, but hope had died for her about halfway through the interview.

'Jacquie, you know it isn't him. He's just not right for it. He'd have got the money off her, for starters. He didn't know she'd handed her winnings back, except what she got from him. He would have thought there would be two and a half thousand pounds in her bag. His greed would have got the better of him. No,' he sighed as he turned for the stairs. 'Back to the drawing board. But not tonight. I'll see you in the morning.'

'What about . . . ?' Jacquie gestured towards O'Malley's interview room.

'We've got another . . . twenty-one hours to go,' Hall said. 'Let's not waste them. I'm sure the sandwiches will be delicious and we can see him again tomorrow. Now go home!'

'You too, guv,' Jacquie said. 'Perhaps Margaret has saved you some cauliflower surprise.'

Hall gave her an old-fashioned look and went up the stairs, feeling suddenly old and tired. This case had a taste to it which he was not liking so far; he would even go so far as to say it was worse than cauliflower surprise.

# CHAPTER TWELVE

Peter Maxwell was used to odd hours. He was married to a Detective Inspector, for a start, which meant that odd hours were not odd at all to them, but more the norm. And before he had started sharing his home with someone of the police persuasion, he had had no one to please but himself, so if he wanted to stay up all night, painting and gluing, reading or sleuthing, or even — Heaven forfend — marking, then he could. He was therefore wide awake and as chipper as could be when the doorbell rang at nearly midnight. Jacquie was out for the count beside him, having got back home exhausted and monosyllabic not many minutes before. He knew better than to probe when she was like this. He knew that Jeff O'Malley was not the guy, as Monk would have it, and that was it. It could wait.

He wriggled into his dressing gown and padded downstairs, feeling every tread in advance for lurking felines or — worse — the little gifts of mice and similar that the feline may have deposited there. The snow had curbed Metternich a bit, but Maxwell was afraid that, like Francis Bacon, he had discovered the secret of freezing food for later using snow. He and Jacquie were expecting a vole glut around St Valentine's Day.

Maxwell's front door had a peephole in it but he had never used it until today. The thought that Jeff O'Malley may be rampaging through Leighford was almost too much to bear, but the thought of him rampaging through his house was much, much worse. So he checked and found that his gut reaction had been partially right. The distorted face on the other side of his door lens belonged to Hector Gold and the semi-conscious shape he was supporting just had to be Alana O'Malley.

He opened the door and prepared to catch the woman as she fell forward. 'Hector,' he said. 'You're very welcome, of course, dear boy, but what the hell are you doing on my doorstep at midnight? Some quaint Minnesotan custom?'

'I'm sorry, Max,' the historian said, hefting Alana into a more comfortable carrying position before attempting the stairs. 'You'll have heard about what happened, I suppose?'

'Some,' Maxwell told him, guardedly.

'Well, after Jacquie and Mr Hall took Jeff away, Camille went into meltdown and Alana just passed out. By the time I had Camille on a bit more of an even keel, I went to check on Alana and she was still out for the count. So I took her to the hospital, and they took a look at her. There wasn't any immediate danger, well no more than she has always been in; liver's like a piece of shoe leather, has been for years. They did a blood alcohol level and they nearly passed out. But I showed them her usual level and they said in fact she wasn't quite so bad as usual. It's just she's not eating and her liver really is on the fritz, and the stress and everything . . . well, I couldn't take her back to Paul's house. If Jeff is out . . .' There was a question in the sentence.

'He's not,' Maxwell reassured him.

'Well, if Jeff *isn't* out, Camille is going to be going nuts. She has decided that her father's behaviour is all her mother's fault. That if she was more of a woman, and can't you just hear the quotes and where it comes from, if she was more of a woman, Jeff wouldn't stray and all the rest. So I was stuck. I can't afford a hotel, the money just goes nowhere over here, and so . . .' They had reached the top of the first flight and he stopped for breath. He straightened up and looked Maxwell in the eye. 'I'm sorry, Max,' he said. 'This is a mistake. You've got Nolan and all. You don't need this.'

'Hec. Don't be silly. Jacquie is in bed, but she would say the same. Come through into the sitting room. If I can work it out, the sofa turns into a bed. You can have that and we can put Alana to bed in the spare room. Actually, belay that. There's another flight of stairs up to the spare room. You can have that, and we'll pop her on the sofa.'

'Don't worry about the spare room, Max. I don't want to leave her. She might . . . well, I don't know. Choke, or something.'

'Do you want to ring Camille to tell her where you are?'

'No. She'll have taken her tablet and we won't get anything out of her until ten tomorrow. If I could just borrow a comb tomorrow and perhaps a quick squirt of deodorant . . .'

'Of course. We probably have some new toothbrushes somewhere. Jacquie is very organised on the personal-hygiene front. Well,' Maxwell looked at them, the semi-conscious woman and the slight, slightly dishevelled man. 'She's lucky to have you for a son-in-law,' he said.

'I hope she makes the most of it while it lasts, then,' Hector said. 'Goodnight, Max. Thank you.'

'Goodnight,' he said, and closed the door gently behind him. It wasn't until later that he realised what the exchange teacher had said and wondered how Camille the Cougar would take it. 'Gentlemen of Leighford, now abed,' he muttered to himself, paraphrasing as he went, 'shall think themselves accursed that she is here. And hold their manhoods cheap . . .'

Jacquie turned over. 'Max?' she muttered. 'What's going on? Is someone here?'

He leant over and in the dark kissed what turned out to be an eyebrow. 'I'll tell you in the morning. Sleep tight, sweetheart. Sleep tight.'

'Hope the bugs don't bite,' she said, adding a little yelp as he put his cold feet on the backs of her nice warm thighs.

And with a sigh, the Maxwells were asleep.

* * *

Someone was singing. Not totally in tune, although that was just a guess, as it appeared to be no tune known to man. It was something very modern, with a contrapuntal harmony in the tenor. Jacquie was impressed, even as she slept. 'Contrapuntal' was not a word she used too often when she was awake. As soon as she realised she was dreaming, it disappeared like a soap bubble in the sun and she was awake.

She poked Maxwell in the ribs.

'Max, Max, wake up,' she hissed. 'There's somebody in the house.'

'Just us chickens, chicken,' he murmured, pulling the quilt over his head.

'Someone's singing. Listen.'

He uncovered an ear and did as he was told. She was right. Someone was singing. Unless he missed his guess, it was *Somewhere Over the Rainbow*, but sung very, very slowly and rather flat. Someone was talking as well. It sounded like a very small gospel choir being led by a very hesitant and rather secular minister. Then the previous evening came back to him and he rolled over to face his wife, her eyes shining in the faint light of the clock numbers which glowed from his side of the bed. He knew his face would be in deep shadow and so all he had to control was his tone of voice. He opted for lightly jocular.

'Not exactly Judy Garland, is she?'

'No.' The reply was very flat. 'But if not Judy Garland, then who?'

'Alana.'

Jacquie was bolt upright with the light on in seconds. '*Alana*? What on earth is Alana doing here? And where is she?'

She looked wildly round as though the woman might suddenly pop out from behind the wardrobe, shouting 'Banzai!'.

'She's in the sitting room, on the settee. Don't worry, Hector is with her.'

'So, let me get this straight. A woman, the wife of a man currently helping the police — that would be me, by the way — is sleeping with her son-in-law in my sitting room.'

Maxwell mulled it over. 'Quite correct. Except that when you say "sleeping with" that is more in the way of being watched over by her son-in-law to prevent her choking on her own vomit. Not,' he raised his hand quickly, 'that she is vomiting as such, but these things happen. He had to take her to the hospital and they said she is on a knife-edge, essentially. He couldn't bear to take her home to Camille, so he came here.' He paused and looked searchingly at her. 'Quite sweet, I thought. That he came here. Isn't it? Quite sweet?'

Jacquie snapped her light off and lay back with a sharp exhalation. 'Peter Maxwell, if I live to be a hundred you will never stop surprising me.'

After a suitable pause, he asked, 'But that's a good thing, isn't it?'

He sounded so like Nolan in the dark she couldn't stay even mildly annoyed. She reached out and stroked his cheek. 'A very good thing,' she said softly. Then, a littler sharper, 'What's the time? No, don't rear up like that, I'm trying to see the clock. Oh, damn and drat. Half past three. I hate it when it's half past three.'

'It's when most people die, or so they say.'

'Always a mine of curious and uplifting facts. Thank you, dear.'

'No problem. Any time. At least we know Alana isn't dead.'

'That's true,' she agreed. 'She's on *Candle in the Wind* now. We've just got *My Way* to go and then she will have treated us to all the karaoke favourites.'

'At least she sings them slowly. Let's pretend they're lullabies.'

She turned over and nestled back into his body, already in the spoon position to receive her. He kissed her shoulder and they let the lullabies claim them, for the last few hours of the night.

* * *

Jim Astley should have retired years ago. He already played golf, so you'd think, wouldn't you, that he'd want to spend still more time on the links. That's what Donald thought, certainly, but Donald had failed to factor in the Marjorie Dilemma. Marjorie was Jim Astley's wife, survivor (somehow) of too many lost weekends. She had a season ticket to rehab and a wagon parked behind the house off which she'd fallen more times than Jim Astley had carried out post-mortems. So, all in all, Astley had elected to overlook the creaking hips and tired eyes that the years had bequeathed him and continue to spend time with the dead, as opposed to the not-very-quick.

Alison Orchard was a different kettle of fish. Dr Astley wasn't sure he really approved of women in mortuaries and knew that between them *Silent Witness* and *Bones* had a lot to answer for. For her part, Alison saw herself as a budding Emilia Fox but nobody else did. She was a head shorter, with dark frizzy hair (which Astley insisted she tie back) and a rather irritating falsetto laugh. Not even Donald fancied her, and bearing in mind his usual proclivity for anything with a pulse, that didn't say an awful lot for Alison Orchard. Still, her mummy loved her and her daddy and all the other little Orchards, so there probably was a God.

That morning, God was gowned up but taking something of a back seat watching Alison go through her paces over the last mortal remains of Sarah Gregson. Pinned to the wall to Astley's left were the police photographs of the crime scene: the body *in situ*, looking like a discarded shop window dummy; the blood which had pooled beneath the head and started to run into the gutter before the frost had seized it; white tents with dates and times that marked the hour, should Henry Hall be sharp enough to get this one to court.

Astley listened impassively as Alison spoke into the microphone hanging down from its fixture on the ceiling. Sarah Gregson had been measured, weighed and photographed. Her clothes had gone to the lab for checking where Angus would do what Angus did best — search for telltale fingerprints, fibres, alien saliva, sweat or blood; *anything* that would underline yet again the famous dictum of the great Edmond Locard — 'Every contact leaves a trace'. The removal of the organs would come later — Astley would do that, it was beyond the remit of the student in front of him. She was focusing, rightly, on the head, shattered as it was where Sarah Gregson and the pavement had met at a terrifying gravitational speed.

'Cut to the chase, my dear,' Astley advised. He could patronise for England and time, as always, was of the essence. Sarah Gregson wasn't going anywhere but everyone else connected with the case was. And her murderer, if there was one, might have gone altogether. 'Cause of death?'

'Er . . . massive trauma to the occipital—'

'Yes, yes.' Astley cut the girl short. 'She went off the roof face forward. Whether she jumped or was pushed, she'd have turned once before she hit the deck. A longer drop would give more turning time, but this is . . . what . . . three storeys. Donald?'

The big man was used to carrying all of Astley's knowledge inside his own head. He thought of himself as a kind of external hard drive, where all the important stuff was stored in case the mainframe went down. 'Thirty-seven feet, four and a half inches.' Donald knew his man — Astley had never really embraced metric.

'So,' Astley continued, 'in a nutshell, *Ms* Orchard, did she fall, did she jump or was she pushed?'

'Urm . . .' It wasn't Alison's day, but in a macabre sort of way, it was Sarah's.

Astley got up and peered closely at the measurements in the photographs. He smiled and tapped the one taken from the south, in line with the kerb, that showed the position of the body in relation to the building.

'Learn,' he said to the girl without turning to face her, 'and prepare to be amazed. If the deceased had fallen from the balcony up here,' he waved in the general direction of the third storey, 'she'd have landed not more than ten feet six inches from the building.'

Alison did a lightning calculation in her head to translate the distance into modern-speak: three point two metres.

'If she had jumped, the distance would have been fourteen feet.'

Four point two metres Alison calculated silently.

'But if the SOCO boys have got it right, and I'm sure they have because I believe that Donald himself was on tape measure duty yesterday, then this young lady landed head first sixteen feet from the building. That makes it murder.'

Alison Orchard was so impressed that she didn't even bother to calculate the distance in metres.

'Now, if young Angus does us the courtesy of finding a fingerprint or two, we can all go home and yet again Henry Hall will get his collar at our expense. The drinks that man owes me.' He tutted and laughed at the same time.

Alison Orchard had her mouth open behind the green mask. It wasn't exactly rocket science. Iris Seager had died in similar circumstances in Baltimore, Maryland in the early seventies when Jim Astley was approaching his first mid-life crisis. Alison Orchard wasn't even born then. True, the Seager case was in all the textbooks, but Alison hadn't got to those chapters yet. Had she looked more like Emilia Fox, Donald would probably have tipped her off, but her genes had been against her from the start when it came to getting any help from that quarter. So, yet again, it was Dr James Astley, one; rest of the world, nil.

* * *

The Maxwell temporarily extended family were in the dining room that morning, being too numerous to fit around the kitchen table. Alana looked surprisingly well for someone who had been knocking on Heaven's door the night before, although mercifully the song of the same name was not in her repertoire. It was Hector who looked as though he had been through the wringer, though only to someone who was familiar with his usual high level of immaculacy. Nolan was delighted to have a new audience and Jacquie and Maxwell were running back and forth with toast and Coco Pops, throwing remarks to one another as they ran.

'I have to get to work, Max. Hector can take you and Nole if that's OK, but what about Alana?'

The next time they passed in the doorway, Maxwell asked, 'Could you not pretend it is Take Your Drunk To Work Day and take her with you?'

'Flippancy will get you nowhere,' she said, a rack of toast later. 'She can't stay here.'

'Why not?'

Because Maxwell had thrown the remark to her as he ran for the boiling kettle she had time to consider her reply, but it still struck her as a little lame. 'Because she can't.' What a mistress of wit and repartee.

They finally both arrived at the table together and sat down to a hurried breakfast. Alana was speaking, in her careful way, tasting and weighing each word before she let it out of her mouth to make sure it would give no offence.

'How is your lovely neighbour, Jacquie?' she asked. 'Mrs Troubridge. She sent us such a lovely greeting card for Christmas, didn't she, Hec? I really loved meeting her at your Christmas soirée.'

Maxwell smiled at Jacquie, the smile of a man who has just been given the answer to his problems on a plate. 'She gets lonely, Alana,' he said. 'In fact, I'll tell you what, why don't I run down now and see if she's in today? I'm sure she would love your company.'

He suited the action to the words and soon the sound of delighted twittering echoed up the stairs as Mrs Troubridge said that indeed she would love to have Alana as her guest for the day. And so, as is often the case with important things, it was decided in an instant and that was how Alana O'Malley, Californian drunk, became the house guest of Mrs Jessica Troubridge, possibly the most unlikely rehab facility proprietor in the world.

* * *

'So, do you think he did it?' The question was not unreasonable, but Maxwell was surprised nonetheless to be asked it so bluntly. He was still trying to buckle himself into the Mossmobile and they had been driving for ten minutes.

'I don't think Jacquie thinks so,' he hedged.

'But do you?' Hector swept the Mosses' car into a space very deftly. He turned off the ignition, but made no effort to get out.

Maxwell pondered for a moment. With the involvement of Mrs Whatmough this case was a lot more complicated than it first appeared and he had a feeling he was just skating over the surface. He just had to hope that the ice didn't get too thin. 'Well, I hardly know the man . . .'

'You don't have to know Jeff to know what he is,' Hector said, dismissively. 'He might as well have a neon sign on his head flashing "asshole" in big red letters. Even so, though,' and he looked thoughtful, 'I don't think he would murder a woman.'

'He isn't exactly what you would call in touch with his feminine side, though, is he?' Maxwell pointed out.

'No. And that's what I mean. Apart from Camille, who I think he loves just because she is half of him, not for any other reason, he doesn't think women are worth anything. That's why he wouldn't risk the chair for one.'

'We don't have capital punishment in England,' Maxwell pointed out. 'We haven't executed anyone since 1964.'

'Ah, Max,' breathed Hector. 'A mine of information. But perhaps I should have made myself more clear. That sign I mentioned? It should read "stupid asshole" to be totally accurate. Jeff O'Malley has never sought a piece of information in his life if it doesn't immediately result in more money or power for himself. His whole world has a population of one — well, two when Camille is in sight, otherwise I don't think even she crosses his mind very much.'

'What will he do when he finally gets home and finds Alana gone?'

'A lot will depend on how soon he notices. He'll notice when he goes to bed, I guess.'

'Oh, so they do still—'

'Jeff does, certainly. I'm not sure Alana is often there in spirit, though. Oh, yes . . .' Hector trailed off, his cheeks faint pink at the memory of the embarrassing nights in the Moss house, just one wall away from his rutting father-in-law. Then he gave himself a shake. 'Well, for good or ill, Max, all that seems to be changing. So, here's to change.' They clinked invisible glasses. 'Let's see what today brings at Leighford High School.'

Some distance away, across the still frozen grass, knots of schoolboys (and girls) crawled unwillingly to school, although there wasn't a satchel between them. Rona Whatserface was holding court already at the centre of a gaggle of Year Nine girls and mobile phones were flashing in all directions. There was some talk of new governmental powers being drafted in to allow teachers to take such time-wasting trivia away from students; which struck Maxwell as rather odd because he already had a drawerful and added to it every day.

Maxwell unbuckled his seat belt — having only just managed to do it up — and slid down out of the high passenger seat. The weekend had held surprises enough and he doubted that even Leighford High could top it. The place had not burnt down and there were no red crosses on the doors. No doubt Legs Diamond was in his Heaven and all was right with the world.

He was still only halfway through the side door when a panting Pansy Donaldson rushed up to him and hauled him bodily into the foyer.

'Mr Maxwell, Mr Maxwell,' she said, shaking him by the arm as a terrier would shake a rat. Noticing Hector Gold she gave him a smile and a nod. He couldn't help noticing she was checking out his footwear, for suitability. Turning her attention back to Maxwell, she gave him a final shake which dislodged his hat finally and he caught it with an unusual display of manual dexterity.

'Mrs Donaldson,' he said, equably, twitching his sleeve back into place. 'How can I help you?' He was secretly glad that the kids weren't allowed to come through this way and that the usual daily haul of wearers of trainers and denim had not yet built up in the hinterland to Pansy's domain.

'I have an urgent email which needs your attention.'

Maxwell had been under the distinct impression that Pansy was on the wagon, but this seemed not to be the case. Why otherwise would she be asking him to deal with one of her emails? 'I don't quite understand what I can do for you, Mrs Donaldson,' he said reasonably.

She turned her back on Hector Gold and waggled her eyebrows furiously at Maxwell. Hector Gold had not been an O'Malley in-law for nothing, and with a flash of a smile at Maxwell, he turned down the corridor which housed the History Department. Into the jaws of death, into the mouth of Hell sauntered Hector Gold. Soon, he could be heard telling a kid its fortune and Maxwell sighed the sigh of a proud parent.

'Right, Pansy. He's gone. We're alone. Whatever is this email about?'

'You'll have to come and see,' she said, pulling on his sleeve again. It looked like the Queen Mary towing the Isle of Wight ferry.

It was easier to go than resist and Maxwell followed her into her office, passing the morning receptionist on the way.

'Morning, Thingee,' he cried as he was carried away on the tide.

'Morning, Mr Maxwell,' she carolled back, deftly handling the myriad flashing lights of the switchboard already and it wasn't even nine o'clock.

'I wish you would learn the names of my staff, Mr Maxwell,' Pansy Donaldson snorted. 'It's very rude otherwise.'

Maxwell turned as she pressed him down into the chair in front of her monitor. 'Mrs Donaldson,' he said. 'I not only know Emma's name, but I also know the name of her hamster. I used to know the name of her goldfish, which sadly died during last half-term. I know that she doesn't like cheese but she does like Marmite, I know that—'

'Yes, yes.' Pansy Donaldson was testy. She didn't like to be upstaged. 'Just look at this email. Look away first, though, while I enter my password.'

It amused Maxwell, sitting there, pressed to one side by Pansy's encroaching bosom, that she should feel it necessary to hide a password from him. He had to have his own password written on the inside of his desk drawer in his office and had begged IT to remove the necessity, but it was apparently impossible. Finally, the login was accomplished and he could sit up again, bosom-free.

The email was on the screen and he read it through quickly once and then, an icy hand around his heart, again, more slowly.

'Mrs Donaldson,' he read. 'I have sent this to you because I know Mr Maxwell rarely opens his emails and I didn't want to trouble him with this at home. Max — sorry to dump this on you, but Manda and the kids, and me as well, I suppose, all want to come home. It really isn't turning out as well as we had expected and everyone is very homesick. Manda is worrying about the house, you know how house-proud she is. The place here was a tip and we got the impression it had been tidied up a bit, so she is beside herself wondering what they are doing to our place. The kids are hating school, they are way ahead of the others and are bored to sobs. Tell Hector that I am very impressed with his classes, by the way. They are the best in the school, even if they are a little confused over the causes of the American War of Independence. If it was just the homesickness and the mess and the boredom I think we'd still stick it out. The weather is fabulous, of course, and the kids are really enjoying the beach, which is a completely different experience from the beach at home. The teaching is fine, I'm really enjoying it and mainly the kids are OK. I have a few reservations about the whole system out here, but I can't change that, so not to worry. But it all took a bit of a nasty turn this weekend . . .'

Maxwell turned to Pansy. 'Have you read this?' he asked.

'I caught the odd word,' she admitted, meaning that she had avidly taken in every sentence.

'Well, please treat it as confidential and don't tell a soul. And that means not telling Legs Diamond or Bernard Ryan, despite the fact that they have no souls.' He screwed his head round to look at her. 'Seriously, Pansy. This is me talking — I am being serious and you know how serious that is.'

'But—'

'But me no buts, Pans,' he said. 'Hector has had a horrible weekend and his week is going to get worse. He doesn't need this. He's happy here.' He played his trump card. 'He really likes you, you know.'

Pansy Donaldson allowed herself a small preen. 'He's a very nice man, Mr Maxwell,' she said. 'I won't tell anyone.' She caught his eye. 'I promise. I really do.'

'Thank you, Pansy. You are a wonderful woman.' Whatever the others say, he added silently in his head. 'Shush now, while I read the rest of this.' He turned back to the screen.

'But it all took a bit of a nasty turn this weekend. We were in bed on Friday night and the kids were finally asleep. This house is on quite a main road — all the roads are main around here, no one walks anywhere, they all drive — and they have taken a while to get used to the noise. There was a tremendous banging at the door and voices shouting for us to come out. Max, you see it on the telly, but having it happen to you is terrifying. I went down and opened the door and there were these men, in bulletproof vests and helmets, all down the drive and running round the house. One burst in through the back door while I was at the front. They were looking for Jeff O'Malley. Something about information from some bloke. I tell you, Max, we have got to come home. The Principal is finding us a new house, but I can hardly get Manda to go in the garden, let alone to the shops, and the kids were freaked out by it as well. They say they don't want to go to school tomorrow and who can blame them. Can you sort it at your end, and I'll see the Principal first thing Monday? Tell Hector I'm sorry to let him down, but you can see how I'm fixed, I hope. Love to Jacquie and Nolan. Paul.'

Maxwell sat for a moment and then turned to Pansy, still at his elbow. 'Can you forward this to my wife?' he said. 'I think this may well have a bearing on something she is working on.'

'Confidentiality,' sniffed Pansy.

'Mrs Donaldson,' Maxwell said. 'My wife is a Detective Inspector of the West Sussex CID. I think that she knows more about confidentiality than you have had hot dinners. Her email address is secure; it goes straight to her desk and nowhere else. I'll phone her to let her know it's on its way, if that helps.'

'Can she unzip?' the woman asked, mystifyingly.

Maxwell blinked. 'I must assume that you are talking about something computer based,' he said, 'since otherwise that question makes no sense and may even be construed as offensive.'

'Encrypted files. Can she unzip them?'

'Again, I am at a loss. Why don't you just forward it as it is, there's a good manager? It's come all the way from California without self-combusting. I'm sure it can make it across town without further harm. Or, if you like, I can print it out. Well, clearly I mean that *you* can print it out.'

Pansy Donaldson pointed with a trembling finger to a printed notice on the wall, exhorting staff to only print things out when necessary. The irony pleased Maxwell, but seemed to pass the woman by. This was, in fact, the third notice that Pansy had pinned there, the other two having been scrawled on by Peter Maxwell with the words 'Big Brother is watching you. G. Orwell'.

'I will send it, Mr Maxwell, but it must be on your head if anything goes wrong. What is Mrs Maxwell's email address?'

'I have it here,' Maxwell said, proudly, and fished it out of his wallet. 'She is jay dot carpenter at leighford police all one word all lower case dot gov dot you kay.' He watched as she wrote it down. 'Excellent. I can leave that with you, then, can I? I'll ring her from Mr Moss's office. Thank you for helping me on this, Mrs Donaldson. And remember — not a soul.'

Sweeping through the outer office, he enquired about Thingee One's hamster, which was thriving after a slight case of bumblefoot. She offered a Hobnob which he gratefully accepted and he was soon off down the corridor, in search of Hector Gold. A little bit of forewarning was on the menu, and it would need some delicacy.

Even so, there were other fish to fry. 'If that's a football in your grubby little mitt, Callaghan, I'm going to hang you from the school flagpole. If we had a flagpole, of course.'

# CHAPTER THIRTEEN

Jeff O'Malley had finally gone to sleep at around three-thirty that morning, at almost the exact moment that his wife was waking Jacquie and Peter Maxwell. He was still asleep as the day shift started to arrive and Jacquie for one hoped that would remain the case for a while. She thought she had better bring Henry Hall up to date and went up to his office. She was about to knock on the door when it flew open and Bob Thorogood barrelled out, red in the face, with a vein throbbing threateningly at his temple.

'Morning, Bob,' she said, stepping back.

'Oh, yes, morning to you as well, *Inspector*,' he spat and headed down the stairs. As he reached the half landing, he shouted, 'Bastard,' and was gone.

Tentatively, Jacquie went into Hall's office, half expecting him to be lying unconscious on the floor, but no. He was sitting in his usual imperturbability behind his desk, signing a pile of letters. He looked up.

'Good morning,' he said. 'Sorry about that. Just had to give Bob a bit of bad news.'

'Redundancy?' Jacquie asked. Bob was a bit of an idiot, a dinosaur but not in a good way, but he was harmless enough.

'No, no. Redeployment. Traffic. Quite high up, actually. Desk job, of course. No night stuff. No on call.' His words were fairly heavily laden, but his face betrayed nothing. 'He seems to prefer that kind of job, so I made sure he had it.' He clicked his pen to retract the nib. No patches of ink on his shirt for Henry Hall when a little forethought could prevent it.

Jacquie sat down. 'Traffic, though. He'll miss the overtime.'

'Will he?' Hall was dubious.

'Well, the overtime money, then. He always seems quite strapped for cash.'

'Indeed. Well. I'm sure he'll soon have all those traffic wardens on full alert. His department budget will soar, I'm sure. Teach them a few tricks, I shouldn't wonder. But that's enough of Bob Thorogood. More than enough. Any updates for me?'

'Yes, guv, I have to tell you—' The *Flight of the Bumblebee* filled the room. 'Sorry, guv. Do you mind if I take this? It's Max and we had a funny start this morning . . .'

Hall nodded and turned back to his signing.

'Hello. DI Carpenter-Maxwell.' This greeting was their personal code for 'I'm in Henry's hearing'. They didn't need a code for when Jacquie phoned Maxwell, because he never had his phone with him.

'Are you near a computer?' Maxwell sounded hurried and harried, an unusual situation for him, but he was bouncing a confiscated football on one foot as he spoke, to his own amazement. Well, if David Beckham could do it, how hard could it be?

'Are you all right? You sound—'

'Not a good time. I'm waiting in Paul's office for Hector and when he gets here it's not going to be pretty. Are you near a computer?' He lost control of the football and it ricocheted off a bookcase and disappeared behind a pile of boxes. He decided to let it go; ball skills were not for everyone and if young Callaghan came calling for it at the end of the day, Maxwell would just deny all knowledge.

'Max, you know what it's like here. I'm never more than a few yards from one.'

'Well, log on or whatever it is you young people do. Pansy has forwarded an email to you. When you've read it, phone me back. I'm in the History Suite, tell Thingee.'

'Max, I—'

'He's here. Must go. Speak in a minute.' And the phone went down with a clunk.

Jacquie put her phone back in her pocket, looking thoughtful.

Hall looked up. 'Problem?'

'I don't know. He says that Pansy Donaldson has sent me an email. Can I log on over here?' She pointed to the computer in the corner.

'Help yourself,' he said. 'Do you know what it's about?'

'No. It seems to involve Hector, but I don't know how.' She pressed the 'on' button and the computer wheezed into reluctant life. 'Oh, why are these things so slow?'

'Monday morning, or so I'm told when I complain. Or Tuesday, or whatever day it happens to be.'

The blue screen inviting her to log on appeared and eventually she was in her emails. 'Here it is. Hang on . . . Guv, you'd better read this.' She scrolled back up to the top and leant sideways while he leant on the back of her chair to read over her shoulder.

'Well,' he said, when he was done. 'This puts a bit of a different complexion on it, I suppose. Does Paul Moss know exactly why they wanted Jeff O'Malley, do you suppose?'

'He doesn't say so, and he has said everything else. I was going to try to find out a bit about him anyway. This is even more reason to do it, don't you think?'

'At least you've got something to ask about directly, rather than just random suspicions.' He glanced up at the clock. 'How far behind us are they? Six hours, is it?'

'Eight,' Jacquie said. 'It's only half one in the morning there. I'd only get the night staff if I rang now.'

'Try all the same. You might get more out of the night staff. They usually have more time. Do you have the address?'

'Yes, I do. Down to the zip code. Paul's wife is a bit of a tidy freak and with that goes all sorts of control stuff. She had cards done before she went. I've got one in my purse. Hold on.' She rummaged in her bag and came out with a small card. 'Here we are. It's in Long Beach, zip code 90999. That's ironic, but not to them, of course. They use 911, don't they?'

Henry Hall was not a xenophobe like Maxwell. He just pretended that the rest of the world didn't really exist. 'Well, find out the nearest . . . precinct, is it, they call them? Give them a call anyway, you might come up with something. Don't worry about coming to the meeting today; get on with that. There's nothing much to add since last night. We've tracked down the other two at the card school. One is a personal trainer with so much muscle between his ears I can't believe he understands poker at all. The other one is a bit brighter, a bit mouthy. O'Malley was almost right about his job. He's a traffic warden. Bit of a keen one, apparently. There is a rumour that he ticketed a pram while the mother was unloading the baby from the car. Obviously only a story, but stories like that don't start for no reason. He was on duty yesterday, checking the machines were all working, so he's off today. He's coming in later. The bodybuilder is coming in in his lunch hour. He could certainly have thrown her, no problem. The other one is not so certain. He's got some kind of back problem, or so I gather. He might not have been able to do it. We'll see.' He walked over to the door. 'I'll let you get on, then.'

'Hold on, guv. I came in to tell you; we've got Alana O'Malley staying at ours. Well, not strictly at ours. She's with Mrs Troubridge. She had to go to casualty last night, out cold, according to Hector. He brought her to us, because Camille was making it difficult at home.'

'What a family!' Hall really had had just about as much as he could take of the O'Malleys. 'She's next door, you say?'

'Yes. Mrs Troubridge was delighted.'

'As long as she doesn't come back to stay at yours, that's probably all right. What about the son-in-law?'

'We haven't discussed him. This email rather changes things, don't you think?'

'True. Anyway, let me know as soon as you know anything. I'll be in the big conference room if you need me before I get back.'

'Right, guv. I'll just ring Max back to see if he has got any more information from Hector, then I'll get right on it.'

Hall lifted a hand in agreement and was gone.

Jacquie dialled the number for Leighford High School and was put on hold. The music was a recording of the Leighford High School string quartet playing, ironically, *The Flight of the Bumblebee*, but rather slower than she was used to, more like the flight of the dodo. Finally, the phone was answered.

'Leighford High School. How may I direct your call?'

'Emma. Hello. Mrs Maxwell here.'

'Oh, hello, Mrs Maxwell. Do you want to speak to Mr Maxwell?'

'Yes. He's—'

But before she could tell Thingee One where her husband was, she had been put through to his office, up on the Mezzanine, where the vultures, Maxwell told the new Year Sevens every September, picked clean the bones of those who had 'forgotten' their homework.

'Hello. Helen Maitland, Sixth Form.'

Helen Maitland was known as 'The Fridge' on account of her always wearing white and being eight-feet wide. On the plus side, she had been Mad Max's Number Two now for so long they'd all forgotten when she'd started and she had a heart the size of the great outdoors.

'Helen. Hello. It's Jacquie Maxwell here.'

'Jacquie. Hello. He's not here, I'm afraid. Can I take a message?'

'No, I need to speak to him. He's in the History Suite. Can you transfer me?'

'Not from here, I'm afraid. We're on a different loop. Can I put you back to switchboard?'

'No, look, Helen. I'll ring off and perhaps you could then get him to ring me. Tell him I'm in Henry's office.'

'OK, Jacquie. Will do. Nolan well?'

'Blooming. A chip off the old block.'

'Well, never mind,' Maxwell's deputy laughed. 'You can't have everything. I'll pass on the message. 'Bye.'

Jacquie put down the phone and waited for it to ring. Maybe Maxwell was right, when he said that before phones made everything so easy, people took more care with plans before doing anything, and also that ignorance was bliss. If all this had had to be done by letter, it would have all been resolved before anyone knew there was a problem. The phone rang.

'DI Carpenter.'

'Was it something I said?'

'DI Carpenter-*Maxwell*, I beg your pardon, Mr Maxwell.'

'All rightie, then. Thanks for ringing back, heart. What do you think of the email?'

'I'd like to say I'm shocked, but I can't, because I'm not. Manda is right to worry about her lovely house. When we got there last night there was quite literally cheese stuck to the wall.'

'I can quite see why you wanted to palm Alana off onto Mrs Troubridge, then. We don't want cheese on *our* wall, do we? But what about the police raid?' He sounded like a man with the phone tucked well in and an eye on the door behind him, because that was what he was.

'I was rather hoping that you might enlighten *me*, if you've had a chance to speak to Hector,' she said.

'I have spoken with him . . . did you hear that? I mean, spoken *to* him.' Maxwell toyed with putting a bullet through his brain then and there, because he had just kissed goodbye to all that was sacred, civilised and grammatical. 'He doesn't know anything specific, but thought that Jeff was keener to come with them to England than he would have expected, so he may have known it was a possibility at least. He doesn't know the details of how he came to leave the police, because it was before his time, but it is odd that he hasn't had some cushy security number; most ex-cops do. The Studios lap them up, apparently.'

'What about money? Does he know anything about O'Malley's finances?'

'Again, only that they are a tad ropey. Camille's nail bar does very well, not that Hector sees much of the proceeds. He thinks she bails her father out from time to time, but on the few occasions he has mentioned it to her, she has flown off the handle and said that her father put the money up in the first place, so it's only right.'

'That is fair enough, I suppose, if he was the original investor. It may be money laundering, though. Hmm . . . well, thank you for that. Have you given any more thought to Mrs Whatmough?'

'I try not to, on general principles. General "principals", get it? Never mind. I digress. Oh, hang on, there's la damn bell sans mercy. I can't hear you.'

Jacquie could hear the electronic jangle and beneath it Maxwell singing a little song to fill the time. It was the stereotypical, but already unseasonal *Jingle Bells*. Then he was back.

'Sorry about that. I'm sure the bells are getting louder as I get older.'

'That's good news. At least you aren't going deaf. Oh, hang on. Now it's me getting a noise. There's a call on the other line. Hold on.'

She put the phone down on the desk and stretched across to pick up the one on Hall's desk. He could only hear her faintly, but it sounded important, whatever it was. Then, suddenly, her voice was back in his ear.

'Sorry, Max. I've got to go. Bit of a scramble. There's been another one.'

'Another one? So this is a series, then?'

'Sorry, Max. Got to go.' And his ear was full of buzzing.

* * *

The screaming had stopped by the time the police got there, but it had been going on for so long that it seemed to have left an imprint on the air. The girl who had been screaming could feel another in her throat and was only keeping it at bay with extreme concentration, so that she had to bend over, hugging herself, to keep the hysteria in. First, no one had come. Then, finally, the old man who kept the jeweller's downstairs had come toiling up the stairs to the office. Then, suddenly, from just him coming in, the world seemed piled into the tiny room and the scream got nearer and nearer her mouth.

Jacquie got there just in time to prevent another outburst. As luck would have it, she was the first woman on the scene and the girl ran and clung to her as if she was the last lifeboat off the *Titanic*. Jacquie just patted her for a moment, and gradually the secretary started to relax.

Jacquie looked over her head at one of the SOCOs. 'Is there another room we can use?'

'Wouldn't recommend it,' he said, dryly. 'There's only the office and I don't think she'll be up for going back in there, somehow.'

'You can come downstairs and use my back room, if you want.' No one had noticed the jeweller was still there, but Jacquie was glad he was. He was an inoffensive little man you'd pass a hundred times a day and never notice. The room was oppressive and the smell that attends any violent death was beginning to ooze out of the inner office and overwhelm the other smells of wet humanity rising like steam from the professionals on the case.

'Thank you. That would be useful,' Jacquie said.

'Oops, hold on,' said the SOCO. 'I'll have to have those shoes, I think.' He pointed with his felt pen that he had been using to label possible clues. 'Blood. DNA.'

Jacquie could have felled him for being so crass. The girl had come in to work and had walked into the inner office to find the very thoroughly disembowelled corpse of Jacob Shears, Solicitor and Commissioner for Oaths — in short, her boss — sitting at his desk as if to start the day like any other. She didn't need it pointing out that she had blood, at the very least, on her shoes. She started to tremble and Jacquie squeezed her tight.

'Don't worry,' said the jeweller. 'My flat is above this office. All we need do is go out onto the landing and up a flight of stairs. No shoes needed.'

Jacquie helped the secretary slip her shoes off and ushered her through the door, with a sharp look at the forensics guy, already off on another chase, this time a paper clip that could be really significant. As she left, he was bagging it carefully and labelling it. No wonder Angus smokes things, she thought. All this stupidity must really do your head in after a while.

The jeweller — 'Call me Michael, my dear' — led them up a narrow stair hidden behind a piece of false panel into a scrupulously neat little flat. Manda Moss would have definitely approved. There was a stunning view from the big window which spanned almost all of one wall, over a snow-speckled Leighford and over the dunes to the sea, sparkling in the distance in the frosty air. Despite the circumstances, both women were drawn to the view.

'It is lovely, isn't it?' the jeweller said. 'These last few days when people have been kept in by the weather have been a real bonus for me. I just shut up shop and come up here and enjoy the view. Just sit yourselves down there and I'll make us all a nice cup of tea. Would you like that, Tia?'

The girl nodded. 'Can I have a tissue, please?' she whispered. 'This one's all . . .' She opened her hand and showed a shredded bloody tissue. 'I'm sorry,' she said. 'I felt a bit faint. I touched the desk. It was all sticky . . .' Her eyes rolled up into her head and Jacquie just caught her as she pitched forward.

'Put your head between your knees, Tia,' she said. 'Come on. Deep breaths, now. You'll be fine.' She crouched there, with her hand on the girl's shoulder while she took a little time out in merciful oblivion, down there between her own knees. When the tea arrived, she motioned the man into the third seat in front of the window. When she felt the secretary trying to get back up, she stood back, watched her for a minute and then sat back down. 'OK now?'

'Sorry,' the girl said again. 'Just a bit woozy.'

Jacquie reached into her bag and brought out some antiseptic wipes and passed them over.

'Do I need to give this . . . this tissue in downstairs?' Tia asked.

'No, they've got enough things to keep them busy,' Jacquie said. 'I'll flush it, if Michael can just point me the way?'

He gestured behind him, and through a door Jacquie found a miniature hall, with two doors off, the first of which was the bathroom. She flushed the tissue and washed her hands. She was trying to get her bearings of how this flat meshed with the one below.

Back in the lounge, the two were sitting in companionable silence, as the old and the young often do. Jacquie had become aware that they knew each other quite well, and of course, why not, when they worked in the same building? She decided it needed to get on to a less informal footing and sat down, taking out her notebook from her bag as she did so.

'Are you Mr Maxwell's wife?' the girl asked suddenly.

'Yes, I am. Were you taught by him?'

'I was in the Sixth Form. I didn't do History. He's lovely, Mr Maxwell is.' The girl looked at the old man as she spoke, wanting to share the warmth. 'He often told us about you. And Nolan. And Metternich. That's the cat,' she added to the man. 'And their little boy.'

'I assume that Metternich is the cat, rather than the boy,' he smiled at Jacquie.

'Yes, but it was touch and go for a moment, there,' she said, clicking her pen. 'Now then, if I can get some names?'

'Tia Preese,' the girl said. 'Do you want my address?'

'Later, if that's OK.' She looked at the man, pen raised.

'Michael. Melling, as in the name of the shop downstairs. And this is my address, as you can see.'

'Did you hear anything last night?' Jacquie asked him. 'You must be directly above the office here, surely?'

'In fact, no. The turn on the stairs has confused you, as it has others. This is in fact a flying freehold over the building next door. It is the same all down the street. The third floor is above the second floor of next door, almost like dominoes threatening to fall over. If you want to check about noise, you will have to ask next door, that way.' He pointed to his left.

'Is that a flat as well, or just storage?' Jacquie asked.

'No, it's a flat. Students, though, from the Art College in Brighton, so they may not be back yet for the start of term. I don't hear them, because my bedroom is next to the stairwell of the other side and that *is* just storage. I'm sorry I can't help you more.'

'Not to worry, Mr Melling. If you can come down to the station later today to give a brief statement, I would be grateful. Now, Tia. Was it normal for your boss to come in on a Sunday?'

The girl gave a huge sniff. 'He worked all sorts of hours, really. He didn't have a partner in the business, so if there was something urgent, or if someone rang him at home, he would come in whenever, really. He had the office phone on divert, so that if anyone rang out of hours, he wouldn't miss the call.'

'What kind of practice did Mr Shears have?'

The girl looked blank.

'Did he do a lot of criminal cases? Conveyancing? Divorce?'

'Yes.'

'Which?'

'All of them. He didn't specialise. Sometimes, he'd ask a friend for advice, you know, if a case was quite difficult. And he didn't do the court work, although they can now, if they like, solicitors. He didn't do that, though. He said he wasn't Perry Mason . . . whoever that is.'

Jacquie felt her age as the theme song went through her head, the thumping arrangement by Dick de Benedictus. 'Was he doing anything difficult at the moment?'

'I don't think so. He had a few of those no win, no fee ones, people slipping up on the ice, that kind of thing. But nothing lately that he has had to bring anyone else in on, if that's what you mean.'

'No enemies, then?'

'Not that I can think of.' The girl furrowed her brow. 'No. I can't think of anyone who would want to hurt him.' Her lip quivered again. 'He was such a nice man.'

'How old was he?' As soon as she asked the question, Jacquie knew it was useless. Tia chewed her lip and tried to come up with a number that sounded reasonable. Michael Melling answered for her.

'Mid forties, I would say. Divorced.' He gave a significant look across to Tia. 'His last secretary but one, I gather. Bit of a scandal. Wife came in. There was a client in the office. All very unprofessional. I had to call the police in the end.'

Jacquie made a note. 'That will be on our system, then.' She closed her notebook. 'There's not a great deal more I can do, until we know more from forensics, that kind of thing. So, if you would pop in later, sir, and you, Tia, unless you would rather we came to see you at home?'

'No,' she said, hopelessly. 'I'll come in. But I've got no shoes . . .'

'I'll go and get you some. There's Shoe Express two doors down. What size are you?' Michael Melling was on his feet and reaching for his coat.

'Five,' Tia said. 'Trainers will do. Thank you ever so much, Mr Melling.'

'You're welcome,' he said. 'Just you wait here and finish your tea. I won't be long. I'll just make sure that the Detective Inspector makes it down my rickety stairs all right.'

'Thank you,' Jacquie said, following him out. 'I thought my husband was the last gentleman left standing.'

'Oh, there are still a few of us around,' he said, leaving her on the middle landing. 'I'll see you later, perhaps.'

She watched him go down the stairs, carefully but clearly well practised on their steep treads. She turned to see Pete

Spottiswood standing behind her. 'What a nice man,' she said.

'Old paedo if you ask me,' Spottiswood said. 'All over that girl like a rash. Probably did for matey in there as well. You can't trust his sort.'

'What? Nice people?' Jacquie was by definition much less naive than the average person, but found Spottiswood's constant jaundiced view very wearing.

'Nice. Yeah, right. Fred West nice.' He went back into the room and peered through to where the body had been. Fortunately, they had removed it while Tia had been upstairs and that bore out Melling's assertion that you couldn't hear anything from the office in his flat. They would have certainly heard that, even if only Jacquie would have recognised the sound.

'Do we know what happened?' she asked him. In fact, she didn't want to talk to him at all, but everyone else seemed to have gone home, except a few lingering SOCOs.

'Stabbed.' Spottiswood was always monosyllabic, except when concocting complex sickie excuses, when he could become quite lyrical.

'Not just stabbed, surely?' Jacquie said, teasing out the information.

'Disembowelled,' he said with relish. 'All the guts on the desk and in the drawers, as neat as you like. But they didn't just fall out. Somebody took them out. They cut all the ligaments, split the mesentery, really did the business.'

'My word, Pete. You're very informed about anatomy.'

'Well, I was a nurse, wasn't I? When I left school.'

If he had suddenly started to fly round the room, Jacquie could not have been more surprised. 'A nurse? You?'

'What? Why not? I'm a caring sort of bloke, I reckon. I was doing all right, but then I had to do this stupid test, one of those psychological things, and they suggested I might be happier doing something else. I was gutted. Bit like matey! Ha!'

'I expect it was your sense of humour that they couldn't handle, Pete. A bit too sensitive, I expect.' Shaking her head, Jacquie Carpenter-Maxwell left the building.

# CHAPTER FOURTEEN

The phone was still in Maxwell's hand when Hector Gold popped his head around the door. The bell had gone, but bells to Maxwell these days were a serving suggestion. He always told GTP students to be there ahead of classes, laptop on, PowerPoint ready, interaction all over the place, the eight-phase lesson oozing from every pore. None of that applied to him, of course. Three hundred years at the chalkface had given him an edge that made all that unnecessary.

'Team teaching, Max?' Hector reminded him. 'Eight Eff Three.'

'Team teaching it is,' Maxwell smiled. 'The high spot of anyone's day. Isn't this what we all came into the profession for?' And he led the way.

Eight Eff Three weren't a bad bunch as psychotics went. Jamie in the corner had more neuroses than brain cells but he meant well. Only behind closed doors and in hushed tones did Maxwell refer to him as Daft Jamie, the last victim of the Resurrection Men Burke and Hare. Kylie had a make-up obsession but Maxwell's promise to rip her nails out had had the desired effect and now she saved the full makeover for Double Science.

The general babble ceased as the two men entered the room. For once, all eyes were not on Mad Max, the Monster of the Mezzanine, but on the small balding bloke with him.

'Everybody,' Maxwell said. 'This is Mr Gold. He is from the Colonies. And no, Jemma, he doesn't know Brad Pitt or his granddad, Justin Bieber, so don't pester him. Mr Gold is a Historian, like me and, for the next forty-five minutes, like you. He's going to walk among you now — don't be alarmed — and he will give you a number.'

Hector smiled a rather weak 'Hi!' to the twenty-nine twelve-year-olds (actually twenty-eight, because no one but Children's Services and the Ed Psych had ever seen Angel Hargreaves, although her name was still on the books) and wandered around the room, numbering them all off. Jemma grinned up at him hopefully, just in case Mr Maxwell was wrong about Justin Bieber. But then, her case was hopeless. Mr Maxwell was never wrong.

Mr Maxwell was mentally miles away from the job in hand. Two murders in a sleepy seaside town out of season was bizarre, but three bordered on the unbelievable. Maxwell knew his serial killers. Sociopaths of that calling were driven by phases, mood swings that took everybody by surprise. They withdrew into themselves, seemed distant, elsewhere. They were fighting the lust to kill but they couldn't fight it. So the search began, like some mad treasure hunt in which the prize was a human life. But there was something odd here, something that didn't fit. Serial killers adopted a pattern, used an MO that worked for them and they stuck to it. They might embellish and perfect as their deadly toll mounted, but essentially it was same old, same old — which gave the good guys some kind of chance of catching them. Peter Sutcliffe used a screwdriver and a ball-pein hammer; Aileen Wuornos a handgun, Vacher and Jack the Ripper were into strangulation followed by mutilation with a blade. But the Chummy who was stalking the streets of Leighford had used a gun and a push. Had he run out of bullets? Left his Peacemaker at home? And the old fifties song refrained in his brain. 'Don't take your guns to town, son. Leave your guns at home, Bill. Don't take your guns to town.'

'Mr Maxwell?' Hector Gold brought him back to reality.

'Right!' Maxwell clapped his hands, astounded at the American's ability to count so fast.

'All the Number Ones over here in the corner.'

There was pandemonium as the chosen ones scraped back their chairs and made for the door corner.

'Number Twos,' (it wasn't a joke to anyone over four) 'back of the room.' More chaos.

'Threes this corner,' he pointed to his bookshelves where the projector was gathering mould.

'And Fours — last but by no means least — front and centre.'

The noise was indescribable. 'Which is why,' Maxwell screamed in Gold's ear, 'I don't do team teaching unless we have a visiting celebrity.'

Gold grinned. He waited for the multi-choice papers to be given out like back home, but it didn't happen. Instead, Maxwell placed two fingers in his mouth and his whistle almost shattered the glasses of a ginger child now in Group Three.

'Let me take you back,' the Head of Sixth Form said. 'It is 1785. Who is the king, George?'

All eyes turned to the luckless lad in Group Four. He didn't know.

'Tell him, everybody,' Maxwell commanded.

'George!' most of them chorused. He overlooked the solitary voice which said 'Victoria'.

'George the what?' Maxwell was a stickler for accuracy.

'The Third,' two or three voices said. The others were too fly to embarrass themselves as the 'Victoria' girl had done.

'Correct,' Maxwell nodded. 'You four groups are businessmen — and women, of course, Cassandra — and you are what they used to call joint stock companies. Your job,' he lapsed into *Mission Impossible* in spite of himself, 'is to set yourself up in business. You've got to decide what you want to make, how you want to make it. Remember . . .' he held up his fingers for the slower learners, 'you'll need to sort out where the money's coming from, where you'll make whatever it is you're making, how you'll transport the stuff and where you'll sell it. Now, we talked about all this last lesson, but that was a while ago, so you'll find some reminders on the sheets on the desks. I want one of you to be a scribe, to write ideas down, and one of you to be the spokesperson, because later on, Mr Gold and I will want to hear your ideas.'

The groups fell to with a will. Henry Barnard wanted to be scribe *and* spokesperson for his group and Gold spent several minutes trying to sort that one out. Nobody in Group Two wanted to be the scribe so Anna Dove was going to have to speak off the top of her head. No change there, then.

'Yes, wigs are good,' Maxwell told Group Four, peering over a shoulder at their jottings. 'What'll you make them out of?'

'Um . . . hair?' Jonathan Armstrong had a City and Guilds in Obvious.

'Certainly,' Maxwell said.

'Yeuch!' Cassandra was never comfortable outside her own century.

'But that will cost and you may not have enough money. Think about what else you could use.' And he passed on. He was just reminding Jack Twelvetrees in Group One that 'Terms and Conditions Apply' appeared nowhere in eighteenth-century-speak when the balloon went up.

'What the fuck is that supposed to mean?'

The silence was deafening. No one used language like that in Mad Max's classroom, least of all other teachers. Hector Gold was almost purple in the face. 'Cell phones in 1785?' he screeched. 'You have got to be shitting me!'

'Keep it real, Alan,' Maxwell advised the offending child. 'The best you can do communication-wise in 1785 is a letter — or perhaps a loudhailer for short distances. Er . . . Mr Gold. A word?'

He shepherded Gold into the doorway and glanced back to find all four groups buzzing. He was fully aware that they were not galvanised by eighteenth-century joint stock ventures, but were busy analysing what had just happened.

'What just happened?' Maxwell asked. It wasn't his favourite film, but then he had no idea that Hector Gold had Tourette's either.

'Sorry, Max,' Gold grinned sheepishly. 'It's all a bit of a strain, I guess.'

'Eight Eff Three?' Maxwell checked. This was bad news. Gold would be facing Ten Aitch Six later.

'No, it's not the kids,' Gold told him. 'It's me. Well, us. Oh, hell. Look, I'll just get along to the staffroom.'

'No, you won't,' Maxwell told him. 'You'll go back in there, with me and we'll carry on. Just act normally.'

'Er . . . there won't be letters or anything, will there? To the Principal, I mean.'

'Legs Diamond wouldn't know a principle if it got up and bit him,' Maxwell assured him. 'If it should arise, I'll just plead communication problems. As I always say,' and he patted the man's arm, 'America is a foreign country where they just happen to speak English. Some of the time.'

* * *

Angus sat disconsolately at his desk and looked at the motley collection of detritus that had just arrived from Leighford by motorcycle courier. The main roads had stayed open throughout the snow. It was just the side-jobbies that remained treacherous. Angus wanted sometimes to just take the idiots from SOCO and knock their heads together. Angus wanted hairs, he wanted swabs, he wanted the esoteric and the arcane. What he appeared to have was a selection of office rubbish that had missed the bin. There was a chocolate wrapper, heavily bloodstained; a half page of newspaper which could only be the *Leighford Advertiser*, judging by the typographical errors and the content, stained with something which was presumably a by-product of disembowelling; some photographs on a memory stick of various bloody footprints and one very smudged thumbprint (also sent as a lifted-off print in a bag); a pair of girl's shoes, size 5 and a paper clip.

Where was the single flake of cigarette ash, from a cigarette handmade to order by a bespoke tobacconist in Guatemala? Where was the wisp of fabric, caught on a protruding nail, that came from a couturier gown made for a crowned head? A paper clip! A chocolate wrapper! Who did they think he was? Some kind of miracle worker? At least there was no cuddly toy.

But of course, Angus was some kind of miracle worker. He squared what could only be called his shoulders, although they were not much wider than his head, buttoned up his white coat and set to work. The lifted bloody thumbprint was obviously in the dead man's blood, but where there was a thumb there was sweat, in Angus's experience, and so the swab went off for DNA testing down the corridor. Angus was in two minds about DNA; finding little bits of people's dandruff and spittle might look easy on the telly, but in fact there were so many bits of so many people in any room it was still looking for a needle in a haystack, except they could now put a label on the needle. Finding out who the needle belonged to was still a job for the cops. Angus just gave them the information, they had to work with it.

Right. Next were the shoes. Quite handy, these. He could lift some DNA so he could exclude the secretary from his results. Few quick swabs, done and done. The newspaper was so fouled with intestinal contents that it was almost unreadable. He put it aside, gently smoothed out, to dry out a bit more and then he might be able to establish exactly what issue it came from and also what it might have on it. It was certainly cut, not torn from the main page, so was almost certainly a valid clue.

So, what did that leave him? He stood looking down at the paper clip and the chocolate bar wrapper. He remembered he was hungry. Starving, in fact; he shrugged off his white coat and meandered into the corridor and stood looking aimlessly at the machine full of snacks of all kinds, crisps, flavoured maize curly things and a whole load of chocolate, both with and without nuts and various other inclusions. Angus's mind was a strange place to be and even Angus wasn't sure he liked it there. It was a mixture of very sensible and logical and very weird indeed. He preferred weird, but he had to admit that sensible and logical was the way he was born and the way he would end up one day, looking at his wife and one point nine children. Angus liked to keep abreast of current statistics and being accurate was the nearest he came to religion, if you didn't count that summer he was a Druid.

So, a thought came surfing along the shallows of Angus's mind and sent him, snackless, back to his bench. He smoothed out the chocolate wrapper and swabbed off the blood, carefully numbering and storing each swab as he saturated it. Soon, he could read the name on the wrapper and he was right: there was nothing like it in the machine out in the corridor. He quickly went online and found that in fact there was nothing like it in any shop near Leighford or anywhere else in England either.

This was exciting. It gave him an excuse to ring Jacquie Carpenter — Angus had no truck with the Maxwell bit of her name or life — to tell her his exciting news. As he waited for her to answer the phone, he fiddled with the paper clip, as everyone does at their desk, except that he was fiddling with it through an evidence bag. Just a common or garden central stores-issue paper clip, just like a million others in his drawer. Honestly, what were those SOCOs like?

'DI Carpenter-Maxwell.'

'Hello.' Angus fought against his usual tongue-tied state when talking to Jacquie. 'It's Angus. From Chichester.'

'Hello, Angus. Have you got news for us already? That was quick. I haven't been back in the office long. Aren't you a marvel? What is it?'

She thought he was a marvel! How much better could a day get? 'It's the chocolate wrapper that SOCO picked up at the scene.'

'You're one up on me there, Angus. I didn't even know there was a chocolate wrapper.'

'It was found . . . hold on, let me check . . .' Angus turned over the evidence bag that had held the wrapper. 'Down the side of the deceased's office chair.'

'He was quite a big chap, Angus. Probably ate chocolate while he worked.'

Angus was a little crestfallen, but ploughed ahead anyway. 'It was a bit unusual, so I thought I would let you know about it.'

'Good idea. Thank you.' Jacquie could hear a crest falling at a thousand paces, even down the phone.

'It's a Wonka Exceptionals Scrumdiddlyumptious chocolate bar wrapper.'

Jacquie paused before she spoke next. That Angus was a bit of a pothead was common knowledge and had he been less amazing at his job his collar would have been well and truly felt years before. But surely even he knew that Willie Wonka wasn't real. Before she could frame the sentence, he was talking again.

'I do know that Willie Wonka isn't real, before you ask me. But I have looked up this particular bar and you can't get it here.'

'In Leighford?'

'No. In England. It's an American bar. If . . .' and again he checked his evidence bag, 'Jacob Shears has not been there on holiday recently, it may well be a clue.'

Jacquie was silent on the other end of the phone. She could hardly believe her ears. Had Jeff O'Malley managed to sneak off another one before they took him down to the station? And if so, why?

'DI Carpenter? Jacquie? Are you still there?'

'Sorry. Sorry, Angus. Train of thought. Thank you very much. Are there likely to be prints?'

'Doubtful. It was very screwed up and also was very bloodstained. I've taken swabs, but—'

'Yes, I know,' Jacquie said. 'We have to have DNA on the file to be of any help. Never mind. I know you'll do your best. Was there anything else?'

'Just the usual.' Angus was feeling a happy glow that came to him when he had pleased DI Jacquie Carpenter Forget The Maxwell. 'Fingerprint — well, thumb, but you know what I mean. The shoes from the secretary. A paper clip — just like all the ones we all have in our drawers. I'll have to be a bit careful when I'm testing that; don't want it getting mixed up, but I don't know of any cases of a fingerprint being lifted from anything that small. DNA, I suppose.'

'Well, keep looking, Angus. Thank you.'

The phone went down with what Angus considered indecent haste, but his angel was probably busy, so he would forgive her. Humming tunelessly to himself, he went off in search of his chocolate. He had once had an iPod, but had put it down somewhere and lost it. Now he just hummed. The sound quality was better and Angus was always on random shuffle.

* * *

Jacquie Carpenter-Maxwell sat at her desk, the phone receiver still in her hand, her finger pressed down on the button. She needed more information before she jumped to conclusions, but if she waited, Jeff O'Malley's time helping them with their enquiries would be up and he would be back on the streets. She needed to sort so much out before that happened, not least of which would be getting a watch on Mrs Troubridge's house and logging her number with the nick for rapid response should she need help. She didn't think that Jeff O'Malley liked his possessions wandering off and staying with defenceless old ladies without his express permission. He was likely to get them back by any means at his disposal. She needed to find out what Hector planned to do longer term and also there was the question of Camille. Was she just waiting back at Manda

Moss's ruined house, to see who finally returned? Or had she not even noticed everyone had gone? Camille was a blank to Jacquie for the simple reason that she *was* a blank. Anything beyond nails pretty much left her cold, which left an awful lot of the world unplumbed by her on any level.

But first, and it had to be now, Jacquie must ring the mortuary and find out the time of death. If it was after nine last night, they were in trouble. Please, please, *please* let it be before nine, she intoned to herself as she hit Astley's speed dial number.

'Leighford Mortuary.'

'Donald?'

'Yes. It's Jacquie Carpenter-Maxwell.'

'Oh, hello.' It was Donald's attempt at insouciance and almost passed muster. 'How are you?'

'Well, Donald, thank you. Look, I've just been speaking to Angus and he has made me wonder about something.'

'Angus is always coming up with funny ideas,' said Donald, jealousy making his left eyebrow twitch. 'What would you like to know?' There was a very slight emphasis on the word 'know' to suggest know, rather than to surmise. It was subtle, but Jacquie spotted it.

'Well, Donald, you know what these forensic chaps are like. I just want to know time of death, really. Then we can put this clue in or out of court, as it were, should it come to that.'

'Well, I hope it does come to that, DI Carpenter,' Donald said, severely. 'This was definitely not suicide, you know. Most people don't go for disembowelling these days. Especially not when they then put the liver in a filing cabinet and shut the drawer.'

'No, no I do see that, Donald. It was a figure of speech. Umm . . . do we have time of death?'

'Dr Astley is just getting started, DI Carpenter,' Donald said, formally. 'But the rectal temperature is taken early in proceedings. I don't know whether he has measured the degree of rigor yet. I'll ask.'

The phone was put down and Jacquie could hear Donald's ponderous footsteps retreat, then the creak and slap of a mortuary door. She heard a distant boom, like the guns in Flanders sounded on the coast of Kent in 1914, or so Maxwell had told her. After a moment, the sounds were reversed and he was back.

'Dr Astley says you seem to be in a bit of a hurry, DI Carpenter,' Donald said, because stirring up trouble was his favourite hobby, after eating, and this seemed a good opportunity. 'He says to tell you that the deceased was killed not a moment before ten o'clock last night and not a second after one this morning.'

'That's the very earliest, is it?' she asked, with a slightly plaintive note.

Donald hated to disappoint her but the truth was the truth after all. 'Sorry. He is absolutely adamant. When did you want him to have died?'

'Not at all would obviously be favourite,' Jacquie was massaging her temples with her free hand, 'but assuming that his time had come, I wish that time had been about five hours earlier. Never mind, Donald. Thank you.' And again, the phone went down on a disappointed man. Donald had prepared various witty rejoinders which would now never be said. He sighed and rejoined his boss; he had organs to weigh, even if they had spent some hours filed under 'Pending'.

* * *

Peter Maxwell sat in his office that cold snowy lunchtime, hunched over a warming but not very nutritious cup of instant soup, and thought about his morning. Away across the fields, out of sight of the staffroom and the Head's office, most of the lads of Year Ten were snowballing the Year Seven boys to death. It hadn't done Napoleon any harm when he was at the military academy, so Maxwell let it pass. That he had seen an unexpected side to Hector Gold was in no doubt. The only question that needed to be addressed was whether this was indeed a product of the stress he was under or whether the Hector Gold they had been seeing was just a veneer over the real and rather scary one beneath. He tended to think that it was the former; no one could have kept up a front that laconic if they were in fact a seething mass of anger and fury. Jeff O'Malley was the furious one in the family, Hector was just along for a rather bumpy ride. The psychopath and the cipher, you might almost say. Maxwell gave a little chuckle to himself; why was there never anyone around when you thought of a brilliant thing like that? He looked into his mug and swirled the contents around. What was a Mulliga, he wondered, and was it Tawny in the wild or only when domesticated for the soup trade? There was a tap on the door.

'Yes?' Maxwell carolled. He usually left the door open but the corridor was so arctic that to do so would be to invite pneumonia at the least. 'Who is it?'

'Me,' said his wife, popping her head round the door. 'May I come in? It's really cold out here.'

'Sweetness!' Maxwell leapt up, slopping his sludge over the edge of the mug. 'What brings you here?'

She dropped into a chair and sighed. 'I don't know, really. I certainly shouldn't be here, not with what I've got.'

He sat down opposite and looked grave. 'Two and six?' The old jokes were indeed the best, but he didn't think that was really why she was here.

'Max,' she said, on another sigh. 'I have a problem and I should be sharing it with Henry, or at the last resort Pete Spottiswood, but it is so . . . complicated, I thought that the only person who would understand all my whifflings would be you.'

'Absolutely right, of course,' he agreed. 'Didn't the bit about whifflings come between honour and keep you? I know I was thinking it, even if I didn't say it out loud at the time.'

'I hardly know where to begin,' she said. 'Any chance of . . . what is that, anyway?' She leant forward to peer into his mug.

'It claims to be mulligatawny and I suppose it isn't too bad. You have to watch out for the undissolved lumps, though, or it blows your head off. Want one? There are some sachets over by the kettle.'

'I'll pass, I think. Are there any other flavours?'

'Broccoli and Stilton. They tend to build up a bit. Helen brings in the mixed boxes but she only likes pea.'

'What a strange life you lead, Mr Maxwell, when I'm not here to see.' She flicked the switch on the kettle and tore the top off a sachet. 'I'll join you in a mulligatawny after all, I think.' She stood at the worktop with her back turned. 'I must ask you not to share any of this, Max,' she said, quietly.

'What, that you drink mulligatawny soup?'

'No, idiot. What I am about to tell you. It involves . . . well, people.'

'No, tell me it isn't so. A crime, involving people. Surely not. Now, stop stirring that soup to death and come and sit down.'

'Promise?'

'Yes, I promise.'

'Not even Sylv.'

'I don't tell Sylv much. She usually tells me things.'

'Fair enough. OK.' She took a deep breath and a sip of soup. 'The other murder, the one I heard about this morning first thing.'

'Yes. When you were on the phone to me. What about it?'

'It didn't seem at first to be connected, although it would seem odd not to be, coming so soon after the others.'

'So you are linking Hendricks and Gregson?'

'I don't even know that, yet. It could be the gambling connection. We haven't been able to speak to Linda Hendricks yet, but if ever there was someone who liked to gamble, it would be her husband. So there might be a link there. Also, Sarah Gregson was a social worker at one time, so she might have known Hendricks.'

'It's unlikely she would have played cards with him if she knew his history, surely?' Maxwell slipped into the role of Devil's advocate with hellish ease. You could almost smell the brimstone, although it could have been the soup.

'True. As I say, everything is very tentative at the moment. Then this morning, the victim was a Jacob Shears, a solicitor in town.'

'Shot?'

'No.' She sipped her soup again and tried to forget the charnel house interior of the solicitor's office.

'Thrown from a high building?'

'Uh-uh. Stabbed and then . . . disembowelled, rather thoroughly.'

Maxwell knew his serial killers. He had a working knowledge of all of them, and a specific knowledge of some. He was still undecided about the infantile arson, the bed-wetting and the cruelty to animals, but he was clear on one point: they all had a method they liked and stuck to it. 'So . . . with three different MOs, why are you guys treating it as a series?'

'We're not. But it is.'

'Precious Bane, we have been together now, Teacher and Woman Policeman, for a lot of years, taken by and large.'

'I didn't like you for some of them,' she pointed out.

'Nonsense. It was love at first sight.'

'No. You misheard me at the time. "Loathe", I said. Not "love".'

'Well,' said Maxwell, 'I'm with Christopher Marlowe on this one. Love at first sight it was. But, I digress. We've been together now a long time but I am totally confused. Why is it a series? Before you answer, I should say that I agree with you, but I know my reasons. I need to know yours.'

'First,' Jacquie said, holding up a thumb, 'Matthew Hendricks was killed by having his head blown off by a .44 Magnum.'

'The most powerful handgun in the world,' Clint Eastwood said, through the medium of Peter Maxwell.

'Yes. An American gun.'

'Most are,' Maxwell remarked, mildly.

'An *iconic* American gun,' she added, 'to be precise. Number Two,' and she held up her forefinger, 'Sarah Gregson was thrown off a multi-storey car park—'

'Definitely thrown?' Maxwell thought he would check.

'Yes. So everyone says. Where was I? Yes, thrown off a car park after playing poker. Three,' she held up her middle finger, 'Jacob Shears is killed in his office.' She sat back. 'Shall I tell you the link, now?'

'If you would,' Maxwell said mildly.

'Hendricks, American gun. Gregson, played cards with an American. Shears, an American chocolate wrapper was found alongside the body, covered in blood.'

'American chocolate is hardly a clincher,' Maxwell thought he should say. 'They have Reese's Pieces in the vending machine at the bus station . . .' He caught her eye. The healthy eating new year resolution had not really taken hold as she would have liked. '. . . I would imagine.'

'This was a much more unusual one, available only in America or online. We have someone checking availability back at the nick — the first two websites we tried don't have stock. So it is likely that it is only an American who would have one.'

'Would you stand and eat a chocolate bar while you disembowel someone? I mean, there is casual and casual, surely.'

'I agree that it isn't usual, but what is usual about stabbing an innocent man and spreading his intestines all over the place? His liver was in a filing cabinet.'

'Nasty.' He put down his mug. He seemed to have lost his appetite. 'Apart from the chocolate wrapper, is there any other link with the other two?'

'No, not that we can see at the moment. He has lots of files around the office and some of them are a bit . . .' she settled for 'difficult to decipher. We'll have to check what he was working on. His secretary is in shock. She found him.'

'Poor thing. Young?'

'Yes. One of yours, inevitably. Tia Preese.'

'I remember her,' he said, pointlessly. He remembered everyone he had ever taught. Sometimes all it took was that he had met them in the corridor, but that was only if they had a noticeable feature, like one eye in the middle of their forehead, something like that. 'Business Studies.'

'Well, that would make sense. She was the only secretary working there and her office was impeccable. He was a bit of a slob, by the looks of it.'

'Enough of a slob to leave chocolate wrappers around?' he asked, but she ignored him. 'It's lovely of you to share, Inspector,' he went on, after a pause, 'but why are you telling me this? I know that I would have wheedled it out of you in the end, but it isn't like you to just tell me straight out like this.'

'You're right,' she said and bravely drank the sludge at the bottom of the mug before putting it down on the coffee table between them. She suppressed a shudder and he was impressed. Most people screamed at that point as they got all the curry in one hit. 'I am getting round to it, but slowly. I don't want to say it, that's why. It sounds too silly.'

'Try me. I specialise in silly.'

She smiled at him. 'Too right,' she told him. 'When the Magnum was used, I just thought it was an unusual choice. When Sarah Gregson was killed, I must admit I fastened on Jeff O'Malley with the feeling that it was case closed. Then when Shears was killed, I knew it wasn't him, but I had made the American connection. I don't want to let it go.' She stared at him, willing him to understand.

'When did Shears die?' he asked.

'Between ten and one last night. Give or take half an hour, although Donald says no leeway. That's just the pathology lot, though. There's always a bit of space on either side.'

'So after you had Jeff O'Malley at the nick.'

'Exactly. Which leaves three other Americans unaccounted for. Alana and Hector were at the hospital or so he says. Camille was home alone.'

Maxwell knew what had happened when Cawley McCulkin or whatever the ghastly child was called had tried that, but it was hardly the same. He considered the theory with more gravity than it deserved. 'Alana could hardly toss a fully grown woman off a car park, let alone disembowel a solicitor. Camille could probably do the throwing, if she took a run at it, but I can't see her getting messy with a nasty bit of intestine rearranging. She might break a nail.'

The silence started at that point and grew until Jacquie cracked. 'And Hector?' Even as she said it, it sounded unlikely. 'No,' she got up and reached for her coat. 'Sorry, Max. I don't know what I was thinking. He could no more murder someone than fly.'

Maxwell looked grim. 'Sit down, Inspector. I think I may know something that you don't.'

# CHAPTER FIFTEEN

Jacquie Carpenter-Maxwell had known longer days, but looking back as she sat at six that evening, with the phone in her hand, she could hardly believe that it was that morning that she had been standing in Jacob Shear's office, trying to avoid standing on anything slippery. Her last hour had just been frustrating, trying to get the Communications Department to OK what could turn out to be a very long phone call to California. Eventually, she had got clearance, got the number and was waiting for someone to answer.

'—nth Precinct. Help you?'

Oh, rats! She hadn't been concentrating. What number had he said? 'Could I speak to the senior officer, please?'

'Name?'

'Detective Inspector Jacquie Carpenter-Maxwell,' she said, 'Leighford Police. England.'

'Nice to speak to you, Detective Inspector,' the voice informed her. 'But I mean, the name of the person you wish to speak with. We got lots of seniors here. We got Homicide. We got Drugs. We got Vice. We got Traffic. Which d'ya want?'

'I don't know,' Jacquie had to admit. 'I don't even know if I have the right Precinct. I want to speak to someone who knows about Jeff O'Malley. He used to—'

'Oh, we all know about Jeff O'Malley,' the voice said, dryly. 'And we all know what he used to do. I tell you what. I'll put you through to Lieutenant Schmidt. Harry, he likes to be called, but let him say it first. I'll put you through. If I lose this call, just ring back and ask for Harry.' The phone went dead, apart from a plangent beep every now and again to tell her that someone still cared.

'Schmidt.'

'Lieutenant Schmidt, I am Jacquie Carpen—'

'Yes. Front desk told me. You want to know about Jeff O'Malley. Why?'

Obviously Schmidt was a man of few words. Also, Jacquie realised she had no idea whether he was a friend of O'Malley's or not. He sounded too young to have worked with him, except in a more junior capacity, but it was never wise to judge. 'I am just finding out some background,' she said. 'He is . . . helping us with our enquiries,' she began.

The man on the other end of the phone laughed. He had a nice laugh and Jacquie reassessed her mental picture of him. He turned from Telly Savalas's Kojak to Tom Selleck's Magnum PI in a winking. 'If it's the Jeff O'Malley I know,' he said, 'he won't be helping anyone with anything. The only person Jeff O'Malley helps is himself. So, what's he "helping" you with? Blackmail? Extortion? Bribery? Gambling?'

'Murder,' Jacquie said, shortly. The blackmail and gambling areas interested her. Bribery and extortion didn't really fit, but anyone who had dabbled with them would be someone that would interest the police of any country.

There was a silence on the line, longer than could be explained by the distance.

'Lieutenant Schmidt?' She hoped Maxwell never heard her saying 'lootenant'. He would divorce her on the spot.

'Sorry. Jacquie, did you say your name was? May I call you Jacquie? Please call me Harry. Murder, you say? I can't say I am surprised. It's a surprise he's taken this long. Who was it? Bookie?'

'No. It was . . . it's a bit difficult to explain, really. There's no real link that I can see between O'Malley and the victims . . .'

'More than one? All at once? Driving, was it? Hit and run, that's his style.'

'No. Three separate incidents. Two we could link to gambling, but we're still working on the third. It's just that . . . well, I know him personally.'

'Oh.' In that single syllable, Jacquie could hear Harry Schmidt close down. 'That's different.'

'Let me explain. His son-in-law is working with my husband, on an exchange.'

'I know about that. We had that poor guy who is living at O'Malley's in here the other day. There was a raid . . . do you know about that?'

'Yes. Paul Moss . . .'

'Yeah, that's the guy.'

'Hmm. Well, Paul emailed my husband at school and said about the raid. He was upset. He wants to come home.'

'Don't blame him. Why're they at O'Malley's anyway? Shouldn't he be at Camille and Hector's? More usual, surely?'

'They were told that Camille and Hector's house wasn't big enough for the family. That's why Jeff and Alana came along, so that Paul Moss and his family could have their house.'

Another laugh. 'Still up to his old tricks. Couldn't have got a visa on his own, shouldn't wonder. Had to piggyback on poor old Hec. No, Camille's condo is big enough. Got a pool, everything. The kids would have loved it and . . . Paul, is it? Yeah, Paul could have walked to school. No, Jeff wanted out and he didn't care who he left holding the baby. Just classic Jeff. Sorry you're stuck with him. Tell me about these murders.'

'Can I email you the details? It's rather complicated.'

'If Jeff's involved, it's probably simple. Jeff just wants money. And power, of course, but he has Alana for that. But you're right, an email would be simpler. Unless you got a webcam? It's easier to Skype.'

'This is a police station,' Jacquie said. 'It's a wonder we've got phones.'

'We just got ourselves a new commissioner,' Harry Schmidt told her, with the laugh in his voice. 'He's buying friends right now. Everyone of my rank and above has got an iPad for us to work on at home. Jeff would have sold his. Not only is he a dinosaur, he's a greedy one. T Rex, I guess. Anyway, got a pen?'

'Yes. We do have those.'

'I like you, Jacquie. You have a sense of humour. Not like Morse. That's one of my favourites.'

'You watch *Morse*?' Somehow it didn't fit the picture she had of him.

'Got them all on DVD. Box set on eBay. Got to relax sometime.'

'Well, we're not all like Morse, thankfully.' Jacquie was more of a *Lewis* girl herself, and not just because of Laurence Fox. 'I'm ready.'

'OK. Send the details to schmidt h — that's all one word — at precinct 9 — that's all one word as well, nine as a number not a word — calif police. Do I need to say that is all one word? Dot com. That'll get me day or night. On my iPad.'

'Thanks.' She read the address back to him. 'But before you go, Harry, why were Paul and Manda at the sharp end of a police raid the other day?'

'Got into a bit of a habit, here in Precinct 9,' Harry Schmidt told her. 'If there's anything going on that's a bit shady, where no one's talking, we shake down Jeff. We haven't got him yet, not since the day we threw him out. But we'll get him one day. If you don't get him first, that is. Look forward to your email. 'Bye Jacquie,' and with a click and a brrrr he was gone.

Jacquie opened her emails and read through the few that had come in. One was an invitation to Bob Thorogood's leaving party. Not that he was going anywhere specific, just down the road, but he was making a point. She wondered how many people would attend and already knew she would be one. There had to be someone there to raise a glass, even if it turned out to be the smallest leaving party in the world. Then she settled down to send the email to Harry Schmidt, or Magnum as she already thought of him. It was going to have to be a miracle of not putting words into his mouth, and yet complete in the detail. She wasn't sure on how much of this was legal, but the clock was ticking and if she wasn't careful, O'Malley would be on the streets before she got any details back. She wasn't sure how to start the email. Dear Harry? Hi Harry? Dear Lt Schmidt? She settled for no salutation at all and plunged right in and soon she was in full flow.

* * *

At 38 Columbine, things were not quite as usual. Hector had spoken to Maxwell in his usual diffident way and Maxwell, in his usual hospitable way, had invited him back, for supper at least, to stay if he wanted. The most important thing was to make sure that Mrs Troubridge and Alana were all right and that would take some doing. As a believer that chatting round the table was the best way to resolve anything, Maxwell had also invited the two women to supper. That just left the question of Camille and Maxwell insisted that there Hector had to do his own dirty work. He was accordingly closeted in the study, making the call.

Nolan, a host to his little fingertips, was laying the table. He was laying for six, with an optional set of cutlery to one side, in case Camille arrived against everyone's wishes. Since he privately called her 'Meal', he was smiling with secret pleasure at the pun. Meal, coming over for a meal. He giggled softly and Maxwell stuck his head round the door.

'OK, mate?' he asked.

'Just thought of something funny, Dads,' he said. 'It made me giggle outside when I meant it to stay in.'

As someone who often giggled on the outside, Maxwell understood completely. 'How are you getting along?'

'Are we having seconds?' the boy asked.

'Mate, I don't even know if we're having firsts yet. I'm trying to see what we've got to eat that will feed six.'

'Or seven.'

'Or seven, yes.' Privately, Maxwell wasn't expecting Camille to arrive. He knew a daddy's girl when he saw one and felt that it was more than likely that she would wait at home for O'Malley's return or until hell froze over, whichever was the sooner. But it wouldn't matter anyway. She clearly never ate anything.

'Betty Getti? That always goes down well.'

Maxwell was startled. It was as if his mother-in-law had walked in. Nolan's gift was not for mimicry, but for choosing the very phrase that conjured the person up. Betty Carpenter was not an adventurous cook, but her gregarious daughter had created a skill in her for stretching meals to their utmost when she came home with half a dozen ravenous and unexpected guests. Betty Spaghetti was famous wherever two Carpenters were gathered.

'Betty Getti it is. What a brilliant child you are.'

Nolan beamed. His Dads was not quite like the other dads, but he was glad he was his. Plocker's dad only came home at weekends and then was always playing golf. In the recent snow, he had played golf with orange balls, so they showed up. What kind of Dads was that?

'Can I watch some telly, Dads?' Nothing like striking while the iron was hot.

'Done your homework?' Maxwell could hardly believe he was saying that to a child this age, but Mrs Whatmough ran a tight ship.

'No. It's reading. I've got to read a page to you and then you have to say I've done it.'

'Come and read to me now, then. While I start the Betty Getti.'

*'Dads,'* Nolan whined. 'Can't I do it at bedtime?'

Maxwell had a feeling that by Nolan's bedtime the house might be full of very worked-up people. Although it was tempting to give himself an excuse to get away, it wouldn't be fair. Jacquie had had a bad enough day already, without being lumbered with unknown quantities of Golds and O'Malleys.

'I'll hear him read.' Hector Gold had appeared in his usual flannel-footed way at Maxwell's elbow. 'What's he on? *War and Peace*, perhaps?'

'Don't joke,' Maxwell said. 'That's next term, I gather. He's reading *Magnus Powermouse* at the moment, limbering up for some Tolstoy. You'll have to excuse him if he does all the voices; we've been reading it to him since he was tiny and he knows it off by heart.'

'Then why does he have to read it to you?' Hector Gold was not a stupid man, but he wasn't a parent either.

'Because we have to sign to say he's read it.'

'I know, but—'

'And so if we sign when he hasn't read it, that would be lying. And Carpenter-Maxwells don't lie, you see.' Maxwell winked at him. The boy was still in earshot.

Gold looked suitably abashed. 'Sorry,' he said. 'I think I've been an O'Malley by marriage a bit too long.'

'I understand,' Maxwell said. 'Perhaps the O'Malleys could try being Golds by marriage for a change.' This reminded him and he said, 'I'm sorry, Hec. How did the call to Camille go?'

'Depends on your point of view.'

'From your point of view, then.'

'I told her that I wanted a divorce. That if she wanted, she could go back to LA whenever she liked. So, it went quite well, in that I told her what I wanted to tell her.'

'I sense a but,' Maxwell told him.

'Yes, big but, so to speak, excuse the non-pun. No big butts in our family, except on Jeff. She doesn't want a divorce. Hates my guts, but is so famous among her friends for still being married after all this time, she isn't going to let that go. So, she isn't going back, she isn't going anywhere without Daddy and I can go to hell — as long as I stay married to her. No problems there. Being married to her *is* hell. But don't worry about me, Max. I'll survive.'

Maxwell looked at the man before him, as meek and mild a man as you would meet in a day's march. And yet this very morning he had used the ultimate forbidden word in one of his lessons and for a moment had a look of a man who in two seconds could be ten dress sizes bigger and bright green. The Incredible Hector, straight out of Marvel Comics. He would survive, because Jeff O'Malley would not try too hard to keep him married to his little princess. 'I'm sorry, Hec. It's all gone wrong for you and that wasn't what this year was supposed to be about. Let's put it behind us, shall we? Jacquie will be home shortly and Mrs Troubridge and Alana will be here soon as well. Quickly listen to Nolan's reading and sign his sheet for me, would you? I'll get the Getti on and we'll be eating in no time.'

Hector Gold had quickly learnt that Peter Maxwell always talked sense, even if it sometimes didn't sound like English. He called through to Nolan who rushed off to get his reading book to share with his new best friend. He had been working all day on a new voice for Magnus Powermouse's father and it would be good to try it on a new audience.

Next door, Mrs Troubridge was all of a twitter. Alana was not an easy house guest, but the old lady had not expected her to be. She had got up late and, although very polite, had surreptitiously gone through all of the cupboards in the house, searching for alcohol. The thought of a house where the only booze was a half-empty bottle of Buckfast Tonic Wine was not something she had ever encountered before. A nip of the treacly stuff had given her a caffeine hit like a truckful of Starbucks and the alcohol had hardly stood a chance. She was now almost more sober than Mrs Troubridge, in that she had not been this low on blood alcohol for about three decades and wasn't sure how she was going to cope. Mrs Troubridge managed the shaking by suggesting a game of canasta. By the time Alana had concentrated on the rules for the afternoon, without once having got close to understanding them, the first wave of the hangover had passed and sobriety was well on the menu.

They were primping now in the hall mirror. Although Mrs Troubridge often ate with the Maxwells she understood that this was an *invitation* rather than just joining them for a meal. She had guessed that there was going to be some emotional upheaval, some baring of bosoms — although strictly metaphorical, or she would have to leave — and a lot of repressed feeling let free. Although not a tactile woman herself, she expected some hugging, kissing and weeping. As long as she was able to observe merely, then that would be quite all right by her.

Satisfied at last with the few thin curls teased into being with a dampened finger and thumb she looked without resentment at the reflection of her guest in the mirror. She had no right to still look so attractive, with what she had been through. She should be haggard and grey, but the Californian sun had given her a bone-deep tan and it would be quite a few years under English skies before she was pale.

'Are you ready, dear?' Mrs Troubridge asked. 'We should be going.'

'It is only next door, isn't it?' Alana O'Malley asked. She was a little disoriented, but she was sure she had that right.

'Yes, dear, but we mustn't be late. Punctuality is the politeness of princes as my dear father used to say.' This mantra was gall and wormwood to Maxwell, who always wanted to correct it and tell her that it was Louis XVIII who used to say that it was the politeness of kings. Although Mrs Troubridge was as old as the hills, even she couldn't claim to be offspring of a king who died in 1824. And he was French; she would want no truck with that.

'OK. Fine. If you're sure.' Alana O'Malley did not want to be impolite, but nor did she want to see Peter Maxwell, particularly. He seemed a nice man, but had a habit of looking at you as though he could see through your skin. And Alana O'Malley had spent a long time growing a nice thick skin.

Mrs Troubridge handed her a scarf. It was obviously clean, but it had a slight smell of old humbugs about it, from being in a pocket for a long time with an abandoned Everton Mint. 'Wrap up warm, dear,' Mrs Troubridge exhorted. 'You mustn't catch a chill.'

Alana's lips parted to say 'But', then in the end she didn't bother. 'Thank you, Jessica,' she said instead. 'How kind you are.'

In the mirror the women looked at each other, glad to have at last found a friend.

* * *

Jacquie had actually got as far as putting her coat on and was jingling her car keys in her pocket. She was standing behind her desk doing a mental checklist of everything, because it would be too late once she got to the car; she didn't intend coming back inside this building tonight.

'Can I come in, ma'am?' Sandra Bolton stuck her head around the door. 'I can come back tomorrow if it's too late.'

Jacquie looked at her anxious face. She didn't look as if she had slept at all and she was at a bad age for losing sleep; not a dewy teenager, not a slightly raddled but well-preserved woman of a certain age, but a tired-looking thirty-something with more worries than enough. With a small and she hoped inaudible sigh Jacquie put down her handbag and undid her coat. She didn't take it off, though, and hoped that that would be a hefty enough hint.

'No, Sandra. Come on in. How can I help you?'

'DCI Hall has got them in, the others from the card game, Tim and Mark.'

'Yes, he said he would be interviewing them. Is that a problem?'

The woman blushed, blotchily, to the roots of her hair. 'What will he be asking them, do you think?'

'I should imagine it will be quite standard. Alibi for the time in question, how long they had known Sarah Gregson. He might also ask them if they knew Matthew Hendricks.'

'Matthew Hendricks? Who's he, ma'am?'

'He was the murder victim on Christmas Day. He was also a defendant in a child abuse case last year. We are wondering if there might be a link. Complicated stuff, Sandra. So, he will ask them that. And if they know a Mr Jacob Shears, the man whose body was discovered this morning.' This morning? Oh, God. It felt like weeks ago.

'I heard about that.' Sandra Bolton's eyes were wide. 'His liver was in a drawer, wasn't it?'

Ah, the running liver gag. 'Yes. It was a very nasty murder. We aren't sure whether anything is linked yet; the murders are all very different but they do have a link which we are keeping very quiet at the moment, Sandra. And . . .' Jacquie wasn't sure whether to just come out and say it, and in the end she did. '. . . you are a suspect, don't forget. Has the DCI interviewed you yet?'

Pressing her lips together, Sandra nodded, a fat tear rolling down her face.

'Well, then, that's fine surely. Did he say he had finished with his enquiries as far as you were concerned? Are you back on duty?'

'Tomorrow, ma'am,' the woman whispered.

'Well, for heaven's sake, Sandra. Do try to stop crying.' Jacquie was a patient woman, as behove anyone who lived with Peter Maxwell, but even she had her limits. She looked more closely at her. A thought snagged in her brain as it sleeted randomly through the atmosphere on its way to nowhere. 'You did tell Mr Hall everything, didn't you?' she asked wearily.

For reply, Sandra Bolton shook her head, tears flying in all directions.

'Sandra! Do you want to work in this job or are you trying to get yourself the sack, because you are going the right way about it. I'm going to call down for two cups of coffee. I am going to ring home and tell my family I am going to be late, yet again. I am going to try to prevent myself from giving you a slap as one of the stupidest and most annoying people I have met today. And after all of that I can assure you that you will have pulled yourself together and you will tell me everything. And that means *everything*. You can't bore me. I have sat through *Death in Venice* and lived to tell the tale.' She picked up the phone and punched a number. 'Jim. Could you get me a couple of coffees please, to my office? I hate to be a nuisance . . . You're a gem. Thanks.' She put the phone down and took out her mobile. Again, she punched just one key. 'Max. I'm held up.'

Sandra heard the answer from the other end as a short burst of rhubarb, ending with a very emphatic question mark.

'I know. It is.' She gave Sandra a glance which was not on her usual friendliness scale.

Some more querulous rhubarb.

'Go ahead and eat without me if I'm not back. Put Nole to bed as well. I'll be back as soon as I can manage. What about Camille?'

The rhubarb was positive this time.

'Has he? Well done him. I expect Daddy will be cross. Or possibly not. Something a bit odd there.'

Rhubarb?

'We've got a few more hours and then that's it.' There was a rap on her door. 'Coffee's here, hon. Must go.' She rang off and called, 'Come in,' simultaneously.

A tray with three coffees edged round the door, in the hands of DCI Henry Hall. 'Good evening, Sandra,' he said, affably. 'I wondered if I would find you here. No, don't get up.' When she continued to rise, tears flowing again, he repeated himself. 'No, really, don't get up.' He put the tray down on Jacquie's desk and took a seat in a chair to one side. 'Please go on with whatever it was you were about to say. Unless you had finished. DI Carpenter?'

'No,' Jacquie said, taking her cue from his formality. 'We hadn't started yet, sir.'

He sat down and laced his fingers together across his stomach. 'Well, off you go, Constable. I'm all ears.'

Sandra Bolton sat, crouching down, all big eyes and tears and snot. She shook her head.

'Let me put it another way,' he said, leaning forward, still stony-faced. 'Off you go, Constable. I'm all ears.'

The Constable looked at Jacquie and found nothing there. She drew a huge shuddering sigh and began. 'Since the very first game we played with Jeff O'Malley, I couldn't afford it. My mother had given me some Christmas money and it was to buy things, the turkey and stuff like that, so I used that and didn't tell my boyfriend I'd had it. So he bought all the stuff and that was all right. Then, the next game, I lost everything and I was going home and Jeff O'Malley stopped me.' She looked at Jacquie. 'Do I have to say this?'

Hall answered for her. 'I don't think you will have many surprises for me,' he said. 'Go on.'

She wiped her nose on the back of her hand, like a child. 'He said that he would give me half my stake money back, if I . . . if I would have sex with him.'

There was a silence and the room held its breath.

She continued. 'I said . . . I said I didn't have time to go anywhere, I had to get home. He said he didn't want to go anywhere either, we could do it there.'

'Where was "there"?' Jacquie asked, gently.

'It was in the multi-storey car park,' she said. 'In the stairwell.' She sniffed again, but pulled herself together so that the rest came out in a rush. 'I didn't have any choice. I didn't have any money and I had bills to pay. I . . . I let him do it, leaning up against the wall. Then . . .' the rest came out in a wail, 'then, when he'd done it, he just walked away. He left me there and walked away.'

Jacquie found herself feeling rather uncharitable as she wondered quite what the woman had been expecting. Flowers?

'And?' Hall barked.

'I heard some footsteps, I'm not sure whether it was from above or below. Someone had been watching. Or possibly just listening. But he was very loud, anyone would know what we were doing. What . . . he was doing. I don't know who it was.'

'And?' Hall knew a lot more of this story but wanted to hear it from the horse's mouth.

Sandra Bolton dropped her head into her hands and shook it, mumbling into her palms.

Henry Hall was not an unkind man, as Jacquie knew too well. He stood up and put his hand on the weeping woman's shoulder. 'Since then, up to but not including last Saturday, Jeff O'Malley has given Sandra half her stake money back after each game, in exchange for sex. Last Wednesday, he consented to taking her to his car, as it was so cold. That was the only kindness he has shown. But the worst thing is that someone did see them that first time a few weeks ago. And so they have been blackmailing her for the returned half of her stake money each time.'

'For goodness' sake, Sandra!' Jacquie exploded. 'Why didn't you report it?'

Hall answered for her. 'She had broken so many laws it was not really an option. Prostitution. Indecent exposure. Behaviour likely to offend public decency.

'Who told you?' she whispered.

'Mark Chambers and Tim Moreton.'

'They knew? I can't believe they knew. And so Sarah knew too. Oh, God.'

'And your blackmailer.' He looked down at her. 'Go home, Sandra. Tell your boyfriend as much as you can bear to, but tell him something because this isn't going to go away. Go on. Blow your nose and go home. Are you OK to drive?'

She trumpeted into a handkerchief and stood up. She nodded. 'I'm all right. Thank you, sir, ma'am,' and she went out, still sniffing.

Jacquie sat there, her hands on the desk. Finally, she just said, 'My God. Can we get him on any of this, guv?'

'I'd love to,' he said. 'But what? It wasn't rape, it isn't blackmail. I suppose we could get him for lewd behaviour and procuring, but that puts Sandra in a much worse position than she is now. And it also means we'd have to arrest a reasonable percentage of the population, half the country's footballers and allegedly the Italian Prime Minister.'

'Could he not be the blackmailer?'

'I suppose so, but he agreed with all the details just now when I paid him a visit in an interview room. He didn't know about the blackmail and I don't think he could pretend that well. Laurence Olivier he certainly is not.' Hall was annoyed; he had so wanted to find out something to keep Jeff O'Malley in for longer but time was running out.

'What about one of the others?' Jacquie asked.

'They told me about it straight out. Would a blackmailer do that? I'm not sure but I don't think so.'

'Hmm. You are probably right,' Jacquie agreed. She was thinking of Mrs Whatmough. 'Sarah Gregson, then?'

'Looks like it, no matter what her husband says. I don't know where this is going, Jacquie, to be honest. I'm just going to make sure those statements have been signed, then I'm off. You?'

'I'm off home as well,' she said. 'We have an O'Malley and a Gold for dinner, along with Mrs Troubridge. Rather a mixed bag.'

'Well, enjoy that, then,' Hall said. 'Will you find it difficult at all, facing Mrs O'Malley?'

'I knew he was a shit before, guv. Knowing a bit more won't make any difference. Something is bothering me, though.'

Henry Hall had thought so, but hadn't liked to say. But would it be the same thing that was bothering him?

'Do you remember what Bob Thorogood said after Hendricks' murder? What if it was one of us?'

'Bob! Yes.' He waited for the rest.

'What if it is? What if it's Sandra and she wasn't being blackmailed at all. What if she's our murderer?'

Hall extended an arm to the door. 'You saw the state she was in. Do you really think it could be her?'

Jacquie slumped. 'No. I really think it's Jeff O'Malley. But it can't be, unless he has some kind of clone.' She swung her bag over her shoulder and snapped off her desk light. 'I'm off home, now, guv. Night night.'

He patted her shoulder as she went past. 'Good night, Jacquie. See you tomorrow.'

'Same old, same old,' she said with a wry smile as she went out through the door. 'See if we can catch someone, perhaps.'

'Got to keep fresh for Bob Thorogood's leaving do tomorrow night,' Hall said.

Jacquie was taken aback. 'Are you coming?' she said.

'Wouldn't miss it for the world. How else will I know if he's really gone?' Hall said, switching off the light and following her onto the landing.

# CHAPTER SIXTEEN

Jacquie opened the door to a waft of tomatoes and garlic. Ah, Betty Spaghetti, the very meal she would have made had she been able to get home in time. She hoped they had saved her some. Maxwell had clearly been listening out for her key in the door and popped his head round the wall at the top of the stairs.

'Up you come, you busy Detective Inspector, you,' he said. 'We've saved you some.'

She climbed the stairs on leaden feet and gave him a kiss. 'Lovely,' she said. 'Umm . . . who's here?'

'Just us chickens,' he told her, the standard response meaning no nasty sparrowhawks or O'Malleys, except by marriage.

She let out a breath. 'Thank goodness for that. Today has had enough in it, thanks all the same.' She stuck her head round the dining room door. 'Hello, everyone. Nice to see you. Nolan, you have tomato on your 'jamas.' She forbore to mention that everyone had tomato on whatever they were wearing, Alana particularly looked as if she had been the victim of a particularly vicious stabbing. It seemed unfair to single out her son, but he was her only legitimate target. 'See you in a minute. I'm just taking my coat off.' Everyone wiggled fingers or smiled round a mouthful of spaghetti. Nolan leapt down from his seat and on the rebound was up in her arms. She gave him a kiss and immediately joined the tomato club, by proxy.

Maxwell squeezed past her and disentangled his son. 'Come on, mate. She'll be back in a minute. She just needs to wash the day away.' He plonked the boy back in his seat and ushered his wife across the landing. 'Here you are,' he said, giving her a glass of something sparkling and ginny. 'I thought we could all be teetotal tonight, to help Alana. But it doesn't need to apply in here.'

'You're a lifesaver.' She took a huge swig. 'I wonder who Gordon is? I'd like to marry him and have his children. Look, you go back in and I'll be there in a minute. Dish mine up.'

He gave her a kiss on the nose. 'Unwind for a minute. You look stressed out. You can tell me all about it later.'

'Nice try. Shoo, now. I'll be there in a flash.'

He trotted off back to the dining room. Hmm, that had gone quite well. There would be info coming down the line later or his name was not Gottfried Clutterbuck.

A few minutes later and Jacquie was as tomatoey as the rest.

* * *

It quickly turned out, as the extended temporary Maxwell family sat down after dinner, that Mrs Troubridge was the Trivial Pursuit Player From Hell. No subterfuge was too sneaky, no cheat too outrageous for her and soon her full cheese was whizzing round the board to cries of dismay from the others. Alana secretly believed that the old broad had memorised the answers. Maxwell realised that she knew the History answers because she'd been there at the time. She was approaching the centre and the rest of them had their heads together to choose a really knockout category to keep her at bay for another round when the phone rang.

'Null and void,' cried Maxwell merrily as Jacquie went into the kitchen to answer it.

‘Rubbish, Mr Maxwell,’ Mrs Troubridge riposted, the scent of victory in her nostrils. ‘I’ve never heard that rule.’

‘On the other hand, Jessica,’ Hector offered, ‘I’ve never heard of the rule where you are allowed to look at the answers.’

‘It only applies to the over eighties,’ Mrs Troubridge told him, flicking him with the rules booklet.

Alana, lying back in Maxwell’s favourite chair weighed down by a fully extended Metternich, smiled at her friend. ‘Good one, Jessica,’ she murmured. She wasn’t feeling too well and her empty cheese showed that she wasn’t firing on any cylinders, because she was not in fact a stupid woman. Things she had put to one side for the last few decades were beginning to surface and they made her stomach churn.

Jacquie stuck her head around the door. ‘Darling,’ she said brightly. ‘Could you just come here for a second? Something I need to check with you.’

‘Certainly,’ Maxwell said, equally brightly. He turned in the doorway. ‘Null and void,’ he said. ‘More than one player has left the room.’

Mrs Troubridge’s twittering was diminished as he closed the door. ‘What’s up, duck?’ he asked Jacquie in his best Bugs Bunny. She was standing waiting for him, phone in hand.

‘It’s Henry,’ she said, waving the phone. ‘He says there has been a nine-nine-nine call to say that there is a big bloke in Columbine, shouting obscenities and throwing bricks at a house. He wants to know if we’re all right.’

‘O’Malley?’ Maxwell asked.

‘Presumably. There’s a car on its way.’ She lifted the phone to her ear and spoke into it. ‘Sorry, Henry. Just checking with Max.’ Covering the mouthpiece she spoke to her husband again. ‘Just pop up to our room, will you, and look along the street, see what’s going on? Thanks.’ As Maxwell left on his errand she spoke to Hall again. ‘No, guv. We can’t hear a thing and it certainly isn’t our house he’s throwing bricks at. Are you at home?’

The reply was pithy.

‘Oh, sorry. A hot bath is relaxing as long as you are in it long enough to get the benefit, I agree. I’ll ring you back. ’Bye.’

She put down the phone and went to wait for Maxwell at the foot of the stairs. He came down quietly, so as not to wake Nolan.

'There is some kind of kerfuffle along the road. I can't quite see because it's round the corner, but it looks to be outside eighteen, or maybe twenty.'

'That's O'Malley, then. He can't remember houses or anything, he can't even remember where he lives himself. I can't believe our roads are that different, but there you are. Some cop he must have been.'

'A case of *Car 54, Where Am I*?' Maxwell said, remembering the television of his youth.

'What's he doing?' Jacquie asked.

'I opened the window and listened out, but I couldn't hear much. What I did hear sounds very O'Malley. I know the word "mother" seemed to occur surprisingly often. He's not throwing anything now. He appeared to be widdling on the lawn.'

'Good luck to him in this weather. I'd lost track of time. I thought he wouldn't be out yet.' She looked thoughtful.

'You were expecting this?'

'Weren't you? He's come looking for Alana, I expect. He wants his stuff back. I thought Henry might try and keep him on the charges we—'

Maxwell smiled, the smile of the alligator on its final approach on the unwary swimmer. 'Charges? What charges?'

'Peter Maxwell, you are a shocker. There were a few things that cropped up and . . . well, I might tell you later, if you're good. Meanwhile, what are we going to do about O'Malley? He'll realise sooner or later it isn't our house.'

Through the landing window, they saw a blue light go past and knew that sooner had probably arrived.

'We'll have to tell Mrs Troubridge,' Maxwell said. 'It's only fair, really. She'll have to decide whether it is safe to keep Alana with her.'

'It isn't,' Jacquie said, shortly. 'She'll have to go to a safe house. Or home, for preference.'

'She's in a safe house,' Mrs Troubridge suddenly said, from behind her, making her jump.

'Mrs Troubridge—' Jacquie began.

'Jacquie. As I pointed out just a few minutes ago, I am over eighty years of age. Well over, if truth be told. And if I can't have a friend to stay at my age, I don't know when I can.'

Maxwell chipped in. 'Jeff O'Malley is a nasty piece of work, Mrs Troubridge,' he said. 'He's been throwing bricks at a house down the road.'

'Why on earth would he be doing something as silly as that, Mr Maxwell?' She looked perplexed.

'He thought it was our house, Mrs Troubridge.'

'Well, good heavens, Mr Maxwell. If he can't even find your house, I don't see what risk he is to anyone. The car is parked outside. Surely that would be clue enough for anyone.'

'I expect the taxi brought him in the other end,' Jacquie explained. To Mrs Troubridge there was only one end of Columbine and that was *this* end. Anthropophagi lived in at the even numbers lower down and heaven only knew what went on in the odd numbers. 'I really think you ought to reconsider, you know . . .'

'I have reconsidered,' the little woman told her, drawing herself up to her full height and looking not unlike one of the more feisty voles that Metternich sometimes encountered. 'I've been through a lot in my life, although you might not find it very exciting. The War, for example. The loss of poor dear Mr Troubridge and, of course, all the unpleasantness with my fall and the Incident. So I am not going to send Alana off to a refuge and certainly not back to America. She's staying here with me. We're going to a meeting of Alcoholics Anonymous on Wednesday evening. It's all arranged. I have a taxi booked and everything.'

It was typical of Mrs Troubridge to lump a murder attempt on her and an injudicious act of Metternich's involving giblets and count those two imposters just the same. She was like a lioness, not a vole, Maxwell decided and shocked them both by suddenly planting a kiss on her wrinkled papery cheek.

'It's a deal, then, Mrs Troubridge,' he said, as she leapt backwards, twittering. 'But we'll have to rig up some kind of alarm system. I'll speak to the Design Technology Department tomorrow. Old Ken keeps telling me he was thrown out of NASA for being too darn clever. I'll put him to the test.'

'I don't want wires everywhere, Mr Maxwell,' she said. 'I won't have wires everywhere.'

'It's the deal,' Jacquie told her. 'Wires, or no Alana.'

Mrs Troubridge looked into her eyes and saw she was not moving on this. With a single nod of the head, she trotted back to the sitting room, to check on her single chick.

'Oh, rats! I forgot.' Jacquie exclaimed. 'I must ring Henry.'

'I'll come along,' Maxwell smiled.

'If you like,' she said, poking him in the ribs. 'But you'll learn nothing, I can guarantee it.'

* * *

The Maxwell family were hospitable people and were therefore often at the mercy of guests who didn't know when to go home. This evening was not one of those when the Head of Sixth Form was forced to appear in his pyjamas yawning and carrying a mug of cocoa to convince people it was time to go. By quarter to ten Mrs Troubridge and Alana were back next door and Hector had withdrawn to the guest room, having rinsed out his smalls and put them on the radiator. He was going back to the Mosses' house the next day to retrieve his clothes and books and then the planning would have to begin.

Henry Hall's news had been disquieting. When the squad car had got to Columbine, they had found some outraged householders, some broken windows, a partially uprooted brick driveway but positively no Jeff O'Malley. He had legged it, according to a watching neighbour, as soon as the first flicker of blue light had appeared at the other end of the road. And, big though he was, and although he was not exactly the youngest vandal they had ever seen heaving bricks at a house, he certainly had a remarkable turn of speed. He had clearly worked out in the past and the muscle had not entirely turned to flab.

Jacquie had gently shared the knowledge with Alana and the woman had been almost preternaturally calm. She seemed to look upon Jeff O'Malley as if death by his hands was probably in her stars. She was beyond afraid of him; she was all scared out. Mrs Troubridge, copied in on the information, was as adamant as ever that she could withstand any attempt on her castle. She had so many bolts and bars on every door and window these days that even she was sometimes defeated by them and the locksmith had her address set to 'favourites' on the satnav of all his vans. Hector Gold was merely unsurprised.

Maxwell and Jacquie sat in peace at last in the sitting room, on the sofa as he absent-mindedly kneaded her feet.

'Hard day, Mrs M?' he asked her.

'I've known harder, but let me think. Disembowelled body this morning. Discovery that Hector has hidden depths, Jeff is a money- and power-crazed psychopath, that one of the Constables in my team has been, nominally at least, prostituting herself—'

Maxwell dropped her foot and sat up sharply. 'I beg your pardon?'

'I will tell you that bit of info, but in a minute. I'm whingeing, if you don't mind.'

'It all happens at Leighford Nick, I must say,' Maxwell said, picking up her foot again. 'Leighford High is very boring by comparison.'

'Only this term,' she reminded him. 'It's not usually so quiet. That's the wrong foot, by the way. You've already done that one. I'll be walking funny unless you do the right one.'

'Sorry.' He changed feet. 'So, prostitution, yes. What else?'

'There doesn't need to be much else does there, not really? But, to round the evening off, the psychopath already mentioned has been heaving bricks at one of our neighbours' houses. Thank goodness he has absolutely no sense of direction. And I suppose that's about it.'

'How did you get on with ringing the States?' Maxwell asked, faux innocence dripping from every pore.

'Nicely, thank you. Magnum PI was very helpful.'

'His name was actually Magnum?' Maxwell was amused.

'No.' She flicked him with her spare foot. 'He just sounds like Magnum. Rather laconic. Handsome.' She had gone off into some kind of dream.

'He *sounds* handsome? That's clever. Do I sound handsome?' He fluttered his eyelashes in what he thought might be a winning manner.

'No — now there you are, you see,' she told him. 'You sound like a curmudgeonly old git, which is what you are. So, as he sounds handsome, then I am assuming that that is what he is, too.'

'Well, that told me,' he said, drawing himself up in mock dudgeon. 'What did he say, handsomely?'

'I haven't had a reply to my email yet, but basically, Jeff O'Malley was kicked out of the police, as I suspected, and was and is into anything dodgy that's going. He — Harry Schmidt, his name is — thinks that that is why O'Malley was so keen to come to England with Hector and Camille. The condo would have been big enough for Paul and the family . . . What's that face for?'

'Condo?'

'Well, I was staying in character. What are you humming?'

Maxwell had found over the years that direct questioning was no good. Sidling up was much more productive. 'Bit of Simon and Garfunkel. Before your time, doubtless. *El Condo Pasa*. My Spanish is rather rusty, but I believe it means an old block of flats.'

She gave him a look and continued. 'He said the raid on Paul and Manda was just something they do from time to time on principle because it is likely that O'Malley has done something, even if they don't yet know what it is.'

'Is that allowed?' Maxwell felt sure that barging into people's homes with guns must have some kind of law against it, even Over There, as he continued to think of America.

'I don't think O'Malley complains. The boat won't need too much rocking to tip him out completely.'

'So, if he was thrown out, what about his pension?'

'Doesn't have one. Camille's nail bar does fairly well, and Harry thinks that she gives her father some of the proceeds. I don't know whether it is normal for a nail bar to do so well. I don't even know what they do or how much they charge.'

'I don't look after you properly,' Maxwell crooned, ironically. 'You should be nail-barring on a regular basis, heart.'

'Right back atchya,' she said. 'But the annoying part is that Harry—'

'Magnum.'

'. . . Schmidt has no reason to suppose that O'Malley would be our murderer. He's violent, yes, but only when in a temper and can be quite charming when he wants to be. That's how he gets things done in the first place. Then he gets rough later.' Jacquie sighed. 'He really is a nasty piece of work, but he didn't do any of the murders, I'm afraid.'

'It was clutching at straws, surely?' Maxwell asked. 'He'd hardly been here five minutes before Matthew Hendricks was killed. I can't help thinking that was something to do with . . . oh, I don't know. Drugs? Money?'

'Jeff O'Malley to a tee,' she said.

'Yes, but . . . not so soon, is all I mean. I agree he could look good for Sarah Gregson.'

She shrugged. 'Why, though? Why kill her and not take the money?'

'Anger. Then he thought if he took the money, it would point the finger.'

'Possible. But what about Ja—'

'Jacob Shears. Solicitor, divorced, no children, forty-five, found this morning by his secretary Ms Tia Preece in his office off the High Street, Leighford. It's all over the local news. Neighbour Mr Michael Melling told our reporter that Mr Shears was very quiet and kept himself to himself. They occasionally met on the stairs but that was all.' He dropped the newsreader tone. 'Why on the stairs?'

'Mr Melling's flat is above the solicitor's office. The office is a kind of sandwich in the middle of the shop and the flat.'

'Funny sort of arrangement.'

'Funnier than you would think. The houses kind of lean around there, so the top floor is over next door. Only the ones at the end match up. That's why he didn't hear anything.'

Maxwell thought for a moment. 'Is stabbing loud, as a rule?'

'Not the stabbing, no. The screaming, that can be quite loud, I'm told. There hadn't been a struggle by the looks of things, but there could easily have been screaming.'

'So he probably knew the person, do you think?'

'He was in the office on a Sunday, so we are assuming that it was a specific appointment. Remind me, why am I telling you this?' Jacquie looked at him with a severe expression.

Maxwell had secretly been wondering himself why she was being so forthcoming. Could it be because this was merely the tiniest layer of frost on the tip of the iceberg and in fact she was keeping most of it quiet after all. 'I can't imagine, but do go on.' He still had the prostitution to find out about. 'Could he have been crept up on?'

'Yes. But that still begs the question why was he there in the first place? With all the bad weather he might have missed the odd day and wanted to catch up, but honestly I don't think he was that busy.'

Maxwell decided to bite the bullet. 'You mentioned prostitution.'

'Did I?' She tried to look innocent.

'Definitely. Prostituting herself, you said, someone in your team.'

'Oh, probably I meant that silly girl who is moonlighting at Domino's Pizza. Silly way to behave.'

'Hmm. You seem to be blushing.'

'It's the gin. Anyway, you'll get no more out of me. We're done here.'

'My word. That sounded a bit American. Something you picked up from Harry, perhaps?'

'That's enough,' she said. 'I've had enough Americans to last me a lifetime. I'm off to bed.' Swinging her legs off the sofa, she went to the door. 'Cocoa, sir?' She wasn't wearing a duffle coat, but otherwise she was any Petty Officer in any war film you cared to name. It was her way of telling him that police secrets were told for tonight, the madness of being a Maxwell was back on the menu.

'Good man, Number One. Make that two sugars.' It was Jack Hawkins to a T.

After she had gone across to the kitchen, he sprawled for another minute, thinking. Everything told him this trio of deaths was connected. But try as he might, he couldn't join even a single dot.

* * *

Breakfast was breakfast at 38 Columbine, no matter what the day was likely to bring. Metternich was still convinced that he might like Coco Pops this time and so was in his normal position below Nolan's chair and in the way as much as possible. Jacquie was dressed in full Detective Inspector fig and eating a slice of toast standing up. Maxwell was buttering toast for general consumption and occasionally managing to eat a slice, but was at least sitting down, to give the Boy a good example. Hector Gold was the only unusual feature, sitting at the end of the table, bandbox fresh and tidy, as though his family had not just imploded and his father-in-law was, if only technically, on the run.

'Have you heard from Camille this morning?' Jacquie asked, for something to say.

'I rang her last night,' Hector answered. 'After the . . . excitement. I asked her to let me know when her father got back. I haven't heard. But that means nothing, to an O'Malley.'

Jacquie made a polite question mark with an eyebrow.

'The O'Malleys are secretive to an almost pathological degree,' he said. 'I know Jeff does the big bluff Californian thing, what you see is what you get, but in fact he's real deep. Camille thinks she knows him, but she doesn't. She never stops to wonder why her nail bar does so well, in a street of nail bars all the same.'

'And why does it?' said Maxwell, almost afraid to hear the answer.

'Because all the wives, girlfriends, their sisters, their cousins and their aunts of Jeff's customers all get their nails done and pay over the odds and tip real well. That's how they pay Jeff without it being dirty.'

Maxwell was impressed that the man could quote from Gilbert and Sullivan whilst talking about money laundering in the same sentence. Class!

'You know that for a fact?' Jacquie asked, swallowing a big bit of toast.

'How much do you pay for a set of acrylics over here?' He looked at their puzzled faces and then at Jacquie's nails. 'OK, stupid question. At home, I guess it averages at about sixty, possibly seventy-five dollars. Well, Camille charges a hundred seventy-five. When I asked her how she got so much, she said it was because she was simply the best. I think just simple describes her. Jeff set the prices. Some of these women come in for maintenance once a day and pay for a full set.'

'Aren't the staff suspicious?' Maxwell asked.

'Like I say, these ladies are heavy tippers.' He glanced up at the clock. 'Had we better be going?' he asked. 'Are we dropping Nolan off, or are you doing that, Jacquie?'

'I want to go with Dads and Hector,' Nolan said at once, jumping down and running round his mother.

Jacquie was not used to not being chauffeuse. 'That would be wonderful, Hector, if you don't mind. Nolan, go and get your reading book and your coat.' She turned to Hector. 'Do you mind being called Hector by Nolan?' she asked. 'He should be calling you Mr Gold.'

'Mr Gold's my dad,' the American said with a grin. 'I prefer Hec, but Hector's fine with me.'

‘As long as you’re sure. Max, don’t forget it’s Bob Thorogood’s leaving do tonight.’

Maxwell looked bright but ignorant, hoping for more information.

‘Tonight. After work. Bob Thorogood’s leaving do.’

‘Am I coming to it?’ he asked, plaintively. If there was one thing he hated more than his own colleagues’ leaving do’s, it was someone else’s colleagues’ leaving do’s.

‘You certainly are,’ she said. ‘If you think I’m spending an evening with a whole load of policemen while you are at home in the warm, you’ve got another think coming.’

‘I thought that was what they paid you for,’ seemed a little harsh in the circumstances so Maxwell held his counsel.

‘Can I watch Nolan for you?’ Hector asked.

‘Thanks,’ Maxwell said. ‘It’s Troubridge Tuesday, but he might be home before we are. How long is this bunfight likely to last, heart?’

‘Not long,’ she said. ‘In and out, I hope. I’ll pick you up from school if you can amuse yourself till about five. Thanks, Hector, if you don’t mind being here by about six, that would be great. Mrs Troubridge has a key. Now, you boys had better be off if you don’t want to be late. Pearls before swine, and all that.’

She lined them up to see them off and felt like Snow White sending the dwarves off to the mine — in diminishing order of size, Grumpy, Skinny and Cutie. They thundered down the stairs and she wondered how these mothers of a dozen kids managed it. Three was ample. She poured a second cup of coffee as a treat and flipped open her laptop, logging on to the secure remote server. Now, let’s see what Magnum had to say for himself.

* * *

Compared with the day before, Tuesday was a veritable breeze. Hector Gold managed to get through his lessons with no more profanity and of course had the complete attention of any class he taught, simply because they didn't want to miss a single golden four-letter word should it fall from his lips. But Hector's explosion of Monday morning seemed to have sufficed and so they listened — as they considered it — in vain, although had they but known it, they absorbed some excellent history.

Mad Max had another crooked finger from Pansy Donaldson as he tried to sneak past her office. She wanted to know if he had replied to Mr Moss's email or not. Obviously, the answer was 'not' as he hadn't got any further along the road to sorting it out and also because he really didn't care to embark on sending emails halfway round the world. Down the corridor was not always a guaranteed success. He managed to schmooze her into sending a generic reply to show he cared and that he would be in touch soon.

Nolan was not destined to have a good day. Sarah Gregson had been what passed for a librarian in Mrs Whatmough's establishment, and although everyone had been shocked to hear of her death, those children who were ripping through the book list were already missing her more than most. *Magnus Powermouse* having come to its hilarious conclusion, Nolan had gone to change it in the lunchtime and had come up against the implacable rock that was the Mighty Whatmough. He had heard a rumour that she had actually been *in his house* while he was asleep and this made him nervous. When Nolan was nervous he became rather smart-arsed. Mrs Whatmough didn't like smart-arses and this was the only thing, by and large, that she had in common with the rest of humanity. Nolan ended up with his first ever lunchtime detention and spent the afternoon planning how to kill Mrs Whatmough and yet escape detection; you didn't have parents like his for nothing. It was for this reason that he missed the secrets of long division, laying the foundation for what would become a lifelong hatred of maths.

Jacquie Carpenter-Maxwell was late for work. The email from Harry Schmidt had been long and complicated and she had become quite enravelled in its toils. Essentially, whatever they arrested Jeff O'Malley for, it would only be because he had it coming. Taking and offering bribes, graft, extortion, illegal betting, a tad of pimping when times were hard, money laundering — well, she knew about that — and a lot of other things with numbers instead of words which she had heard on telly but would have to look up to be sure about. About the only thing he didn't have what Harry called a 'rap sheet' for was murder. The final paragraph was perhaps the most interesting.

'This is off the record, Jacquie,' Harry Schmidt had written, 'because it's kind of a personal opinion and I've got no proof. I was only a rookie when I met Jeff O'Malley first, and he took me under his wing. He did that with the rookies, got them on his side so they wouldn't rat on him if they saw him doing a deal, things like that. I'd find a little stash of weed in my lunchbox, something Jeff saw as a favour. When I said I didn't do weed, he said no problem, what did I want? He didn't seem to get it that some people didn't want drugs. Anyway, one night we were out on patrol. He didn't have to come, he just liked being out with the rookies — better if they were girls, but he didn't mind. He said he liked being out on the streets, gave him an edge. So you never forgot where the bad guys were. We saw a guy we'd picked up the week before, pimp, violent, but he got off on a technicality.' Jacquie felt the hairs stand up on the back of her neck. 'Jeff got out of the car, told me to wait and he followed the guy, they weren't difficult to spot, the guy was wearing real bright colours, Jeff was bigger then than he is now, I reckon. I trailed them, kerb-crawling at a distance, and when the pimp took a left down an alley, Jeff went in after him. I can't tell you what happened, because I wasn't there, but I heard later the guy was in hospital for three weeks. I don't know what you can make of that, but I heard later that wasn't the first time he'd made sure someone didn't really get away. I guess he doesn't like to lose — so watch yourselves and Alana. He's a loose cannon, Jacquie. Best, Harry.'

When she had finished reading, she sat for a moment, thinking. Then, glancing up at the clock, she chugged back her cold coffee and slammed the laptop shut. So much for having more time this morning! And now she had to somehow make sense of this email and share it with Henry. Damn Jeff O'Malley.

Henry Hall was, as always, totally organised. He put the statements from the remaining two card school members on Jacquie's desk. She wasn't in yet, but if she was late it was always for a reason. He had a quick staff meeting and went to his office to read the post-mortem report and the witness statements on the Jacob Shears case. He must be getting old, he thought to himself. Some of these names sound as familiar as my own. Have I now met everyone in this town? Is Margaret right? Is it time to retire and move somewhere else and grow vegetable marrows, like Hercule Poirot?

But of all of the people who were having less than perfect days, the one whose day had gone most pear-shaped had to be Jeff O'Malley. He was cold. He was hungry. He was pretty much lost. But most of all, he was really, *really* angry.

## CHAPTER SEVENTEEN

Maxwell was doing some marking in his office waiting for Jacquie when he heard footsteps coming along the corridor. They were accompanied by an uneven trundling, as though a very heavy supermarket trolley with a wonky wheel was being dragged by someone with a gammy leg over cobbles. If it wasn't that, it simply had to be Mrs B, redoubtable cleaner and redistributor of dust for Leighford High, 38 Columbine and any institution not fast enough to say no when she applied for a job. Maxwell hunkered down in the chair and hoped that a cursory glance from the woman would make her assume the room to be empty. This would almost certainly make her miss it out; she only cleaned for an audience and an empty room was a cleaned room, as far as Mrs B was concerned. Opening the door moved the dust around, for heaven's sake, and that was ample. Maxwell held his breath.

The door opened and he could almost hear the eyes raking over the room. This must have been how the first mammals felt, lurking beneath a hollow log as Tyrannosaurus Rex stalked the land, snuffling and sniffing for the taste of warmer blood than his own. The door closed and he exhaled.

'Hello, Mr M,' a voice said, almost in his ear. He thought for a moment that his heart had stopped for good, but it sped up again after a small hiccup. 'Didn't see you there. It's bad for your back, you know, slouching down like that. Doing a bit of marking? That's nice. That Metternich brought in something 'orrible last week I had to clean up. He needs a talking to. That DVD of Nolan at Christmas, ain't it lovely? Mrs Troubridge ain't half proud.' Shortage of breath stopped her and gave Maxwell his entrée. He stood up, public schoolboy as he was at heart.

'Mrs B. Hello!' He limbered up for his serial replies to her monologue. This took concentration and it had been a long day. 'Didn't you? Is it? Yes, I am. I don't really think so. Did he? He certainly does. It certainly is. She is indeed and who can blame her?'

The woman beamed. The world was spinning correctly when she and Mr Maxwell communicated on this special level. No one else bothered like him. He was a gentleman, Mr Maxwell was, of the old school. He might be an old git, but he was her old git and she had missed him over the Christmas holidays when cleaning at 38 Columbine would have been not only pointless but impossible. Normal service had resumed the previous week, not that there was any way to tell, except the three crisp tenners had disappeared from the hall table and the kettle was warm when he got home.

'Innit cold?'

Maxwell waited. There had to be more.

Mrs B flicked a duster with a crack. 'Innit cold, Mr Maxwell? In the school?'

'Oh, sorry, Mrs B. I wasn't ready. Yes, it is cold. I'm sure it's barely legal. Temperatures in the workplace, duty of care, things of that nature.'

'Too right, Mr M. I had to put my coat on yesterday I was that cold. That's not right, indoors when you're working. What are you doing here still, in the cold?'

'I'm waiting for Jacquie. We're going to someone's leaving do.'

Mrs B was all ears. 'Somebody from here, is it? Going? Is it that Mrs Donaldson? Her what drinks? No better than she should be, that one.'

'No, Mrs B. It's someone Jacquie worked with. She should be here shortly. We won't be staying long.'

'Want to be back for little Nolan, I expect,' Mrs B told him. She didn't hold with children being babysat for, unless she was doing the babysitting. She and Mrs Troubridge waged a silent war on the care of Nolan.

'Well, yes, but Mr Gold is going to be there when he gets in from Mrs Troubridge. He goes there on a Tuesday, as you know.' In the whole exchange, Mrs B had not raised a duster and the vacuum cleaner was in the corridor where she considered it belonged. 'Have you met Mr Gold?'

Mrs B sniffed. Her xenophobia was more bred in the bone than Maxwell's and she was not one to forgive. Her mother had made dark remarks about the behaviour of Yanks Over Here in the war and her mother never lied, as everyone knew. Mrs B had been born in 1944 when her dear old dad had been fighting his way through Italy, so it wasn't fair that the Yanks had been over here, safe and sound, while he was laying his life on the line. Yanks! Her sniff said it all.

'He's a nice chap. You'd like him, I'm sure. He's staying with us for a bit.'

The sniff was more resounding this time. 'I understood he was married. That wife of his went in our Beyonce's nail bar last week and created something rotten because her acrylics weren't the right length. Our Beyonce told her, she only stocks the mediums, there's no call for the longs in Leighford. People don't want them, there's just no call.'

'How did Beyonce know it was Mrs Gold?' Maxwell knew that Americans were fairly rare in Leighford, but surely the Golds weren't unique.

'Made the appointment, didn't she? Said her name and where she was living. Mr Moss's wife, she has her eyebrows threaded at our Beyonce's and she'd told her all about it. She's very meticulous, Mrs Moss.'

Maxwell was wondering what eyebrow threading could possibly be and decided it sounded painful. He tried to move the subject on. 'There has been a bit of a problem at home,' he said, settling for the vague option. 'Mrs O'Malley is with Mrs Troubridge, Mr Gold is with us.'

Mrs B's eyes gleamed. She could hardly wait for her next session at Columbine, where she would wheedle details out of Mrs Troubridge, as she gave her a 'quick whizz', as she termed it, before cleaning next door.

Then, just as she had Maxwell on the ropes and about to tell all, they both heard Jacquie's heels tapping along the landing of the Mezzanine. She stuck her head round the door.

'Hello, Mrs B,' she said. 'I thought that was probably your Charles outside.' Catching Maxwell's puzzled expression, she clarified. 'Hoover,' she said. Mrs B drew breath to make some opening gambit that would get more detail about Hector Gold, but Jacquie was too quick for her. 'Must go,' she said with a smile. 'Leaving do. We're not staying long, so we'd better not be too late. Ready, sweetheart?' The last remark was to Maxwell, who was adding scarf, gloves and hat to the coat he had had on all the time.

'Can't wait,' he said and joined her in the doorway. 'See you later, Mrs B,' and he shut the door behind him.

Mrs B, baulked of her prey, flicked her duster at a film poster showing Michael Caine facing down a Zulu warrior. She loved Michael Caine. A lot of her courting had taken place in the cinema and she was a bit of a film buff as a result. She looked with misty eyes at the poster of Yul Brynner lurching through Westworld. He was lovely as well and she only had to hear the theme music of *The Magnificent Seven* to remember the first time she met the first Mr B, in the queue to see the film when it came out. She gave Yul a reminiscent wipe and rejoined Charles for a bit of a trundle down the landing.

* * *

The pub where Bob Thorogood had chosen to hold his farewell party was not what Maxwell was expecting. Somehow, the gastropub with its faux Italian (or should that be *fingere* Italian, he wondered, dredging his memory banks?) was more suited to young things having a glass of chilled cheap Chardonnay than a load of coppers nursing pints. And yet here they were, not exactly crowding into Gino's early on Tuesday evening. The owners — neither of them called Gino — had been happy to give hefty discounts in this usually very quiet couple of hours in the midweek doldrum of the worst month of the year. Jacquie and Maxwell shrugged their coats over the back of two chairs tucked out of the way behind a polystyrene quarter-size copy of Michelangelo's *David*, with pockmarks in his bum where bored drinkers had picked at it, and settled down to be politely convivial.

Bob Thorogood was already at the bar, with a few of his diehard oppos from Leighford Nick. He glared as Jacquie and Maxwell came in and said something derogatory to the men standing next to him. None laughed; Jacquie was a little disappointed by that. Obviously her promotion had made more differences than she had thought. She sent Maxwell to the bar for drinks and to buy one for Thorogood. He had never been known to refuse a freebie.

'Hello, Bob,' he said pleasantly, when they were standing side by side waiting for the *barista* to notice they were alive. 'Congratulations on the new job. What can I get you?'

Thorogood was between a rock and a hard place. He hated this bloke, older than him, without his charm and obvious charisma, and yet able to pull the best-looking woman in the station. Thorogood had once had a small success with a desperate civilian admin assistant in the stores cupboard which had convinced him of his attraction to women, and all the snubs before and since had not been enough to make him see that it had been a strictly one-off occurrence, brought on by overexposure to fumes from the photocopier. Now, here the old git was, offering him a drink. His hindbrain took over, the lizard we all carry within us.

'Thanks. I'll have a pint.' He paused, just for effect. 'With a whisky chaser, if that's OK with you?'

'Of course,' Maxwell said affably and nodded to the girl behind the bar who bent to her task. 'Can you also make that one orange juice and . . . I think I will join this gentleman in a whisky. But no pint with mine, thank you.' He turned to Thorogood again. 'So, change of direction, Bob. Have you started in the new office yet?'

'Yesterday,' the other man growled. 'I was filling a vacancy so DCI Hall kindly let me go.' He picked up his pint and raised it slightly in Maxwell's direction. Drinker's courtesy. 'Thanks. Yes . . .' He leant one elbow on the bar, his prepared story tumbling out, as it would throughout the evening, becoming less coherent with time. Maxwell was lucky to be getting it in more or less mint condition. '. . . Yes, Henry didn't want to lose me, of course, but there was, as I say, this vacancy, and they were pretty desperate. So I agreed to start straight away.'

'I should think Henry was very grateful,' Maxwell said, with no emphasis.

'Yes.' There was no emphasis in Thorogood's reply, either.

'You got this do arranged quickly,' Maxwell remarked, sipping his whisky.

'This is my local,' he said. 'And it doesn't do to linger. If you have your do too late everyone has forgotten who you are.'

'Very true. So,' Maxwell turned to survey the room, 'who's here? Are they all colleagues?'

Thorogood looked round the room. There were about fifteen people, divided into small knots of three, with the odd one standing alone looking awkward and nursing a glass. 'Except those two totties in the corner, yes,' he said. 'You probably know the ones from Leighford Nick by sight. That chap over there,' he gestured with his glass, by now only a quarter full, 'is one of the wardens from my New Department. Seems a nice chap, very ambitious. Should go far. I've got a supervision interview with him tomorrow, see how he's getting on.'

The man didn't look ambitious. He was rather weaselly to look at, with an unresolved spot on one temple. His glasses were mended with a piece of grubby Elastoplast but his coat, which he had opened but not removed, was an expensive one, all pockets and flaps with a designer lining. Perhaps it was a Christmas present. Probably from his mum, Maxwell decided.

'He doesn't look ambitious,' he remarked.

'You're right,' Thorogood agreed, putting his empty glass down, emphatically. Maxwell nodded to the *barista*, who provided a refill. 'Thanks,' continued the Traffic Supremo. 'No, you're right. He looks very ordinary, but he was in my office yesterday afternoon while I was still dusting off the spider plant. Had a lot to tell me about my predecessor. Very useful.' He tapped the side of his nose, meaningfully. It was probably the last time he would succeed in doing so that evening.

Maxwell realised he still had Jacquie's orange juice in his hand, warming up nicely. 'I must go,' he said to Thorogood. 'Better take the old ball and chain her drink, I suppose.'

The Party Boy watched him go. What a nice bloke, he thought to himself, through a haze of beer and whisky. We've all been wrong about him. His ex-oppos flowed back to surround him as Maxwell walked away but didn't stand as close as they had before. Thorogood had started to take on the smell of a dead man walking and that was a smell that could stink up your own career before you knew it.

In the next half an hour Gino's started to fill up and Bob Thorogood was a gratified host. Most people from Leighford Nick were there to make sure he was really gone; most people from Traffic, based at County Hall three doors down from the bar, were there to toady up to the new boss. Bosses didn't last long in Traffic. It was considered, by those who knew the term, to be a kind of Chiltern Hundreds of the division. The place they sent you while they thought about what they were *really* going to do with you, that wouldn't involve tribunals and huge payouts.

Maxwell and Jacquie sat in their David-shielded seat and Maxwell picked a few more polystyrene granules out of the statue's bum, just to show he had been there. When Henry Hall arrived in a blast of cold air, he scanned the room and joined them, bringing drinks with him. They watched him greet Bob Thorogood and buy him a drink and then he nodded to others in the room as he made his way to their table.

'I'm surprised to see you here, Henry,' Maxwell said. 'Not that I'm not delighted, of course.'

'Just need to see that the bugger has really gone,' Hall said, sipping his Virgin Mary, heavy on the Lea and Perrins. 'I can't believe it went so smoothly. Enid . . . what was her name, Jacquie? Not Blyton, surely?'

'Burton,' Jacquie supplied.

'Yes. Enid Burton was finally written off as retired on health grounds last week. She'd been off for nearly a year with stress, so not a moment too soon. We couldn't recruit while she was in post but as soon as we could — well, there was Bob and it seemed ideal.' His glasses flashed in the mock candlelight and Maxwell swore he saw a smile sleet past. 'Well, cheers.'

'Henry?' Jacquie asked. 'Why does that weaselly bloke keep staring at you like that? It looks as though he's coming over. Do you know him?'

Hall screwed round in his chair. 'Oh, no,' he said. 'That's Mark Chambers.' He looked at Maxwell and decided to continue anyway. 'You know, one of the card players. I interviewed him yesterday. Have you read his statement?'

'Glanced,' Jacquie said. 'Flicked, you know how it is.'

'Nothing in there of note,' Henry quickly concluded. 'He's a bit of a police groupie, that's all.' The man was now alongside.

'Hello, DCI Hall.' He looked expectantly at the Maxwells. 'May I join you?'

'Of course,' said Jacquie pleasantly. 'I am Detective Inspector Carpenter-Maxwell and this is my husband, Max. How are you?'

The man pulled out a chair and leant towards her. 'How do you mean, how am I?' he said, earnestly.

She was taken aback. She almost expected him to get out a notebook and jot down her reply. 'Well, nothing, really. I just thought you might be feeling a little shocked. After Sarah Gregson's death; she was a friend of yours, wasn't she?'

'Not a friend, really, no,' Mark Chambers said, pushing his glasses up his nose, right on cue. 'An acquaintance, I should say.' He smiled ingratiatingly at Hall.

The others looked at him. He had met this woman, admittedly in the company of others, twice a week for months. Only that previous Saturday, she had given him four hundred and fifty pounds, which she had won from him fair and square. She was now dead. And he was calling her an acquaintance. Jacquie and Maxwell, who knew Hall, could tell he was seething. But Chambers was not to know; as usual, there were no outward signs.

'It's a shame, of course,' he said, compounding his clichéd appearance with a hearty sniff, 'but she was rather an unhappy woman, I always thought. Flawed. Like Sandra Bolton . . .' He looked around the room. 'Is she here? Or is she suspended? I understand she—' Before he could carry on, Hall stood up, striking David a nasty denting blow with his elbow.

'I must just go and speak to Bob before I go,' the DCI said, brusquely. 'Margaret will be waiting with my supper. I'll see you tomorrow, Jacquie. Goodnight, Max. Love to Nolan.' And he was gone, elbowing through the now reasonably sized crowd.

Maxwell looked at Chambers with narrowed eyes. The man was not physically attractive, it was true, and he had the conversational style of a runaway rhinoceros. Perhaps some people were just born to be traffic wardens and their parents and teachers didn't bother to instil the social graces, knowing it would not be worthwhile. To fill the lengthening silence, he asked, 'Have you lived in Leighford long, Mr Chambers?'

'I don't actually live in Leighford,' Chambers said.

'Oh.' Jacquie was surprised. Most people who worked in Leighford lived there. It seemed pointless not to; it was a pleasant enough town, if a little touristy in the season. The shops were OK, the facilities normal for a south coast seaside town of its size. And she thought she remembered O'Malley saying that one of the men lived above a taxi firm. She was sure it was Chambers. 'Where do you live?'

'I may have given the wrong impression,' Chambers said, with a gap-toothed smile. 'I mean that I do live in Leighford, but I have a house out in one of the villages.' He saw their expressions and smiled more widely. 'A doer-upper, I think they call it Stateside. I don't live in it all the time. And of course, in this weather I haven't been able to get out there so much. It has no central heating at present, in this weather it is a bit of a no-go area.' He sipped his drink. 'Where do you live?'

'Out on the edge,' Maxwell said quickly. There was something about this man that made him not want to give his address. There was something of the stalker about him. He hadn't realised that traffic wardens were paid so well. Perhaps he was in the wrong job. 'Two houses, Mark,' he said. 'You are lucky. We've just got the one.'

Chambers laughed. 'Not two houses, as such,' he said. 'I live in a flat in Leighford, and the house is one my mother left me. She died last year, God rest her soul. We were very close. Even with my extra jobs I'm not sure I could manage two houses. Dear me, no.'

'You live over a taxi firm, as I remember, don't you?' Jacquie said.

Chambers looked puzzled. 'No,' he said. 'A greengrocer's. Very quiet. Not too smelly either, unless the onions go off over a weekend. I was over a butcher's, once. That wasn't so nice. What made you think I lived over a taxi firm? That would be quite noisy, I should think.'

Jacquie shook her head and sipped her drink. 'I don't know who mentioned it,' she said.

The silence lengthened again.

'And then, there's the gambling,' Maxwell threw in.

'Are you a policeman?' Chambers asked, frostily.

'No. Not really,' Maxwell hedged.

'Not really?'

'Only by marriage. I'm a teacher. At Leighford High.'

'How do you know so much, then?' Chambers said, rather snappily. 'Shouldn't all this be confidential?' He looked at Jacquie as he spoke.

'I know Rosemary Whatmough,' he said, for reasons he couldn't fathom.

'Is Rosemary Whatmough a policeman?' Chambers was really on his guard now and on his dignity. Jacquie could smell trouble on the wind.

'She's a teacher too,' she said. 'She was Sarah Gregson's employer and she is our son's Headmistress. You know how people gossip.' She tried to lighten the mood and seemed to succeed.

Chambers relaxed and treated them to another smile. 'Ah, gossip. Yes, my mother never liked to gossip. But we did like a nice game of cards. Whist drives, that kind of thing. I could never get the hang of bridge, but Mother was a demon.'

'Racing demon.' Maxwell made a card game joke and it gave them all an opportunity to laugh nervously. 'But, seriously, the gambling. It must have taken a chunk out of your wages, I suppose.'

Chambers stopped laughing. 'It did, yes, but I never gambled with more than I could lose. And I didn't lose every time, not like the others. They were very unwise. They should have stopped coming if they couldn't afford to lose. That's what I told them, but they thought they could win it back. Gamblers always do. I'm not a gambler, you see. I just like to play cards.'

The silence descended again and Jacquie got up. 'I must just go and have a word with Bob, if you don't mind,' she said to Maxwell, but it was Chambers who answered.

'No, off you go. I'll stay and chat to Max.'

Maxwell gave a rictus smile to Jacquie, who went off towards the bar.

'What a lovely woman,' Chambers said. 'You're a lucky man. I have never married. Never found the right girl. Ha ha.'

The right women could be very fleet of foot, it was true. Maxwell took refuge in his glass while he thought of something to say. 'So, you know Jeff O'Malley?' he asked. 'I know his son-in-law. We work together.'

'I wouldn't say I know him,' Chambers said. 'I just met him a few weeks ago at the game and I can't say we hit it off. He seemed rather a bully. He came back to my flat once, for a drink. A policeman, I gather, back home.'

'Yes, indeed,' Maxwell agreed.

'He told me all about his family. His daughter sounds a wonderful woman. Apparently, she has been in films. Living in LA I suppose you would get that kind of opportunity. I've never had any ambition in that direction. We were never a family to put ourselves forward like that, although I gather my grandfather used to do a humorous monologue sometimes at Christmas. That would be before I was born, of course.'

There was something very soporific about the man's voice and Maxwell could suddenly see with awful clarity how easy it must be to be hypnotised. Perhaps Chambers lulled unguarded motorists into a stupor before he slapped a ticket on their windscreens. He could sense the room receding and Chambers' eyes seemed to glow behind his glasses. He shook himself awake and found that they had moved on from granddad amusing the family to how the present scion of the otherwise defunct Chambers family had had a few disappointments in his career, but was having an important interview with his new boss in the morning, of which he had high expectations.

'I'm sure you'll do splendidly,' Maxwell said. 'And of course, if you get a promotion, you can give up your extra sources of income and concentrate more on your doer-upper.'

Chambers was again on his dignity. 'Who told you about my extra sources of income?' he snapped.

'Um . . . you did, I'm sure,' Maxwell said. He had only been making polite conversation. 'You said you had extra jobs.'

Chambers laughed unconvincingly. 'So I did,' he said. 'Sorry, I get a little defensive. For some reason, people don't like traffic wardens.'

'How silly,' Maxwell said, clicking his teeth. 'Just doing your job, after all. What are your extra jobs, if you don't mind my asking?'

'Traffic warden,' Chambers said, as if clarifying everything.

'No, your extra jobs.'

'Traffic warden,' he said again, as though explaining to a child. 'At weekends, I am a traffic warden, in private car parks. Cinemas. Out-of-town stores. That kind of thing.'

Maxwell was stuck for once for an answer. All of the stock ones — that must make a change', 'pleasant to be in the open air', 'that must be very interesting', 'at least there's no heavy lifting' — didn't seem to do the trick somehow.

'I don't think I'll give them up, though,' the man said, glasses gleaming with enthusiasm. 'I enjoy it. People should obey the rules and then they wouldn't get a ticket. All I'm doing is putting it right.'

Maxwell nodded and smiled. A vigilante traffic warden. Every town should have one.

# CHAPTER EIGHTEEN

Jacquie had been giving him covert glances for the last few minutes and had finally decided to take pity. She squeezed through the crowd and bent over to speak to Mark Chambers. 'I'm going to have to tear Max away, I'm afraid. Babysitter problems, you know how it is.' As she said that, she realised how stupid that sounded. Of course he didn't know how it was. But he nodded anyway and leant back, as if giving Maxwell permission to leave.

They waited until they were outside before either spoke.

'Is it me?' Maxwell asked.

'No, it isn't. He is a bit of a nutcase. But . . . you know how these people get. Lives alone. Has an unpleasant job. Lost his dear old mum.'

'I've lost my dear old mum, but I'm not strange.'

They walked on in silence for a few more steps.

'There should be an answer, there, if you don't mind.'

She laughed and punched him lightly on the arm. 'You're not strange, not really,' she said. 'I do wish I'd met your mum, though. What was she like?'

To answer, he pulled his scarf over his head like a headsquare and tied it tight under his chin. He tucked his sideburns under it and teased a few curls out at the front.

'Like that, more or less,' he said. 'The only bit of my dad I have that's obvious is that funny knee I get in wet weather and a tendency to drool when I'm asleep.' He rearranged himself quickly; he had drawn a few odd glances from late shoppers in the Asda car park.

'I'm sure I would have loved her,' Jacquie said.

'Well, she would have loved you back,' he said, kissing her nose. 'Where did that other chap work, the one in the card school?'

'That was sneaky,' Jacquie said. Maxwell could change tack in a conversation for England. 'Why do you want to know?'

He shrugged. He had forgotten that that was another thing he had inherited from his father: expressive shoulders. 'Just wondered. A bent cop, a silly cop, a teacher, a traffic warden and a . . . just wondered, that was all. So I can do the old joke in the future. Just wondered.'

'Well, you can wonder away, old-timer,' she said. 'As a matter of fact, before the advent of Jeff O'Malley and his ways, the card school was busier by far. A couple of Leighford teachers, in fact. Whatsisface, Science Department — you know him, of course.'

'Whatever would I know a scientist for? But as a matter of fact, he is one of my form tutors in the Sixth Form. Roger Philips. He doesn't strike me as a high roller.'

'Well, he isn't. That's why he dropped out when O'Malley blew into town. Penny a point to five hundred a night was a bit much for him, I think. Don't let him know I told you, for heaven's sake.'

Maxwell smiled. 'Don't worry about it. I don't think he has understood a word I've spoken in ten years. It was when they stopped wearing their white coats that the rot set in. So, what about the others? What did they do?'

She knew she would have no peace until she told him. 'Two housewives; the landlord of the pub, from time to time; another policeman, who will no doubt have had his collar well and truly felt by Henry by now; a fitness instructor; a landscape gardener and a funeral director. Pick the bones out of that, Mr Clever.'

For a moment he toyed with inviting them all, Hercule Poirot-style, to a Denouement Meeting, the sort that could never actually happen because nobody would turn up. Didn't Agatha Christie know some strange people?

Jacquie was rummaging in her pocket. 'Where the hell have I put my keys? Did I give them to you? These pockets aren't very deep.'

'Did you drop them in the pub?' he asked, patting his clothes instinctively.

'Oh, no, did I? Oh, rats. I'll go back.'

'No, heart. Look, you pick up something nibbly for supper so we can have it quick. We never have much Nole time on a Tuesday, what with cooking and all. I'll pop back and see if I can track them down.'

She was still looking hopefully at her feet. 'I'm really cross about that. Sorry, petal. Do you mind?'

'Not at all. I'll catch up with you in there. Mwah,' and he was off at a careful trot. He remembered not to toss the keys triumphantly in the air until he was out of sight.

He scurried along the road and dived into Gino's, almost colliding with Mark Chambers in the doorway. Good timing. 'Mark, I was hoping to bump into you. Jacquie was telling me about that other chap that played cards with you. Mrs Whatmough, Sarah's boss, you know, wanted to know who you all were. For the funeral. She's helping arrange it; she's a wonderful woman.'

'Is she? Sarah never said.'

'Well, she is. So,' Maxwell was hopping up and down with cold and shortage of time, 'can you tell me his name? And where he works as well, if you know.'

'Sandra Bolton knows him better than I do.'

'Is she here?' Maxwell looked around wildly.

'No. But your wife works with her. Why doesn't she ask her?'

'Sandra is off at the moment,' Maxwell extemporised. 'Stress.'

Mark Chambers looked at Maxwell for a couple of heartbeats. 'Tim Moreton,' he said. 'He works for the council, but I'm not sure in what actual capacity. Something to do with health, I think.'

'Excellent. I'm sure I can track him down,' Maxwell said. 'Not that I have ever looked on it, but apparently there is some kind of database, and as a council employee myself, I'm sure I can find him. Moreton, you say?'

'That's right. Tim.' The traffic warden was looking as though Maxwell had been parked in a loading bay for just a tad too long. 'Now, if you'll excuse me, I must be getting along.'

'Of course.' Maxwell let him by. 'And good luck for tomorrow.'

'Tomorrow? Oh, yes, thank you. You can only do your best.'

'How true. Goodnight, then.' And Maxwell hotfooted it back to Asda; with luck he would be in time to add a few illicit treats to the trolley, for later.

* * *

As they pushed open the door of 38 Columbine, the Maxwells held their combined breaths, wondering why there was no noise of thundering feet. Nolan was not a difficult kid, taken by and large, but after a Troubridge Tuesday he was usually pretty hyper, partly from the E-number-laden sweets she plied him with, partly from the muscular effort it took not to knock over her many knick-knacks. But all was quiet. Maxwell felt Jacquie stiffen at his side and her wariness was catching. They prowled up the stairs with every sense alert.

The kitchen and sitting room were empty and there was no sign that either Nolan or Hector Gold had been back in the house since that morning. Metternich's bowl was as empty as it had been when Jacquie had left the house; usually, there were a few random biscuity things lying in and around the bowl, where Nolan had been a little too generous filling it, but there was nothing, just a thread of morning tuna.

Staying together, glued by a nameless fear, they toured the house, and when they reached the attic with still no sign, it was Maxwell who spoke for them both. It was more of a croak than speech.

'O'Malley?'

'There must be an explanation,' Jacquie said.

'It's too cold out to have gone for a walk,' Maxwell said.

'The car's not there. Perhaps they went into town for pizza or chips. Perhaps they went to get a DVD from Blockbuster or something.'

Maxwell let out a rather unconvincing laugh. 'I bet they're next door.' He was more of an ointment man, whereas Jacquie always noticed the fly first.

'They would have heard us come in. And where's the car?' That missing car was what bothered her most. And where was the note? Where were the signs that they had come back here at all? *Where was her son?*

Recognising the rising note that was all mother, the Detective Inspector part of her having been beaten to the tape, he pulled at her sleeve. 'Come on. Let's go and check next door. I bet they're there.' She didn't move. 'Come on. Jacquie. You're overreacting.'

'You wouldn't say that if you knew what he'd done,' she flashed angrily. 'I had his full rap sheet this morning in an email. He's violent when he thinks he has been wronged and who has wronged him more than us? As far as he can see, we've taken his family and he's not having that. He's in a strange country, away from his dodgy friends, with no one to protect him. What better way to pay me back than — Sshhh!' She suddenly covered Maxwell's mouth, as though it had been him talking and not her. 'What was that?'

Down at street level, a door slammed and feet were thundering up the stairs. A distant voice was calling. 'Mums! Dads! Where are you?'

'Oh, God!' she breathed. 'Nolan!'

To prevent a Carry On moment at the head of the stairs, Maxwell let her go first. Not only did it mean no one fell down and broke a limb, but also he got a few precious seconds to dry his eyes on his sleeve.

'Up here, sweetie,' Jacquie called and met her son on the first landing. He leapt into her arms from a standing start and wrapped his legs around her and squeezed his face into her neck.

'Are you all right, darling?' she muttered into his hair. 'Where have you been?' She looked up and saw Hector Gold standing diffidently, still at the head of the stairs, as if too shy to come in further. In a film, he would have been wringing a cap in his hands and polishing the toecaps of his boots on the back of his trousers. 'Hector. What's going on?'

'Sorry, Jacquie. We didn't mean to scare you. It was Jeff. He was . . . Look, can we sort out Nolan first? He's had a fright. I'll tell you later.' He dropped his voice so it was hardly audible and mouthed, 'He doesn't know it all.'

Maxwell, standing behind Jacquie and stroking his son's curly head, nodded agreement. He leant in and kissed his son. 'Come on, mate. Let go of Mums for a minute and let's get you a bit cleaned up. You're a bit teary. Come on, poppet. Let's have you for a minute. Poor Mums, you're strangling her.'

With an extra squeeze for luck, the little boy allowed himself to be transferred to his father and he nestled there with his face hidden, but calmer now.

'It was Mr O'Malley,' he said. 'He was at Mrs Troubridge's when I got home.' His voice dropped even lower, so Maxwell could hardly hear it. 'He isn't a very nice man.'

Jacquie's inner Detective Inspector rose back up and pushed the mother to one side. 'Did he touch you?'

Hector put a hand on her arm. 'Don't put him through all that, Jacquie,' he counselled. 'There's no need for him to know all that stuff. Jeff didn't hurt him. He's a bastard, but he's not that kind of bastard. It was Alana he was after. And me, for causing all this.'

'You? Why you?' Maxwell thought he knew, but wanted to be sure.

'I brought them all here, so it's my fault, by Jeff's reckoning. But anyway, Nolan's just frightened, that's all. He hasn't been hurt or even touched. Don't worry, Jacquie. Just get him cleaned up and in to bed.' He swayed a little. 'Can I sit down? I don't feel too good,' and he slumped against the wall, one arm around his waist.

'Hec?' Jacquie said, holding him up. 'Are you all right? Are you hurt?'

'Just a little of the O'Malley medicine,' he said. 'He made me an offer I couldn't refuse. Alana or me. Even Jeff O'Malley baulked at a child and an old woman, and I baulked at seeing my mother-in-law beaten to a pulp. So I let him have a go at me. I'm just bruised. I'll be fine. Don't fuss; I just want to sit down for a spell.'

Jacquie was torn. She had a small child to soothe, she had an injured man to help, she had two women to question about a crime. Maxwell could recognise agony of indecision in anyone, but in his wife his senses were even more honed. He slid Nolan down to the floor and put his little hand in hers.

'Take Mums upstairs, mate,' he said, 'and let her put you to bed. Have a read and a cuddle and then send her back down when you're ready. But not a moment before you're ready. Is that a deal?'

Nolan nodded but put up his arms again to be carried. Babyhood was still nearer to the surface than any of them realised in normal circumstances and it was breaking through tonight.

Maxwell watched until the two were on the stairs and then he turned to Hector Gold. 'Mrs Troubridge and Alana? Are they all right?'

'Shocked. Mrs Troubridge was like a tiger. She came near to being hit, but O'Malley had me and it is better for his macho self-image to hit a man rather than a woman.'

'But . . . he hits Alana?' Maxwell was in no doubt that O'Malley was a wife beater. He could see it in Alana's eyes.

'Yes. But Alana is just a commodity. Tonight, though, he was apportioning blame, and so I got the lion's share. Nolan didn't see it, by the way. I got this when I helped Jeff to load the car.'

'What with?'

'Food, from Mrs Troubridge's. Bedding, lots of quilts and blankets. Torches; I never knew a woman with as many torches and batteries as Jessica.'

'She likes to be prepared,' agreed Maxwell. 'Founder member of the Girl Guides or League of German Maidens; I can't remember which.'

'He's not going back to the house, that's clear,' Gold said. 'He'll be holed up somewhere. Jeff's a master at disappearing.'

'But he doesn't know the area. He can't even find a particular house for certain. How will he know where to hide?'

'He'll find somewhere. Meanwhile, can I *please* sit down?'

'My dear chap,' Maxwell remembered his duties as host, 'come into the sitting room and we'll make you comfy. Do you want a drink? Painkiller? Or should we wait in case you need surgery or something.'

'This isn't an episode of *Diagnosis Murder*, Max,' Gold reminded him. 'It was just a few punches to the solar plexus. I'll live. I'm a lot tougher than I look.' He flopped down onto the sofa and lay back and closed his eyes. 'Which is probably just as well, you may well be thinking.' He shifted awkwardly and finally found a comfortable position.

Maxwell moved the chair so that he was in the man's eyeline. 'We'll have to ring the police, you know,' he said. 'Mrs Troubridge and Alana need protection, if nothing else.'

'No, please don't. It'll only rile him. And they're safe next door. It's like Fort Knox with all those bolts. They let him in last time because he took them by surprise. That won't happen again.'

'For heaven's sake, Hec! This isn't the Old West. He is a dangerous man on the loose with a bee in his bonnet. He could . . . I hesitate to use the word "pounce" but it fits the bill so well, so I will. He could pounce at any moment. On any one of us. Or a member of the public.' A sudden thought struck him. 'Is he armed?'

Hector Gold still had his eyes shut but Maxwell knew his ears were still working.

'Hec? Is he armed?'

'He left his guns back in LA. Stashed them somewhere; said he didn't want to leave them where the limeys would find them.'

'So he isn't armed? I want to hear you say it, Hector. I know you wouldn't lie to me.'

'Then I won't. Yes, he's armed. He's got a .44 Magnum from somewhere. And ammunition. He showed me it tonight. If you count having it rammed into your stomach with the safety catch off as being shown something.'

'A Magnum?' The word seemed to be haunting Maxwell. 'Who does he think he is? Dirty Harry?'

'I think he thinks he is the man who taught Harry to be dirty, Max. I'm not sure Leighford Police are ready for Jeff O'Malley. Can I just rest my eyes a minute? When Jacquie comes down, we'll talk some more.'

He suited the action to the words and relaxed so suddenly Maxwell was afraid he had collapsed. He had forgotten most of his first aiding. Was it only concussion that made you sleepy? Did he have some kind of internal bleeding that had led to collapse? He watched the American's chest rise and fall, evenly. He looked for swelling around his middle, but he was as skinny as ever. He watched the pulse beat in his neck and matched it to the sound of the blood in his own ears. If anything, Hector Gold was in better shape. He tiptoed from the room and made his way to the stairs to the bedrooms. Halfway up, he met Jacquie coming down. It was bad luck to pass on the stairs, so he backed downwards and they crept along the landing and sat in the kitchen.

At first they spoke in hushed voices, which returned to normal and more very quickly when Maxwell told her about the gun.

'He's got a *what*?'

'A .44 Magnum. He didn't bring it in with him; I don't think he thinks much of us as a nation, but he has at least enough respect to not try to get a damn great gun through customs. He has got it somewhere since.'

'Do we know when?' Jacquie was assembling facts ready for the inevitable phone call to the station.

'I didn't ask. Hector is being cagey. I don't think it is because blood is thicker than water. I think it's because he feels guilty for bringing him here.'

'I should let Harry Schmidt know.'

'Why ever does he need to know? He's thousands of miles away and up to his doodads in his own troubles, I should imagine.'

'I should let him know, nonetheless. What if he goes back?'

'Can't you do the thing they talk about on the news?' he asked. 'You know, put a watch on ports and airports. All points bulletins, that sort of stuff.'

'I'm not sure how good they are, if I'm honest. I'll get a call out for Paul's car. Do you know the number?'

Maxwell sat back. Sometimes he wondered if she knew him at all. 'I know it's blue. I know it's high up. I know it has that ding in the back where Paul reversed into Pansy Donaldson that time.'

'Reversed into her car, you mean, I hope.'

'No, just into Pansy. You can almost see her shape in the rear panel. Quite a work of art in a neo-Impressionist Dada sort of way. She was fine. It would take more than a car to dent Pansy. But in my mind's eye I can't see a number. Sorry.'

'School would have it?'

'Yes, somewhere I suppose. Or Hector might know it. He's asleep but I'm sure we could wake him.'

Jacquie stood and was halfway to the door. 'Should we let him sleep? Is he unconscious?'

'Sit down,' he told her. 'He seems just asleep to me. Breathing normally. Pulse normal. We'll let him have a nap and then wake him up.' He looked at her, standing there on high alert. 'Look, Woman Policeman. Make your phone call. Speak to Magnum PI. Let's get an APB out on this sucker, or whatever the appropriate expression might be.'

She was in a quandary. She should get everything going. But that would mean going in, giving statements. Having a house full of police and, worst of all, having Nolan rousted out of bed and being questioned. She couldn't have that. Definitely not. She sat down and drummed her fingers on the table.

'Suggestion?' Maxwell said, softly.

'That would be nice,' she murmured and reached for his hand.

'Ring Henry. At home. Let him make the decisions. Tell him there is no way on this earth that you are leaving this house tonight. If police come, you won't let them in. You have let down the portcullis and drawn up the drawbridge. The moat is full of piranhas and you'll see him in the morning. How does that sound?'

'I'm a Detective Inspector,' she pointed out.

'Sorry. How does that sound, Detective Inspector?'

She smiled at him. 'It sounds good,' she said, and reached for the phone.

* * *

Henry Hall had put things in place. Jeff O'Malley was now a wanted man. A watch was being kept on the Mosses' poor battered house. Camille could be seen pottering about from room to room but there was no sign of her father and she didn't seem to be interacting with anyone inside. The watchers weren't to know that she wouldn't have interacted if the Band of the Blues and Royals had been sharing her accommodation, but the bottom line was that Jeff O'Malley wasn't there.

A watch was also being kept on Mrs Troubridge's house. A detective was stationed in the front bedroom of a very excited neighbour across the way. He was armed, as far as the neighbour knew, with a walkie-talkie and a pair of high-powered binoculars. The high-powered rifle was still in its bag and hadn't been assembled yet. Time enough to do that when the understandably nosy neighbour was tucked up in bed.

All squad cars had a description of the Mosses' people carrier and a grumpy but secretly excited Pansy Donaldson had been roused at home to see if she knew the registration. She certainly did, she had replied with asperity, as for some time a part of it had been printed in reverse on the top of her leg. So, to cut a long story short, the net was closing in on Jeff O'Malley and it was getting tighter by the minute. He was described as armed and dangerous, wanted in connection with three, repeat three, murders and also some GBH. He was not to be approached if spotted. This was exciting. More LA than Leighford, that was for sure. Something for the permanent record, apprehending a felon of this magnitude. Eyes were peeled and yet still, as the night wore on, there was no sign.

* * *

When all the eyes in 38 Columbine were closed, Maxwell's flew open. He crept to the bedroom door and snuck along the landing to the foot of the attic stairs. The third one up was a bit of a squeaker, so he avoided it carefully and soon was clicking on the overhead light and nestling his modelling ambience forage cap on his wiry hair.

Metternich yawned and stretched on his linen basket. Never one for the great outdoors, when it was cold he was a strictly indoor animal, just nipping out for pees, poos and predation. All three had been dealt with earlier, so he was in the mood to talk.

'Have you been keeping up with this case at all, Count? It has been a bit complicated and I know you are quite fond of Hector in your own way, but you'll have to put that to one side. The finger is definitely pointing at an American so far, but it is pointing so much at Jeff O'Malley, I can hardly believe it could be him.'

Metternich chirruped as he chewed on a particularly recalcitrant tangle in his belly fur.

'Exactly. We don't believe in coincidence do we, you, me and Henry Hall, but we don't believe in big neon signs over people's heads saying "I'm the guy" either. So, we need to look further afield. If it's an American, it can't be O'Malley, because he was in the station when the third murder was committed. But why, I hear you ask, are the three murders being tied together?'

The cat stopped chomping for a minute and looked silently at his human, an eyebrow raised in question. The question was 'are there any cat treats in that drawer?' but as usual, the silly old fool didn't seem to grasp the point.

'The clue of the American chocolate bar is quite unusual, you must admit, and it is strange that in a short space of time following the arrival of a violent ex-cop from California there are three vicious murders, and a lot of distress for ordinary people, if you count Mrs Whatmough as ordinary, as a blackmailer runs riot through the town. There is an element of rough justice in this that is a bit theatrical as well; I think if O'Malley wanted to deal out justice it would be short if not very sweet. But even so, Count, even so, it seems to me that for a man who can't find his way to the front door, to have cut such a swathe is a bit of a hard picture to frame.'

Metternich sat up suddenly and began to wash over his ears, first one side, then the other. Still no treats, but a cat likes to be tidy.

'It may be more of a case, I think, of someone who has lived here for a long time, perpetrating small little bits of unpleasantness now and again, suddenly finding the perfect scapegoat to hide behind while he steps up his campaign. But I think that Jeff O'Malley is not the man to use as a scapegoat. I think this scapegoat might turn out to be the sort of animal who turns round and bites you in the arse. Or perhaps I should say in this context, "ass".' He looked at the animal who had owned him for so long. He was still looking pretty chipper, though in summer now his black bits tended to go a bit ginger. They never mentioned it, though, and the animal himself affected not to notice. He could still kill with the speed of a bullet and toss a fully grown adult field mouse over his haunches with one deft kick, so don't mess.

The big yellow eyes bore into Maxwell's, unblinking. Could the old buffer grasp nothing? They were supposed to understand every word you said, weren't they?

The Head of Sixth Form opened a drawer. 'I'd forgotten about these,' he said, opening a packet. 'Do you fancy a cat treat, Count?' and he flicked one onto the floor.

The cat jumped down and hoovered it up. Finally!

# CHAPTER NINETEEN

Wednesday morning dawned bright and clear and, for the first time in weeks, there was no frost. Much of the snow had disappeared now, it was suddenly clear, with just great grey banks at some major junctions, and the odd snowman which had been packed down hard now looked like a headless and truncated penguin, if it looked like anything at all.

Maxwell opened the door and sniffed the breeze. 'Do you know,' he remarked to the world in general, 'I do believe I will give White Surrey a bit of an outing today. I can always leave the poor old chap at school if it isn't safe this afternoon and hitch a lift with Hector.' He turned and called up the stairs. 'I'm cycling in, chaps. Will somebody throw me my cycle clips down?'

Someone upstairs was on the ball and the two pieces of quite sharp metal whizzed past his ear like a nunchuck. 'Thank you, whoever that was,' he called.

'Getcha next time,' Hector called back, to muffled giggles from Nolan.

'I'm off, then,' Maxwell said and wheeled White Surrey out from the garage and gave himself a moment to acclimatise. Then, he swung his leg over the saddle and pedalled away, filled with his usual mild amazement that it was still possible. He seemed to have got away with it fairly well. Timing was everything, of course, and he was careful to make his departure while Jacquie was checking her emails, to see if Handsome Harry Schmidt of the LAPD had replied to hers of Tuesday inst. In an unusual display of what in another man might be construed as jealousy, he had asked Hector if the Lieutenant was, indeed, handsome. It took a while, as even Hector was not familiar with the correct pronunciation, but eventually he understood who Maxwell was talking about.

'Gee, Max,' he had said. 'I never thought about Harry that way, but yes, I guess he is handsome. Not that young, probably around forty, but very distinguished. All his own hair.' Maxwell had taken time off to preen his own luxuriant locks at that point and Hector had smiled. 'All his own *very stylish* hair, looks a lot like a toupee, but it's all his own. Tan, of course. Yes, I think the ladies like Harry Schmidt a lot. What's the matter? Jealous?'

'Of course not,' Maxwell said. 'Jacquie knows that beauty is more than skin deep.'

'He's a real nice guy as well.' Hector Gold knew how to twist a knife. Then, the clincher. 'He has a lovely family. Just the one wife, that's as rare as your own hair in LA. I think it's six children. Could be more. His wife pops one out mostly every two years or so. Yeah, lovely family, the Schmidts.'

So Maxwell rode away, with one less niggle on his horizon, but already planning the complex manoeuvres that a successful day would inevitably bring.

* * *

Jacquie was also mulling over a complex priority list as she turfed Nolan out at Mrs Whatmough's estimable academy and was so lost in thought she nearly ran the woman over as she suddenly stepped forward from behind a parked car. She wound down the window and leant across.

'Goodness, Mrs Whatmough. I nearly ran you over. Did you want to speak to me?'

To Jacquie's surprise, the woman pulled open the car door and climbed in. 'I just need a word, Mrs Maxwell,' she said. 'I must know how you are getting on with the case. Sarah, you know.'

'I'm afraid we're not any further forward, Mrs Whatmough, really. There was another murder on Monday as well, as you may have noticed in the news.'

'Is that connected?' she said. 'I must admit that I take little interest in crime as a rule, but I didn't see any similarities.'

'You're quite right,' Jacquie agreed. 'But we are looking at this statistically. Three murders since Christmas Day are a lot in Leighford and so we are looking for links, no matter how tenuous. We may be wrong. Please don't worry; we will soon have the killer, I'm sure.' She looked closely at the Headmistress. 'You look very pale, Rosemary. Are you feeling OK?'

With an effort, Rosemary Whatmough pulled herself together and opened the car door. 'Thank you, Mrs Maxwell. I am quite well, but . . . if you could let me know how you are getting on, I would be so grateful.'

'As soon as I know anything, I'll let you know.' Jacquie let the clutch out slightly and gave the accelerator the tiniest press. Rosemary Whatmough could take a hint and slid out of the car door with an elegance rare in a woman of her build. She stood on the pavement and waved Jacquie on her way as though nothing had happened.

* * *

Henry Hall was in Jacquie's office when she arrived, two cups of coffee already installed. Jacquie grabbed hers and took a mighty swig.

'My word, that was welcome,' she said. 'I've just been ambushed by Mrs Whatmough.'

'Has she confessed?' Hall said, with a hint of genuine hope in his voice.

'Sadly, no. But there is definitely more to this than meets the eye. Any news on O'Malley?'

'Nothing, I'm afraid. I'm sorry, Jacquie, but we will be keeping the watch on Mrs Troubridge's house until they get him and they are also staking out the Mosses' house. Oh, listen to me. Staking out. Watching, I mean. This Americana is beginning to affect me adversely.'

'Is the Americana the link?' Jacquie asked.

'Sometimes I think yes, then again, I think no. The problem is that if it is O'Malley, he came here and hit the ground running, with a list of people to blackmail, people who had done wrong — that is if we take the vigilante bit of his personality, and I'm not sure I believe in vigilantes, in fact. Who could have been feeding him the information? He had never met anyone from Leighford. He didn't know until a few weeks before that he would ever come to Leighford. I think he's *involved*. I think he probably knows who it is and he's keeping the facts to himself until he can use them to his own advantage. But I don't think he did it. And here's why.'

He stopped to take a mouthful of coffee. Henry Hall did not believe in coincidence. He did not believe in serendipity, karma, fate or anything else which came under his umbrella of weird and flaky. When he had suddenly realised in the middle of the night where he had heard a certain name before, he had not risen from his bed shouting 'eureka!' He had simply clicked on the small portable reading light he kept by the bed for the purpose, and in the margin of his newspaper, next to the almost completed crossword puzzle of the night before, he wrote one word, switched the light off and went back to sleep with a sigh. Now, he pushed a file, dirty along the spine and rather old, but also rather full, across the desk to her.

'Mind the spiders,' he said. 'It's come over from Records. No one has looked at it since the subject went to prison last.'

Jacquie took it from him and pulled it towards her. She looked at the name and her eyes widened. 'This man isn't in prison, guv,' she said. 'He's—'

Hall couldn't help himself. He had worked this one out and was going to take the credit, but only in front of

Jacquie. 'Yes. He's the neighbour, both above and below, of Jacob Shears, victim of this parish. Mr Michael Melling is a convicted sex offender, on the list for life. I knew I knew the name when I saw the statements.'

Jacquie was appalled. 'He seemed so . . . nice.'

'Many do,' Hall said, 'you know that. It's how most of them are so successful. I honestly think he is harmless these days. His record shows he did all the SOTP courses and the rest in prison and they work some of the time, I hope.'

Jacquie was thinking back. Thinking back to how Pete Spottiswood had had the man taped from the start. Thinking of what a kind man he seemed to be when Tia was so upset. 'Surely, though, guv, he's not the murderer?' she asked, confused.

'No, of course not.' Henry Hall was leaning back, his hands laced in their customary position. 'He is the victim.'

There was only one reaction and Jacquie provided it. She sat up, slopping her coffee and gaping. Then, she said, '*Victim?*'

'I've been giving this a lot of thought and I've even thought about Bob Thorogood's remark about it being one of us.' He glanced across at her. 'It isn't, by the way,' he reassured her. 'And it certainly isn't me, as some people in this nick have been suggesting.'

'I obviously don't keep up with the gossip, guv,' Jacquie said, feeling her rank press on her back.

'You'll get the knack of running with the hare and the hounds, but it's hard work, believe me. Anyway, I don't believe it is a policeman. But I do believe that what we have is a street cleaner, like Peter Sutcliffe. He — or she — thinks that they are the only ones who can clean up the society they live in. We're looking for someone who feels superior. Who thinks they know the lot. A teacher, perhaps. There are inevitably rather a lot of people who have Max in the frame.'

'There are always a lot of people who have Max in the frame,' she pointed out. 'There was a book with him as favourite for doing that domestic, Christmas before last, when that woman cut her husband's head off and then went for a walk with it in a pram.'

Hall looked at her and almost smiled. 'But no one really thinks he did it,' he pointed out. 'They just want to get him on something, for always being right and for having married you.'

She blushed. It suited her, did she but know it.

'Anyway, I think that our vigilante, whatever he is — milkman, brain surgeon, tinker, tailor, soldier, sailor — is picking up on old crimes and putting them right.'

'Sarah Gregson, though. What had she done?'

'She killed her mother.'

'*What*?' Today was certainly piling on the surprises.

'Well, no, she didn't, of course. But her mother was dying and in pain and she killed herself. And just before she did so, she asked Sarah to help her, and she refused. She was living with a lot of guilt. Her demons, her husband called it.'

'And Matthew Hendricks abused his children and his wife.'

'And Michael Melling was a sex offender.'

She sat back in her chair and blew out her cheeks. 'So, we could have loads more still to come. And the field is wide open. It's nothing to do with Sarah Gregson.'

'That's true. But I think that Jeff O'Malley has found who it is, or he is closer than we are, at the very least. If we can find him, we might be able to find the murderer that way.'

'From what I hear, he won't tell us anything he doesn't want to,' Jacquie reminded him.

'We could — we almost certainly will — deport him for what he's done already. We have a bargaining tool right there.'

'Perhaps. Are you putting a man on Melling's shop?'

Hall had considered this, but had decided that the killer was unlikely to return to the scene of the crime. He would probably consider that a solicitor had probably done something dodgy, if only his affair with his secretary, and would leave it at that. 'No. Michael Melling is safe, I think. We need to look at other people who we might have met already who would fit the bill. Who else likes to control?'

'Vicars?' Jacquie asked, clutching at straws.

'Possibly. But not Guy Mattley, if that's who you mean. He is a genuinely nice man. I know he's not the one.'

'He's not the guy.' Jacquie couldn't help it, but Henry Hall didn't watch American TV and had no idea what she was talking about.

'We haven't exhausted teachers,' he reminded her. 'Mrs Whatmough, Hector Gold, to name but two.'

'We haven't exhausted policemen either,' she riposted. 'Sandra Bolton, Bob Thorogood, since you mentioned him. Pete Spottiswood. Did you know he used to be a nurse?'

Hall looked suitably amazed.

'Nurses like to control. All those hospital corners and bedpans.'

This was starting to sound like a parlour game. 'What about doctors?' Hall asked. 'Landscape gardeners, chopping your trees down without asking, and then there's all that space to bury a body.'

'Cleaners,' said Jacquie. 'Tidying up all your stuff you want left out and having all the time in the world to go through your papers and find out all your secrets.'

Hall slumped. 'Let's face it, Jacquie. We could name sections of society from now until kingdom come and we'd never get it. Come on, let's do the morning meeting. Perhaps some of them won't have hangovers and will be thinking straight.'

'Oh, yes, guv,' Jacquie said. 'How did you enjoy last night? Are you convinced now that Bob Thorogood has actually gone?'

Hall looked mildly crestfallen. 'I have a horrible feeling that I've done him a favour. He seemed right at home amongst all those little Hitlers and I understand his office is a picture, spider plants and everything. I'm quite jealous.'

'No, you're not,' Jacquie said, giving him a little push towards the door. 'But it's nice if he's happy. He wasn't a bad copper, just a lazy one.'

'Right now, I'd rather have a lazy one than a renegade one with a .44 Magnum in his pocket. But let's join the others. Perhaps there'll be news some little old lady has caught him by knocking him out with her handbag.'

Jacquie leant down and peered at the sky.

'What are you looking at?' he asked her.

'Looking for pigs,' she said. 'This is their flight path, you know.'

Hall couldn't resist a look out of the window. The world of Maxwell was a strange one, but it was nice to visit, once in a while.

* * *

The main indigenous species of the world of Maxwell was busy that Wednesday lunchtime. He had left Helen Maitland to deal with all of the problems a Sixth Form was heir to and was pedalling off down the school drive, a damp cold wind in his face. He was going to visit somewhere he had hoped he would never have to go, the municipal sports centre and swimming pool, to meet Tim Moreton and hopefully find a murderer. A sports instructor sounded just the ticket for a spot of light disembowelling with no struggle, not to mention hurling a fully grown woman off a car park roof and squeezing the trigger of a .44 Magnum and hitting his target first time. Maxwell was hoping that the visit would not involve undressing. He hadn't brought any games kit, as he still tended to call anything you wore to exercise in, and he hadn't got a note from his mother. Never mind; he would cross that bridge when he came to it.

The sports centre was not too far from Leighford High and looked like a gulag. Apart from wide low windows along one side which gave swimmers a bleak view out at the ring road, it was grey concrete blocks under a flat roof. Anything more calculated to depress and least likely to make a person want to fling themselves about in a flurry of exercise was difficult to imagine. A handwritten sign, laminated but, because of the many drawing pin holes, no longer waterproof, told him in weeping letters that Reception was away to the right. This led him right round the building, past various grey doors going nowhere and some wheelie bins overflowing with old Christmas decorations, to a door about six feet to the left of the notice.

Pushing the door open, he was assailed by a wall of warm chlorine- and feet-scented air. He tried to breathe through his mouth as school-day horrors revisited him. He was worried even more now that he didn't have his kit. And none of his name tags were sewn in.

'Can I help you?'

Well, she seemed friendly enough. 'Is Mr Moreton in?'

She looked at a board to her right. It was divided into squares and in one of them Maxwell could see a scrawled 'TM' and a tick.

'Yes. He's in the building but he'll be at lunch at the moment. Can I ask why you want to see him?'

Maxwell thought quickly. Although the Mrs Whatmough subterfuge had not been a million per cent successful with Mark Chambers, he decided to try it again. He explained and the woman looked suitably doleful.

'He told us about that. Terrible. He said she was such a nice woman as well.'

'I understand she was. I didn't know her, but my son did.'

'Boyfriend?' she asked, grimacing understandingly.

'Reception class,' he told her. 'Could you call Mr Moreton, I wonder?'

'You can go through,' she said. 'He's in the canteen. It's open to the public. It's just through there.' She pointed to a double glass door in the opposite corner of the lobby.

After his experience of finding his way into the building, Maxwell was moderately surprised to find himself immediately in a large room smelling vaguely of tuna sandwiches, overlaid still with the smell of chlorine and old gym shoes. He had thought that Tim Moreton would be easy to spot but he had not taken into account that at the sports centre pretty much everyone would be there for the purposes of pec enlargement and glute firming — Maxwell sometimes watched the QVC shopping channel for amusement in the middle of the night if he was experiencing one of his rare dark midnights of the soul, so knew the jargon — and so the room was full of big men and frighteningly firm women eating mounds of green stuff, laced with seeds and various nutritional additives. He assumed the tuna sandwiches were consumed by the staff serving behind the counter.

There was nothing else for it. 'Mr Moreton?' he called. A big man in the corner looked up.

'Yes?'

He was big in a way that Jeff O'Malley had once been big, hard and firm without a wasted inch. The receding hairline and expression of general discontent took something away from the impression of discreet strength, but even so, he was a very powerful-looking bloke, and easily capable of any of the murders so far committed.

Maxwell crossed over to him. 'May I join you for a minute?' he asked.

Moreton assessed him briefly. Not a potential customer for any of his services, whether council sanctioned or not. 'I'm nearly done with my break,' he said, to cover himself should the guy be a Jehovah's Witness of unusual persistence.

'This won't take a minute,' Maxwell assured him, pulling out a chair and sitting down. 'I'm just here to get your address for Mrs Whatmough, Sarah Gregson's Headmistress, you know. She's arranging a small tribute to Sarah—'

'Let me stop you there,' Moreton said. 'I happen to know that Sarah's husband is arranging all that. Perhaps you ought to let this Mrs Whatmough know she will be doubling up. That could be embarrassing for her. And we wouldn't want that, would we?'

Was that the kind of remark a blackmailer would make? Was there a hidden agenda or was this a perfectly nice man who didn't want to see someone embarrassed? Maxwell found it hard to tell. 'My word, she doesn't know that, obviously. I'll certainly tell her. I expect she would like to thank you herself. Where did you say you lived?'

'I didn't. I don't need thanks, just glad to be able to help.' Moreton was starting to think that he had been right in the first place. This man *was* a Jehovah's Witness, with a brief to collect names and addresses. Had he read something about that, once, or was that the Seventh Day Adventists? He often got them mixed up and had once enraged a hapless door-knocker by accusing him of polygamy when all he was doing was delivering the *Watchtower*. He mopped up the last of his no-fat no-taste dressing with a piece of gluten-free bread and drank the last of his power drink in one mouthful. 'I must be getting back. Very nice to have met you, Mr . . .' Some hidden synapse reminded him that if you met someone who seemed like a stalker it was a good idea to try and identify them, although the name was likely to be false; stalkers were tricky and in his heyday Tim Moreton had had a few. Mainly deranged menopausal women who had taken his attentions for genuine love, but nevertheless, he was an expert by most people's standards.

'Maxwell,' Maxwell told him. At this stage, he had no reason to lie.

'Well, Mr *Maxwell*,' Moreton said with heavy-handed sarcasm, 'Thank you for coming. Give my thanks to Mrs . . . Whatmough, was it?'

Maxwell nodded.

'Mrs Whatmough, but I really do recommend she gets in touch with Sarah's husband. Reverend Mattley, All Souls. He'll give her all the details.' He stood up, stowing his plate and glass neatly on his tray. 'Nice to have met you, goodbye,' and he was off, with a springing, power-filled step, to the door.

Maxwell sat there for a moment, undecided. He was a judge of people, of all ages. No one could survive for five minutes, let alone for five centuries as he had, in the teaching profession without being a good judge of people. And

Maxwell was pretty sure that he had just spoken to a rather nice, if limited, totally honest man. Damn! He wasn't sure how he was going to get the details of the others — the funeral director, the landscape gardener and the rest — out of his reluctant wife. He would have to think of another way.

* * *

Another way didn't present itself. All evening there seemed to be something else to do. There was Nolan to get to bed, which for the first time was proving to be a struggle. The events of Troubridge Tuesday had had a profound effect and he tried every trick in the book, and some he appeared to have invented himself, to prevent bedtime arriving. Hector Gold took turns at reading to the child, taking glasses of water and then supervising the subsequent trips to the loo. The only thing that stood a chance of working was the ancient ploy of going to bed with him, something they hadn't had to do for years. Eventually, he was tucked up in the middle of the parental bed, looking very small and vulnerable, his curly hair damp from the bath.

'It's no good, Max,' Jacquie said, as they were finally sitting down in front of the fire. 'I can't keep this pace up. Work is mental and it seems to have come home with me. Nolan doesn't see enough of me, and then there's this latest—'

'Don't be daft, woman. Whisht and bejabers, as our various Celtic cousins would no doubt advise. If we are being precise, then it was me who brought this lot home with me. Hector and all that. In fact,' Maxwell continued on his search for six degrees of separation, 'it is all Paul Moss's fault. Or, let's say, his kids, who wanted to live in the land of the foot-long hot dog. I would go further — it is the fault of Margaret Thatcher and Ronald Reagan, who made us all think that the Special Relationship was really special.' He looked up to see if she was smiling yet. Almost there. 'Then there are the colonists in Boston all sitting round that bar and shouting "Cheers!" . . . Need I go on?'

'I know,' she said. 'I'd make a rubbish housewife. It's just that these murders . . . they are so grubby, somehow. They demean the victims and make them seem as guilty as the killer, somehow. I don't like it. Then there's this weather. Will it ever stop being cold?'

'It's been a long old winter, that's for sure. But, how do you mean, the victims are guilty?' He saw a revelation poke its nose out of its hole. Time to tease it out with a promise of a nice piece of tempting cheese.

She had closed her eyes but now she opened them. The man sitting opposite her was as mad as a cake, but perhaps the wisest fool in Christendom. He had taken a girl and made her into the woman she was today, not afraid to let her education show, not afraid to cry when she was sad and laugh like a drain when she wasn't; in fact, she often ended up laughing anyway. She would tell him just one thing. That couldn't hurt and knowing him he was halfway there already.

'We think we have a vigilante on the loose. Not O'Malley, someone else. That means that from a very small selection of possibles, we have the whole damn county to choose from.'

Maxwell tried to look amazed.

'You knew already, didn't you?' she said, deflated.

'Not knew, no. But if Matthew Hendricks is the first murder, then you have to consider it. I mean, whatever the cause of his behaviour, he was hardly Mr Goodbar, was he? I'm not sure of the other two, but is there such a thing as an innocent solicitor?'

OK, perhaps not just one thing. In for a penny, in for a pound. 'Sarah Gregson was battling with the fact that she had considered helping her mother to kill herself. She didn't, but it was her demon, her husband told Henry, and so she told everyone she met, practically. It was pretty much common knowledge among anyone she had ever known socially. She was doing talking therapy to anyone who would listen. Henry also thinks that the solicitor was not the target. He thinks the man who lived below, and also above, his office was the victim. He is a sex offender with a long history, now reformed, but who knows? So, there you are. You know what we know.'

Maxwell was stunned. Usually he had to tweak the knowledge out in fits and starts. 'Thank you for telling me,' he said, simply. 'I know now why this case is getting to you. The list of potential victims is . . . endless.'

'The murderer is a blackmailer as well, we think now. If he finds out something he can make money from, he does. If he thinks the person needs a . . . lesson . . . he gives it to them. Simple as that.'

Maxwell sat in silence. This was bigger than he thought. Bigger than Jeff O'Malley, at any rate.

There was a tap on the sitting room door and Hector Gold stuck his head round it. 'I've just checked that Jessica and Alana are back from their AA meeting OK,' he said and smiled. 'I think Alana is going to find Jessica a rather strict jailer, but it will all be fine in the end. Be prepared for leaflets is my advice. Anyway, I'd like to clear my head a bit, so I'm going for a walk. Don't wait up, I've got Jessica's spare key. Goodnight.' And with that he was gone.

'He's no trouble,' Maxwell remarked after they heard the front door slam. 'It's rather like having a hamster.'

'I even wonder if he can possibly be that nice,' Jacquie said. 'My confidence as a people watcher has taken a bit of a knock, after my mistake with the sex offender; I thought he was a thoroughly nice man. Pete Spottiswood knew, and I didn't. Pete Spottiswood wouldn't usually recognise a baddie if he was wearing a badge saying "I Did It".'

Maxwell slipped out of his chair and knelt beside his wife. He leant over and gave her a kiss. 'Look, go and have a bath. A nice, long, soaky one. It won't fix anything, but you'll feel better for it.' He shuffled back to let her get up. 'Go on. Off you go.'

She smiled at him. 'Do you know, I think I will. I'll go to bed, then. Have an early night.' She glanced at the clock. 'Earlyish.'

'I'll be up later. I'll probably watch a bit of telly and then call it a day myself. See you later.' He settled himself down with the remote. What he was looking for was something quite mindless, to wash over him and clear his head. So why was it, with about four million channels to watch, there was nothing on but *QI*?

# CHAPTER TWENTY

Starry, starry night. Robbie McKittrick yawned and tackled the next Sudoku. He was getting rather good at them and understood now why his sister had bought him the Monster Book of the same for Christmas. He saw the people carrier cruising along Columbine, headlights dipped, registration plate grey with the filthy spray from the treated roads and was alert at once.

McKittrick noted the time as the vehicle slowed to a halt down the road. Ten thirty-eight. A dark figure got out and he saw the lights flash as the electronic lock clicked. A big man, dressed for winter. He saw him half turn, wave and call something to somebody on McKittrick's side of the road before entering the garden gate of Number 28. Another false alarm and he got back to the Sudoku. This one was a bitch.

Peter Maxwell was thinking of calling it a night. Nolan was sound asleep in the middle of their bed and would have to be relocated before he and Jacquie hit the hay. It wasn't that they had strong views of children sharing a bed with parents, but the child was like a windmill to sleep with and it wouldn't be comfortable for anyone if he stayed. Jacquie was dozing in the scented steam of a well-deserved bath, trying to soak away the cares of the case gnawing away at her. He had just watched for the thousandth time at least the final shootout in *Shane* when gloved grinning Jack Palance goes down in the blaze of Alan Ladd's .44 and gun smoke drifts along the bar.

'Maybe one day the bastard won't beat him to the draw.' Maxwell spun away from the screen to face a .44 of his own. It wasn't a Peacemaker and it wasn't smouldering Alan Ladd in his buckskins standing there. It was a Magnum and the gunfighter was Jeff O'Malley.

The American put a finger to his lips. 'Where's my sonofabitch son-in-law?' he asked. Maxwell genuinely had no idea. Hector had gone out over an hour ago and hadn't come back yet.

'How did you get in here?' Maxwell asked.

'Back door, Max, just like a regular neighbour poppin' round to borrow a cup of sugar.'

'I don't appreciate having *that* pointed at me in my own house,' Maxwell told him.

'I don't appreciate being hunted by your goddamn police force for something I haven't done.'

Maxwell's brain was whirling. Feet from him, on the floor above, the dearest people in the world were wrapped up in their own little cosiness. This was 38 Columbine, a new-ish, average town house on the edge of a little seaside town that had managed to miss every exciting event in history. That was then. Now, it was a potential crime scene filled by a psychopath the size of an outside toilet and the man was holding in his hand the most powerful handgun in the world.

Maxwell knew his *Dirty Harry*. The thing held six bullets in the chamber, and close as he was to O'Malley, he didn't have a hope in hell of reaching him before the American pulled the trigger. A novice might miss because the gun had a kick like a mule, but O'Malley handled a .44 like Maxwell used to handle chalk. He was deadly at any range in the classroom, but 'deadly' was only a word and a figurative one at that. His only hope was to keep the lunatic talking until he could distract him. Jacquie wouldn't be down; she was turning in for the night once she was out of the bath. Nolan getting involved in the crossfire didn't bear thinking about. And where was that black and white tough guy when you needed him? Maxwell realised anew that when the going got tough, the tough got voling.

'Is that what you killed Jimmy Hendricks with?' he asked, edging slowly to the window.

'Me?' O'Malley growled in outrage. 'You stupid limey sonofabitch. I was a beat cop for more than fifteen years. I know a vigilante killing when I see one.'

'Vigilante?' Maxwell frowned.

'You people!' O'Malley snapped. 'You arrogant bastards. OK, I may not be the brightest apple in the barrel, but I recognised the signs. This Hendricks — wife beater, wasn't he? Went to work on his kids as well? What kind of a man does that?'

'You, for one,' Maxwell said, looking his man in the face. The muzzle of the gun jolted upwards and he heard the hammer click. 'I never laid a hand on Camille in my life,' he hissed, barely audible.

'What about Alana?'

'Well,' the gun lowered a little. 'Maybe a slap or two. There was nothing in it. This Hendricks was a fucking animal according to the locals. They were talking about it at the card school.'

'So you killed him?' Maxwell had his back against the window pane now. He knew there was a surveillance officer across the road, watching his house and Mrs Troubridge's. He'd be bound to see the odd position, perhaps even O'Malley and his gun. The houses opposite only had two storeys. The man with the binoculars was on a level with the Maxwell's sitting room window. Surely he would see a man pressed against the window?

'If I'd done it, I'd a shot the bastard's kneecaps out first. Make him suffer. No, that Sandra had it right, that female cop.'

'She did? In what way?'

'Said you pinko-liberals over here are so fucked up with red tape and political correctness you never convict anybody. Hendricks would be doing ten to twenty in Folsom back home.'

'Ten to twenty?' Maxwell echoed.

'Sure. It's the tariff for attempted murder. I'd get him on that, with a little help from the redneck DAs I know. You bastards bleat about his broken home and his syndromes and extenuating circumstance. Somebody wasn't happy with that and somebody killed him.'

'But not you.'

'I told you, no. Now, for the last time, where's Hector?'

'For the last time, Jeff,' Maxwell said slowly. 'I don't know. Why do you want him?'

'I got my reasons,' O'Malley said.

'I hope you have,' Maxwell said, 'because there's a police marksman across the road. He'll have your head in the cross wires by now.'

O'Malley looked beyond the Head of Sixth Form to sleeping Columbine, the houses half lit across the road. But there was one window in total darkness, the one in line with the Maxwells' living room. 'Shit!' He jammed the gun into the shoulder holster under his coat and dashed for the stairs. Maxwell spun to the window. Marksman, my arse. He couldn't see anyone at all.

He heard O'Malley clattering down the stairs and the furious scream of a black and white cat as the pair briefly collided near the door.

'Max?' Jacquie called from upstairs. 'Is anything wrong?'

'Popping out for a minute, sweets,' he called as though he was off to get a paper or top up his stash of Southern Comfort. Jacquie sat up in the bath, frowning. That didn't make sense.

At the door, Maxwell saw O'Malley lumbering down the road towards the Mosses' people carrier outside Number 28. White Surrey flashed briefly in his mind but even when both of them, man and bike, were in their prime they were no match for a two-litre engine driven by a madman. There was nothing else for it. He didn't want Jacquie putting her life on the line and whoever was supposed to be watching across the road had clearly gone to sleep. Without thinking he snatched Jacquie's car keys hanging by the hall stand and was out into the night.

Across the road, a startled Robbie McKittrick was gabbling into his mobile. 'Guv? McKittrick. Sorry to bother you so late but you said you wanted to know if we sighted O'Malley?'

'Where is he?' a tired Henry Hall wanted to know.

'Driving south along Columbine in a people carrier, silver, I think. Registration number's illegible. Maxwell's after him.'

'What?'

'Peter Maxwell, guv, he's chasing him.'

There was a long pause. 'On his bike?'

It was McKittrick's turn to pause. 'Ha, ha; like it, guv.'

'How is he chasing him?' Hall's voice was stern at the other end of the phone.

'In his car, sir,' McKittrick had a lot of time for Henry Hall, but this took the biscuit. What *was* he on? The line went dead.

And as it did so, Jacquie Carpenter-Maxwell, wrapped in a housecoat and head towel, reached her sitting room window. Below, she saw her car kangarooing down Columbine and she screamed.

* * *

Peter Maxwell had not driven a car for more years than he cared to remember. Not since that mad wet day that he had let his wife do the party run while he roared England on at Twickenham from the comfort of his settee. They had collided, his wife and child, with a police car in pursuance of a suspected felon, or so they had said in court, and Maxwell's world had turned upside down. He'd tried, in the days and weeks afterwards, to turn the ignition key, to grip the wheel and release the handbrake. He couldn't do it. Instead, his mind went numb and he found himself sitting there, tears trickling down his cheeks, a driven man who could not drive.

Something changed all that. Tonight. This one night. And that something was Jeff O'Malley, with a gun under his armpit and murder in his heart. Maxwell had no clue where he was going but he had to follow him, stay in sight of those taillights flashing red as he hurtled round corners. He ran a red light at the corner by the library. So did Maxwell and they were out across the Dam making for the sea.

One by one the patrol cars picked up the message. People carrier driven by Jeff O'Malley, murder suspect, armed and dangerous. Possibly pursued by Peter Maxwell, deranged and equally dangerous, in his own way. Proceed with caution.

Caution was the last thing on Henry Hall's mind as he roared through the night to 38 Columbine. Jacquie was waiting for him. There'd been no time to wake Alana and Mrs Troubridge and of Hector Gold there was still no sign. Robbie McKittrick found himself off surveillance and babysitting Nolan. His rifle was now unpacked and ready, just in case. And he wasn't playing Sudoku now.

Sharp left, swing right, taking the roundabout at a ludicrous speed, Maxwell was hanging onto the wheel as though his life depended on it. Somebody else's did. He saw the brake lights of the people carrier explode in a flash of scarlet and watched as O'Malley, breath snaking out in the night cold, hit the ground running and hammer on the nearest door. Maxwell hit the brakes too, killed the engine and the lights. Funny how it had all come back, the driving. Like falling off a bike, really.

He slipped out of the car and crouched beside it. A light came on beyond the frosted glass and a figure was outlined by the porch light. O'Malley's gun was in the man's face and he pushed him backwards. It was vital that Maxwell get there before that door closed — ringing the bell once it was wasn't likely to elicit much of a response and it wasn't the season for carolling or trick or treat. He didn't know he still had it in him and his lungs were bursting as his shoulder hit the glass. Anybody else caught in the back by a flying door would have been catapulted sideways, but this was Jeff O'Malley and he just recoiled, the gun still in his fist, but waving at both men in front of him.

'Mr Moreton.' Maxwell eased his suddenly painful shoulder. 'Hope you don't mind us calling in?'

O'Malley slammed the door shut and held the Magnum's barrel horizontally against Moreton's head, leading him by the shirt sleeve into his lounge. The television screen still flickered in one corner, the sound on mute.

'You alone?' O'Malley asked him.

'Yes,' Moreton said, eyes wide, wondering what to do.

Maxwell tried to read the situation. There were folderols of the female persuasion dumped on the settee and a rather nasty sepia wedding photo on the sideboard. O'Malley was ahead of him. 'Little woman not home?'

'Staying at her mother's.' Moreton was thinking on his feet. Janet Moreton was in fact snoring quietly in the second bedroom to the left at the top of the stairs.

'Just as well,' O'Malley said. 'She wouldn't like what's going to happen now. On your knees.'

'Jeff—' Maxwell tried to intercede.

'Shut up!' O'Malley barked and forced the fitness instructor to the ground. He clicked back the hammer and pointed the gun. 'Left knee first? Or right? I've been told it hurts more when the victim is in this position.' Something about the way he said it made it clear that his information was first hand and on the spot.

'Are you mad?' Moreton gasped. 'What's going on?'

'Why'd you do it?' O'Malley asked him. 'Hendricks, Gregson, Shears?'

'Who?' Moreton blinked. 'Do you mean Sarah Gregson? I just played cards with her, that's all.'

'OK,' O'Malley shrugged casually, but there was a murderous glint in his eye. 'I don't need the whys. I'll settle for a confession.'

'I didn't do it!' Moreton was shouting now, beyond trying to keep Janet out of all this. Perhaps she'd wake, realise what was going on, call the police from the upstairs phone.

O'Malley jerked the gun upwards, locking the cold muzzle under Moreton's left ear. 'I'm not a cruel man,' the American said, 'despite what some guys say about me.' He flashed a glance at Maxwell. 'So we'll dispense with the kneecaps. Better meet the guy upstairs with a clear conscience, fella.'

'For the last time,' Moreton was nearly incoherent by now, 'I didn't kill anyone.'

Maxwell stood, flexing his fists. He still faced the same problem. O'Malley's trigger finger was faster than any part of the Head of Sixth Form you cared to name. He wouldn't be able to cross the carpet in time.

'OK.' O'Malley relaxed his thumb, clicking the hammer back gently and he stood upright. 'So . . . what is it you limeys say? I know a man who did.' He holstered the gun and was gone.

'Call the police,' Maxwell barked at the quivering heap on the carpet and he clattered out into the night.

* * *

Hall and Jacquie knew these lonely streets in the early hours. So did the patrol cars circling the Dam, purring down St Martin's Street and beyond the Tesco site. There was no one on the streets now, no one on foot. It was too late for revellers staggering home from the Vine, too early for the most ardent dog walker. Only in the cars was there a hive of activity, the radios crackling. Hall was coordinating it all while Jacquie drove. He didn't want her to do it in the state she was in but he couldn't trust her with the coordinates either, for the same reason. At least with the mechanics of driving, she'd be able to focus on one thing at a time.

'Emergency call, guv,' she heard Hall's radio crackle. 'A Mr Timothy Moreton. Just been threatened with a gun. It's Jeff O'Malley and somebody claiming to be called Maxwell.'

'Oh God,' Jacquie said through gritted teeth.

'Any direction from Moreton's?' Hall asked.

'West along Barlichway Road. Two men in a people carrier. Licence number . . . we haven't got that, guv. Sorry.'

'We've got it. Don't worry. Put everyone on it, Phil. They're making for the town centre.'

There was a squawk as the police radio flicked to other channels. Hall looked at Jacquie, staring cold-faced, resolutely ahead. 'We must accept,' he said quietly, 'that we are looking at a hostage situation.'

Even at moments like these, DI Jacquie Carpenter-Maxwell could keep her sense of humour. Just. 'That'll be OK,' she said. 'Max won't hurt him.'

* * *

'Where are we going, exactly?' Maxwell asked. O'Malley had been crawling along this street for what seemed like hours.

'You invited yourself along,' O'Malley grunted. 'So shut the fuck up.'

'That's no way to talk to someone from a country that let you people join two world wars,' Maxwell smiled.

O'Malley glowered at him, then he laughed. 'You goddamn sonofabitch, Maxwell. You know, if things had been different, I coulda gotten to like you.'

'I'd like to say the same, Jeff,' Maxwell said, 'but you having a lethal weapon in your armpit rather put that out of the realms of possibility, didn't it?'

'I shoulda left you at Moreton's. Where is this goddamn apartment? It's over a cab rank, I know it is.'

'If it's the place I think it is, it's over a grocer's. And this is Juniper Street. The last grocer here went out of business in 1934, if my *A Brief History of Leighford* is anything to go by.'

O'Malley looked at him. 'You know who I'm looking for, dontcha?'

Maxwell nodded. 'If it wasn't Moreton . . .' he said.

'Right.' O'Malley hit the brakes. 'Then we got just one other place to go.' And with a scream of tyres, the Mosses' people carrier squealed off into the night.

* * *

'Juniper Street.' Hall repeated the radio's message to Jacquie, though she'd heard it plainly enough.

'That's where . . .' she suddenly realised.

'. . . we should have been looking all along. Phil?'

'Guv.'

'Get a couple of cars to 28, Juniper Street. Flat 2B. Mark Chambers. Traffic warden. And don't let the ticket machine fool you. This man is armed and dangerous. We're on our way. No one is to enter the premises until we arrive.'

* * *

'Jesus,' Maxwell whispered. 'I didn't know we paid our traffic wardens so well.'

He and O'Malley sat in the people carrier in front of a large detached house, dark with rhododendron bushes and willow. Only the drive gleamed pale in the half-moon.

'Of course,' he said, 'it could be that Mr Chambers' dear old mum was rather better heeled than he let on.' He glanced at O'Malley. 'Or the blackmail business is definitely taking off.'

'Blackmailer. Killer. This guy's into multitasking big time.'

'How did you know it was him?'

'I didn't,' O'Malley admitted, 'but it had to be somebody at the card school. Some sonofabitch trying to frame me. That meant it was somebody I knew, and apart from you and your little lady, I don't know anybody outside of the card school.'

'I must admit,' Maxwell said, 'I was beginning to suspect Hector.'

‘Hec?’ O’Malley roared with laughter. ‘That pantywaist! And here I was thinking you were some judge of character. Wait here.’

‘Jeff.’ Maxwell held the man’s arm. ‘Think about this. You’ve got your man. You and I reached the same conclusion at the same time. Henry’s not going to be far behind. Leave it now. We’ll call Henry, put him in the full picture. All right, you’re facing assault charges with a deadly weapon etcetera etcetera, but that’s a long way from murder.’

‘Yeah,’ O’Malley said, almost sadly. ‘And I’m a long way from home. I’m not gonna crease your skull with this,’ he patted the pistol butt, ‘but I ain’t taking no responsibility for what happens in there.’

‘Fair enough,’ Maxwell said and the two of them approached the house.

It was locked, front and back. There were burglar alarms at various vantage points on the walls, but no obvious sign of CCTV cameras. And no security lights. Perhaps Mark Chambers didn’t expect any visitors. Maxwell was still peering in through the wobbly glass in the front door when O’Malley nudged him aside with a crowbar in his hand. He caught Maxwell’s look.

‘He ain’t gonna open up like we was collecting for the Blue Cross.’ And he slammed it forward, shattering glass and barging the swinging door aside.

The burglar alarm screamed into the darkness, warning half of West Sussex of intruders, and O’Malley hauled open a cupboard by the door and jammed the flat of his hand down on the control panel. The screech stopped as soon as it had started.

‘No chance of a l’il lady here,’ the American growled to Maxwell and he made for the stairs, flicking on lights as he went. O’Malley moved quietly for a big man and he was already on the landing behind a door when a bleary-eyed Mark Chambers stood there in his pyjamas, blinking in disbelief as he saw Maxwell below him, halfway up the stairs.

‘Mr Maxwell?’ he said, frowning. ‘What are you doing here?’

Chambers had a gun in his right hand, a .44 Magnum which Maxwell had seen rather a lot of in the past hour. It was the old television police drama cliché again, the last words of a victim in dear old Midsomer before the credits rolled or the advert break came on. Maxwell glanced imperceptibly at O'Malley, who flattened himself against the wall, raising a finger to his lips.

'Just passing,' Maxwell played along. 'Thought I'd arrest you for murder.'

A bemused smile crossed Chambers' face. 'I'd heard you were something of an amateur detective,' he crowed, 'with the accent on the amateur.'

'Where did you hear that, Mr Chambers? On the police band? You remember Jeff O'Malley, don't you? American gentleman? Card player?'

'Get to the point,' Chambers snapped.

'Well, he thought your flat in Juniper Street was above a taxi rank because he heard the radio broadcasts. But what he really heard was the police band you habitually tune into, wasn't it?'

'I could have been one of them.' Chambers' face was a livid white. '*Should* have been one of them. I applied to the police, not once, but several times. And they turned me down. Some nonsense about unsuitability. So what do they do? They let bastards go. Like that shit Hendricks. That Sarah Gregson who'd killed her own mother. How do you do that, Mr Maxwell? Kill your own mother.' He shook his head at the injustice of the world.

'I don't think Jacob Shears deserved the treatment you gave him, did he?'

'Ah,' Chambers shifted a little nervously. 'That was my bad, I'm afraid. Mistaken identity. I meant to take out that child molester, Melling. Still, it's early days.'

'Why did you change your MO?' Maxwell asked. And why, he heard the question screaming in his head, didn't O'Malley *do* something?

'To keep the rozzers guessing, of course. I'd been planning this for years, but when Jeff O'Malley arrived, I thought,

"What a perfect patsy." So,' he waved the gun, 'what better pointer to an American than this? I didn't need to waste a bullet on Sarah Gregson when a simple push would do the trick. Shears was a little messy, but I was running out of methods by then. You, of course, will die as a result of a break-in. Bizarre, they'll all say, for a respected member of the community, a teacher, but there it is. Bit of night-prowling, perhaps, to boost his salary — bit too much like hard work if you ask me. Not quiet and sophisticated like blackmail.'

'You won't get away with it, Mr Chambers. The police are on their way.'

'Oh, yes, they always are, aren't they? Do you know, I even lost my job today — the day job, that is. That stupid bastard Bob Thorogood said I was too . . . what was the word he used? — Overzealous, that was it. He didn't actually fire me. I resigned. Told him where he could stick his bloody job.' His face relaxed from the mask of fury to a self-satisfied smile. 'No, I have a permit for this,' he waved the gun again, 'and the mood of the country is at last starting to swing my way. It will be self-defence. Intruder. Dead of night. An Englishman's home is his castle and all that. I called out to you, Mr Maxwell. I said, "Who's there? I've got a gun and I'm not afraid to use it."'

The lights suddenly went out. There were two shots in the blackness, blasting as one, and the roar and flame of a pair of .44 Magnums briefly illuminated the landing. When the lights came back on again, Jeff O'Malley was slumped against the wall, his hand on the light switch, the other still holding the gun but with blood dripping off his fingers and along the barrel. At the top of the stairs, inches from the crouching Maxwell, Mark Chambers lay face down, a dark stain spreading from his side, out across the carpet and down the first riser.

'Sonofabitch,' O'Malley muttered and Maxwell gingerly took the gun from his hand.

They heard the police sirens wailing in the distance and both men sat down while Maxwell checked Chambers for signs of life. There were none.

# CHAPTER TWENTY-ONE

Jacquie Maxwell looked out of the kitchen window. 'It's hailing,' she said. 'Makes a change.'

Maxwell glanced over his shoulder and through the kitchen door — across the landing he could see out of the sitting room window. 'It's snowing out the front,' he remarked.

There was a silence. A perfect Saturday morning in 38 Columbine. Another piece of toast popped up and Jacquie caught it deftly. Maxwell was treating himself to a croissant.

Eventually, he spoke again. 'Where's Hec?'

'Seeing Camille off at Heathrow. She flies this afternoon, but she wanted to be there in plenty of time. Also the press might catch her if she gets there early.'

'Surely you mean the press might miss her?'

Jacquie smiled at him indulgently. 'Max,' she said. 'It's Camille.'

'Sorry,' he said. 'I wasn't thinking.'

'It's snowing out of this window now,' she said. 'I'm so tired of this weather.' She buttered and jammed her toast. 'I had an email from Harry last night.'

'That's an odd coincidence. I had an email from Paul yesterday afternoon.' Sounds of spreading, tearing and munching according to their season filled the kitchen. Metternich's purr was almost the loudest thing in the room. 'Did he have anything exciting to say, Harry? Bet he was pleased we got Jeff O'Malley on something concrete.'

'Yes, he was. Er . . . as a matter of fact, he had a proposition to put to me.'

'What a very odd coincidence,' Maxwell said, wiping jam off his chin. 'Paul was also talking propositions. I don't usually enjoy being proposed to by my colleagues — not the male ones anyway. He has met Harry, by the way. He popped in to apologise for the raid.'

'He seems very nice,' Jacquie said.

'Paul? Of course he's nice.'

'Max! I mean Harry.'

'Paul seems to like him, from the sound of it.' Maxwell got up and went to his wife, still staring pensively out at the snow. 'If you want to go, I'll give it a try, you know,' he said.

She turned in his arms and looked into his eyes. 'Try what?' she said, trying to sound light and unconcerned.

'The sabbatical year in LA. Teaching at the university. Giving seminars on British police procedure. All that.'

'How long have you known?' she asked him, poking him in the chest.

'Since Paul's email arrived.'

'Pig! You didn't say a thing.'

'Nor did you,' he pointed out, 'until just now. And then it was only when I said it first.'

'But . . . but . . . it's abroad. It's full of Americans, talking with accents, with funny grammar. Think of the *spelling*!'

'It's near Hollywood. The West, or what's left of it. Disneyland for Nole. Skunks for Metternich to play with. Sun. Lots of sun.'

'They don't walk anywhere, they only drive.'

Neither of them had mentioned that mad Night When Maxwell drove. He had just handed Jacquie her keys and the whole thing had never happened.

'All the more pavement for me,' the eternal pedestrian said. 'Look, you won't put me off now,' he said. 'I've already told Bernard Ryan. He's started the paperwork.'

'My God! What did he say?'

Maxwell looked down. 'He seemed rather pleased, as a matter of fact. Asked how soon we would be going. I told him it was up to you. You can expect the bunch of flowers any day now, I should imagine. When will you tell Henry?'

It was Jacquie's turn to look down. 'I spoke to him yesterday, when I got the email.'

'And what did *he* say?'

'He wasn't as pleased as Bernard, perhaps, but he was supportive. He's thinking of a sabbatical himself, trying out retirement, I think. Margaret's idea. I give it a week, myself, but we'll see. This O'Malley case has given him a lot to do, of course. The blackmail victims run into the hundreds. Mrs Whatmough was the tip of the iceberg.'

'Well, that's it, then. We've just got to tell Nole.'

'Mrs Troubridge.'

'Metternich.'

'He knows,' Jacquie said. 'He's been under the table listening all the while.'

'Your mother.'

'Do we have to? Can't she just find out?'

'Come here, you clever girl. Need any pointers for the lectures?'

'I was hoping you'd be giving most of them.'

'Try and stop me.'

* * *

It wasn't exactly Spring when Henry Hall drew up outside 38 Columbine, but it wasn't as bone-freezingly cold as it had been for the last two months. The tableau in front of him could only be happening there. Mrs Troubridge, all of a tremble, was hugging the Maxwells one by one, even Mad Max himself, and then passing them on to Alana for a hug, as though on a conveyor belt. Hector Gold was standing in the doorway of Number 38, dapper in an apron and slippers, passing out the Maxwells' luggage. Metternich was in a large and palatial cat carrier on the path, the label clearly showing that he was travelling with the people, not the luggage. A phase of Henry's life, a long phase, a happy phase, was laid out in front of him. He had loved Jacquie Maxwell as Sylvia Matthews had loved Maxwell all those years, as a good thing in his life, someone to make him keep on trying. Margaret and the boys were his world, but Jacquie Carpenter-Maxwell was his star.

Hector stepped forward and everyone feared there may be a speech. 'Thank you for entrusting your home and dear Mrs Troubridge to me,' he said to Maxwell, meaning every word. 'I feel privileged to live here and before I go I will apply to the appropriate office in government to make sure there is a plaque on both your houses.'

Maxwell stepped away from his front door, content. He had passed the mantle of Leighford and Columbine into the right, if rather zany, hands. The Sixth Form had given him a laptop, their way of trying to drag him into their century. But they all knew it wouldn't work.

Blowing kisses, Henry drove them away, Metternich spitting just for the look of the thing. Everyone was quiet on the drive, even Nolan appreciating that, however huge the ice creams were, he was going to miss Mrs Troubridge, Plocker and even Mrs Whatmough. He pressed his nose to the window and committed his world to memory.

At Heathrow, Jacquie and Maxwell hugged Henry Hall with equal fervour. Nolan was swung round and Metternich given a tentative stroke before he was borne away by a besotted air hostess, who would be bleeding profusely before she got beyond the gate.

Maxwell looked at Henry. This was a seminal moment in their lives. Something memorable must be said. 'I'll be back,' Maxwell said, in a perfect Arnold Schwarzenegger.

Hall stepped back, waving, as the little family went through the gate marked 'Departures'.

'Yes, indeed you will,' he muttered to himself. 'You're my star witness — I'll see you in court.'

And his Raymond Burr was flawless.

**THE END**

# THE JOFFE BOOKS STORY

We began in 2014 when Jasper agreed to publish his mum's much-rejected romance novel and it became a bestseller.

Since then we've grown into the largest independent publisher in the UK. We're extremely proud to publish some of the very best writers in the world, including Joy Ellis, Faith Martin, Caro Ramsay, Helen Forrester, Simon Brett and Robert Goddard. Everyone at Joffe Books loves reading and we never forget that it all begins with the magic of an author telling a story.

We are proud to publish talented first-time authors, as well as established writers whose books we love introducing to a new generation of readers.

We won Trade Publisher of the Year at the Independent Publishing Awards in 2023. We have been shortlisted for Independent Publisher of the Year at the British Book Awards for the last four years, and were shortlisted for the Diversity and Inclusivity Award at the 2022 Independent Publishing Awards. In 2023 we were shortlisted for Publisher of the Year at the RNA Industry Awards.

We built this company with your help, and we love to hear from you, so please email us about absolutely anything bookish at feedback@joffebooks.com

If you want to receive free books every Friday and hear about all our new releases, join our mailing list here.

And when you tell your friends about us, just remember: it's pronounced Joffe as in coffee or toffee!

Printed in Dunstable, United Kingdom

65366766R00170